Of Bodies Changed

Cliff James

Published in 2014 by FeedARead.com Publishing

Copyright © Cliff James

First Edition

A CIP catalogue record for this title is available from the British Library.

All characters in this compilation are fictitious.
Any resemblance to actual persons, living or dead, is purely coincidental.

The ancient Poets animated all sensible objects with Gods or Geniuses, calling them by the names and adorning them with the properties of woods, rivers, mountains, lakes, cities, nations, and whatever their enlarged and numerous senses could perceive.
And particularly they studied the Genius of each city and country, placing it under its Mental Deity;
Till a System was formed, which some took advantage of, and enslav'd the vulgar by attempting to realise or abstract the Mental Deities from their objects – thus began Priesthood;
Choosing forms of worship from poetic tales.
And at length they pronounc'd that the Gods had order'd such things.
Thus men forgot that All Deities reside in the Human breast.

- William Blake, *The Marriage of Heaven and Hell*

Acknowledgements:

My special thanks are due to the first readers, Caroline Howlett and David Booth, for magic and realism; Daniel Cutmore, for competing against a formidable mistress; Ros Hunt and Gunaruci, for an essential education in equality and solidarity; Jacqueline Hodgson, for Celtic memories; Adam Clark, for the gentle gifts of time and space; Sigrid Fisher, for feistiness and other indispensible materials; Claire Burton and Judith Stone, for asking three times; Mel Rhind and Matt Hall, for choosing to fight; Neil Walden for shining so brilliantly; Colin Wolfe and Ayan Dasvarma, for inverting the upside-down world; Torsten Hojer, for giving a chance; Adam Baird, for countless rants of occasional genius; Janet Farrell, Baz Inquai, Jo Hickman and Jamie Beagent, for postage stamps, patronage and permanent fellowship; Holly Hero and Andy Dixon, for providing a safe space; Anne Irvine, for a fine pair of eagle eyes; and J, for the moon that never quite set.

CONTENTS

I – Of Air 7

II – Of Fire 21

III – Phaethon 39

IV – Diana And Actaeon 54

V - Teiresias 69

VI – Niobe 92

VII – Daedalus And Icarus 108

VIII – Alcmene 126

IX – Echo 148

X – Venus And Adonis 163

XI – Orpheus 188

XII – Eurydice 211

XIII – The Fall of Troy 230

XIV – Glaucus 250

XV – Scylla 269

XVI – Of Water 288

XVII – Of Earth 305

I
Of Air

18th October 1999

I journeyed all night to grieve in the south after scattering my mother's ashes over the North Sea. Behind me, the husks of her memory surged in a storm that rent the land asunder. I fled the shapes she made in the air. Now dust is all I remember.

My mother used to say that the north wind blows when the earth grieves for its lost daughter. She said that the days become darker and the sky colder because Proserpine has been taken by the king of the underworld into his subterranean realm. For half the year, the sky will weep and the world will wail its loss until the wheel turns, the seasons shift and Proserpine returns with the spring.

I do not know the stories of other people, nor the myths they tell their children. I do not know what reasons they give for the turning of the wheel. I only remember what I think I know: a simple tale told at bedtime, whispered in the flickering candlelight of an October storm. A goddess-child taken to the underworld. A world locked in winter for six months of the year. My mother spoke quietly in her sing-song Greek inflections, smoothing out the long vowels and softening the consonants, until I slept and dreamed of Proserpine's return. In spite of the gale, I dreamed of the spring.

She told me that tale more than twenty years ago.

I came south this month as the north wind tore trees from the earth and tossed them in my path. The rivers roared over stone bridges and flooded the streets of sleepy towns. By dawn, I saw the devastated countryside for miles around. The morning revealed an eerie wilderness, a world laid waste by the autumn storm. The radio catalogued incoming reports of tragedies around the country, warned parents to keep their children locked safe inside, told motorists not to venture onto the roads.

'Fuck you,' I told the radio and fumbled to light a cigarette with one hand, holding the steering-wheel with my elbows. I pushed an old, scratched CD into the player and silenced the news with sepia-coloured folk music from my mother's country. I had been driving since midnight; it was now seven. I had not stopped since leaving Whitby. My eyes still flickered with the dancing sparks of my mother's ashes. I felt through the rubble on the passenger seat, among the empty cans and ancient

Diazepam and even older Lorazepam wrappers for something to soothe the storm. All of the packets were empty. I groped the lid off an unmarked container, most probably Benzodiazepine, and swallowed three dry tablets without a drink. The car veered across two lanes, hammered by the gale. I struggled to steer against the elements.

They say that the Earth Mother went in search of the underworld where her daughter had been taken. She hunted for the gateway into Hades but was denied access. Whether she overdosed on sedatives and drove through the greatest storm in living memory, I cannot say. I did and like her was refused admittance.

Once upon a time, one evening in April, I remember my own mother driving a car, my brother and I huddled under a duvet in the back seat. We stopped at a petrol station to fill up the tank. She came back from the counter with past-sell-by-date sandwiches for our tea. I remember the excitement, the feeling that the world's wheel had turned again, that my mother was now steering.

'Now, people, listen' she announced. At difficult times, she often spoke to us as her nation, as though she were a tribune addressing the commonwealth. We, Chris and I, were her two citizens. 'We're on a voyage, an adventure. We're off to explore the world. The universe is laid out before us. We can go anywhere and do anything. Jackie, Chris – where shall we go? You tell me the destination and there we will go.'

I sat up and looked out of the window. A motorway sign blazed in the darkness. I read the words as we passed.

'What's in The North?' I asked.

'Good girl, Jackie. The North it is. What about you, Chris? Any preferences? We can take a vote. This is a democracy now, *agapi mou.*'

'When's Dad joining us?' asked Chris. He was examining the ham in his open sandwich. He was only three years older than me, but I remember thinking at the time he sounded more cynical than his years. There was a maturity in his voice, a scorn behind his words. He would not be bought with talk of democracy, promises of citizenship. This night-time quest did not thrill him as it did me. He held my mother's eye in the rear view mirror. I turned away to look at the southern lands we were leaving behind, to cling onto the dissipating excitement of our great drive north.

All that happened a generation before I lost my family, before my mother's death, before I scattered her ashes over the murderous sea.

I lit another cigarette and tuned the radio back on. More news of accidents, more victims of the storm. The hurricane had swept down the spine of the country, drawing me on its journey south. I followed in its wake, never quite catching the wild eye of the storm. By the time a bloodshot sun heaved over the plains of East Anglia, the hurricane had thrown itself into the English Channel. The radio was still telling motorists to stay at home.

I became skilful at avoiding flying debris. Trees had tumbled like dominoes over the landscape. Swathes of the roadside forests had been levelled by the hurricane; upended trunks blocked the road. I drove on grass verges and into the opposite lanes to circumvent branches, bins, abandoned vehicles. The first evidence of life I passed were two ambulances at the Dartford Crossing screaming towards a fatality.

The night my mother took us north was very different. The air that evening was quite still and the stars had come to watch over our escape. The tense land held its breath for our great flight to freedom. She drove swiftly, stealthily, under the cover of darkness. She said we were following the Evening Star beyond the next horizon. I asked her how far that was.

'Can't you see Venus?' she said, gently teasing my excitement. I looked out of the window and felt afraid. The sky was immense. The stars had been unloosened and now danced across the unruly universe. When the car shuddered over potholes in the road, gravity evaporated. At any moment, we too would drift up and away into the unshackled darkness. Sinking back into my seat, I hid from the vast wilderness of sky.

'Yes, of course I can see it.' As soon as I had said it, I knew that such a lie carried bad luck.

She looked at the clock and said we were making good time; we could stop for a breather. The car pulled into a wooded siding and we got out to stretch our legs. The sudden silence of the engine was startling. She took my hand and called over her shoulder for Chris to follow. He kicked at stones and glared after us. I saw his cold eyes shining in the headlights.

She led us through the trees and up a steep grassy slope. It was dark, a darkness more pure than I can ever remember – and yet I felt safe, concealed. I listened to my mother's breathing beside me, felt my hand in her warm, secure grip. We scrambled up the incline and over the edge until our faces were slapped by the wind. The trees ended abruptly at the ridge of the hill.

'That,' she whispered quietly so her accent would not be carried in the soft breeze, 'that down there, that was Balwick. That was your father's country. The fields, the churches, the thatched cottages, the fences, the gates, the locks. That – all of that – was your father's kingdom. Say goodbye to Balwick, people.' She swept her hand over the twinkling landscape, brushing aside the swarm of lights. The declining line of the South Downs reached around the low-land towns like the arms of a jealous giant might cradle his treasure. A slim rib of waning moon hung over the landscape.

'The world is now before us,' she said. 'We can go wherever we want. You see those hills snaking off into the distance? That is a great wall that has kept us divided from the world. Those lights, those houses: that used to be our country, people; our prison. Feel the wind. See, even the air out here is free.'

She stood tall and surveyed the county, her face posed and defiant. In my mind now, I see her looking as proud as Alexander the Great contemplating the Indus Valley for the final time before he turned his back on it forever. The breeze lifted her hair and she was beautiful, an angel burning softly in the starlight. I know that this is only my memory, a myth I have created to ease her parting, but that is how I choose to retell it. I have power over nothing if not the past.

My mother pointed at Venus. The planet hesitated above the smooth ridge of the Downs.

'When that star is overhead we'll stop driving and make our new home, wherever that will be.'

'How far is that?' I asked, electrified again by the late-night adventure. 'What will the people be like? Will they speak the same language as us? Will we be able to understand them?'

My mother laughed and knelt down beside me. 'Yes, *agapi mou*, they speak the same language as us. We will live by the seaside and go down to the beach to collect shells every day. In winter, it will snow so hard that we will build a snowcastle as high as these hills. Higher. And when the north wind blows, we'll curl up in front of a fire and tell each other the very best stories. We'll invent new tales until that old grey wind grows weary of its wailing and falls asleep.'

'But what about Dad?' said Chris. At that moment, I hated him for breaking the spell. I wanted to kick his shins for being a traitor, for speaking in that new adult voice. My mother stood up and searched for the keys in the pocket of her jeans.

'The wind's picking up.' She turned abruptly towards the trees. 'We'd best make tracks.'

I took one last look at Venus winking over the Downs. Chris came last, dragging his heels. His face was turned back towards the lights of the low-land towns. I could not understand why he seemed so hard, so determined to loiter. It made me afraid.

We followed my mother's voice down the slope and into the woods. I no longer felt safe and concealed by the darkness, but hunted by the eyes of hidden beasts in the undergrowth. Something was waiting to scream our names, to wake the sleeping birds and warn the giant that we were trespassing in his forest. The trees would march us back to my father's house. Branches lifted and leaves dropped heavily around us.

'You know why she doesn't like the wind?' Chris whispered conspiratorially close to my ear. 'It's because she's afraid. She knows that the wind carries our scent on the air. She knows that every wolf in the forest can smell us. She knows they're watching us from the darkness, waiting to pounce.'

'She isn't afraid,' I said loudly to shame him. 'There are no wolves are there, mummy? Chris says there are wolves.'

She did not look at me but told us to keep close.

I thought I had embarrassed Chris and exposed his tale. Instead, he laughed at both of us. I clung to my mother's hand. Looking back at his dark silhouette, I felt more afraid of him than of the approaching wolves in the undergrowth.

That was the last time I saw the South Downs, my father's country. Even now when I dream of it, there are wolves among the trees.

Coming back to this place in the wake of the hurricane, I saw those hills for the first time in more than twenty years. Many of the trees had been pulled up by the storm. I recognised the curves of the land, the way the road wound carefully over the arms of the Downs, a dangerous path over the muscles of a sleeping giant. I remembered the place from a starlit scene, fantastically clothed with layer upon layer of memory. Now, in the stark light of morning, the ridge seemed bald and humble, the fantasy stripped away with cold recognition. The myth shed its skin. I did not know what I would find lurking beneath.

I parked the car on the roadside and fought the wind for control of the door. That old remembered grove had been combed flat against the earth and now only the hardiest trunks remained standing. The wind forced me against the roots and between sharp, splintered branches. It was easier to clamber on my hands and knees. It hurt to open my eyes; it hurt to listen. I scaled the steep bank, sometimes crawling beneath the shelter of an uprooted trunk, always on the watch for a pair of red eyes among the branches, a twitching black nose, a jagged grin.

As soon as I looked over the ridge, I was hit by the fury of the gale. The county lay stretched below, a patchwork quilt pulled flat and taut between the Downs. Beneath the shelter of the ridge, I stole quick glimpses of my father's country. Those sprawling suburbs, lonely steeples and up-turned woods all conformed to familiar patterns, but they had been reduced in substance by the passing of years. Balwick lay in the valley, pummelled by the winds and diminished by time. The county had declined in my absence and now seemed exhausted, deprived of its threats and magnitude, beaten into submission.

I stayed for a minute or two, trying to match the landscape to the memory. I could not see the tiled spire and white tip of the house where I grew up, my childhood home. The house was an oast-house, a 17th century hop kiln where beer-makers had once turned dried hops into ale. Sometime in the last half century, the Church had turned the oast-house into a vicarage and the alcohol was converted into blood. My father moved in when he took charge of the parish, years before he was married. He lived there alone long after my mother had run away with us to the north to the uncertain sanctuary of Whitby. He spent his last days in that place, our prison, hoarding his old family wealth under his mattress, a goblin-king enthroned on a treasure trove. I barely remembered my father at all. I did not go to his funeral.

We used to tell stories about the haunted oast-house. We used to say that the building had a dark, pagan mind of its own. It hated its forced conversion to a sober religion. It hated its Christian occupiers and their sterile creed. It tried to harm us by moving furniture, twisting loose rope into nooses, breaking glass on the carpet. Anything it could touch, it would. My mother told us the story of the fork that flew across the kitchen, cutting her cheek and jamming so deeply into the wall that it had to stay there as a permanent reminder. Chris said that his bedroom chair would walk over the carpet each night, lodging itself against the door handle and locking him inside. I had sworn never to go back.

Family ghost stories. Childhood fears. I climbed back into my car and pulled the door against the wind. The radio announced several deaths during the night, but assured me that the storm was abating. I lit another cigarette and started the engine.

After our father died, Chris bought the oast-house back from the Church. Reassuringly, he was no longer a Christian; far from it. Surely now, I had thought when I heard the news, the building could rest in peace. Surely now, the forks would lie still in the cutlery drawer.

I drove over the ridge of the Downs and entered the maelstrom of the weather side. The car rocked from side to side, harried by storm-devils. I tried to brake but the wind shoved the car harder and faster down the hillside. I prayed – to what? to the sky? to the earth? – that no vehicles were coming up the other way, that no trees were lying in my way. I lost control of my descent. Through the window, I saw the oast-house steeple jolting over the landscape and wondered if that would be the last thing I should see. I thought, vaguely, that this is how you get access to the underworld.

My cigarette fell on the passenger seat and I tried to smother it. Among the prescription packets and empty cans, I stumbled upon the container of unknown tablets. I took the last two pills and flung the bottle over my shoulder. If this is going to be it, I thought, I might as well go out in style: a car crash and a cocktail of unknown barbiturates. Monroe and Diana in one. I tugged the sleeves of my cardigan over my knuckles. It was the one my mother knitted me one blustery February when the power lines were down. I pressed its comforting roughness between my fingers and wished I had been wearing my black graduation dress instead. It was the only smart outfit I had ever owned. That way, when they lifted my body from the wreckage, the men – handsome firemen, all of them, of course – would want to kiss me and the women of Sussex would weep into their black mourning shawls. No one in this part of the world would weep for a premature spinster in a frumpy woollen cardigan.

And then I laughed. As if a dress could make men swoon and women weep. I laughed at the leaping car, the furious wind, at the madness of my night-time journey. I laughed at my mother's death, her ashes dancing over the North Sea, the seagulls that swooped in for the pieces. And then I laughed tears over the steering wheel as an oncoming car veered out of my path and bounded onto the grass verge. I swerved into a spin and watched the sky come tumbling down, the dark land dissolving in upturned clouds.

They say that the Earth Mother went mad with grief and wandered the universe in search of her lost daughter. They say she was refused entry to the underworld until she reached that moment of awakening, that precise point of despair when she herself was ready to die. Then, they say, and only then, was Proserpine released from Hades and spring returned with her mother's unbounded delight. That, at any rate, was my mother's version of events.

She became silent and concentrated on the cardigan she was knitting. The February gales moaned outside the window, like the ghosts of sailors returned from watery graves. I turned my back on the glass, afraid of their pale, bloated faces. My mother rocked in the lamplight. It was an image she cultivated: the old Greek widow of the sea, knitting clothes for her unborn grandchildren in a rocking chair. But she was neither old, nor likely to ever have any grandchildren.

'When will the power come back?' I hugged my knees and swayed to the rhythm of her creaking chair. I pretended to be her shadow.

'Probably in the morning. We won't have it tonight, not with this weather.'

'Where will Chris be now?' I stole a peek at the window.

She stopped knitting to look at her wristwatch. I was glad when she resumed, filling the room with the click-click-click of her reassuring needles. I believed in her magic, her power to keep the dead sailors of the storm outside our house. Her knitting spell was my favourite.

'It's nearly nine. He'll be in London now, changing trains.'

'Will he ring us when he gets there?'

She frowned to count the stitches on her needle. She answered quietly, 'No, *agapi mou*. He won't.'

Hecate, the cat, padded into the room and circled the coffee table, mewing querulously. I gathered her into my arms and held her face against mine.

'Will he ever come back?'

A sudden thump shook the bookshelves on the wall that faced the sea. I screamed and the cat bolted out of my grasp. My mother stood up and glared fiercely around the room.

'It's just the shed door knocking in the wind.' She smiled and rubbed her tired eyes. 'Go outside and close it for me, would you, darling? I'll make some hot chocolate.'

I looked at the bleached faces of the ghost sailors. Their fish-mouths gasped against the window.

'Go, Jackie. Take this for good luck.' She handed me a knitting needle. I looked up and saw tears in her eyes.

* * *

The car horn droned monotonously. It seemed to be somehow responsible for the aching in my head. I felt a tight pain around my stomach, squeezing the air from my lungs. I was upside down, curled in a foetal position and pressed hard against the inside of the car roof.

I heard a man's voice close by, speaking gently with a soft accent. He asked if I could hear him, if I could move my hand, if I could open my eyes. I thought of the dead sailors at the window, their eyeless sockets and skinless fingers pressing against the glass. I clenched my eyes in dread, refusing to look at the ghoul, and answered yes to all his questions.

I smelt not seawater but aftershave as he reached across to unclip the seatbelt. He supported my neck with one arm and gently lowered my shoulders to the roof. The pain around my stomach eased as the belt gave way. With the help of his guiding hands, I crawled out through the window into the gale.

'Do you hurt anywhere?' I recognised his accent as Irish. When I opened my eyes, I saw a fully fleshed man in his mid-thirties anxiously looking me up and down. He stared at my temple, at the aching point where the blood trickled freely.

'I think we need to get you to a doctor, miss,' he said. I fingered the wound he was frowning at.

'Really, it's nothing.' I looked at my bloodied hand and tried to stand up. 'It's just a cut. I'm fine to drive, really I am.'

I leaned against the car to steady myself, barely comprehending that the vehicle lay upturned in a field several metres from the road.

The man put his hand to my elbow and said something about concussion. I thought of my smart graduation dress, of Sussex women weeping and handsome firemen sighing. I laughed but the pain cut me short. It's just shock, I thought. It makes you say and do ridiculous things, like laugh when you could have died.

He walked me to his own car that was parked on the grass verge where he had swerved, and handed me a handkerchief.

'You're lucky not to have killed yourself,' he said sternly. 'And me with you. You'd best come home with me. We'll call you a doctor from there.'

'Your accent. You're not from Sussex, are you?' I pressed the handkerchief against my head. 'You're not a fireman by any chance?'

He stared blankly, unsmiling. Of course he wouldn't smile. How could he smile at the fool who almost killed him, who might keel over at any moment with some internal haemorrhage? He mentioned concussion again, but I simply stared back at him. Looking at him was like looking at the uncomprehending face of some animal, I thought; the blank pupils of a goat or a sheep perhaps. Or something that had wandered from the menagerie of dreams: a fabulous hybrid, half-human half-ibex. He returned my gaze but there was no connection. The moment, whatever it was, passed quickly enough and he held the passenger door of his car open for me to get inside.

'Are you married?' I asked, bending carefully and climbing in.

'No. I live with Jake. And he'll be wondering where I've been all this time, that's for sure.'

'Who's Jake?'

'My partner, my significant other, if you will,' he answered shortly and climbed into the driver's seat without looking at me.

He reversed down the verge and turned towards Balwick. I could see the white tip of the oast-house poised on the edge of the cluttered houses, its steeple pointed at the fast-moving sky. Turning the wheel briskly, my rescuer dislodged a photograph from the dashboard. I caught it as it fell on his knee. It was a photo of him, looking at least a decade younger, and his boyfriend, I assumed. They were standing outside what I recognised as St Patrick's Cathedral in Dublin, my Irish hero resting a proprietorial hand over his lover's shoulder.

'Is that your Jake? He's very good-looking. Quite a catch. What's that white streak in his hair?'

'It's a white streak in his hair.'

'How strange. Is it natural? He doesn't look that old.'

'Yes, of course it's natural.' His tone told me not to ask any more. I glanced at his face and thought him very handsome, though uptight and tired. Grey hair sprouted prematurely behind his ears and dark stubble peppered his pronounced chin. From the side, he looked like a goat more than ever.

'I'm Jackie,' I said, and when there was no response, 'do you have a name?'

'Martin. Why, what's got into you? What's so funny?'

'I couldn't say,' I said, laughing again. 'Concussion, most probably. And all those mysterious pills, I shouldn't wonder. I actually can't help it.'

Martin sighed. 'So, you've been taking drugs?'

Clearly a bad sign, this inappropriate mirth. I felt immature in his presence, incompetent and not at all myself. I knew what he thought of me as clearly as if he had said it aloud. I was an irresponsible driver who ventured into hurricanes despite the dire warnings, probably unbalanced because I laughed without cause, and partial to unmarked pills to top it off. It was written in his tight lips. It was evident when he rolled his dull, animal eyes. I was metamorphosing into the cluster of things he imagined me. Realising this, I found him instantly unattractive.

'I asked you a question,' he said, staring at the road ahead.

'Only prescription. Why, does it worry you, having a mad woman in your car?'

'No, my dear, I'm just wondering whether I've made a mistake, not leaving you in that ditch.'

Fuck you, I thought, and turned to the familiar landscape. Trees stretched across garden fences, tiles were scattered over the road. We passed a house where the rafters had fallen in, another where a huge bough crushed the front porch. I watched the steeple of the old vicarage grow closer.

'So, is everyone in this town gay?' I asked, changing tack.

'Why? Who else do you know?' Now there was a nervousness in his voice, an unease that had not been there before. It made me feel more relaxed.

'My brother, Chris. He lives at the old oast-house, the one that used to be a vicarage. He's gay too. Chris Mavrocordatos? You might know him?'

Martin slowed the car and turned to look at me. He frowned and pursed his lips unpleasantly. Could it be spite? Had he recognised something in me, some resemblance to my brother? Accelerating again, he turned to the road.

'No, I don't know him. But I know of him. I'll drop you off there – at that place – instead.'

There was an undisguised resentment in his voice now. He was not simply unfriendly, but resolutely hostile. His goat-like eyes remained on the road. He pushed harder on the accelerator.

'You don't like Chris.' I stated this as a fact.

He did not answer but clicked his tongue in irritation.

'Are you scared of him?' I asked mischievously and smiled at his discomfort. For whatever reason, he hated Chris and, by association, that loathing extended to me. As he turned down the old familiar lane towards the house, he frowned.

'Does your man – Jake, is it? – does he know Chris?'

The car finally pulled up beside the great iron gates of the oast-house.

'We're here,' he said firmly and I recognised something like fear in his voice. There were beads of sweat on his forehead. He refused to look at me.

'You really are afraid,' I said and looked up at the old house. The spire reared against the eddy of running clouds. From the safety of the car, I heard the weathervane creaking in the wind. I remembered that sound from my childhood. Chris used to creep into my bed at night and say it was a banshee, the Old Woman of the Downs, climbing onto the roof to steal away a soul. He said he had seen her face once, shrieking through the window as she swung from the gutters. The gutters now lay splintered on the lawn.

'This is where you get out, miss,' said Martin. 'Get out of the car, now. Please. Now.'

I pushed the door against the wind and climbed out. Leaves and litter gathered around my ankles, seeming to recognise me.

'Wait a minute,' he called. 'I'm sorry, if you don't mind, my handkerchief please.'

I looked at the bloody cloth in my hand and wondered if he could really be so petty as to demand it back. Evidently he could. Before I knew what to say, he reached across the empty seat, grabbed it and then closed the door. He drove away without a backward glance.

I remembered those iron gates. They were intricately designed, so finely constructed that a child could barely fit her hand through the tight spirals. My father kept the only set of keys to that padlock in his cassock at all times, and would draw the chain between the bars before setting off on his parish rounds. As a girl, I would stand at the gates like a statue, as still as Midas's golden daughter, watching his black cassock disappear down the wooded lane. When his footfalls had faded beyond earshot, I became flesh and bone again and tried different needles in the lock. My mother gave me a new needle to try each day and mounted a watch from her bedroom window, scouring the lane for a sign of the priest's return.

One day, one clear morning in April, she gave me a knitting needle, the last in her box. It was a long, thin, metal needle, cold against the skin, powerful as a sword in my little hand. I pressed it secretly against my belly until it grew warm under my blouse. I watched at the gates as my father's bald head disappeared down the lane. I counted his footsteps into silence. My mother nodded the all-clear from her window and I penetrated the keyhole with the stick. It clicked loudly, so loudly I thought the whole town had heard. I held it with trembling fingers, waiting for the gates to scream and the Old Woman of the Downs to wail her banshee cry. But the weathervane remained still and I stood in the spring sunshine of my mother's smile. That evening, she drove us out beyond the Downs, having locked the padlock firmly behind us.

Now, as then, the gates were locked, the chain pulled tightly between the railings. I rattled the bars but they refused to yield. Through the iron palisade, I watched yellow leaves spiral-dance over the weed-ridden drive. The great oaks in the neighbouring cottage had been stripped of leaves by the force of last night's storm. Barren and without colour, the grounds of the oast-house reminded me of the Selfish Giant's garden.

The few windows of the house were barred and shuttered, giving it the appearance of a closed face, a dead expression. Paint peeled from the wooden door and window frames. It was rotting with neglect. The building lay upon the tired earth, lonelier than the carcass of a once-powerful dinosaur, blind and decrepit with age. It heaved in the gale, the wind seething through the corridors like a tide through a shipwreck. The tiles lifted with a sigh.

I called through the bars, but my words were swept into fragments by the wind. Not a shutter lifted on the house, though I felt the unmistakable discomfort of being watched.

'Hello? Chris? Is anybody home?' My voice echoed harmlessly off the walls. Only the circling leaves on the lawn whispered a response. I felt snubbed, as though I had hailed a stranger I mistook for a friend.

Still, my skin prickled at the sense of being watched. For some reason, I felt myself blushing.

Walking beside the immense stone wall, I circled the house westwards towards the jangle of wind-chimes from the neighbouring cottage. It was on the border of the two gardens that I first saw the boy.

He was perched, gargoyle-like, on the cornerstone of the wall. Sticking out his chin, he scowled in a way that might have been aggressive in an older teenager, but on him was simply precocious. In his hand, he flicked a cigarette lighter unsuccessfully in the wind. I suspected that this was meant as a threat.

Approaching him, I saw the hostility in those eyes, the menace in that sneer. His cheeks were not, as I had first thought, smeared with dirt, but camouflaged with streaks of boot polish. Lowering his face, his fierce blue eyes still holding me, he spat in my direction. The wind caught the spittle and trailed it back down his chin.

'What you looking at, shit-face?' he said, smudging the black polish and saliva with his sleeve.

'A very ferocious gargoyle, I think. Or a goblin that hasn't learned how to spit properly. What's your name?'

'Shit-face,' he repeated, and turned away to gaze at something more fascinating on the distant horizon.

'Well, Shit Face, it's nice to meet you. Do you live there?' I pointed over his shoulder at the cottage next door to the oast-house. He kicked his heels against the stonework and began, tunelessly, to whistle.

'Are you parents at home, Shit Face?' I looked over the fence at the cottage garden. Overgrown thyme and rosemary bushes rocked in the wind, half-revealing stone statues of assorted satyrs and centaurs. An ancient elder tree bowed over the path, dangling wood-chimes from every branch. More wind-chimes and shapes woven from willow branches swung from the porch and the windows around the cottage. The house and garden were alive, animated by dissonant currents.

I raised a hand to my temple, now pierced with renewed pain, and felt the wound moisten. The garden rippled unsteadily, shifting as the wind whirled the shrubs and bells. I leaned against the wall as the earth shifted and the grass heaved beneath my feet.

The boy leaped to the ground in one lightning movement and touched my arm.

'You feeling alright?' he asked in a kinder voice. I tried to focus on his changed face. His dark eyes waxed full as he saw the blood running down my cheek. The ferocious gargoyle on the wall had been transfigured into something brighter, more innocent, by his fall to the earth.

He pressed the sleeve of his sweater against my brow and wiped away the blood. I closed my eyes and felt the world turn sideways, the soil surge upwards and strike the side of my face. In the darkness, I tasted the bitter earth on my lips, heard the rustle of lice and beetles among the roots. Here, in the land below consciousness, among the leaves and secret stones, I was sheltered from the wind that carved the slopes and curves of my body. Like the giant of the South Downs, I arched my arms around my head and buried my face in dust.

A long way away, like a voice lost on the hills, I heard the cry of a child calling for his mother. It was Proserpine, I thought, ranging among the worm-hole labyrinths in search of the grieving Earth Mother. It will be a long season and a sad path through the elements before she gets there, I knew. But for now, that lonely cry echoed like a lullaby through the caverns of chalk and rocked the Downs to sleep.

II
Of Fire

27th October 1999

Catriona Holt is a beautiful woman. From the dark juices of her garden herbs she conjures healing potions and scented compresses, love perfumes that make the heart beat faster and pungent, rowan-berry curses mixed with mandrake root of which she speaks little but smiles, sidelong and mysterious.

Catriona is a big woman. Not fat, but awesome in the true sense of the word. When she laughs, the air cackles around her; when she growls, the furniture cowers. You feel her immense presence before she appears. Full as the fruitful autumn, she arrives in swirling chiaroscuro dresses and carries a sweet sense of the equinox in her rippling wake.

Sitting beside my bed, she stirred her magic fingers in a wooden bowl and whispered spells. Her dark-red lips stretched into a smile when she saw me reach from beneath the blankets and rub my eyes. She placed the bowl on a bedside table and poured tea into a mug.

Touching the sun brooch that was pinned between her breasts, she told her son to put some parsnip soup on the wood-burning stove. Somewhere in the house, above the jangle of wind-chimes and the murmuring radio, I heard the boy's answering call. Catriona passed the mug into my hand and held her warm fingers over mine.

'What is it today?' I asked. 'Dragon-wing tea? Frog-skin coffee? Something hallucinogenic and highly illegal, maybe?'

Catriona smiled and shrugged her shoulders with exaggerated modesty. 'Just a little something from the garden. How are you feeling this afternoon?'

'Is it the afternoon already?' I leaned across the bed to part the curtains. Outside, the dark clouds lumbered towards the Downs. Catriona's herb garden was overshadowed by the imposing walls of the oast-house next door. 'What time is it?'

'It's nearly five, darling. You've been dreaming. Your eyelids have been dancing like fairy wings. I was beginning to wonder what dream could possibly tempt you away from me for so very long.'

'Is it so late already? Have I been asleep all day?'

'And the clocks went back last night, so you missed the extra hour. You're a confirmed slug-a-bed,' she laughed and stood up to throw another log on the fire. The bedroom glowed yellow as the fire hissed. She lit three candles on the mantelpiece and the oil-lamp beside the bed.

The electricity lines had been down for more than a week, since the day I returned to Balwick. The peculiar, archaic, fairy-tale comforts of Catriona's cottage seemed to cast an otherworldly spell over me, playfully stripping life to its bare essentials. Such everyday things as electric lights and television sets and internet connection would have seemed vulgar and out of place here.

'What on earth have you been concocting, Catriona?' I asked. Her fingers were stained purpley red. She raised her mixing bowl and held it under my nose. I scented some spice – saffron, perhaps – and a sweet, earthy odour.

'I hope you don't expect me to eat it.'

'Goodness no, darling,' she smiled, resting the bowl on the bedside table, and perched on the edge of my mattress. Her thighs were warm against my toes. 'It's eye shadow made from the finest beetroots in the land. You'll look good enough to eat when you wear it.'

'I'm your walking, talking living doll, am I?' I poked her with a toe beneath the blankets. 'Or are you having a bit of a do?'

'All these questions,' she laughed. 'I'm not spilling any beans, not just yet. Not until you've tried the tea. Drink it up before it gets cold.'

I tasted it. Catriona's eyes, keen and curious, searched my face for a sign of approval. The tea was detestable.

'I knew you'd love it,' she said. 'I have a talent for these things.'

'Catriona, it's unspeakable. You've made it undrinkable on purpose. Something this foul is surely no accident.'

'You love it really.' She spooned honey into the teapot and stirred. 'And we are agreed. No more nasty pills from the doctor?'

'No,' I said. She had purged all prescription drugs from my car and given me a lengthy talking to. As a convalescent in her care, I was in no position to argue. 'No, more nasty pills.'

The bedroom door was kicked open and her son entered carrying a tray of bowls. He passed the soup around and refused to make eye contact. He was flushed with the importance of his task. We ate in contented silence and listened to the fire singing in the grate.

In Whitby, during power-cuts like this, my mother and I would gaze into the fire and tell stories. On the night that we returned from the solicitor's office after changing our surnames to her maiden name, Mavrocordatos, she lay her knitting beside the rocking chair and stared into the fire. She began as she would always begin by saying the heady, hallowed words as casually as she could make them sound.

'In the old days, when I was a high-priestess in the sacred temple of Delphi, I would gaze at the flames and see the shape of the future and the ghosts of the past.'

'What did you see?' I asked, full of faith and wonder.

'I saw the fall of Athens to the Spartan army. I saw the rise of the spiteful Christian god in the east, his jealous eye cast over the islands of my pagan Aegean. I saw the Ottoman wield his scimitar like a high-flying spark over the embers of my homeland. And I saw my own people, *Ellenis mou*, tear themselves apart in the wreckage of their own, much fought-for freedom.'

'What do you see now?' I asked, enchanted by her tales but never fully understanding her words. She bit her lower lip and stared with glassy eyes at the fire.

'I see a man, very tall, perhaps a titan, holding his head erect, majestic and proud. He lifts his eyes to the bright stars above and raises his fist against the empty heavens. His name is written in a red glow among the ashes. He is Prometheus, the fire-thief, he who made humanity from fistfuls of red clay. He spits flames and fury upon the gods, but they remain silent, disdainful. He has wings formed not of feathers but of fire. They sparkle and hiss and sweep higher and higher, lifting him into the air. There, can you see him rise, Jackie? Can you see his wings of fire, right there?'

I leant forward on my knees and felt the heat against my face.

'Don't get too close. You don't need to try too hard. Let the pictures make their own shapes. He is flying straight at the sun to steal a brand of fire to warm the frozen people of the earth. There now, in the heart of the blaze, I've lost him and can't see him. But now there, on the other side, he has returned with something in his hands. What is it, Jackie? What can it be?'

'It's a piece of the sun,' I cried in delight and remember seeing the titan fall among the logs, clutching a flaming torch of sunlight to his chest. 'He landed on the mountains and gave armfuls of fire to the cold people. I saw him there, I really did.'

Chris came silently from the shades of the settee to kneel beside me on the carpet. He too leaned forward to look at the embers. I watched his eyes reflect the flames, fireworks on water. I remember noticing, for the first time, that a soft black fur had begun to bristle down his cheeks and above his top lip.

'What do you see, Chrissy?' my mother asked, without shifting her eyes from the fire. Chris did not reply. He remained transfixed beside me. Only the crackling wood and wind outside echoed in this little room. I could hear him breathing, the slight rustle of his clothes as he inhaled deeply and held his breath.

'I see something too. Something dark, like a shadow,' he began uncertainly. 'It's rising over the woods at the back of a house. It's rising above Dad's house. It has eyes, deep red eyes. It's looking for someone.'

My stomach tightened. The flames danced higher, spouting at unnatural angles from the gaps in the logs. Outside, the wind hammered against the roof and blew smoke back down the chimney and into our faces. I wiped my eyes and turned to my mother.

'The shadow, it has horns,' Chris went on. 'No, not horns but flames coming from its head. I can see his face now. He looks familiar, but I don't know him. He is smiling, but he is mean, cruel. His eyes are vacant and dead, as dead as a shark's. Deader. He's looking for me. No, he's looking at me. I know him now. It's the Devil.'

The wind pushed the fire down and the room filled with smoke. At once, all three of us stood up choking, waving the fumes out of our faces.

'Can't you smell it?' Chris cried. 'Can't you? It's sulphur. He's here, he's with us now. He's in the room.'

Chris stepped towards the door and then backed away, cowering. Something awful stood in his way. In the palpable shadows of the room, in the corners where the fire threw no light, I saw the quick movement of faceless shapes, of figures too quick to grasp. The room darkened and closed in around us. The wind stifled the fire. Like Chris, I could almost see the presence standing in the doorway.

'Mum,' Chris whispered in a voice I had never heard from him before. The sound horrified me and I ran to my mother. Her nails scratched my arm as she hurled me to the rug beside the fire. Quickly, she grabbed Chris's wrist and swung him to the floor beside me. The movement was unexpectedly harsh. Her fear startled me. It confirmed the presence of evil in the doorway.

'Look at the fire,' she hissed, her voice thick with fear. 'Look at the fire. Keep your eyes on the flames. Don't look anywhere else in the room. There, where the wood burns most fiercely. Look at the brightest part until it hurts your eyes, but do not blink. Do it.'

Chris hugged his knees and stared into the fire. His lips uttered quiet words over and over again. I caught the consonants and understood. He was muttering, 'God, God,' over and over again as a mantra, a charm to save him from his terror.

I heard my mother run out of the room and into the kitchen. She touched the walls to find her way in the darkness.

'Are you looking at the fire?'

'Yes,' I shouted back.

'Is Chris looking at the fire?'

I glanced at him. His prayer became louder and his eyes were now closed. He prayed with absolute concentration. Behind me, the shadow breathed upon my neck. I crept towards the fire and searched for a sign in the red ashes.

This is where my memory plays tricks. It is a mis-remembrance of the way things happened. It is something from the years I have spent mythologising the past. Night after night I would remember that evening, the night the Devil came for us, as Chris would later call it. I can still see the dark hand – or was it a woollen glove? – lowering over Chris's head, gripping his hair, dragging him backwards over the carpet, his arms and legs thrashing. I remember his screaming, his cheeks streaked with tears and his hands frantically trying to grab the wall as he was pulled relentlessly towards the open door.

My mother ran in from the kitchen, carrying the blackthorn broom she had made herself from garden twigs. She slammed the door behind her, just in time to prevent Chris being dragged out by his hair. He crashed against the panel and fell down, unconscious. Hard-faced and fierce, my mother swept the floor around him, spitting as she went.

'*Hey dirla, dirladada, hey dirlada,*' she sang quietly, brushing Chris's hair with the tip of the broom.

> '*Hey dirla, dirladada, hey dirlada,*
> *Farewell, sir; it's over.*
> *Farewell to the child you're leaving too.*
> *I have only one friend, the river.*
> *She goes dirla dirladada.*'

She waved the broom over his body, spat three times and continued to sweep the carpet in wide clockwise spirals, wheedling the unwilling shadows out of the room.

'Jackie,' she said, dusting the skirting-board with the bristles. 'Look into the flames and sing along with me. Do it, *agapi mou.*'

I turned back to the fire and saw, or thought I saw, a name written in the ashes. My mother swept the floor, the walls, the air and the ceiling around the entire room, her accent growing more pronounced and rising powerfully over the wind outside, until her English words were replaced with unbroken Greek. I joined in, singing an unsteady descant and watched the flames grow tall again until they licked the base of the chimney flue.

When she had finished her circuit of the room, she swept the shadows through the hallway and out of the front door. Chris shifted on the floor and crawled onto the settee without making a sound. My mother returned with candles and incense sticks that she placed around the hearth.

That night, I slept in the armchair. Chris rested his head on my mother's lap. Drifting between nightmares, I woke occasionally to the sound of Chris's voice. The candles had burned low and the flames flickered faintly among the embers.

'It's the only thing to do,' I heard Chris say. 'I know it's what God wants me to do.'

'God wants this, god wants that,' my mother replied, softly singing and smoothing his fringe. 'And all the while, we both know it's nothing to do with any god we can imagine. Unless you think that your father's will is God's will. We had to leave him. You know that.'

'You left him,' he said. 'I was taken.'

'I left him for all of us, Chrissy, *agapi mou*. I left him so we could all be free. You remember what he did; you know what he does. It was only a matter of time before he started on Jackie.'

'How is this free?' His voice became angry. 'Free for the Devil to take us. We were protected there; we were a family. It was as it should be, but you broke that up and now we're damned. You've damned us.'

'Is that what you think happened tonight?' My mother leaned close to his face, looking directly into his eyes. 'Do you honestly think that was the Devil?'

Chris remained silent for some time. When he did speak, it was so quiet I could barely hear the words. 'It was the Devil,' he said. 'We're not safe here on our own. It doesn't matter where we go. We'll never be safe. We're beyond salvation because you took us away.'

'Salvation? *Malakies.*' *Bullshit.* Her voice lost the softness she had been using to soothe her son. She spoke abruptly, starkly, with the surety of one who knows a hard truth and will speak it regardless. She glared ahead, frowning at some unpalatable vision beyond the walls. 'Let me tell you what happened tonight. When you open your mind and your imagination takes you on the highways of the stars, you can stray into the path of other people's dreams. Most people have weak thoughts, hungry little trolls that limp along the highways like blind old beggars. But some people have stronger imaginations, powerful enough to influence the minds of weaker ones.

'Your father has a strong mind, *agapi mou*, a livid mind. When he is angry, as you know too well he can often be, why, I have seen the hands on the kitchen clock spin out of control. I have seen chairs somersault and tables walk and spoons fly through the air. And all the while, his fists stay coiled in his pockets. Your father has a strong will and he can master it. You know, he used to say that it was his god or his devil doing those things. But it was him alone, just him and his dark will, his jealous mind.

'Tonight, Chrissy, you looked into the fire and you opened your mind to the universe. You wandered along the highways of the stars and on the way you happened to meet your father, for he is always looking for us, hunting us. He tried to pull you back with him. You have those bruises to prove it. And because you are afraid of him and of his fairy tales of salvation and damnation, of heaven and hell, some part of you surrendered. You are afraid of his might; that's understandable. But you mistake his might for victory. He has not won; he will never win. Not unless you hand the victory to him on a collection plate, like the dutiful acolyte you used to be at Sunday Service. Not unless you give in.'

'He could have taken me,' Chris said matter-of-factly.

Still gazing through the wall, my mother smiled. 'Do you honestly think I would have stood by and watched him drag you all the way back to that house? Do you think you would have let him? He only stands a chance as long as you overestimate him, Chrissy. As long as you underestimate us.'

They were quiet for a very long time, gazing in opposite directions. Eventually, Chris broke the silence.

'No. It was the Devil. I know it was the Devil. I know we'll be safe if I go back to him. I have to go back.'

'The sacrificial lamb, eh? The prodigal son? How sweet, how noble.' She lifted Chris's head from her lap and stood up. Stepping away from him, she leaned an elbow on the mantelpiece and gently kicked the wall with her tip of her slipper. 'Go back to him, if that's what you decide. I won't stop you.

'But,' she sought for kinder words and, failing that, spoke the harsh ones slowly. 'As long as you're there, as long as you are with him, you are no longer alive to me.'

Chris did not reply.

In the silence that ensued, my mother remained at the fireplace. I heard the wind grow calm outside. The last of the embers died in the grate.

After some time, perhaps half an hour or more, Chris rose from the settee and went to his bedroom. I listened to the sound of him packing his clothes, the rough zipping of his suitcase.

'Mum,' I whispered from the darkness of my armchair. My mother flinched, perhaps thinking that I was still asleep, or maybe forgetting that I was there at all.

'What is it, Jacks?'

'I saw something tonight in the fire.'

'I know. Don't think about it now.' She stood at the window and parted the curtains. A blackbird began to sing of the early arrival of dawn, though the sun still lay buried beneath the horizon. All was still and in darkness.

'No,' I insisted. 'I saw something else, when you were sweeping that thing outside.'

She did not answer immediately but seemed to be listening to the blackbird. I wondered if she had heard me at all. 'What was it?' she asked at length.

'I saw it, his name in the grate, written red in the ashes.'

'Whose name?' She turned to me, her expression both tired and angry.

'It was his name. I saw it written in the place where Prometheus fell. I saw Chris's name.'

* * *

Catriona finished her soup and, fully satisfied, she let the spoon drop in the bowl.

'An exceptional meal. Well done, Lionheart,' she said to her son and patted her stomach. 'I fancy some chocolate. You need anything from the shop, Jackie?'

'I've run out of cigarettes. Would you mind?'

'No way, not in this house,' she said, pulling a comic face in disgust. 'Why should I go to the effort of healing you, just so you can kill yourself with those dirty little sticks?'

'They're my lungs, Catriona.'

'Pay no attention to her, Lionheart.' She turned to her son and waved a magisterial finger in my direction. 'She's neither big nor clever. Take everything she says with a pinch of salt. In fact, ignore her altogether. She's a bad influence. I'll be back in a minute.'

She dismissed us with a ceremonious wave and drifted out of the bedroom. Conspiratorially, Lionheart and I waited for the sound of the front door closing. When it did, I climbed out of bed and he threw a dressing gown at me.

'Jesus, Jackie,' he said, pointing at the ancient scars on my arms. 'What happened to you?'

'I've had these since forever.' I glanced down at the faint red lines that criss-crossed my wrists. 'Since I was a child. Don't remember how I got them. Must have been very clumsy, I guess.'

'Chris has them too,' he said. 'He won't tell me what they are, neither.'

'Honestly, Man-Cub; I really don't remember.'

Instinctively, I pulled the sleeves over my wrists and headed to the window. Lionheart pulled a pack of cigarettes from his army combats and opened the latch.

'Don't say anything.' He handed me a cigarette.

'I won't tell if you don't. '

We inhaled deeply and he showed me how to blow smoke rings into the afternoon air. From here, I could see the west wing of the oast-house, the windows shuttered and blind. Chris still had not returned to Balwick from his wanderings.

'How old are you, Lionheart?' I asked curiously, my gaze lingering on the house. A long dark stain ran down the corner of the wall, below where the guttering had broken. For years now, the rain had poured through the hole, stripping the paintwork and plaster away. It was not how I remembered this immaculate house of nightmares, but that did not reassure me.

'I'm seventeen,' he replied after a deep intake. 'What's it to you?'

'Sure, and I'm a hundred and nine. Come on, if we're going to be friends, we should at least try to be honest. You said you were fourteen the other day.'

'I had a shit-load of birthdays while you were sleeping. You snored a lot.' He stared moodily at the tops of the Downs beyond the wall and flicked ash into the garden.

'I'd hazard a guess that your birthday is in four days' time. At least, it better be. I've been making a little something for it.'

His face lightened at these words and, once again, that instant transformation of wonder came over him. He glanced around the room. 'Where is, Jackie? Come on, show me.'

'I don't think so,' I said. Lionheart shrugged, faking indifference. 'Very well, if you won't tell me how old you are, then tell me about your name. Why Lionheart?'

'Tell me why you're called Jackie,' he said, mimicking my voice.

'Fair exchange: my name for yours. Okay, my mother named me after a convent in Paris, on the Rue St Jacques. Now your turn.'

'You're named after a fucking convent? How crap is that? What was she, a nun?'

'Not as crap as it sounds, Man-Cub. It happens that some rebels met in that convent to plot a revolution. They decided to cut the heads off the king and queen of France, and all of the aristocrats. They even invented a new machine, the guillotine: the most efficient way of chopping off so many unnecessary heads. And they came up with a drinking toast, something like: *May the last of the kings be strangled with the guts of the last priest.* Come on then, your turn. Where did Lionheart come from?'

'Fuck, wow. Was your mum one of the rebels? Did she cut the king's head off?'

'No, Man-Cub. That was two hundred years ago.'

Lionheart lost interest and spat onto the garden path below.

'Anyways, me and Mum were doing history one day,' he said after a pause. 'We were talking about tyrants and we looked up the kings of England. I don't go to school, you know.'

'I know,' I smiled. 'You're home educated. The local grammar school is "ideologically unsound", right?'

'Too right,' he said, glancing at me sideways to check I was not teasing. 'It's, like, a total fucking Ideological State Apparatus. Anyways, Mum called me Richard when I was born. But she always said I could choose my own name whenever I wanted. So we were looking up about Richard the Lionheart and Mum said he was gay, like Chris. You know, they don't tell you about that in school. They don't tell you a lot of things. It's like they don't want you to know stuff that,' he thought for the right words for a moment, the words that Catriona might use, 'that might challenge the dominant discourses, you know? So, I called myself Lionheart.'

'But why?'

'Why wouldn't I?'

'Do you want to be – like Chris?'

'I am like Chris, don't you think?' He looked down his nose at me.

'I like Lionheart; it suits you. On the downside, though, it makes you a monarchist, while I'm a republican. Things could get very uncivil between us.' I smiled and gave him time to work this one out.

'You make no sense,' he said after a while. 'You're so like Chris.'

I glanced at the oast-house and wondered if that were at all true.

'Do you think so, Lionheart? I asked, but he just shrugged. 'Do you know when he's coming back?'

Lionheart leaned over the ledge and stared at the house.

'We don't see him much in the winter because he stays with Conrad in London. And then he goes to Greece for ages, like for months. He comes back at Yule for a bit and then disappears until spring.'

'Comes and goes with the seasons, does he? So, who's Conrad?'

'Don't you even know Conrad? It's Chris's oldest friend from university. Chris visits him on his way to Greece each year. I look after the house while he's away, keep it safe. Can't believe you don't even know who Conrad is.'

I nodded, remembering the watchful gargoyle-boy on the wall when I first arrived.

'Do you miss Chris when he's away?' I asked.

'Mum says you don't know him at all,' he barked, flicking his cigarette butt down to the herbs below and turning on me. 'She says he's a completely different person from when you knew him. You won't even recognise him. She says you should find out about him before he gets back.'

'Find out what? I did grow up with him, don't forget. I do know my own brother. Better than you. Or anyone else.'

'If you know him so well then tell me, what happened between him and Jake?'

'Jake who?' I asked. Lionheart's cold laughter was humiliating. The sound echoed through the caverns of my memory and resonated with something familiar: another youth in another time. I thought of Chris clambering through the undergrowth of a forest and laughing at imaginary wolves. The similarity was uncanny.

'Lionheart, who is your father?'

He drew another cigarette out of the packet and offered it to me. Lifting a match, he held my gaze and shrugged.

'What does it matter? Mum said I can choose who I want it to be.'

'You can choose who you want your dad to be?' I processed this fragment of new information. 'And have you chosen anyone?'

Before he could answer, we heard the front door slam. Catriona sang her greetings along the hallway. Lionheart and I threw our cigarettes into the garden and closed the window. I rinsed my mouth with cold tea and slipped beneath the blankets. Lionheart collected the empty soup bowls and left the room with a sly wink.

Bustling through the door, Catriona entered with an enormous slab of chocolate.

'A present for my patient,' she said. 'Jesus, how stuffy is it in here? Let me open the window for you. Are you warm enough, sweetness?'

She threw the chocolate onto the blankets and glanced at the dressing gown I had not taken off.

'Sure, I'm warm enough,' I said, shrugging off her quizzical look. She paused, sniffed the air and shook her head.

'Catriona, just how old will Lionheart be next week?' I asked, trying to change the scent.

She opened the window and glanced at the ash on the windowsill. The smoking cigarette butts among the twigs of the rosemary bush did not help. 'He'll be fourteen, if he doesn't die of lung cancer before then.'

Fourteen, I thought. A year older than Chris was when he returned to his father's house. I say *his* father, not mine. I discarded that man the moment I unpicked the padlock on his gates with a knitting needle. Twenty years later, those same unforgiving gates had refused to let me back inside, and I found myself being carried into the neighbouring cottage by a strange woman and her son. During those intervening years, I have at times thought about him, of course: the pantomime priest in a black cassock looming over my childhood, the wicked count from a family fairytale. I have felt his mythical presence standing beside my bed, whispering in the autumn winds for me to come back to the oast-house, to leave my mother and return to him. But he died before I could or would, and the fairytale remains just that: a tale.

I remember Chris as seeming more mature than Lionheart at his age: more hairy, more sombre and infinitely less awkward with adolescence. Chris made a decision that I could not imagine Lionheart making at the same age. Chris chose to return to his father. I never fully understood why.

'Is that why you've come back,' Catriona had asked on my second night under her roof, 'to find out why Chris left you and your mother, why he came back to live with his dad?'

I lay on Lionheart's bed with my head swathed in bandages. The doctor had visited earlier that morning and prescribed painkillers. He said I would be okay, that I needed to rest for a couple of weeks and, with a suspicious glance at my hostess, added that he would check up on me from time to time. Catriona shooed him out of the house and returned to the room.

'Wank-doctor,' she hissed. 'Knows sod all about healing.'

I talked with Catriona about Chris until the early hours of the morning.

'There's so much I don't understand,' I replied to her question. 'Why did he come back to the oast-house? Why did he hardly ever contact us, even after his father died? Why did he shut me out of his life, Catriona? You know, in the last ten years, I've maybe spoken to him three or four times, probably less. And now, Mum's dead.' I stared at the fire and let the tears stream down my cheeks. Catriona gently lifted my chin to look at my face and stroke the tears away.

'And now Mum's dead and there's nobody left. I've no one but Chris. And now you tell me that even he's a stranger?'

'You're not alone, darling,' she whispered. 'I'm here now. It's all okay.'

I rested my head on her lap and sobbed helplessly. She combed my hair with playful fingers and hummed a familiar tune.

'*Hey dirla, dirladada, hey dirlada,*' she sang softly. '*Farewell, sir, it's over. Farewell to the child you're leaving too. I have only one friend, the river. She goes dirla dirladada.*'

'Why do you sing that?' I asked, drying my nose on her sleeve.

'I don't know. I suppose because Chris always sings it when he's feeling lost and lonely. It's like a lullaby; it's soothing. These little things are contagious'

I laughed and wiped my eyes. 'My mother always used to sing that to us when we had bad dreams. Chris can't have forgotten everything then. Does he really sing that, even now?'

'Of course.' Catriona puckered her cherry-red lips into a smile. Throughout my prolonged convalescence, the brilliance of Catriona's make-up showered my dreams with colour. She made me giddy with her perfumes, her aura of exotic herbs and vital spices. Sometimes I could almost swear that her smile cast rainbows over the ceiling of my sick-room. As though reading my thoughts, she told me that she concocted her own make-up from the wild storehouse of her garden.

'It's all home-grown, darling. I'll make you something spectacular to cheer you up,' she promised.

'Anything at all,' I said, patting the bandages around my head. 'I feel like a hard-boiled egg, one that nobody wants to eat.'

'More like a golden egg that the golden goose laid,' she said, the mischief twinkling in her eye. 'And there are many who would want to eat you. I'd have you, for starters.'

Each night that week, Catriona settled in her chair beside my bed and told me about the neighbourhood politics: which houses had had their electricity restored since the gale; how the ladies of the parochial church crossed themselves when they saw Lionheart and her walking down the street, and how they referred to Chris, quite openly in the parish newsletter, as the Devil.

'That delights him especially,' she said. 'He intends to replace the Old Vicarage sign outside his house with a new name: "Pandemonia". When I first told him about his nickname among the old dears, he laughed. "Seriously, though, I wish they would get it right," he said. "It's Lucifer." He said he thought "the Devil" was much too common.'

This worried me. It seemed that my brother was now a victim of village prejudices. Catriona agreed wholeheartedly.

'And, how he loves it,' she laughed. 'Every time he overhears the cashier in the post-office whispering to her co-conspirators, or catches sight of the blue-rinse brigade crossing the street to avoid him, he gets wicked and descends on them with a vengeance. "Mrs Lawson," he says cheerfully, "how's that vaginal infection of yours?" They shift their tits and turn to each other in disgust, clutching their handbags. "Do tell me how it is by the end of the week," he goes on. "It would be most unfortunate to see it spread amongst your friends." Sure enough, by the end of the week a fungal infection has ravaged the entire Women's Institute. The doctor's surgery is inundated. It's the power of his will, you see. He afflicts them with a suggestion.'

'He hasn't changed, then.' I remembered the wolves in the forest and the Old Woman of the Downs screeching on the roof. 'Still the same old Chris. He scared me senseless when we were kids.'

'Oh no, sweetness,' Catriona said sensitively, almost ashamed. She threw a warning glance that I knew I should have taken seriously. 'He has changed.'

For some reason, possibly because I have no other family left alive, I grew possessive of my older brother. I felt threatened by the silent distance of years between us. I had returned to the south to find some sense of refuge in the land of my childhood. Now, this stranger was telling me that nothing was the same, least of all Chris.

'He is my brother, Cat, not yours,' I said, flushing with rage. I wanted to raise the tension between us. I wanted her to retract her knowledge of my brother. More than anything, I wanted reassurance. 'People don't change that much. Deep down, he's still the same Chris I grew up with. People are who they are, that's all there is to it.'

'You yourself called him a stranger,' she said simply and I resented her for it. I needed to be consoled by the familiar, comforted by the familial, to find relief in the easy, unchanging, commonplace things. I was outraged by Catriona – the foreigner in my childhood country. Her words were presumptuous. Her knowledge of my brother was invasive, exclusive. She had no part in my history.

'So, exactly how many days have you known my brother, Catriona?'

She lowered her gaze and poured tea into the mugs on my bedside table.

'We recovered your car this morning, sweetness,' she said, shamelessly changing the subject and diffusing my fury. 'Day has a pick-up truck, you know. He and Lionheart rolled the car over and towed it back to his garage. My boys are strong. He says he can repair it within a couple of weeks, depending on the power lines, of course.'

Catriona's partner, Day, lived in a lonely shack on the Downs. He was a quiet, studious man who rarely spoke and watched the world through bright green eyes. He wore his long golden hair loose and I admired his gracefulness, the elegance of his every movement. He was like a human cat, instinctively never putting a foot wrong. He had helped Catriona carry me into the cottage on the day I collapsed outside the oast-house, and had remained sitting silently beside my bed until the doctor arrived. Later, Catriona told me that Day was wary of other men, especially self-important professional types, which was why he had left when the doctor arrived. He returned at odd times to check on me and hold my hand.

'So, what exactly does Day do with his time?' I sighed. Catriona had won, but not in a way that made me feel defeated. I let her steer the conversation away from Chris. 'Is he a mechanic by trade?'

Catriona shook her head. 'No, darling, he's a philosopher, but he does enjoy tinkering with all things mechanical. He made these lamps,' she said, turning the gas-lamp flame higher, 'and an ingenious watering system for the garden. Now he's researching for a book about Spinoza.'

'Is that a skin disease?'

'No, but it should be,' she laughed. 'Ethics and philosophy. It's something he and Chris have great arguments about.'

She was interrupted by Lionheart who burst into the room and declared that he would be collecting firewood from the garden in preparation for a Halloween bonfire. 'To which you are cordially invited,' he added with a slight bow.

'How fabulous,' Catriona clapped her hands. 'I'll come up with something sensational for your costume, Jackie. It will lift your spirits. Plus, Day's homebrew should be ready for Halloween. Is there anyone special you want to invite for your birthday, Lionheart? That friend we've been seeing so much of lately, perhaps?'

'Will Chris be back in time?' he asked.

'No, not until Yule, I shouldn't think.'

Lionheart's face fell. He left the room for longer than was necessary to retrieve Catriona's book on herbal cosmetics from the kitchen.

Tonight, Catriona's fingers worked magic in her wooden bowls. The scent of lavender and rose petals carried through the house. She hummed a folksy melody, which conjured visions of the North Sea and memories of Whitby. I gazed into the fire and recalled Lionheart's words from earlier. Chris is your brother, he had said, and you don't know him at all.

The candles on the mantelpiece burned low. Hot wax dripped onto the hearthstone. Above the fireplace, Christina Rossetti's face gazed down at me with secret sorrow from her picture frame. In the alcoves on either side of the fireplace, stacks of hardback books weighed down the bowing shelves. I had borrowed from this library during the past two weeks, re-reading Mary Shelley, Ann Radcliffe and all the Brontës. Now, I needed something new, something to answer the questions I had borne for twenty years, perhaps something to help me frame the right words to ask them.

'Is there anything I can browse through?' I asked Catriona when her tune had reached the end, or beginning, of another bar.

'Like what? An obscene bestseller from pre-Revolutionary France?'

'Or a photo album. Do you have any pictures of when you and Chris were at college together? Anything like that?'

I did not need to say much more. Catriona knew this was my form of apology. Quietly delighted, she dried her hands on her dress and disappeared with a knowing smile. Moments later, she returned to my bedroom with her arms full of scrapbooks. She laid them on the blankets between my legs and opened the foremost book. Each album had been lovingly covered and bound with old paper sketches, charcoaled images of forests and houses, half-finished faces among the trees, coastlines turning into cheekbones.

'These,' she said, stroking the first page of photographs. 'Here's Chris on the day he moved into his house in Sunderland. It became our house. You never went there, did you?'

'He never gave me the address. He just said he was living in digs and would much prefer it if I didn't visit.' Looking through the photos, I was surprised at the relative splendour of his student home. 'This house, these rooms, they look enormous. I thought he had no money as a student.'

'He didn't.' Catriona turned the page, smiling fondly at the memories. 'The house belonged to a priest, a Father Cuthbert who had been lusting after him for years. The priest and his wife lived in a vicarage across the city. They let him rent this house for buttons, practically. The only condition was that the priest could come and stay there on his day off, in order to "relax with those charming young men", as he put it.'

'Chris didn't sleep with him, did he?'

'No, not that one, but he did shag his way through most of the Durham diocese. That's Joseph, there. He was Chris's first boyfriend before I met him at university.'

'Another priest,' I said in disgust. 'What was it about the clergy? I thought he'd find them as repellent as I do. Especially after growing up in the vicarage. Was he still religious when he was dating this one?'

'His faith was waning at that time, I guess. Joseph was the final nail in the clerical coffin. And there, that's Jake with the white streak in his hair. They met at college in the first term. Love at first fuck.'

I studied the photograph carefully. The smiling young face reminded me of someone I had seen, perhaps even as recently as returning to Balwick. I could not fuse the connection, but the sight of him troubled me.

'He has a kind face; very handsome,' I said, touching the photo, and then the memory returned. 'This Jake, I've seen him before in that man's car, the one who drove me here. He had a photo of Jake on the dashboard. He told me that Jake was his boyfriend.'

'That would be Martin,' said Catriona. She pursed her lips. 'If anyone in this town should be known as a devil, it's him. But he attends church every Sunday and helps with the collection plate and the readings, and the blue-rinse brigade think he's more respectable than their messiah. It's an easy mistake to make and frequently done.'

Her face softened as she turned the pages of her scrapbook. Her eyes glazed over with memories and her words were uttered quietly. She talked of Jake as though he had died, as though a great friend had been taken early from her life. Jake, the one who played the piano, who soothed Lionheart to sleep when he was an infant. Jake, the missing name in the twenty year silence that separated my brother from me. Jake, the only one that Chris had ever really loved.

'Chris and Jake, they met at university,' she said. 'We all fell in love in those days. It was the only lesson we properly learned, the one thing we remember now when all other references and footnotes have been erased. How to cast the spell of magic eyes, how to turn a lover into another form, a wolf or a unicorn, with a simple, electric touch. And, of course, how to change ourselves into other forms, better forms: a heroine, a titan, or a weeping statue of stone. The alchemy of love, I suppose. We all fell in love, but with Chris and Jake it was more than that. It was like a religion.

'Each day was a new spell for them to cast. In the evenings, they would come home with a more colourful tale. Running wild along the December beach until they turned into seagulls; skimming stones that never sank but flew over the sea to the frozen fjords of Scandinavia; finding dragons in the cliffs where they made secret love and promises, safely hidden away from the hostile eyes of the city. Love was their creed. Nowadays, it's Chris's enduring faith in these myths that make his doubt so unbearable.'

Catriona placed the albums tenderly on the floor and rubbed her tired eyes.

'I think I'm ready for bed,' she yawned and flapped her arms for a goodnight hug. I leaned forward to kiss her cheek, but she turned unexpectedly and brushed her lips against mine.

'If there is anything else you want to know. Anything at all, darling,' she left the sentence unfinished and, smiling to herself, left the room.

In Whitby during power-cuts like this, my mother and I would gaze into the fire and tell stories. Tonight, I searched among the glowing embers for a glimpse of Chris. The logs hissed and collapsed in the grate, leaving the room in darkness. I gathered the blankets around me and curled up to the sound of the weathervane, the Old Woman of the Downs, rocking herself to sleep on the spire of the oast-house. Wreak, wreak: her voice echoed across the fields, chanting the rhyme of the inconsolable. Wreak, wreak, wreak, she cried throughout the night. A childhood ghost, unforgiven by the grave, unsettling my dreams.

III
Phaethon

31st October 1999

Lionheart stirred his finger around a wooden bowl and raised a painted tip to my face. I closed my eyelids and let him spread the colour beneath my brows. He rested the bowl on his knees as Catriona handed him another clay pot with a cotton bud.

'Okay, now pucker your lips like this,' he said and demonstrated how.

When he had finished painting my face, he grinned and went away to do his own. Catriona handed me a plastic tiara and a pair of diamond earrings. I slipped the sleepers through my ears.

'I feel like the Pope,' she said, crowning me solemnly with the tiara. 'I name thee Josephine, Empress of the World. Look on her works, ye mighty, and despair.'

We raced each other into her bedroom, to where a great mirror stretched the full width and height of a wall. Illuminated by the candles that she had placed throughout the room, I approached the mirror feeling every bit as grand as the Empress Josephine.

'It's beautiful,' I said, swirling the white gown she had made especially for the celebration. I had never worn anything like it. 'Utterly beautiful. I don't feel myself. Thank you, Your Holiness.'

Catriona crowned herself with a somewhat more magnificent tiara and posed beside me. Her eyes flirted mischievously with mine in the reflection.

'Madame Bonaparte, I presume,' she said with a curtsy. 'Allow me to introduce myself. I am the Great Empress, Catherine of Russia. You may now kiss my ring.'

'And you,' I answered, curtseying with equal dignity, 'may kiss my devoted arse.'

Catriona licked her lips. She was about to speak, but paused uncertainly. I met her curious gaze and felt a quick, unnerving thrill. The glance was momentary: a lightning flash that cast silence on the house, a magic grain falling unnoticed by the world through the hourglass of the evening.

'But, Madame,' she said, in a softer voice, 'your devoted arse is much too tempting.'

'Your highness is too modest,' I replied slowly, surprised by my own daring. ''Tis no more tempting than yours, though maybe of a somewhat silkier texture.'

Once more, I held her eyes and she mine.

'Is that a challenge?' She touched my waist so lightly that my skin prickled. Her fingers ran gently upwards. I trembled at the contact. 'Or an empty promise?'

In one swift movement, she laid me upon the duvet and stroked my sides until I laughed ridiculously. I shivered at the breeze of her warm breath against my neck, her scented hair falling over my face as her tickles became caresses and my throes subsided. Her fingers searched gently, expectantly, towards the sensitive flesh between my thighs and I tempered my resistance.

'I have you now,' she said quietly, 'Your Grace.'

I dropped my head to the sheets and turned sideways to the mirror. In the warm glow of the candlelight, I barely recognised myself as the woman with wide, dark eyes, painted lips parted, breathing heavily. I was Marie-Antoinette in some decadent painting. I watched Catriona move stealthily over the body of the woman in the tableau, her fingers working strange magic beneath the petticoats.

'It's curious,' she whispered, catching my eye in the reflection. 'We should have kissed long before we got this far.'

Too soon, a knock at the bedroom door prompted Catriona to unhurriedly remove her hand. She readjusted her tiara and resumed her languid, imperial pose.

'Enter, minion,' she said casually.

The door opened and Lionheart entered in full make-up and jewellery, wearing one of his mother's evening gowns. His dress trailed along the carpet as he pranced towards the bed and curtsied.

'Tonight, mother dearest, I'm Richard Cœur de Lion, King of England, Duke of Normandy, Gascony and Aquitaine, recently returned from the fucking awful crusades,' he said. 'You got any nail-varnish I can borrow?'

* * *

Catriona's garden is sheltered by a row of ancient oaks. She has baptised each of them with the name of a nymph – dryad, she corrects me – and to each she bowed in turn as we processed arm in arm up the garden. Lionheart followed with Kevin, his friend from an estate on the other side of town. Kevin stubbornly refused to wear a frock for the celebration, though Lionheart did persuade him to wear a tiara and to hold his hand during the pageant. Kevin stared uneasily around, perplexed but equally enchanted.

Day sauntered at the back of the parade, raising his red dress above the wet grass with one hand and clutching a demijohn of ale with the other. Catriona and I were both spellbound with how seductive he had become after Lionheart's makeover, although he was undecided about which monarch he should be. Consequently, Catriona and I entitled him 'Ethel the Unready', which he accepted graciously.

'Merry meet and hail to thee, Eurydice.' Catriona bowed to the last oak. 'We salute you at Samhain.' She led us between the stone centaurs and satyrs that decorated the lawn, towards the stone benches that circled Lionheart's bonfire. Day lowered himself onto the bench beside me and complained about his sore feet in those heels. I glanced over the wall at the spire of the oast-house which towered into the starry sky. Without a wind, the weathervane behaved quietly, as I had hoped it would.

Catriona gave an elegant birthday speech for Lionheart, during which she speculated on the names he might choose for himself in the following year. She welcomed any non-physical entities that may also wish to join the celebration and concluded by wishing everyone a Merry Samhain. Day poured his potent ale into wineglasses and handed them around.

'Happy birthday, Man-Cub,' I said, and gave him his present. He ripped away the paper and examined the gift.

'It's a picture of you,' I explained. 'I sketched it when you were asleep at the end of my bed. How is it for a likeness?'

'It's fucking ace,' he cried and hugged my waist so tightly I had to steady myself against the bench. He pressed his cold face against mine, leaving a lipstick smudge on my cheek, and flounced towards Kevin to show off the picture. Catriona crouched beside the bonfire and sheltered a lighter in her hands to light a joint. As the paper flared, the diamonds on her tiara reflected the flame. Her earrings glistened. She winked secretly in my direction and roused a responsive fire within me.

'You know, you do look like Titania tonight, my empress,' Day called to Catriona and I agreed. 'Shouldn't we have some music to summon the faeries?'

'Sure, faeries,' Kevin scoffed, spitting into the fire.

'Kevin's quite right,' Catriona said, lowering her face dangerously close to the teenager's ear. 'The faeries are already here. But we need music to summon the witches, of course. On your marks, Lionheart. Drums!'

Lionheart lifted the long train of his dress around his knees and raced his shrieking mother into the cottage. Kevin skulked around the fire, kicking stones at the statues. Day courteously poured more ale into my glass. I felt a sudden pang of awkwardness in his company, embarrassed by our solitude and still warm from Catriona's lingering touch.

'How long have you and Catriona been together?' I asked, admiring Day's gentle, kindly face. In the spreading glow of the bonfire, I saw him blush. I sensed the tension rise between us, as though kindled from a spark of his delicate shyness, and I too blushed in sympathy.

'Fifteen years or thereabouts, I suppose,' he said, frowning into the flames. The fire crackled with expectant desire. I felt like a Jane Austen character, Senselessness courting Sensibility in an English rose-garden. I wondered why Catriona had not yet returned.

I dried my lips with my sleeve lace and surveyed the quiet scene. Kevin had disappeared among the dark oaks, lost beyond the firelight which cast dancing shadows upon the lawn. The statues shifted on their hooves, lifting the weight from one tired leg to another. I stared with a mixture of horror and some delight at the oversized penis of the stone satyr nearest to us.

'Jesus Christ, where did she get these monsters?'

Day followed my gaze and laughed. 'I sculpt them.'

'I shouldn't ask, I know, but who on earth is your model?'

Day shrugged. 'I use a well-placed convex mirror.'

'In that case,' I raised my ale, 'here's to the real thing.'

It's just the alcohol talking, I thought, startled by my audacity. The alcohol, the firelight and the magic of the garden. We clinked glasses and Day smiled, relieved, I think, by my flirtation. The tension dispersed like sparks of fire in the autumn air. The heat of the ale rose to my head, and yet I allowed Day to refill my glass.

'Are you Lionheart's father?' I asked suddenly, again surprising myself with the bluntness of the question that I had wanted to ask for days. He shifted closer to me along the bench until our thighs were touching. In Catriona's enchanted world, I thought, these people followed their own codes, unmoved – perhaps even amused - by the conventions and disapproving whispers that fomented in the narrow streets beyond their garden walls. I felt myself becoming seduced by their ways, thirsty to discover more.

Day adjusted his dress and leaned back to look at the stars.

'His biological father? No, probably not.'

'Does Lionheart ever wonder who his father is?'

'Not to me he doesn't.'

'But he wants to know, surely?' I searched Day's face for a flicker of interest. He shrugged and sipped his ale. He felt no compulsion to answer.

'I'm not saying he needs one, of course,' I added quickly, irritated by the conservative stance I appeared to be taking. 'I just wondered why he hadn't been told. Surely every child wants to know who their parents are, don't they?'

'Do they?' Day lifted the demijohn to fill my glass again.

I sighed, exasperated, and turned towards the cottage. The oak tree known as Eurydice rustled, shook, and ejected a sprawling Kevin upon the lawn. Distracted by his entrance, I watched the boy readjust his tiara and amble away from the trees. Day placed his glass on the paving stones and began the ritual of rolling yet another joint.

'Suppose you haven't considered Chris?' he said, waving a lighter under the lump of dark resin.

'Surely, you don't mean it.' I stared into his reticent eyes. 'Chris can't be Lionheart's father, can he? But, I thought – Chris told me – he's gay. Isn't he?'

'If you're satisfied by such definitions.' Day smiled and licked the cigarette paper. 'But does that necessarily mean he can't be Lionheart's father? Course, it doesn't necessarily mean he is, either.'

Bewildered, I stared at the fire. The flames warmed my already flushed face. Day lit the spliff and put it into my hand, his fingers vaguely touching mine as he did so. I inhaled and allowed the tender rush to take effect.

From the cottage, we heard the clash and patter of approaching music. Catriona and Lionheart chased each other across the fire-lit lawn, rattling the night with tambourines.

'Suppose you could talk to Catriona,' he suggested quietly,' if you were interested. Ask her about Jake. Learn about Chris before he comes back from Greece. You might find he's quite different from what you remember. Possibly. Just a suggestion.'

'I keep telling people, I already know him. He's my brother.'

Day shook his head, but was interrupted by the arrival of Lionheart. Catriona seated herself on an opposite bench and tapped her drum. She grinned excitedly and seemed very pleased with herself. The mischief in her bright eyes indicated some dastardly plot.

'So, have you overcome your coyness yet?' She looked at me and then at Day. 'Thought we'd given you plenty of time to get flirting.'

'Catriona,' I said with an effort at indignation.

'Well, it is Samhain, after all. The ancients would have lost no time to celebrate the season in – how shall we put it – heathen ways.'

'She means fucking,' Lionheart cackled and danced like a puppet around the fire. Kevin sat beside Catriona and gaped stupidly from Day to me and back again.

'Lionheart, please,' I cried. 'Day is your partner, Catriona. I'm your guest here. What kind of game are you playing?'

'Don't you agree that Day is beautiful? Unconscionably so? Are you saying you wouldn't want to seduce him? Seriously, Jackie?'

Day raised an eyebrow at Catriona's words and concentrated on the spliff in his hands. Kevin fidgeted and gazed from one adult to another, while Lionheart whooped around the flames. The weathervane on the oast-house began softly to whistle.

I took the joint from Day and exhaled smoke towards the stars. I felt self-conscious, teased by their attentions, betrayed by my own transparent attraction to Day. And to Catriona. The tension spread like the rising heat in my cheeks. I considered my response.

'I wouldn't dream of seducing Day,' I replied coolly, provocatively, 'unless I had already conquered Catriona.'

Catriona cheered and waved her tiara above her head. Lionheart wolf-whistled and hammered his tambourine. Kevin's jaw dropped.

'Welcome to the clan,' Day said quietly to me. 'You can stay.'

The voice of the weathervane rose steadily above Lionheart's drumming. Catriona lifted her face and caught a scent on the breeze.

'I do believe we have company,' she declared and took up her drum. Kevin and I glanced uneasily at the shadows in the garden.

'Over there,' Kevin shrieked, pointing at the garden wall. I looked between the oaks and saw arms and feet appear on the wall. Someone was climbing into the garden. The oak trees rustled as bodies dropped upon the lawn. I sensed movement in the darkness surrounding us, mutterings in the dark places, and caught glimpses of fire-lit faces in the shrubbery.

'Fucking hell,' I said, stepping closer to the fire. 'They're everywhere. What's going on, Catriona? Who are they?'

Catriona laughed and sat back upon the bench, her arms outstretched in wide greeting.

'Witches, faeries, maenads and hags,' she proclaimed theatrically. 'Welcome, dear ladies of the night, to the feast of Lionheart, child of Samhain. Smoke, drink, be stoned and be merry, for tonight we fly with the stars.'

The figures approached the bonfire. Some wore black capes and held pumpkin heads under their arms, others were dressed in purple togas and carried heavy demijohns full of wine. Four women frolicked in red ball gowns, playing leap-frog on the lawn. I simply stared at the spectacle.

'Relax,' said Day, passing the spliff again. 'It's just a party.'

I accepted the joint, giggled and gazed at the colourful people. Candle wicks were lighted from the flames of the bonfire and placed around the lawn. A man in a top hat and tails approached Catriona and asked something. Catriona shook her head.

'Day and I have made other arrangements for tonight,' she replied with a wink at me.

Taking my glass, I curtsied my compliance to my hostess and moved among the throng. Groups of fantastical people sat cross-legged on the grass and chattered. I sat beneath an oak tree and listened to fragments of conversation. An adolescent girl with blonde dreadlocks sat beside the fire and strummed a guitar, badly. Lionheart leaned against her back and kept the rhythm with his tambourine.

'You having a moment to yourself, sister?' a rusty voice muttered behind me. I turned to the shadows and faced a woman in a leather coat leaning against the other side of the trunk. 'Got a light?'

'Here.' I handed her my lighter. 'I'm Jackie.'

'Sure.' She inhaled deeply from her spliff and breathed smoke into the night air. 'Take it.'

'Thanks,' I said, accepting the joint. 'And what otherworldly creature are you?'

'I'm a goddess, girlfriend. I'm your salvation.'

'From what?'

'From the enemy, sugar. From the fucked-up system that screwed you just as clearly as it screwed Eve. From men, of course. All of them, every last fucking one.'

'All of them? Even Day?'

'Jury's out on that one, babe. Hey, I'm Suede.' She leaned back to shake my hand and retrieved the joint from my fingers. 'You've probably met my daughter, over there. Or at least heard her. She's determined to discover chords that no human could ever imagine.'

She pointed towards the dreadlocked adolescent playing the guitar. Lionheart danced erotically around the girl, thrusting his hips towards her face as he beat the tambourine.

'Do you allow that?' I asked, nodding towards the teenagers.

'And it hurt none, do what you will. Hell, anything's allowed, as long as they don't get hitched. Besides, she's safe with him. He's not totally interested in girls. Can't keep his eyes off that lad.'

I followed Lionheart's gaze to Kevin's excited face.

'See? Thinks with his dick, just like Chris.'

'You know Chris?'

She chuckled to herself. Crouching down on her haunches, she blew smoke rings into the branches. 'Chris and I go way back, back to the dark ages, the ice age of Jake. I was there when it all kicked off.'

'When what kicked off, Suede?'

'Jeez, if you don't know what happened, sister, then you don't know Chris at all. Listen, I need a slash. I may be some time.'

Suede rose unsteadily from the grass and staggered towards the house. I rested my head against the bark and turned to the stars. Venus glittered beyond the muscled shoulder of the Downs. How long has it been since I had seen that star over this landscape, I thought. How long since I had heard the weathervane creak in the wind? Chris used to say it was the Old Woman of the Downs, singing a song for lost souls. Tonight, the sound was comforting, a lullaby for the stoned.

I thought of Suede's words. And Lionheart's and Catriona's. Chris has changed; Chris is different. Find out about Jake; learn about Chris.

I struggled to think of the last time I had seen my brother. It must have been more than a decade ago when he had finished university but was still living in Sunderland. As always, he refused to let me to visit him there, so we met in neutral territory in York. I remember we had coffee in a café near the Minster. That was when he told me he was gay. He seemed uncomfortable so I tried to be supportive, but it was still a shock. I told him that I was still his sister, but perhaps I said other things too. I was only twenty and more naïve than I should have been. Now, I am just ashamed of that conversation.

'Get over it, Jackie,' he had said. 'It's nothing sensational.'

'You can't tell Mum,' I said, thinking of her reaction. 'She'll blame herself. She'll blame your father. How could she understand something like this at her age?'

'She already knows. I told her when I was thirteen, that evening the Devil came to visit. She understood so much more all those years ago than you do now.'

'But how can you be sure?' I asked. Chris drained his cup and left some coins on the table.

'Fuck off, Jackie,' he said through the cigarette between his teeth. He stood up to leave. 'I came to talk to you about something else, but we didn't even get that far. I never imagined you'd be such a fucking bitch.'

He shoved his way past the chairs. All the eyes in the café turned and stared as he left. I called out after him, but he would not look back.

It was a scorching summer day, I remember, the hottest on record. I watched him disappear down the blinding street, fading in the glare of sunlight on windows and stone walls. After he had gone, I stayed in the teashop until it closed, then caught the last train home to Whitby in the dark.

In ten years' absence, I had only spoken to him a few times on the phone, the last time on that evening when my mother died. He refused to attend her funeral. I insisted that I come to see him. He said I could do what I pleased.

* * *

'What's wrong, darling?' Catriona asked, slumping beside me and draping a shawl over my shoulders. 'Your mascara's run and your tiara's askew. So undignified. Certainly no way for an empress to behave. What is it, sweetheart?'

I rested my head on her shoulder and gazed at Venus over the Downs. The witches had dispersed and the fire had died down. I wondered if I had dreamed the whole fairytale evening.

'Where is everybody?' I stared drunkenly around the empty lawn.

'The nymphs have all flown away, Day's in bed waiting for us, and Lionheart's taken Kevin to his chamber. It's just you and me, my little star.'

'Tell me a story, please, Catriona.'

'What story do you want to hear?'

'Tell me about Chris. Tell me about Jake.'

'That's a long one,' she sighed, gently wrapping an arm around me, 'and it takes a sad heart to bear it. Are you sure you want to hear it tonight?'

I nodded. Catriona lifted my head carefully from her breast.

'Not out here, it's too cold. Come inside and we'll talk over a hot chocolate.' She helped me stand, although I tottered on my heels. She walked me into the warmth of the low-lit cottage.

I sat in Catriona's armchair and took off my jewellery. She emerged from the kitchen with two steaming mugs of chocolate and sat beside the fireplace. Outside, the wind-chimes jangled in the early morning breeze. I heard the ancient wail of the weathervane. The hallway clock ticked quietly to itself, but all else was hushed and sleeping.

I curled catlike in the armchair and sipped the chocolate, waiting for Catriona to begin.

* * *

'Some memories get fainter as they age,' Catriona said, lighting a candle and placing it on the hearth, 'like the colours in ancient cave paintings. Some things are harder to recall, so I can only improvise. Others grow brighter with the retelling and take on new sheens as we invoke them, as we paint over their faint lines with our own, personal strokes. But I do remember the colours of Chris's house in Sunderland, especially on a grey northern evening when the streets outside were washed black with autumn rain. I remember the red and purple hallway, the grandeur of the antique furniture and the immense height of the ceilings.   The stairs stretched upwards into the deep throat of the building, where darkness lurked in the doorways of the bedrooms.

The house was Victorian in almost every way, except for its post-modern tenant.   The bronze wall-lamps and chandeliers resembled authentic oil burners. Various Van Gogh and Gauguin prints hung framed in the hallway; it was all very *fin de siècle*. The coal-fired AGA range in the kitchen heated the water and radiators. First thing in the morning and last at night, Chris carried fuel from the coal-shed to the AGA to keep the heart of the house pumping. When the fire went out, it took days to get the heating going again.

Of the two main reception rooms, Chris loved the yellow drawing room most of all. A vast mirror hung over the fireplace, giving the room a false impression of magnitude. He would lie sprawled like a panther in the great yellow armchair and hold court over his fellow undergraduates: a prince of the golden age. For all his talk of socialist comradeship, he reigned like a Sun King from that throne.

It was difficult not to be impressed by Chris's house or intimidated by his arrogance. He made many enemies in our first year at university through his implacable pride. He went out of his way to offend people who bored him, particularly those who made a virtue of their blandness. To be honest, even I hated him in that first semester. I thought him self-important and insensitive. He *was* self-important and insensitive, a creature of ice and stone, proclaiming liberty, equality and fraternity while claiming the higher ground for himself. He saw me as the bourgeois enemy; I thought him pretentious. We were both reading Literature, and the weekly seminars became our battleground.   He accused me of driving the likes of Virginia Woolf to suicide; I accused him of drowning Shelley. It was pitiless, pretentious stuff at that age.

At Christmas, however, Chris threw a Solstice party for the Literature undergraduates. Earlier that same evening, I had just ended a month-long relationship with a girl from the LGBT Society. I gate-crashed Chris's party to assure myself that there were worse things in the world than failed relationships with mediocre women. I was in self-destruct mode, I guess.

When I arrived at his house, Chris was in the bathroom lying fully clothed in the bath, a bottle of white wine propped against his chin. He summoned me to enter and invited me to join him in the warm water. He said that earlier that day he, too, had ended a three-year relationship with a guy called Joseph. He was drowning his sorrows as demonstrably as an exhibitionist could.

I climbed into the water and grabbed one of the bottles that surrounded the bath. We embarked on a competition to decide whose ex-lover was more revolting.

'What is her name? What *was* her name, I should say.' He pointed fingers at the three of me that shifted before his drunken eyes.

'Gail,' I said. 'Grim Gail. Grotesque Gail.'

'Sounds like a deadly storm. What was wrong with her?'

'She never read. She never read anything. She thought *David Copperfield* was a book about magic tricks. She thought *The Bell Jar* was a gay bar.'

'Neither did Joseph, apart from *The Daily Mail*.' We both winced. 'Must be why he hated everything, including himself. Wait, he also read magazines about model villages. He was obsessed with model villages. He loved the way that nothing ever moved or changed, that the little plastic people stood obediently where they were put. You go away for weeks and when you come back, the people are just where they were, good as gold. He liked that about model villages. And about people.'

'Gail farted in bed,' I said.

'Is that how she got her name?' We both cracked up, splashing water onto the carpet. He reached for a bottle, found it empty and stretched over the edge to uncork another.

'Joseph,' he continued, catching hold of another recollection, 'Joseph spoke in farts. See, it's a secret language they learn at private school. It's how our pupal rulers communicate with each other in the dorms when the lights have gone out.'

'Like when evangelicals speak in tongues?'

'Similar, but apparently they all understand it. It's how they run the country. It's like a secret frequency only they can hear.'

'The whiff of corruption,' I pondered, accepting the bottle from his hands. 'You know, Gail admitted to voting SDP once.'

'Joseph voted Tory.'

We both flinched and continued the competition until Chris laid down his ace.

'Was Grim Gail religious?' he asked.

'No, darling; not as far as I know. Why?'

'Because Joseph was. In fact – and wait for it – Joseph was a fucking priest.' He laughed and thrashed the water. Nothing I could say about Gail would trump that revelation. Chris had won.

From the time of the Solstice party, Chris and I became inseparable. I stayed at his house for Christmas and New Year, as we both shared an instinctive aversion to family gatherings. On the morning of New Year's Eve, I tried to persuade him to come with me to a gay club in Newcastle.

'I despise New Year's Eve,' he said, 'and I hate gay clubs. And I hate gay men. If I go, you know what'll happen. I'll end up shagging some unspeakable drunk and hate myself in the morning. Besides, I'm celibate now.

'Celibate?' I flicked his ear. We were sharing a bed as we often did at that time, especially when the fire in the AGA had gone out. It could take hours, even days sometimes for the house to get warm again. I gathered the duvet into my arms and peered pathetically over the top at him.

'Please, Chris,' I pleaded. 'Listen, if you come tonight, you'll meet the most beautiful man you've ever seen. He'll be loving and sweet and never fart. And he'll never have read *The Daily Mail*. He won't know what a model village is or have seen the inside of a church. And he'll spend the rest of his life with you, happily ever after. Honestly, how could you turn down the possibility of such endless love?'

'Is this your prophecy?'

'My promise and my threat,' I nodded.

As the day wore on and the house gradually grew warmer, the sky outside became overcast. Chris was reading the last few chapters of *Anna Karenina* in fingerless gloves. He occasionally peered out the window at the frozen world.

'It's going to snow,' he said. I flicked through the television listings and ignored him. He repeated himself three or four times until I responded.

'We're still going.'

'Why don't we look into the fire?' he said, laying aside his novel. 'Fire-gazing. I used to do it with my mum. You look in the fire for an answer to your questions. It's called scrying. It's like fortune-telling.'

To pacify him, I agreed. We kindled a fire in the grate from old essays and the legs of a broken kitchen chair. Chris went out to the coal-shed in his slippers.

'It's too cold, it's too cold,' he sang, 'we're all going to die.'

I nurtured the fire until it could take the coke. When the flames were high enough, Chris brought me a cup of vegetable soup that I sipped before the hearth. Then, without explanation, he moved slowly in a circle around me, pausing at the four-quarter points of the compass to summon what he called his elementals.

'Shall I call the exorcist now?' I glanced uneasily around the room when he had finished his circuit. 'Or when your head stops spinning?'

'It's to protect us,' he said, surprised by my ignorance, 'to keep us safe from uninvited guests. You really don't want your visions to be distorted by malevolent energies. Now, look at the fire. Look into the darker parts where the pictures come quick and easily. Down among the embers where the shadows flicker with a life of their own. There, Cat, look. Can you see anything?'

'Only myself, looking like a right fanny.'

'Well, that's true enough. What else do you see?'

After a moment's silence: 'I see a seagull flying over a man's head. And a unicorn. A rodent scratching at a door. A very high tower and a very stormy sea. There's something else, skulking in the dark corner of the grate. Oh, naturally, it's a man with a Bible in his hands: a priest. Your turn.'

Chris sipped his soup and passed the cup to me. He took the rusty poker and disturbed the embers. The coke wheezed.

'I see a tall man with willowy hair gliding through a forest,' he uttered mystically. 'He's speaking to every tree, asking for their names.'

'Oh yes, I suppose that you can actually hear that, Nostradamus.'

'I see a circle in the ashes surrounded by stars,' he continued without listening to me. 'It's worn as a crown on someone's brow, another man. He rises like a moon in the sky and the circle-crown sheds light around the hearth. He shines like a god in the night. In fact, he is a god.'

'Where exactly is all this?'

'In the mountains to the east.' Chris rocked slightly and his eyes narrowed. 'In the mountains to the east where the morning sky grows pale is a chariot of gold and bronze. It rises, more glorious than Lucifer. The axle grinds as the charioteer takes the reins and spurs the horses over the stars. He's Phaethon, Child of the Sun. Look, his name is written in red lights on the ashes. He mounts the constellations, but it makes him proud. Looking down, he sees the continents far below and loses perspective. He's blinded by his own fire. He lets the reins go and falls like a meteor down, down to the earth. Through the earth's crust, through the lairs of ancient dragons. He falls to the underworld where neither sunlight nor moonlight will ever reach him. He is in darkness.'

Chris leaned forward and rubbed his eyes as though waking from a dream.

'What about the moon-man? The one with the circle-crown?'

Chris peered blindly into the grate. 'I can't see anything else,' he said and reached for his favourite woollen jumper, his comfort sweater.

'Right, so this helps us how? Does it mean you're coming tonight, or not?'

Chris simply shrugged and picked up his book.

'Maybe you'll meet your Phaethon if you come.'

Chris stared blankly over pages. He was about to speak, seemingly to correct me on some obvious point, but changed his mind.

'Well, whatever,' I said, losing patience with the whole exercise. 'Perhaps you'll meet your moon-god or your willow-tree man, or whoever. Come on, Chris. You must. You really have no choice in the matter.'

Chris shook his head and continued reading his book.

* * *

At eight o'clock, it began to snow. We walked briskly to the railway station, our faces smarting in the icy air. Chris muttered curses against the cold, against his change of mind. The streets were deserted but for a notable number of cats stalking along walls, marking their territory with warning mews.

We skidded down the long hill into the city centre and watched the full moon rise over the tower-blocks. Without speaking, we paused at the zebra crossing and gazed at the scene. It was one of those unexpected moments when the city is hushed in unnatural silence, as though the world is frozen in a timeless spell. The entire sky of falling snow seemed to sparkle in the moonlight.

'How can it do that?' I asked, staring at the canyons of the white cityscape. 'How can it snow when the moon's out?'

'I don't know if it can. But it is.'

'What does it mean? There must be a Red Indian name for it.'

'Amerindian,' he corrected me, taking my hand and leading me across the empty road. '"Red Indian" is so colonial.'

'You know what I mean. There must be a name for it."

Further into town we passed a troop of bellowing men in T-shirts and women in little more than bikinis. Chris locked his arm in mine and swaggered with unconvincing machismo.

'I feel like a southern poof in this coat,' he said against my ear.

'You are a southern poof.' I sidestepped an empty beer can that had been kicked across the pavement.

The railway station windows were dark when we arrived. A uniformed guard was drawing the last shutters down.

'Oh, very well done, Catriona. You didn't check the train times? It's New Year's Eve, for fuck's sake.'

I looked around the streets at the drunks lurching in the snow.

'There's a bar in Roker,' I suggested, feeling vulnerable in the open precinct. 'It's called Diana's. A guy from the LGBT Society says it's mostly gay, if a little sleazy. Wouldn't hurt to check it out, would it? We're out anyway.'

'I've been before: it's shit. And I despise New Year's Eve.'

'Excellent, then we're bound to have a wonderful time.' I took his arm and marched him away from the city centre.

Eventually, he led me down a side road towards the cemetery. We entered the hushed graveyard and left the streetlights of the road behind. Chris claimed that this was a short cut to Roker. I had my doubts and pulled him closer to my side. The cemetery was criss-crossed with moonlit shadows and a ruined chapel rose amid the tombstones. Chris wanted to explore the abandoned ruins and fallen pillars, but I pulled him back, unsettled by the screech of a barn owl in the rafters.

'Wait till you're old and unloved, Chris. Then you can haunt this place as much as you like. Just like that lonely owl. For tonight, let's get the fuck out of here.'

We left the cemetery at the east exit and followed the coastal road towards the club. Sometimes, above the rumbling song of the rowdy city, I heard a chorus of wailing police sirens. Out at sea, the foghorn droned a warning to sailors, mindful of the rocks that had claimed many a wreck. Strange, I thought, how the original sirens, those harpy sisters of Proserpine, had abandoned the rocks and moved inland when the foghorn drowned out their lure. Strange that dry land had transformed the seductive sea hymn into a warning cry.

Sometimes now, when the moon is full and the land is hushed by a sheet of untouched snow, I remember the voices of those sirens and I wonder why we never listened to their warnings. At the time, we felt that the moonlit ice had wiped the old year clean and the world was starting over again. It was eerie and strange, and yet all so new. We felt that the sins and the loves of the past had been purged from our lives and a new age was beginning. And in one sense, for both of us, it was. For Chris, it was to become the age of Jake.

IV
Diana and Actaeon

In days when dragons roamed the earth, Chris used to say, they burrowed deep into the cliff-sides beside the sea to lay their sacred eggs and hoard their stolen treasures. The golden age of the world was the time when dragons built their palaces underground.

'This is one such lair,' he said, climbing down the steps into Diana's bar. Following him, I touched the cool rock walls that dripped with moisture and withdrew my hand. It felt like the lungs of some great beast. We had strayed into the throat a dying Leviathan.

Smoke and music echoed up the stairwell. The stones vibrated with rhythms from the underground cavern. I pressed myself against the wall to avoid a sleek young man that emerged from the depths. My clothes absorbed sweat from the rocks.

'Chrissy, sweetie,' the man cried, laying a kiss on both of Chris's cheeks. 'I thought you never visited such sordid little holes like this anymore. And, I see you've brought a female? How very cosmopolitan of you, my dear.'

He lifted a cold, languid hand for me to kiss. I declined.

Chris said nothing and continued to descend.

'You know, I was just about to leave this godforsaken dive,' the rat-like creature pawed my sleeve. 'But now that Chrissy's here, wild horses couldn't drag me away. How do you do, my dear? I'm Dane, of course. Of course I'm Dane. No doubt you've heard all about me. And most of the rumours are true, I can assure you.' He stood on his toes to kiss my cheek.

I recoiled from his Tequila breath and hurried after Chris. Dane skipped along behind, his little shoes clipping like castanets down the stairs.

We passed under an archway and into the main bar. The room receded into private alcoves, shaded in the smog of countless twinkling cigarettes. Constellations of the underworld, I thought wryly. Strobe lights flashed across the walls and tables, flickering with the vigour of a weak, infernal sun. Battered mirrors hung around the walls like battle-shields, endlessly reflecting the ruddy, topless bodies on the dance floor.

Dane shoved me aside and slid his limp hand through Chris's arm.

'Now, sweetheart,' he whinnied, 'you absolutely must come and sit at my table. Let's pretend you're with me and we'll set the whole place ablaze with gossip. Imagine. Me and Chris; Chris et moi.'

Chris prised Dane's clinging fingers from his arm and reached out for my hand.

'Stay close to me, Cat, and don't let me out of your sight. If you lose me, I'm done for.'

'And you said you never frequented these places,' I said, observing the familiar nods and winks Chris received as we meandered around the edge of the dance floor.

'What, Chrissy?' said Dane, raising both hands in mock disbelief. 'He's always out. Correction: *was* always out. Strutting his stuff in leather and ripped denim. Playing hard to get. Hard as a cock, aren't you sexy? It's all very intoxicating. So macho. A proper James Dean, aren't you, poppet?'

'Dream on.' Chris pulled me towards the barmaid, the only smiling face I could see. 'What do you want, Cat?'

'Gin and tonic, and a shot-gun.'

The girl behind the bar winked at Chris and poured the drinks. She wore a pair of glittering wings on the back of her blue dress, which slipped every time she reached across the counter.

'Who's your lovely friend, Chrissy?' she asked, tipping ice into my glass. 'Introduce us, handsome. Where are your manners?'

'Catriona, my guardian angel for the night.' He nodded at me and then leant across the bar to kiss the girl's cheek. The barmaid blinked her dark eyelashes and adjusted her shoulder straps.

'Catriona,' the girl tasted the name. 'That's lush. I'm Cyane, but you can call me Cy, as a special favour. Why haven't I seen your pretty face down here before?'

'Probably because I've never been here before. My first time.'

'A Diana virgin, eh?' Cyane's fairy wings trembled when she laughed. 'Well darling, you're in experienced hands. I'll be exceptionally gentle with you.'

'Cy never goes above ground,' Chris said, carrying his Guinness to an alcove and successfully losing Dane in a pack of oily youths. 'Says there's too much sadness in the world for her to go back up there. Although, they say she's been seen running along the beach at night when the moon's full.'

'As it is tonight.' I glanced back at her gaze that was still on us.

We shed layers of coats and relaxed in the intimate shelter of the alcove. Chris talked about the underground palaces of dragons in the golden age. He insisted that this was one such place.

'How often do you come here?' I asked. After all this time, I was beginning to realise he had many more aspects than I had imagined.

'Hardly ever now. Used to come a lot when I needed to stray from Joseph's dog-collar and leash. He never came to such places. He was scared shitless of being outed. God forbid he should lose his stipend and pension, or the adoration of his flock. This underworld became something of a sanctuary for me.'

'A sanctuary from what?'

Without answering, he half-stood and waved to a figure passing under the archway.

'Isn't that Bisexy Andy?' he asked. 'He's coming over.'

Bisexy Andy was a timid philosophy undergraduate from our year who rarely spoke. When he did, he twitched nervously and apologised profusely. It was Andy who first told me about this bar. I moved the coats along the bench so he would have room sit down.

'Hi Cat, Chris.' He spoke so quietly I had to lip-read the words. He avoided my gaze and stared down ferociously at the table. 'I didn't want to interrupt. I mean, if you're having a quiet evening, that's cool.'

I patted the empty seat beside me. 'Sit down, Andy. You're not interrupting anything. We've not come here for a quiet evening.'

'Cool, but see, it's not just me. I'm with a couple of people. Hardly anyone at all. There's probably no room, so we'll sit – somewhere else?'

'Bring them over,' said Chris. He was staring at Andy's friends who lingered in the shadow of the arch. I was conscious of the limited space at our table, but Chris avoided my eyes. He beckoned for them to join us.

'There's your willow-haired lover from the fire,' I whispered to Chris. We both eyed the two figures that approached from the doorway. The taller one moved gracefully between the tables. His thick blonde hair was pulled back into a pony-tail. He wore a pair of gold-rimmed spectacles which reflected the flickering lamp in our alcove and hid his eyes.

'I'll let you have the tall one,' Chris said into my ear as they arrived, nodding. 'Just so long as you let me have his little friend.'

'I prefer something in a dress.' I glanced briefly at the ever watchful barmaid, Cyane. Chris stood up to shake the newcomers' hands.

'Ok, right. Chris and Catriona.' Andy pointed nervously at our faces and tried to remember everyone's names. 'This is Richard and this is, um, Jake.'

'I think I've seen you before,' Chris smiled at the smaller man with the baseball cap. 'You were outside the library on the steps this evening. You're Richard?'

'It's Jake,' the baseball cap answered, beaming broadly. 'Jake Edlestone. Yeah, we were there earlier. You're a first year too?'

His teeth shone like tombstones in the strobe lighting. He spoke with a soft Durham accent, which I cannot pretend to imitate. Well done, Chris, I thought; your chosen one is very cute.

Chris nodded and eagerly indicated that Jake should sit close beside him. The golden, graceful Richard laid his gloves on the table and perched on the cushions beside me. My personal space retreated in a swift, incoming tide. Apologetic as always, Andy offered to go to the bar and left us, paired and cornered, in an awkward silence. Richard turned uneasily towards the dance floor. I glared at Chris's bright, lupine eyes.

'What do you study?' he asked his prey. I cringed inwardly at the banality of his question, hoping he would not ask about A-Levels next.

'Music,' Jake answered, removing his baseball cap. His face was smooth and unblemished, but for a faint mole on one eyelid. His mouth was broad and when he smiled – which was frequently – he had dimples in his cheeks. I judged, perhaps too harshly, that his nose was rounded like the snout of a dog. A friendly canine, but a dog nonetheless. Without a doubt, his most notable feature was the white streak that shone at the front of his mousy blonde hair. Having been smothered by the baseball cap, the streak curled and gleamed in the disco lights like a sliver of moonstone.

'Is that real?' Chris leaned close to investigate the streak. I had never seen him so resolutely amorous before. His unashamed eagerness left me somewhat disillusioned. He became upright and tense, as though touched by a quiet electric current. His sharp teeth gleamed excessively white in the shady alcove. His desire was as palpable as the strobe lights on the table. I would never again see him as the cool, sophisticated panther he pretended to be.

'Yeah, it runs in my family,' Jake replied, delighted by Chris's attention. 'My da and granda have it. You can touch it, if you want. It won't come off.'

Chris played with Jake's forelock, his touch lingering a heartbeat or two too long.

'It's real.' Chris turned to me, enraptured. His eyes were hungry, though I knew he could see neither me nor any one else except Jake.

Andy returned from the bar with the drinks, apologising for no apparent reason as he passed the glasses around. Clumsily, he grabbed a stool from the neighbouring table and positioned himself at the entrance to our alcove. My confinement was complete.

'There's a karaoke later,' he said, adding hard labour to my sentence.

'Oh, a karaoke,' a thin voice hailed from nowhere. Dane slithered from behind a pillar and rested a wrist on Andy's shoulder. 'Everyone knows how much I adore the karaoke, don't they? We must sing something together, my dear. I'm Dane; you've probably heard of me. All the rumours are true.' They shook hands. 'And what do they call you?'

'An – An – Andy,' stuttered the philosophy student.

'Why, would you listen to that. I do believe there's an echo in here, An-An-Andy. You'll have to be a gentleman tonight, mind. There's nowhere for little old me to sit, so I claim your knee as my personal stool. Hello, gorgeous,' he turned to Jake. 'I don't believe we've met. I'm Dane, of course.'

Dane-Of-Course held out his knuckles, expecting them to be kissed. Jake ignored the hand and reached instead for his bottle of lager. Andy spent several minutes introducing everyone again. Dane kept his beady eyes fixed on Jake.

Chris whispered something into Jake's ear. They both laughed unkindly, exclusively, at whatever was said. They would have laughed whether they heard what was said or not, so long as they could breathe on each other's cheeks, inhale the other's delicious new breath. Jake returned a word into Chris's ear and a spell seemed to fall over them, a barely visible mist that partitioned their otherworld from ours. On the sidelines of tumescent romance, I sat uncomfortably close to my silent, golden-haired neighbour. The interminable evening seemed to stretch into the distance, towards the early hours of a gaping New Year.

At some point, Cyane emerged from behind the bar to wheel a veteran karaoke machine across the dance floor. Jake and Chris grinned at each other, their noses touching as they tried to hear what the other said. Dane pawed the shrinking Andy. The dragon's lair dripped with oily sweat. A thousand miles above our heads, an ice age paralysed the surface of the earth. And I will surely die here, I thought.

'The karaoke, the karaoke,' Dane clapped and dragged a traumatised Andy to the stage. 'We absolutely have to sing my song, *Endless Love*. Everyone knows it's my song, my dear. It's mine.'

'Poor Andy.' Richard spoke for the first time, surprising me with the warmth of his voice. 'He didn't deserve the Dane treatment. No one deserves the Dane treatment.'

I noticed that Chris had successfully draped his arm around Jake's shoulder. Jake lowered his hand tenderly upon the other's knee. They contrived to talk, nose to nose, as though oblivious to the sensational development of this touch.

'You're hating this evening as much as I am, aren't you?' Richard continued, leaning towards me.

'I'm not a very obliging gooseberry, no. And you?'

Richard shook his head. 'I suppose we could ruin the evening entirely by dancing. What do you think?'

The first weak strains of Dane's funereal voice wafted across the bar. Defeated, the last dancers returned to their tables. Andy's surprisingly deep bass joined the duet. On the table, the glasses trembled.

'I think it would be the nail in the coffin of my evening,' I said, taking Richard's hand and leading him to the deserted dance floor. 'Something truly awful must be done.'

I rested my head against his apple-scented hair and inhaled deeply. He may not be wearing a dress, I thought pragmatically, but he does have remarkable hair.

We moved purposefully, unselfconsciously and without the slightest coordination. As I turned in Richard's arms, I spied Chris and Jake gather their coats and sneak towards the archway. Dirty buggers, I thought, wincing at Dane's unforgiving tenor. So much for being celibate.

* * *

There are a few, rare times when, despite the punishments inflicted on your body the night before, you wake feeling like Snow White. The New Years' sunlight beamed through the half-open curtains, revealing a cosmos of swirling dust motes over my bed. Shivering, I gathered the spotless sheets into my arms and watched my breath create vapour clouds in the air. Fuck, I thought, the heating. The AGA's dead again.

I wrapped a blanket around my shoulders and stepped between the ashtrays and mugs on the floor. The guest bedroom, which I mostly inhabited, was next door to Chris's room. On the landing, I heard secret whisperings behind his closed door.

'Afternoon, Catriona,' he called mischievously. 'Would you mind ever so much putting the kettle on, please?'

'What time is it? And what did your last slave die of?'

'Three o'clock. Why's it so cold?'

'The AGA's gone out. Make sure you and your little friend are both decent when I come back with the coffees.'

The low winter sun shone through the stained-glass panels above the front door, painting the walls with coloured circles and rectangles. As I came down the stairs, there were unaccountable sounds in the Yellow Room. Inside, I found Richard kneeling in his underpants and a sweater, tending a fire in the grate.

'It was cold,' he said, poking the coal. 'Had to do something.'

'Good thinking.' I could not think why he was here, in this house, in his underpants, poking the fire. I tried to put together the pieces of the evening. 'Were you – did we? So, you stayed the night?'

He nodded and turned back to the fire.

'Look, I'm sorry,' I said, conscious that my hangover had decided now was the best time to kick in. 'I don't remember much of yesterday evening. But if we did anything – if we did do anything – you need to know that I don't usually. At least, not with men. It's not just you. So, if you were hoping that there's more to last night – '

'Don't flatter yourself,' he said, smiling at me so kindly that I blushed. 'I slept on the settee. You did try valiantly to get me up the stairs. I resisted. And I don't usually stay for more than a coffee.'

'Coffee,' I agreed and retreated from his smile.

In the kitchen, I took two painkillers and swore. Richard joined me beside the AGA, hugging himself to keep warm. The sunlight rippled down the golden hairs of his smooth legs, soft and slightly tanned like an almost-baked loaf. I turned my attention to the kettle and broke the silence with banal questions about his course and his favourite philosophers, which he answered in monosyllables.

'What's that?' he asked, looking out of the window into the back yard. 'A sign-post?'

I glanced at the snow-covered path leading to the coal shed. The reflection of the sun on the frozen world was dazzling. Richard had seen the wooden pole which stood upright in the centre of the yard.

'Oh, that's Chris's dream-tree,' I said. 'Every time he has a wish or a dream, he ties a crystal onto those cross-bars. At the full-moon, he says, the moon-goddess sifts through the wishes and grants him one. It's really quite cute, if a little insane. And the wood creaking in the wind, he says, reminds him of a weathervane or something at the house he grew up in.'

'The moon-goddess? Diana?' He looked at me sideways through his glasses. His loose hair was longer than I imagined and glowed like threads of gold in the afternoon sun. And what big lips you have, I thought.

'Artemis in Greek,' I said. 'Diana in Latin.'

'Same as the bar last night.'

'So it is. I wonder if Chris made a wish to find his moon-lover last night. Appears to have come true, if he did.'

'His moon-lover? You mean Jake?'

'Diana's not the most appropriate goddess for lovers, is she?'

'Meaning what?' Richard carried our coffee mugs into the Yellow Room. We crouched beside the fire and felt the heat spread shivers down our cold bodies. I could smell his flesh ripen at the heat, sweet as a honeyed oatcake, warm as rising dough. The blanket slipped softly from my shoulder, baring my cleavage. I did not readjust.

'You know the tale of Actaeon, don't you?' I rested my mug on the hearth. 'Actaeon was a hero, a hunter who worshipped Diana. He hunted deer and led a pack of faithful hounds through the forests in search of his prey. Remember, the hounds are faithful: that's important. One evening, he came across Diana bathing naked in her sacred underground cave.

'Diana is, supposedly, a chaste goddess. She dismisses love as a mortal failing. She doesn't have a heart; she has a cold, immortal moonlight fire inside her body. Anyway, Actaeon spied the bathing goddess and was enthralled, unable to move, utterly entranced. When she realised she was being watched, Diana turned Actaeon into a stag. Ironically, it was his own loyal hounds that caught him and tore him limb from limb. See, she's not a promising goddess to invoke for love.'

'Wouldn't say that Jake was chaste, though,' said Richard smiling.

'But he does resemble some breed of hound. A grinning Labrador, perhaps. Or a Jack Russell.'

We turned to the ceiling at the sound of raucous laughter in the room above. I was going to speak, to say that I did not mean to associate Jake with the moon-goddess but the doorbell chimed and we both jumped. I pulled the blanket around my shoulders and went to the door. After telling the story, I half expected to meet a furious deity with a bow slung over her shoulder. It was no less surprising that a balding priest in a black cassock was standing on the doorstep, fingering his collar.

'Is Christopher at home?' he asked miserably. His sad eyes glanced behind me into the dark house.

'Yes, he is,' I said too quickly and then recognised the priest from Chris's photographs. It was the revolting ex-boyfriend, Joseph. 'No, actually, I don't know. I've just got out of bed, you see.'

'I see.' He was very disapproving. 'Would you be so kind as to ask if he will see me? You can tell him that it's Joseph.'

'You'll have to wait there. I'll only be a minute.'

'I'd rather wait inside, if it's all the same. You won't have noticed; it is rather chilly out here.' He laid a black boot on the carpet and waited for me to move aside. I held the door open and backed away as a blast of Siberian air brought the clergyman into the hallway.

He said nothing but glared miserably around. His extraordinarily large head was bowed down. He moved like an overburdened ox. I ran up the stairs and tapped on Chris's door.

'Chris, there's someone here to see you,' I shouted in a deliberately loud voice – and then quietly, 'it's Joseph, your revolting ex. What shall I tell him?'

'Shit,' he whispered. 'Tell him I'm out. Tell him I'll be back later. Tell him to piss off.'

'Hello, Chris? Are you in?' I repeated loudly again, and then returned to the hallway. 'Sorry, Joseph, he doesn't appear to be here. Maybe you should try again tomorrow?'

The priest raised his bovine chin and glared at the print of Van Gogh's *Sunflowers* on the hallway wall. He looked at his watch, at the *Sunflowers*, at his watch, and then at me. None of these things seemed to please him.

'I do have Evensong at six,' he said, as though I had suggested the opposite. 'I don't have time to rearrange my services around his comings and goings. Would you tell him I'll come back after seven, perhaps seven-fifteen. Can you remember that?'

Without another word, he opened the front door was sucked out by the cold draught. The door slammed of its own accord.

At this noise, there was movement around the house. Richard emerged fully clothed from the Yellow Room. Upstairs, the bedroom door creaked open and Chris peered cautiously over the banisters.

'All clear,' I said and returned to the warmth of the Yellow Room.

Chris and Jake abandoned the sanctuary of the bedroom and joined us in the drawing room. They had wrapped themselves together in a single duvet. They sat in the great yellow chair, their bare feet hanging over the arms of the throne. The king has a new consort, I thought, eyeing the newcomer with interest and not a little resentment.

'Hey, Richard,' Chris smirked. 'Didn't know you were staying over. You two have a good night?'

'He slept on the settee,' I cut in before the insinuations began. I offered Chris a cigarette to distract his mouth.

'No thanks. I've given up.'

'Since when?'

'Since last night,' he said, kissing Jake's cheek.

'Not because of me?' Jake asked, a little too earnestly. 'I don't want you to change a thing. You're perfect as you are.' His soft musical accent washed over me, endearing me, against my will, to the usurper in the house.

'I'm giving up. You're good for my health.'

'Excuse me, guys, but what about this priest?' I interrupted the mawkish performance. 'He'll be back later, around seven, so he said.'

'This priest is your ex?' Jake feigned disinterest and stared at the fire. Behind the complacent mask, his jealousy was evident to all. 'Does he come round much?'

'He didn't deal with the break-up very well,' Chris shrugged. 'He lives in a clerical bubble; it's a psychiatric condition. He's cushioned from reality by a clique of adoring parishioners. Acolytes revolve around his every pronoun. People are only there to be an audience, to admire his performances. They cease to move in his absence, like figures in a model village. And they certainly don't have their own free wills. My leaving has created something of an existential crisis in his universe.'

'What will you say when he comes back?' asked Jake, his wide eyes betraying his uncertainty. I remember thinking that I had never before seen such clear blue irises, bright as sapphires. It was no wonder that Chris was thoroughly smitten. Those eyes could tame the devil.

'I'll tell him I've got a gorgeous new boyfriend, of course.'

'Have you?'

'Haven't I?'

Richard and I shared a nauseating glance. Without a word, I picked up his thoughts and mumbled something about making another pot of coffee. We retreated into the kitchen and abandoned the two-man theatre of the romantically absurd.

* * *

In days when dragons roamed the earth, Chris used to say, they burrowed deep into the cliffs beside the sea to lay sacred eggs and hoard stolen treasures.

'I discovered Jake in an ancient dragon's palace,' he said, wiping hot chocolate from his lips. Both guests had since departed: Jake to his mother's house for a New Year's roast, and Richard to his philosophy books. 'A thousand miles beneath the sea, I found the last unplundered treasure of the earth. Have you ever seen eyes so blue? And his body? Christ, he stood up in the full glare of the sun this morning and looked like a statue. It could have been Michelangelo's *David* standing there, stark bullock naked in my bedroom. He is beautiful, isn't he, Cat?'

'Like a god.' I waited for him to reference the white streak.

'And that white streak in his hair. It's so unusual, isn't it? Have you ever seen anything like it? And so warm, so utterly gentle. What do you think?'

'Where were you guys at midnight?' I had sidestepped his repeated question for the two hours since Jake had left, and still he did not notice.

'When you and Richard abandoned us for the dance floor, we decided to go for a walk along the beach. We walked for miles along the coast in the snow, just talking about everything under the moon. I told him about my father and all about the house where I grew up.'

'What about your father?' This was new. At that time, Chris had never talked to me about his family. Once again, he had excluded me from the hidden chapters of his life.

Chris stared at me as though I had said something uncouth. He moved his lips, considering the things he could say and the things that should be withheld. Deciding to say as little as possible, he kept it simple.

'Everything. And then Jake told me about his parent's home in Elliston, his childhood in a coal-mining village, the strike, the hardship, the breaking of the community. Everything.

'At midnight, we sat on the harbour wall near the lighthouse. We listened to the church clocks chime twelve and then the roar of voices from the town. People began to cheer 'Happy New Year' in the streets as though everybody knew each other. Jake missed his last bus home, so I offered him the spare mattress in my room. We walked slowly back to the house as the city fell silent. We sat talking in the kitchen for another couple of hours. I was trembling with anticipation, Cat, actually trembling. The suspense was unbelievable. For the first time in my life there was, I don't know, a correspondence. He's the opposite of Joseph. He's my equal. It's there in his eyes, Cat. Joseph never looked at me like that. None of the priests did.'

Chris moved to the fire and contemplated the flames as though they held the mystery of Jake. Outside, the crystals on the dream-tree sounded in the breeze. A police helicopter droned far above the houses, flashing the streets with its wide reaching beam, slicing the silence of the midwinter sky.

'We went to my bedroom as the first blackbirds began to sing,' he continued. 'It was still dark outside. I tried to pull the spare mattress out, but Jake touched my arm and said we could share my bed. It's a king size, after all. As long as you keep your hands to yourself, he laughed. I promised I would. We undressed in darkness and climbed under the covers.

'We were silent for about half-an-hour before I whispered his name. He was still awake and he turned his face towards me. I could feel the heat of his body less than a hair's breadth from mine. Our toes touched. I could smell his soapy skin beneath the duvet, the toothpaste on his warm breath. Then he shifted closer.

'When he spoke, the words seemed to come from a long way away, like a roll of thunder on the Downs. For some reason, I thought of my father's oast-house in Balwick, the house where I grew up. There used to be a tree in the garden, a single dog-rose tree beside the great wall. When the house was still and my father was in bed, I would creep out into the night and curl up beneath its thorns. I would whisper my guilty desires into the soil. Jake's words took me back there, to the empty garden where only a rose-tree grew, where I made my first wish.

'Can I kiss you, he asked me and, after all this time, I remembered my father's garden. Can I kiss you. Just that. I didn't say anything but he understood my answer and he moved his lips to mine.'

Chris stood up and walked to the window. The night had fallen. The crystals on the dream-tree glittered in the helicopter's searchlight as the beam swept over the roofs of the houses.

'I tied a spell on that tree, last night,' he said, looking at the winking crystals. 'Before we went out. I didn't tell you. A wish that I would meet Jake.'

He turned his back on the night and pulled the curtains. 'I never believed in that kind of magic before,' he said, more to himself than to me.

He rattled the iron poker in the grate. A swarm of pent-up sparks flew up the chimney. At the same moment, the doorbell chimed as though it too had been roused from the fire.

'I'll get it,' Chris sighed. He went into the hallway with his head bowed down, his excitement gone.

Chris usually moved with feline dignity. Before I knew him, I had noticed him. He would prowl into our seminars with his first college friend, Conrad. Both figures walked with the sexual grace of Abyssinian cats, turning their whiskered faces from the adoring eyes of most first-year girls and every other boy. It was that arrogance that had fuelled the early friction between us. Tonight, in contrast, he moved like a beast of burden, resigning his neck to Joseph's plough.

I listened to the sound of the front door being opened. A wave of sharp air swept into the house, riling the flames in the hearth to a dangerous height. As the front door closed, the flames slunk low in the grate and drew smoke down the chimney and into the room.

'You know, Christopher, it was very inconvenient of you to be out when I called earlier,' Joseph complained as they marched past the Yellow Room and into the kitchen. The door closed and I heard nothing more of their conversation.

I hold a secret memory of Chris, one that I bury for bleaker evenings. It falls on our first night of term, the night when everyone is a stranger and nobody wants to be alone. A ball had been arranged for the homesick freshers. As the clocks struck eight, we all flocked to Wearmouth Hall, summoned like a host of excitable butterflies.

When I arrived, I saw Chris smoking on the steps of the hall. He was standing on his own like an unhappy, brooding statue as the chattering guests bustled past him. He stalked into the dining hall as the last man to enter and sat opposite me. He did not speak, although I made several blithe attempts at conversation. He glared around and shrugged occasional responses to my questions. Eventually, I turned my attention to others. As the alcohol flowed, I bonded with those around me in hostility to the silent misanthrope on our table.

After dinner, I strolled alone to the balcony to light a cigarette. The humming city stretched down to the sea, twinkling in the cold September breeze. I was revived by the night's freshness.

'You know, my sister hates the wind that blows in from the sea,' a voice uttered close behind me. 'She says it brings the ghosts of drowned sailors inland.'

I turned, surprised, as Chris glided beside me. He leaned against the balcony, his face dour and saturnine, hardened by the north wind.

'So you can speak,' I replied as disdainfully as I could. 'There was me thinking you were far too important to converse with the likes of me.'

'I was expecting someone would come with me tonight,' he said by way of apology. 'My partner. I hate turning up to these things alone.'

A sudden roar of male laughter drifted through the balcony doors. We both turned and glanced at the row of ruddy faced youths, dancing a can-can across the tables. The waiters implored them with exaggerated gestures to climb down, but the whole assembly clapped and cheered the burlesque performance.

'Everyone else came on their own,' I said. 'What makes you so special?'

'I was the only one expecting to be disappointed, I guess. Do you have a light?' Chris reached inside his jacket for his cigarettes.

'No.' I dropped my cigarette butt over the edge and abandoned him on the balcony. The can-can dancers came crashing to the floor, dragging the table-cloth and cutlery with them. The entire room rose clapping and called for an encore. In the furore, I saw Chris skirt the edges of the hall and disappear through the main entrance.

I felt a pang of remorse as his downcast face avoided my eyes. But then I caught sight of Gail for the first time. Evidently drunk, she beckoned me to her table with an impressive profiterole.

* * *

The front door slammed and Chris returned to the Yellow Room wearing the same expression as on that first night we met.

'What is it about Joseph that makes you do that?' I asked crossly, frowning at his posture.

'Do what?' Chris sat on his throne and closed his eyes. I offered him a cigarette, but he shook his head. Jake still rules, I acknowledged.

'Every time after you've seen him, you look like you've been told off. It's a terrible posture, like you've been condemned. Or your spine has buckled. How does he do it to you?'

'How he always does it. He negates whatever I say. He denied the existence of Jake. He said I was trying to make him jealous. Then he sobbed and asked me to hold him as he needed a "friendly" hug – which I steadfastly refused. Finally, he grew angry and said I would be sorry.'

'What did you do?'

Chris yawned and rubbed his forehead as though it ached.

'I said that he would be the sorry one if I went to his Bishop and told him everything. I told him to get out of my house and never contact me again. He got his coat and stood up without a word. Just before opening the door, he turned and leaned close to my face. You can smell the incense on their clothes, you know. His teeth are stained with the blood of his Christ. He whispered a curse on the doorstep. "What your father did," he said, "will be nothing compared to what I will do to you, Christopher." Then he left.'

'Fucking hell, are all priests such drama queens?'

'All the ones I've ever known,' he laughed, the sparkle returning to his eyes. 'And I've known quite a few. I used to sleep over at the theological college when Joseph was in training. Naturally, I was hidden from public knowledge like a secret concubine. I was summoned to his bedroom for his evening pleasures. One night, there was a fire somewhere in the college and he ordered me to stay hidden in his room so I wouldn't be seen. How he would have explained the charred corpse in his bed to the authorities, I don't know. Fortunately for him, the fire was put out.'

Chris leaned back in his chair. He looked weary.

'Joseph began to sleep around with the other ordinands at college,' he went on. 'Secretly at first, but then it became more obvious and he no longer denied it. He explained himself with faultless logic, poking at my distress like a curious mortician. I retaliated by shagging every priest who made a pass at me. The theological college was my brothel. When the Church offered him his first parish in the north, I followed. What else was there for me? The Durham diocese became our sexual battlefield.'

'I think the battle's over now.' I moved closer to Chris and laid a hand on his shoulder. 'We should have a glass of wine, love, to celebrate the new reign of Jake.'

I returned from the kitchen with two glasses of wine and noticed that Chris was sweeping around the front door with an old broom.

'Wouldn't the Hoover would be more effective. You're dropping twigs all over the carpet.'

Chris shook his head. He was murmuring a tune under his breath. Just another one of his moments, I thought, and curled up on the settee.

I listened to the helicopter fade gradually into the night. The crystals on the dream-tree stopped twinkling and fell quiet. The front door clicked open and closed, and Chris returned to the Yellow Room alone, rubbing his hands, satisfied.

'Who was at the door?' I asked, looking over his shoulder.

'No one,' he smiled, brimful of some mystery. 'I was just seeing the shadows out.'

V
Teiresias

Spring came that year with the vigour of a goddess returning from the underworld. Beneath the great iron bridge in the centre of town, the banks of the River Wear were aflame with daffodils and crocuses. The North Sea glistened with the sea-god's pleasure and the nesting gulls barked ahoy from their roosts along the cliff-edge.

Inland, Chris and I planted lupins and night-scented stock seeds in the window boxes. I rarely slept in my own college room now, and casually evacuated the halls of residence throughout February, dismantling my life piecemeal and rearranging it in the new order of Chris's sanctuary. Of course, Jake also became a permanent feature of the house, bearing his suitcase, computer, and even furniture on endless bus trips.

As the seed heads in the window boxes rose with the soft promise of heat, so Chris also seemed to thaw and unfurl. The stony loner with the dark-eyed stare from the first term had shed his permafrost frown and become something other, something changed. The adamantine statue had become organic flesh and smile, warm to Jake's touch, tender by March.

On the morning of the vernal equinox, Chris readied the house for their third "lunniversary" party: there had been three lunar cycles since the full moon when he and Jake had first met. Chris was vacuuming the rarely used green-wallpapered drawing room. He was considering what costume to wear for the evening shindig, when a removal van pulled up outside the house. Jake jumped down from the driver's cabin wearing a tight white T-shirt.

'Special delivery for my boy,' he called, bounding through the front door. He wrapped his strong arms around Chris. I had already seen Jake emerge from the bathroom steam in his underwear and, as Chris had insisted on many occasions, he did have the body of Michelangelo's *David*. Although he was short, he was stocky and had muscular arms. It was a physique to admire, and no one admired it more than Jake himself.

I dropped the dusting cloths I had been busy with and joined Chris at the window. We stared at the removal van in the street like two excited children trying to guess a Christmas present.

'It's something special for the house,' said Jake. At times like this, when he could barely contain his excitement, his Durham accent grew pronounced and his voice swept up and down several octaves. 'It's from me for the house. Can you guess what it is?'

'For the house?' Chris repeated. 'A four-poster bed?'

'No. Here's a clue. I'll be playing with it more than anyone.'

Your cock, I thought, but said nothing.

'A piano?' asked Chris. Jake grinned widely and pulled Chris into the street. It was a clear March morning, the sky was as blue as Jake's eyes, and a warm breeze swept the old year's leaves down the pavement.

Jake climbed into the rear of the van and leaned wooden boards against the bumper so the piano could roll down. Chris and I heaved against the weight as Jake rolled it safely to the road.

'It's fantastic,' said Chris the animated, the ever-encouraging. Jake lifted the lid and began to play an imperfect, quirky composition.

'My folks bought it for me,' Jake explained. 'It's only second-hand. They say I can pay them back when I'm rich and famous. I told them not to hold their breath.'

'How rich do pianists get?'

'Rich enough to buy a small island for my Greek prince.'

'Lesbos?' Chris turned to me and winked. 'Or Crete perhaps?'

'Isn't that a type of pancake?' asked Jake, slowing his rhythm and frowning thoughtfully.

'We can get pancakes too.' Chris turned Jake's baseball cap backwards. 'As many as you like, when you're an Honorary Member of the Royal Academy.'

'Then we'll live in Crete and eat pancakes on the beach.'

I smiled and listened to his playing. It was a simple tune that flowed clunkily in repetitive rounds, a Norwegian folk dance, I think – one of Grieg's country dances that Jake was trying to master at that time. My thoughts followed the rhythm along its lively course, over the houses and into the cloudless sky, then down the iron drains to the dark tunnels of the earth. I think he said it was called *Spring Jig* or some such thing but the name has long-since been forgotten, as have Jake's musical ambitions.

* * *

Carefully, Jake placed a vase of roses on the piano in the Green Room. He stood back to appreciate his arrangement. He had sketched a stylised portrait of the moon with charcoal, which Chris had framed and hung on the wall over the piano. It was the same symbol they had had engraved on the rings they exchanged at a commitment ceremony in January. Of course, this was all before even the Scandinavians had dreamed up equal marriage rights. This was back when such commitment was a radical stance against an overtly hostile world. At that time, barely a full lunar cycle after they had met, I remember complaining that January was too cold to hold a wedding, especially at night on the north-east coast. We were walking along the harbour wall in the blast of a wintry gale. The moon cast a silver path over the dark, churning sea.

'It's not a wedding,' Chris turned around, smiling at Jake. 'It's a hand-fasting. To last a year and a day, or so long as our love shall endure.'

'Beautiful.' I had to shout above the roar of the waves that crashed on either side of the walk. 'But it's still too cold, whatever you call it. How far are you going out?'

Jake pointed at the dark tower at the end of the harbour wall.

'The old lighthouse.'

We reached the broken fence where I was to wait for their return. The lighthouse loomed at the end of the causeway. Lone fishermen kicked their feet over the edge of the wall and struggled with rods and tackle in the wind. Chris and Jake climbed through the broken fence and laboured against the elements along the unlit path.

I crouched behind the fence for shelter and waited for the lovers to finish their secret ceremony. Above me, a handful of shredded clouds streaked across the constellations. From the direction of the town, the church clocks chimed the midnight hour. A siren's wail echoed between the tower blocks and drifted over the waves. I counted the twinkling lights of ships on the black horizon, and was surprised by the sudden flare of a falling star.

As the clocks chimed twelve-thirty, Chris and Jake returned from the causeway. I congratulated them and asked if they had seen the shooting star.

Chris shook his head. 'We were otherwise engaged,' he explained, smirking.

'You were shagging? In this weather? Guys, really.'

'Consummating the vows,' said Jake. 'We had to keep warm somehow.'

He linked his arm through mine and I tensed at the over-familiar gesture. He spread his hand in the blaze of a streetlight and invited me to admire the gold band on his fourth finger. It was the first time I had seen the simple engraved symbol.

In the green room two months later, the same design was hanging as a framed sketch above Jake's piano.

'Where did you get the idea?' I asked, polishing the piano lid.

'Chris wanted a simple waxing moon. I wanted a full moon with a crater. So we combined the two.'

'Well, aren't you the talented one?'

Jake leaned against the piano and looked anxiously at me. I felt ashamed and lowered my eyes, but he fixed me with those baby-blues.

'You don't like me very much, do you?' he asked. 'Sometimes I feel that – I don't know – maybe you think I'm not good enough for him.'

I was not expecting such candour. I had no where to look but back at him. He was beautiful, that I admitted, and I could not help but understand how Chris had become addicted to his body. Sometimes he astounded me with his naiveté, listening with wide uncomprehending eyes when Chris and I argued politics over the kitchen table. At other times, such as now, I was surprised by his insight. He could read me like sheet music.

'Why do you say that?' I knew that my voice was too shrill, my avoidance too obvious.

'Because you won't answer me. Because I don't know the stuff that you and Chris know. I can't talk politics or books. Perhaps because Chris could do much better than me. He could, though, couldn't he?'

I sighed and laid the dusters on the piano. 'You want the truth?'

'The truth,' he said, folding his arms to shield his chest from the barbs of my honesty. Despite his brawn, he looked vulnerable. My grievance against him dissipated with the dust in the sunlit air.

'The truth. I think that, because of you, Chris is happy. He might very well be the happiest he's ever been. I think that this is the first time he's been in love, really in love, and that you're helping him bury whatever demons he has in his past. The truth is, you remind me that I'm alone. I'm the sad old gooseberry left on the shelf.'

'Has he said he loves me?' Apparently, Jake only heard selective fragments of my truth.

'All the time. Hasn't he told you yet?'

Jake shook his head and gazed at me with those clear blue eyes. 'I hope he does. But I don't expect anything from him.'

'Come on, man,' I said, somewhat sharply. 'Chris adores you. The truth is that I'm terminally single. It's not easy for me to be around either of you when you're smouldering with passion all the time. And, yes, I am aware how outrageously selfish that sounds.'

As I spoke, I formed a vision of Chris blazing in the flames of his emotions. The image faded and Chris appeared on the street corner, summoned by my imagination.

'You're not a gooseberry, Cat,' Jake said gently. He stood beside me at the window to gaze at his boyfriend. 'Everyone wants you.'

'Yeah, sure. Like Grim Gail.'

'Or Cyane at the club?'

'She lives underground,' I sighed at the memory of the beautiful nymph behind the bar at Diana's.

'Or Richard? He's a bisexy fucker, don't you think? He can't take his eyes off you.'

The warm flavour of Richard's golden body came back to me in faint waves, subtle as the scent of Jake's roses on the piano. I remembered his golden hair, his shy but curious glances behind the glasses. I sighed again.

'Perhaps it's best if I'm not here so much,' I said quietly, changing the subject. 'Perhaps you and Chris should have this place to yourselves.'

'But you're like a sister to him. More than a sister. He's said so, many times. You're a sister to us both.'

When Chris came in, we talked of other things.

* * *

'My father's garden is a barren place,' said Chris. He was dabbing gold paint onto his lips and eyelids. 'A row of old oak trees is the only living thing in that wasteland. There's a dilapidated tenant's cottage next door, separated from his vicarage by a great stone wall. I sheltered in that cottage during the warmer months, though the rain dripped down the cracks and the wind whistled through the broken windows.'

'Why did you stay there?' Jake asked, smearing silver paint down his cheek bones.

'To get away from my father, but it didn't work. In spite of the inconvenience, he still pottered down the drive in his dressing-gown at midnight and scratched at the cottage door until I woke. I was led, taken, still sleeping into the garden and told to strip off among the nettles. There, we cried out the penitential psalms until his god became bored.'

'Why did you strip off?' asked Jake.

'It was my Gethsemane, my place of anguish. He said it was what his god wanted. He called me his offering. After we finished and he returned to the vicarage, Joseph would park quietly outside the cottage and scratch at the door for his turn.'

'His turn at what?' I asked, lifting the blindfold I was wearing for my costume. 'Saying penitential psalms?'

'How do I look?' Chris held out his palms. 'Take the blindfold off, Cat. How do I look?'

'Stunning,' said Jake.

'Like a god,' I concurred. He had draped a loose white toga over his shoulder, exposing the dark hairs of his chest and one pink nipple. His entire body was painted gold and gleamed in the lamplight. 'Who are you?'

'Here's a clue.' He waved a torch over his head.

'The Statue of Liberty?' Jake suggested, struggling to hang a quiver of arrows from his silver belt.

'Ah, Prometheus, bearer of fire, of course,' I said, pulling the blindfold back over my eyes. 'Well, guys, who I am?'

'A blindfold, a toga, an enormous pair of tits and a banana down your knickers,' Chris listed the items. 'Teiresias, I presume?'

'Absolutely. Man-woman prophetess, shifting between the sexes with the fluid grace of a transvestite. Now, give me your hand, Diana.' Blindly, I stretched out my fingers until they touched Jake's bow. 'I prophesy that you shall open the wine.'

I was considering what Chris had revealed about his father's garden while Jake uncorked the wine. In blindness, I felt along the kitchen surfaces until I found the back door. The evening was cooler than it had been earlier and a breeze rattled the dream-tree. The voice of the wood creaked as softly as an old woman's whisper.

'Not too cold for you out here, is it, my transexy prophet?' Chris asked, sliding stealthily beside me.

'I was just thinking of your story,' I replied, resting my head against his shoulder. 'Of your father's house. Tell me, how long did you live there?'

He said nothing for a moment and I wondered if he would answer at all. 'My mother took us to Whitby when I was eleven. I went back to live with him when I was thirteen. Why do you ask?'

'Because I don't understand why you went back.'

He laughed, but the sound was too harsh, too forced. 'What is this, Cat, the Spanish Inquisition? Take that blindfold off. Teiresias has gone to your head.'

He wrapped his arms around my waist and I held his fingers. I waited some time before asking, 'Why did you go back to that house?'

Chris sighed and let go of my waist. 'My mother didn't want me to. She said that my father had been twisted by his religion. I thought I knew better than her. I was afraid of his Devil: I needed his God for protection. I suppose I went back because I didn't want to be what I am.'

'And what are you?'

'I like men,' he said facetiously, as though this were news.

'You felt guilty about that?'

'Bronze-age superstitions can still be relied on to make people feel guilty, even after thousands of years.'

'Is that why you stripped and said penitential psalms? Guilt?'

'Amongst other reasons.' He steered me towards the back door. 'Enough for now, Cat. This is no theme for tonight. It's meant to be a wild and unruly party.'

As he walked me inside, the doorbell rang. I heard Jake skip lightly along the carpet.

'Have you ever seen such a butch Diana before?' asked Chris.

'Nor one so unchaste,' I agreed.

I felt my way into the kitchen and found the open wine bottle. As I poured myself a glass, Jake stampeded into the room, laughing wildly.

'It's Richard,' he cried. 'He's come dressed as a woman. He's gorgeous. Cat, you have to see this.'

I took off the blindfold and beheld the erotic apparition that was Richard. He glided into the kitchen, seductive and nymph-like, dressed in a tight scarlet evening gown and feather boa. His eyelashes were coloured darkly with black mascara; his lips pouted with exaggerated passion. Voluptuous, I thought. Delicious.

'Do you want me to seduce you?' he asked deeply, resting his rouged cheek against the doorframe. I savoured the apple-scented fragrance of his golden hair which hung loosely over his bare shoulders. The banana stirred in my knickers.

* * *

They say that the blind seer Teiresias was a wise prophet in the ancient city of Thebes. They say that he warned the king of Thebes that the city would be destroyed if the king did not worship the god of wine, Bacchus. The sober king despised Bacchus's drunk and disorderly devotees. He refused to heed Teiresias's warning and outlawed the worship of Bacchus. There is an irony that infuses all morality tales, a poetic justice in the whim of the gods. Bacchus intoxicated the people with wine and provoked a riot in their hearts. The people went wild, the city was destroyed and the king was ripped apart by his own drunken subjects. Such is Greek tragedy and such was the story I was telling when the doorbell chimed at seven o'clock.

'It's too early to be anyone special,' I said, handing a glass of cheap claret to Chris. 'It's probably the Jehovah's Witnesses again. Richard, you go. You'll convert them as soon as they see you in that frock. Chris, you stay here with me and Jake. Let us worship the god of wine instead.'

Chris ignored the wine and went to get the door in his toga. We heard the front door slam and muffled voices drifted closer.

'This,' said Chris, returning to the kitchen and evidently embarrassed, 'is Father Cuthbert, our landlord. The honourable master of this house.'

Behind Chris loomed a middle-aged priest in a dog collar and a shiny black suit. He laid his extraordinarily long fingers around Chris's bare arm and moved him aside. Placing a leather-bound Bible on the table, he moved to the vacant chair and lowered himself down with the grandeur of a mediaeval cardinal.

'How do you do?' he said, taking in Jake's naked chest. 'You must be the famous Jake Edlestone that we've all been hearing so much about.'

He reached across the table and clasped Jake's hand.

'And you, my dear, must be Carolina.' He took my hand and pressed his cold lips against my skin. It took all my resolve not to recoil visibly from the touch.

'Catriona,' I corrected him. He smirked.

Ignoring Richard, Father Cuthbert fingered the pockets of his jacket and produced a cigar. Richard turned his back upon the priest and blew smoke rings into the air. So cool, I thought, admiring his pouting lips. So debonair.

'Now, Christopher, my wife and I have had a perplexing telephone conversation with Father Joseph. You do you remember Father Joseph, don't you?' Cuthbert raised an eyebrow and crossed his skeletal legs. 'It's all very awkward, this business. You see, Joseph says that you're not living alone in this house, my house, as per our original agreement. Indeed, Joseph is concerned that those parishioners of mine who happen to live in this neighbourhood would be, shall we say, unsettled to learn that two overt homosexuals were in flagrant occupancy of my property. Being a man of the cloth, of course, a reputation is unfortunately something one does have to safeguard. Not for myself, of course, but for the unsullied character of my employer.' Vaguely and almost inadvertently, the priest crossed himself. 'Whatever my personal sympathies, it would not be proper for me to be seen to condone such unorthodox arrangements, if you catch my drift.'

Having come towards the end of his homily, Father Cuthbert took a puff of his cigar and tongued the smoke behind his jagged teeth.

'I am certain you will appreciate my predicament,' he concluded, tapping the cigar against the rim of the ashtray.

Jake and I exchanged glances. In the ensuing silence, Chris strolled casually to a cupboard and collected a crystal wineglass for the priest.

'Red or white, Father?' he asked, placing the glass on the table.

'As it happens, I have just finished all my rounds. A decent nip of the old red wouldn't go amiss. And then, of course, there is the issue of the guest bedroom. I know I haven't made use of it as frequently as I would wish, but the stresses and strains of my vocation are – '

'Unimaginable, I would guess,' Chris completed the sentence, his empathy deep and convincing. He filled Cuthbert's glass to the brim and then, to my horror, proceeded to massage the priest's angular shoulders.

I sensed some scheme fermenting, an unspoken performance calling the actors into place. His strategy ticked in the air like the clinking crystals on the dream-tree outside.

'You do need somewhere to retreat, to reinvigorate yourself. That's only natural.' Chris winked at Jake. 'We do understand.'

Jake returned the smile and rested his hand on Cuthbert's bony fingers. 'I imagine the choristers can be hard to manage, too,' he said, soothing the priest with his soft Durham accent. 'Are they quite a handful?'

Those eyes could enchant a cobra, I thought as Jake gazed down at the priest. Cuthbert uncrossed his legs and leaned back into Chris's massage.

'Of course, you could increase the rent,' Chris said reasonably, 'backdated to December. And Catriona wouldn't mind having the smaller spare bedroom. Then you can come and stay in the room next to our bedroom whenever you need. Problem solved. Everyone's happy.'

'Whenever you want,' Jake agreed.

'It would be very cosy.'

'It is tempting, don't you think?'

Cuthbert twitched his thin lips into a boyish smirk. 'I believe it is, Jake. Very tempting.'

Chris slapped Cuthbert's shoulder. 'Why not come next weekend? We'll be visiting Jake's cousin in Coventry, so you would have the entire house to yourself.'

'Now, how relaxing would that be?' said Jake, physically taken aback by the excellence of the idea.

'But wouldn't you both want to be here?' Father Cuthbert sounded hurt. 'It would be so much more fun if you two boys were around to keep me company.'

'We've plenty of days ahead to spend together,' said Chris.

Jake refilled his wineglass and smiled like a cherub.

'I could arrange it with Constance,' he said, draining his glass, 'my wife. That will not be a problem. It never is.'

Chris helped Cuthbert into his coat and escorted him to the front door. Jake and I leaned behind the kitchen door, listening to his parting words.

'I do look forward to seeing more of you,' he said through the cigar between his teeth. 'And, especially, your charming young friend, Jake. What a revelation he is. And it would be delightful to meet more of your acquaintances. The girls can go wherever girls go and do whatever girls do, but we boys could make a night of it. I do look forward to it. Good evening, Christopher.'

As the front door closed, Jake and I wept with stifled laughter.

'You two are shameless,' I said. 'Hookers have more discretion. How did you manage it?'

'You saw what happened; you were here.' Chris swaggered to the sink and rinsed Father Cuthbert's glass clean. 'Softly, softly, catchy priesty. You know you can't complain. We've established a commune.'

'Oh yes, the smaller spare bedroom for Carolina,' I mimicked, returning to my place beside Richard. 'How very generous of you. And what, pray tell, will happen when he actually stays?'

'Leave that to me.' Chris's face was triumphant. 'He won't stay more than once, I guarantee you that. What do you think, Richard? Talented bunch of hustlers, don't you agree?'

Richard turned to the ceiling, manifestly unimpressed.

'Possibly.' He blew a smoke ring across the table and then turned to me. 'I'm afraid I was distracted, attention elsewhere.'

* * *

Richard was a beautiful woman when he chose to be. He reclined in Chris's throne, pouting, sucking on the end of an extended cigarette holder and blithely contemplating the party. His blonde eyelashes flickered like butterfly wings as one admirer after another drifted into his orbit, curious to find out who this glamorous apparition could be.

'So sophisticated.' I said, handing him a cocktail glass. 'I could almost fancy you. Almost, I said.'

Behind the rouge, Richard blushed. I perched on the arm of his chair for much of the evening, poised like his paramour. The hungry fire of his gaze warmed my cheek.

'Fucking hell, that's her,' I hissed in Richard's ear when Grim Gail strolled into the Yellow Room brandishing a sausage roll. 'Who summoned the Ghosts of Girlfriends Past?'

'Cat,' my ex-girlfriend said simply when she noticed me. 'Didn't expect you here. Bit grand, this joint, isn't it?'

She lurched awkwardly at my face in an attempt to kiss my cheeks, showering me with pastry crumbs in the process. I returned the air-kiss and smiled.

'Gail, how splendid to see you.' I rested an easy hand on Richard's knee. 'Yes, this is where I'm living now. What a delightful surprise to see you here.'

'I came with Dane and Andy.' She glanced keenly at Richard's furry legs. 'Those silly boys are showing off. Think they're in love. We never did all that handholding and kissy stuff in front of people, did we? God, I hope not. We didn't want people to know we were together, did we. None of people's business, that.'

'Absolutely.'

Dane scurried into the Yellow Room with Andy trailing in his wake. The huddle of Chris's literature friends quickly dispersed as Dane gibbered about the dearth of attractive young men in the world today. I asked Gail how long Dane and Andy had been together.

'Since New Year's Eve.' She shrugged indifferently and regarded my hand on Richard's thigh. 'Cat, you ever going to introduce me to your new friend? Don't think I've met her before.'

Richard leaned forward with seductive grace and lightly touched his pouting lips against her cheek.

'Enchanted,' he whispered in a deep, ambiguous voice.

'My name's Gail,' she laughed, ineptly tossing her hair as maybe she might have once seen an actress do in shampoo commercial. 'We haven't met before, have we? What's your name, darling?'

Richard relaxed back into the throne and raised the cigarette holder to his barely parted lips.

'Aurora,' he answered, slowly exhaling smoke through his teeth. 'Aurora Bathsheba Delilah Day.'

'My girlfriend,' I explained, draping a possessive arm around Richard's shoulder. 'She's finally agreed to move in with me. I'm so pleased you two have finally met. I can't keep my hands off her. Isn't she divine?'

Richard tugged my waist and rested his hand on the banana, teasing the stalk with his fingers. I lightly rapped his knuckles.

'Have you ever seen such devotion?'

Gail glanced suspiciously between me and Richard until Dane interrupted us, pulling Andy along by his trouser-belt.

'Cat, darling.' Dane flapped his free hand in my general direction. 'Have you seen Chrissy or Jakey anywhere? I have to complain about the lack of talent at this dreadful party. It's a catastrophe. What were they thinking? Where are those dreadful boys?'

'In the Green Room. Next door. Jake's entertaining the troops with his new piano.'

'He didn't waste any time moving in with Chrissy, did he? I always said it was animal lust with those two. Bound to end in tears, disaster in the making. I'm always right. Especially after Jake's little infidelity with Gorgeous Gary, of course, but we're not allowed to talk about that. Maybe I'll be proved wrong. There's always a first time. Who knows where those two birds of paradise will end up?'

'Gary?' I asked. 'Which Gary?'

'Hush my mouth.' Dane covered his lips with both hands. He leaned close to my face so I could see his flint-like teeth, smell his Tequila breath. 'Best forget I said anything, sweetheart.'

I found Chris leaning against the piano in the Green Room, concentrating on Jake's performance. It was another piece by Grieg, I remember clearly, "In the Hall of the Mountain King" from *Peer Gynt*. It should have been played mischievously. The gnomes and goblins of the troll king should have come creeping out of the shadows, tentative and on tip-toes at first before they unsettled the room and caused a riot. But Jake was still learning this piece and it sounded clumsy and ponderous. Blind to any imperfections, Chris toyed erotically with the silver bow and gazed at his lover's fingers on the keys. I stood in the doorway behind a crowd of patient undergraduates and waited for the performance to end. Perhaps only I felt awkward. Perhaps I was simply discomposed by Dane's troublesome rumour. It would not be an easy thing to contrive some way of raising the matter with Chris.

'They look like a tableau from the Romantic period, don't you think?' a soft voice asked in my ear. 'A daguerreotype from the golden age. A scene from the Villa Dioadati. When Jake's famous, we'll look back and remember how beautiful they were this evening.'

Conrad leaned against the wall and rolled a cigarette. He was Chris's closest friend, a gentle, self-possessed presence who seemed to appear out of nowhere and evaporate at a moment's notice. Tonight, he lurked in the corner of the Green Room, smiling unconvincingly at Jake's music. There was a trace of steel in his voice whenever he talked about Jake. Though never substantiated, I did wonder if he secretly desired Chris – in his own, interminably straight way.

'Sometimes, Conrad, I could swear you were longing to be in Jake's shoes. How long before you spill the beans?'

'About what?' He smiled and held my gaze.

'Oh, the usual: ambiguous stirrings, man on man fantasies?'

'Sorry to disappoint you again, Cat.'

'You really must do something about this denial. It's so disappointingly conservative.'

Conrad smirked and turned towards the piano. 'Have you heard about Chris's grand plan for a coven? He wants to start some new college group, a Society of Heathens.'

'Of course, he's been talking about it for weeks. Congratulations on changing the subject, by the way. I barely noticed. Do you think anything will come of this pagan project?'

'Sure, people will join. He's written an article for the college paper. No doubt you've seen it? Not bad; even possesses literary promise. Says he wants a society founded on free love, an Epicurean revolution. We'll all be Greek gods, and so on. He's even persuaded me to be the group secretary. You know how persuasive he can be.'

'And you wouldn't refuse Chris anything, would you? I thought you were a materialist, Conrad. Have you suddenly found a spirituality?'

'The gods are metaphors, you know as well as I do. No, it's the free love that attracted me to his coven.'

'Is he planning orgies now? How very bohemian. And I thought the group was about retelling ancient myths. I never imagined he had a different kind of oral tradition in mind.'

I could not imagine Jake taking kindly to Chris's idea of free love, but then I remembered Dane's dark hint. I asked Conrad if he had ever heard of someone called Gary. Conrad shook his head and lit another cigarette.

'I think Dane mentioned that name earlier. Naturally, I paid no attention. Why do you ask?'

'I heard him mention it too. I don't imagine it's anything.'

* * *

Jake knelt on his bed, flushed with the exertion of his performance, while I, Teiresias, wise man-woman prophetess, tied the blindfold around my eyes and took his warm palm into mine. Conrad sat close to Chris on the floor. He flicked a lighter and inhaled deeply from the spliff they shared. Downstairs, I recognised the cry of Dane's hacking hyena laugh. Outside, the wind began to rise. It ruffled the curtains and jingled the crystals on the dream-tree.

Jake's palm was sweaty between my fingers.

'The love-line is your strongest feature,' I noted, stroking his hand. 'But it breaks in three places. I can feel a name written at the first break, but it is secret. I shall return to this.

'There are two figures around your head-line. One stands upon your intellect, raising the line upwards. The other lurks below, whispering lies and subterfuge. This is a warning: you must drag the lower figure into the light to expose him before he causes untold damage to your relationship.

'The life-line is vague and broken with choices. These are choices for you to make, though you feel that they are outside your control.

'I come back to the name that breaks your love-line. It is a name of four letters, and begins with G. You must articulate this name, reveal him to Chris before the figure lurking beneath wreaks havoc. The name has come to me now. It is Gary.'

I lifted the blindfold and looked at Jake. He was grinning, nervous and embarrassed. Failing to find words, he ran his fingers through his hair.

'Dane's been spreading rumours about you and this Gary,' I explained. 'He and Andy are promoting themselves as the romance of the year. I think he sees you and Chris as the competition. He's trying to stir up trouble.'

Chris exhaled deeply, his dark eyes glinting in the low-lit room. Jake rose slowly from the bed and led Chris by the hand into the bedroom next door. After they had left, we could hear their hushed voices as Jake explained whatever he had to confess about the mysterious Gary. I accepted the joint from Conrad.

'Can you do mine, oh wise Teiresias?' He held out his palm for me to inspect. 'You've been pretty accurate so far.'

'Thus speaks the sceptic.' I pulled the blindfold over my eyes and held Conrad's dry hand.

'The strongest line is your head-line. It dominates your palm like a streak of lightning. The heart-line is straight at first, but becomes more curious as you age. There is an unusual bend in the sex-line, a queer shape which you must come to terms with.'

Conrad laughed and withdrew his hand. 'Not close at all,' he said. 'I don't know much about witchery, but I do know there's no sex-line.'

'Still, I am troubled by a repressive tension in your aura. There is a question that needs to be addressed before you can truly be at peace. Maybe some sexual inhibition that needs to be overcome?'

Conrad was rescued by the return of a sheepish Jake. He came gingerly into the bedroom and flopped onto the bed.

'Chris is throwing Dane out,' he said. 'Gary was the guy I was seeing the night I met Chris. I ended that relationship the next day, I really did, but didn't see the need to tell Chris about it. It turns out that Gary and Dane know each other. I think they were trying to sabotage us.'

'A pair of serpents in your Eden?' I smiled and held Jake's hand.

We listened to the fracas downstairs. Dane's high-pitched howling sounded uncannily similar to his rendition of *Endless Love*, though I could not think why he would be singing that. I never did find out what happened downstairs, but Chris returned to the bedroom with a wolfish grin.

'Dane has had to leave unexpectedly,' he announced. 'And Jake and I will be having some time away together, starting with Coventry next weekend. Then off to see my mother in Whitby. And, finally, I get to meet his parents in Elliston.'

Chris lay upon the bed and looked up at Jake's face.

'Everything's okay now, love,' Chris said softly, stroking his lover's hair. 'The rats have been evicted from Hamelin.'

'I am sorry.' Jake wanted to say more but Chris laid a finger on his lips.

'We've seen the last of Dane. And we can forget about Gary.'

Conrad and I exchanged an uncomfortable look. We were about to leave when we heard stilettos on the landing. Richard strutted into the room, readjusting his bra-strap.

'Gail's not one to take no for an answer, is she?' he said, sitting cross-legged on the floor beside me. 'She had to feel my subterfuge –' he nodded down at his crotch, '– before she finally got the message.'

I too put my hand between his legs. Only, the message I received was very different.

* * *

March continued to be exceptionally warm. By the following Friday, we were waiting outside Chris's house and sweating in the spring sunshine. The tops of most garden walls in this neighbourhood had been cemented defensively with shards of broken glass, which reflected the sunlight like prisms. Jake poked his fingers into the window boxes where we had buried lupin seeds. Chris stood beside him with one hand on his shoulder. Richard frowned up the street.

'Here comes Father Cuthbert,' he said, lifting his rucksack. 'You can recognise his penis-substitute a mile off.'

The priest's black BMW pulled into a parking space. Father Cuthbert emerged wearing a biretta and expensive sunglasses.

'You do know that this is a very small town.' He peered over his glasses at Chris and Jake. 'I would prefer it if you two didn't appear so, shall we say, overt in public.'

'Isn't that how Jesus finished the Beatitudes?' I asked.

'Some of us do have reputations and the sanctity of our employer to maintain,' he continued, ignoring me. 'And I have absolutely no intention of courting trouble with the diocese because of your peccadilloes, Christopher. It would be embarrassing if I had to remind you that this is not your house.'

'There's milk in the fridge and clean sheets on the bed.' Chris attempted to give Cuthbert a peck on the cheek. The priest recoiled from the kiss and darted towards the shelter of the open door.

'For God's sake, Christopher, never do that,' he hissed, dabbing his face with a handkerchief. He glanced nervously at the other houses before closing the front door behind him.

We travelled to Coventry by train. The sun glistened on the North Sea and bathed the fields in golden green. Richard rested his head against my shoulder and snored softly as he slept. His eyelids fluttered as the dark shadows of passing houses flashed across his features.

On the night of the lunniversary party, after all the guests had gone home, Richard went downstairs to the Yellow Room, hugging his sleeping-bag to his chest. I waited for silence to descend like a dark angel upon the house before I crept onto the landing. I heard Chris murmur in his sleep, disturbed by bad dreams, and Jake grumble into his pillow. I avoided the one treacherously loud floorboard outside the bathroom and stalked down the stairs.

For all lovers, the first night is always possessed by mythopoetic symbols. The streetlights through the curtains, the patterns on the carpet, the humming of the fridge: these things become more potent than mere incidental memories. They take on the substance of legend. The quick breathing in the darkness; the meeting of skin with warm skin; the taste of his tongue against mine, tentative at first, and then hungry when it finds a welcome. Mundane they may be to every other creature, these memories are my totems now and always shall be.

It was the same for Chris and Jake, although I can never approach the inner sanctum where their totems lie in undisturbed slumber. When they undressed in darkness, when they spoke in whispers, when Jake asked if he could kiss Chris: those things are locked in the holiest caverns of their beings. No one can ever fully appreciate another's sacred love-myth. No one else can ever feel the power of the images that linger, beyond separation or death, in a lover's memory.

I remember the first night I spent with Richard through image and sensation. It is a legend I often revisit and each time I return, I know that somehow I alter it. I can try to recreate the past. I can try to make it live again as it did the first time around. But it is always a replica, always at a further remove from the real thing. No one can ever adequately give life to the heart-filled moment that has passed.

The morning after the party, Chris and Jake knocked quietly on the door to the Yellow Room and brought tea and oranges for our breakfast. We talked about everyday things. Chris cuddled Jake on their throne in his usual way; Richard stroked my back as though it had always been like this.

At one moment, Chris and I exchanged glances and a slow realisation spread like the imperceptible dawn over my skin. I understood clearly that Chris had changed fundamentally in the past three months, just as I was beginning to. A metamorphosis had come over us. It was something internal, an electrical pulse in the brain, some slight variation in the aortic rhythm that had forever altered our states, transformed our external structures. We were not who we had been, nor yet what we would become.

As the train passed through a tunnel, I watched Richard's sleeping face mirrored in the window. Opposite me, Chris rested his head on Jake's knee and gazed at his own dark reflection.

'Being on a train is like being an immortal,' Chris mused.

Jake looked up and smiled his confusion. 'How's that?'

'See, as the train accelerates, the landscape speeds up. The hills become fields, become valleys, become towns, become hills again. The body of the land grows wheat fields, then forests, then houses, then back to forests. The sea covers the land and then retreats, leaving wheat fields again. In the time it takes me to buy a cup of coffee, vast cities have been replaced by trees. And we haven't aged at all.'

'Does this mean that the gods travel by Intercity?'

Chris gazed over the midlands as a lion surveying his plains. 'These ones do.'

Jake's cousin, Claire, met us at the station and walked us to her car. She was a tense woman, I would say, a strained woman. She had bleak eyes and a rigid smile. I was not surprised when, within five minutes of arriving, she expressed her hope that we would accompany her to her Baptist Chapel on Sunday morning. Chris's eyes flashed; the ghoul within had been awakened.

'Do you go to church, Claire?' he asked. 'How splendid.'

'It's a nine o'clock service, so you can have a lie-in beforehand.' She was delighted by his interest.

'You know, Claire, I haven't been to church for four years. The last time I went was at my father's church. He was a priest. He still is, for all I know.'

'Then you must come on Sunday. Everyone has doubts, Chris. You mustn't let years of grace be broken by momentary lapses of faith. They pass, but the joy of returning to the fold is so much sweeter.'

'Oh no, Claire. The pleasures of fallen angels are by far the sweetest.' He slapped Jake's arse. Jake threw a warning glance, but this only incited Chris further. 'I can't remember any pleasures of going to church. See, I have an enduring memory of my father smothering the mouth of a choirboy and thrashing him with a broom handle. And Jesus just looked down from his crucifix and did nothing. I'm sure he had other things on his mind. What things do you do in your chapel, Claire?'

Claire's cheeks paled to the shade of her Whitsun blouse. Her eyes smarted with the insensible martyrdom of a Christian mocked. She led us in silence to her car. I lagged behind with Chris and sensed his triumph.

'I'm going to enjoy this weekend.'

'Chris, was your father's village church large enough to have a choir and choirboys?'

Claire had reached her car and was opening the door for Jake and Richard to climb inside.

'As it happens,' Chris said quietly so the others would not hear. 'I was the only boy in my father's choir.'

As Chris had predicted, he thoroughly enjoyed spending two nights in the company of Jake's devout cousin. Claire summoned cohorts of her brethren on both evenings to wage war with the demon she had welcomed into her house, but this only encouraged him.

'It's all too easy,' he laughed, pouring another glass of wine for me. We were on our own in Claire's kitchen, evaluating the battle so far. 'Where's the intellectual challenge?'

'Go easy on Claire. You've drained her of blood. And Jake's looking bored, really bored.'

Chris winked and returned to the fracas in the sitting room.

'So, Claire,' he said innocently enough as he sat beside her. 'I wondered if you could help me on the path to enlightenment. Why is it, exactly, that I'm going to burn for eternity in Hell?'

'I didn't say you would burn in Hell,' she replied, patiently as an angel. 'Only Our Lord knows who will be saved and who will be damned.'

'Damned for eternity in the painful fires of Hell?'

'No one knows what Hell is like,' one of Claire's bright-eyed brethren leaned forward. 'We imagine there will be eternal fires because that's the most painful form of torture we can think of. It's like a metaphor.'

'So, God invented the most painful form of torture imaginable for me because I love Jake? Isn't that a little unreasonable? And, what does it say in the First Epistle of John: "Whoever does not love, does not know God; because God is Love."'

'Our Lord loves the sinner, but hates the sin,' said Claire, resting her chin on her knuckles. 'He knows the world is full of temptation and He loves us all the more for resisting it. I love Jake and I love you, because I'm a Christian, but it would be wrong of me to love your sin.'

'So, my love for Jake is a sin.' Chris scratched his head. 'But it's okay for me to rape a virgin, as long as she's female? I don't know why you'd want to choose this particular religion, Claire. I don't think I can respect your sense of right and wrong.'

'No, Chris, it's not okay for you to rape a virgin. Where on earth did you get that idea?'

'It says so in the Book of Numbers, when God orders the Israelites to keep the young girls of the conquered tribes as rape-slaves. And it happens about four times in Deuteronomy, and again in Judges, and Samuel, and in Exodus – '

'Ah, yes,' Claire's friend clapped her hands. 'But that's the Old Testament. When Jesus came, he fulfilled the law of the Old Testament.'

'So, raping slaves was fine with God until the last century BC, but then he had a change of heart about everything in the first century AD? Apart from gay sex, of course, which still wasn't to his taste.'

'It's not as simple as that.' Claire retreated to the corner of the sofa. 'The scriptures explain everything much more clearly than I can.'

'Why can't you explain what you think?'

'Because the scriptures are the word of God,' she said, holding her head in her hands.

'So, at the turn of the third millennium, you have chosen to base your principles on a collection of contradictory texts – written by various men years after the death of your man Jesus – that have been edited and selected out of hundreds of other documents, and bound together into one hotchpotch volume, under the orders of a political primate, Pope Damasus. And, you're still content to condemn the living love I feel for Jake, here and now, because of that dusty accident of bad editing? Why?'

'Because I love Our Lord and I know it will all become clear.'

'That must make you feel very special, Claire.'

'You know, I think you probably will suffer, Chris,' she said quietly and wiped her eyes. 'I think you may well end up burning in the fires of Hell for eternity. I will pray for you.'

'Or I will simply die, as you will simply die, when our hearts stop beating. And instead of the fires of Hell or the clouds of Heaven, there will be a chorus of hungry worms or fish, depending on how we go. Isn't that what really terrifies you most of all, Claire, why you force yourself against all reason to believe in such tales? It's because you're afraid of the nothingness at the end. You're ashamed of it.'

'I will pray for you, Chris.'

'Have you ever wondered why we bury and cremate our dead? Nothing to do with hygiene, it's just so we don't have to see the reality of death. You know, the Zoroastrians used to leave their dead in open places for the birds to eat. Now that's a far more honest way to go, don't you agree? Everyone can see what happens. It makes us live our lives more potently. That's how I want to go, at my end: openly. Not ashamed of death, but embracing it.'

'You will burn, Chris. You will burn at the end.'

She stood up and left the room. Jake glared bitterly at his lover and chewed his thumbnail. Until that moment, I had never seen such hate on Jake's face. I never imagined he would ever look at Chris that way. Our eyes met for an instant and, in that flash, I felt afraid.

'I think it's time for bed,' he said and went upstairs.

'Badly done, Christopher.' I shook my head. 'Very badly done.'

* * *

The strangest events of the weekend occurred on the Saturday evening. Claire was brooding on a bean-bag, nursing her wounds and pouting at a glass of mineral water. Chris was standing on the doorstep and saying goodbye to the brethren when the phone rang. It was answered by Claire. She held the receiver to Chris without looking at him.

'It's a Father Cuthbert, for you,' she said.

Much later that evening, Chris told me the substance of the priest's call.

Cuthbert had sounded disturbed, scared even. He said there was a something in the house, a presence that had steadily increased as the afternoon wore on. He had spent most of the Friday writing letters at the kitchen table, but was disturbed by a sense that someone was standing behind him. Each time he turned to reassure himself that he was alone, he noticed that the temperature gauge on the AGA had dropped. He loaded more coal into the grate and let more air into the vent, but the temperature plummeted.

As darkness fell, he turned on all the lights in the house. The presence now extended to every room, particularly around the stairs. He closed himself in the Yellow Room and tried to watch television.

He said that the dream-tree in the garden began to creak. After a while, it was rocking so violently that he could barely hear the television. The breeze was only slight, yet the wooden pole grated harshly in its concrete hole. He claimed that it rasped like the voice of an old woman. He could not drown out the noise, so he decided to go to bed.

The temperature of the AGA had now dropped so low that he could see his own breath as he climbed the stairs. Rationalising it all in his own mind, he said it was the cold that made the hair on his neck rise as he walked over the landing. In the guest bedroom, he said his prayers and felt somewhat safer. He even managed to drift off to sleep for a couple of hours before he was woken by the noise downstairs.

At first, he thought he had imagined it. As he listened, he could clearly make out the sound of cutlery being shaken. He lay still for a while, listening to the disturbance. When it stopped, he breathed again until he was terrified by a thunderous crash in the Yellow Room. Mustering all his courage, he crept out of his bedroom with a Bible in his bony hands and forced himself through the hideous sensation on the stairs.

When he reached the Yellow Room, he turned the handle and entered. Turning on the light, he looked around the empty room. Nothing had changed, nothing had been moved. The house now lay in silence. The only sound he could hear was the manic creaking of the dream-tree outside. There was a bitter taste in the air, he noticed; perhaps the smell of burnt hair. He moved towards the window to look outside but, as he did so, he saw – or thought he saw, or rather felt – someone standing behind the curtains. He could make out the shape of a head behind the folds of the material.

He stood motionless for several minutes, staring at the figure behind the curtains. The clock on the mantelpiece ticked the loud seconds away, the dream-tree continued to convulse and the smell of burnt hair grew stronger. It may simply have been a draught that made the curtains shift, but as it did Cuthbert retreated through the door and turned the key in the lock. The blood pounded in his ears as he listened for any movement. Nothing happened.

Summoning all his courage, he pushed his way through the heavy presence that misted the stairs and locked himself in the bedroom. Although the noises had now ceased, he lay awake until the first birds began to whistle.

He could explain the sounds and the invisible presence of the night as the products of an overactive imagination, he said. But when he rose with the first weary grey smear of dawn, he had no explanation for the offering on the landing. He opened the bedroom door to find his coat hanging from a picture hook opposite his room. As he went out onto the landing, his bare feet stepped on fragments of burnt paper. He searched the house for any signs of forced entry, but found none. The security chain remained drawn on the front door; each window was bolted from the inside.

'Is he staying tonight,' I asked.

Chris nodded. 'I sincerely hope so.'

* * *

On the Sunday morning, Claire came into the sitting room where Richard and I were sleeping on the floor. She coughed politely to wake us.

'I'm going to chapel now,' she said. 'It's too late for you to get up and join me now, even if you had wanted to come.'

I made my belated apologies as she closed the front door.

The sun was bright through the gaps in the curtains and cast a soft blue glow over Richard's shoulder. He lay like an indigo Hindu god, like Vishnu reclining beside his paramour. I listened to his soft breathing and traced light spirals with my fingernail on his skin.

'Richard. Are you awake?'

'The name's Aurora Day,' he said sleepily. 'Not Richard.'

'Are you my goddess then? My rosy fingered goddess of the dawn?'

'As you wish. Cat, do I have to keep wearing that dress?'

I kissed him and tasted the delicious warmth of his mouth. He reached for my shoulders and drew me towards him. At times, he reared high into the slim stream of sunlight and shone like Aurora, my dawn, my saffron-clad Day. Then his face set swiftly, deep between my thighs and I could no longer see him, only feel his tongue lapping like a dark, swelling tide of underground waters.

The curtains trembled in the morning breeze and cast shadows over our slackening limbs. When time returned, I lifted myself from the tide of his body and whispered his name softly. I called him Aurora, my sunrise. I called him Eos, my dawn. I called him Day and he liked it, and so it remains his name, even all these years later. We spoke of small matters and lesser things, until our thundering hearts eased and we dozed in each other's arms.

'I slept the sleep of the innocent last night,' I said, running my fingers through the golden hairs of his chest. 'Sleep to knit up the ravelled sleeve of care.'

'I didn't,' he said. 'Chris woke me up, coming and going all night.'

'Chris? What was he up to?'

Day pressed his face into the pillow and mumbled something. I rose from the nest of warm sheets and padded into the kitchen to make a fresh pot of coffee. When the phone rang, Richard – now baptised Day – answered it. I heard him climb the stairs and return with Chris. I stayed in the kitchen, listening to Chris murmur an occasional response on the phone. Ten minutes later, he joined me in the kitchen.

'That was Father Cuthbert again,' he said, flattening his bed hair. 'He won't be staying at the house again.'

'What happened this time?'

'I don't know. He said stuff about more noises. Something about a knife or a fork stuck into the kitchen wall, someone grabbing his hair and pulling him down the stairs. It didn't make much sense.'

Chris sipped his coffee. At the same time, we both noticed a smudge of ash on his fingers. He rinsed his hands in the kitchen sink.

'Chris, what's going on?'

'What does it matter? He won't be back.'

'But the house – the noises.'

In the front room, Day groaned and covered his head with a pillow.

'If it's haunted, it's only haunted by us.' He dried his hands on a tea-towel. 'We take our own ghosts with us wherever we go, Cat. Sometimes, we can even leave the odd one behind.'

Heavy grey rainclouds draw steadily across the sky as we walked towards the train station. Chris and Jake stood silently on the platform and waved farewell as the train took me and Day back to Sunderland. Jake had hardly spoken all morning. Occasionally, he cast a vacant glance at Chris while they waited for their train to Whitby. The next stage of their grand tour was Chris's mother's house. Jake appeared less than keen to be going. The weekend at Coventry had been a bad move.

I watched the landscape grow bleak and barren as we travelled back to the north-east coast. Day rested his head against my shoulder and muttered in his sleep. I thought of Father Cuthbert's phone call and the disorder in the house while we had been away. The details of Cuthbert's tale grated with some memory from the morning, something I had seen but which I paid no attention to. I listed the various events. Day had seen Chris get up in the night. Chris had washed ash off his fingers in the morning. And – and what else?

As the train pulled into Sunderland station, I remembered. When I was making the coffee in Claire's kitchen, I had glanced outside. On the patio lay some black fragments in a ring of stones. At the time, I had peered through the window and wondered at the burnt paper and hair that shifted in the breeze. I did not think of it again until I remembered the words Chris had spoken before we set out on this ill-fated trip.

'Leave Cuthbert to me,' he had said. 'He won't stay more than once. I guarantee.'

VI
Niobe

Sometimes it is hard to remember Jake as he was in those early years.

Other memories are easier to grasp. Some people and places are painted as bright as icons on the walls of my mind. I walk up to them and marvel at their colours, vivid as the day they were created. Sometimes at night, when the mood is right and my eyes are closed, I can reach out a hand and touch the fabric of those days. The pictures flow like a silent tale told in a mediaeval tapestry; the faces stare across time like portraits in a Roman mosaic. I lend the faces my voice and the history becomes myth, but the texture is as real as ever. With Jake, however, it is different. I shall try my best to restore him, to piece him together again as I think he really was.

He was attractive, but never the flawless god that Chris made him out to be. He was vain. He took every opportunity to flaunt his body and often walked through the house with a just small towel wrapped around his waist. He never got on with Chris's university friends. He thought they treated him like a friendly but unintelligent household Labrador who smiled at their clever talk, occasionally walked on his hind legs and even played the piano. He lacked academic confidence, having barely scraped through college. Increasingly, he retreated into his body-building as though superficial muscle were the best he could achieve, as though external excess compensated for an internal absence. It was a facade but we all came to believe it to some extent. And I know we were wrong to do so.

Jake's only personal ambition was to play the piano. I suppose we all knew that he had a passable talent, but nobody really believed he would ever be an alumnus of the Royal Academy or perform in the Albert Hall, or even the Sunderland Empire for that matter. But it did give him a sense of accomplishment that he lacked in other spheres. The picture I have of our life in the commune is of unending evenings in the Green Room, of Chris and Conrad surrounded by books and deconstructing ancient myths, of Jake struggling to perfect a chord sequence. When Chris took up a fancy for the Romantic poets, he persuaded Jake to take a corresponding interest in the Romantic composers, particularly Mendelssohn and Liszt, regardless of what Jake was supposed to be studying. Chris knew nothing of this music, but he wanted Jake to complement his own journey into the Romantics. Whether this held Jake back in his academic course or not, it gave Chris the background music he required for his bohemian evenings. If Day and I were trying to have our own space in the Yellow Room, we would sometimes ask Jake to keep the music down. On those occasions, Chris growled and told us not to interrupt his genius at work. Good boy, Jake; clever boy, Jake.

Although he had not spoken the word as yet, Chris's love was ever present; it was like a palpable presence in the house. It lingered in the air like a cigarette that had just been extinguished, it settled on the skin like evening dust. Jake's love was of the quieter kind, glimpsed in secret looks and more subtle touches. His eyes were the mirrors of his heart, blue as moonlight on a winter lake. It was his eyes that said everything, sometimes reflecting the fire of Chris's devotion, other times clouding darkly when he thought no one was watching. Conrad was also aware of these secret glances.

'What are you thinking, Jake?' I asked when we were alone. 'When you look like that, so wistful and sad. What is it?'

'Just wondering,' he smiled. 'Wondering what Chris sees when he looks at me. I can't imagine. Can you?'

* * *

One week after Day and I had pulled away from Coventry railway station, Chris and Jake returned to the house. Their grand tour had taken them to visit Chris's mother in Whitby, where she had given them the gift of a kitten for our house. Chris was in town, buying food and a basket for the cat. Jake and I were petting the kitten in the Yellow Room. The little fiend, Circe they called it, sniffed warily at Jake's feet before pouncing on his toes.

'Little fucker.' He was not fond of the kitten. 'It knows I hate it. Have you seen how it looks at me?'

'How can you possibly hate kittens? See how she looks at you.'

'She looks evil. They piss on everything like it's their god-given right. And they look right through you, like they don't respect you. And they never come when you call. They're not faithful, not like dogs.'

'Dogs stink, Jake. You can't stroke one without your hand reeking. Cats, on the other hand, are too cool to obey orders. They're too independent. They're the atheists of the animal world.'

'Too evil, more like. Chris's mum has this old black moggy called Hecate, the mother of this little bitch. She hogged the settee and spat whenever I went near her. I couldn't move without getting hissed at.'

'While we're alone, Jake, tell me everything. What's Chris's mum really like?'

Jake rolled his eyes. He adjusted the towel he wore around his waist to make the bulge of his packet appear larger. He was as vain as Chris was proud.

Jake related the events of their week in Whitby. I listened keenly to the hidden side of Chris's life, the side he concealed from even his closest friends. With the exception of dark hints about his father, I knew nothing of his parents or his past.

I can try to tell it the way I was told, but the words have been corrupted over the years. All I can do is lay my own colours where the fabric has faded, to re-imagine the threads where the memory is weak.

Chris's mother met them in her sea-blasted garden, where she was building a wall with stones from the beach and cement from a kitchen bowl. The wind was too wild for her to hear their greeting as they approached. Jake watched the woman stand up to brush the long silver hair out of her face. She paused and opened her mouth slightly when she caught sight of Chris.

Jake was struck instantly by the similarities between mother and son. They both shared the same straight nose, although hers was larger and more classically Grecian. Her brow was noble and her expression as proud and commanding as that of the mother of the Greeks gods.

'Hera?' I asked, but Jake stared blankly at me. 'Sorry, go on.'

Her dark eyes penetrated Jake's façade. She disregarded his pre-prepared smile, cauterised his tight T-shirt and close-fitting jeans, and dissected his muscles. He turned away from her fierce gaze. She tied her hair back with a length of crimson ribbon and rested her hands on her hips.

'You look well, Chris.' She eyed him coolly up and down. 'You don't look bad at all.'

'You haven't aged a day,' he replied. 'Your hair has, but the grey suits you.'

'You must be Jake.' She turned to him with a flicker of an ironic smile and held out her hand. 'I'm Calliope. I don't want you calling me Chris's mum, or Ms Mavrocordatos, or any nonsense like that, just Calliope. Okay? I'm very pleased to meet you. I haven't often been graced with a glimpse into Chris's life. You must be something special.'

'A hidden treasure,' Chris added, 'from a dragon's lair.'

She clasped Jake's fingers firmly. Her leathery palms felt hard and blistered against his soft skin.

'Really glad to meet you at last,' he grinned warmly.

'What remarkable eyes you have, Jake. I can see why Chris is captivated. Indeed. We should go inside, people. It's too windy out here. I don't expect you remember the house very well, Chris. It's not big, but we'll be warm and cosy.'

Jake followed the strident Calliope towards the whitewashed cottage. Chris remained outside and gazed thoughtfully at the sea. He lingered there, resting against the wall until sunset, staring at a sun-bleached tree that marked the boundary of Calliope's land. When the first stars shimmered on the dark waves, Jake came out of the house looking exasperated. He called Chris in for the evening meal.

'Do you see that?' Chris pointed at the many coloured ribbons that flapped from the branches of the dead tree. 'That's her own dream-tree, tied with the rags of a hundred tattered wishes. Wonder what she's wishing for?'

* * *

'You can have Jackie's room, both of you,' Calliope said, peering over the rim of her wine glass. 'She's got an interview at York University. She won't be back until early next week. I know she'll be sorry to have missed you, Chris, but needs must when the devil drives.'

Chris sliced through his nut cutlet without looking up. Jake glanced between mother and son. He knew he was on the outside of some complicated mind game in which the rules and objectives were unknown. Calliope sat straight in her chair, her dark eyes surveying the cluttered table as though it were a chessboard.

'When was the last time you saw each other?' he asked awkwardly, steering a neutral course through their guarded exchanges. Chris continued to chew a mouthful of food and shrugged his shoulders.

'Eight years in February.' Calliope turned the glass between her fingers. 'Chris matured quickly in this house. He was always encouraged to use his own mind, make his own choices and trust his own will. And I always respected his decisions, whatever they were.'

'As I always respected yours.' Chris fired a glance at his mother.

Without returning the look, she smiled graciously and pushed her plate away.

'Would you care for any more vegetables, Jake? I'm afraid there's only fruit and cream for dessert.'

Jake declined with a modest shake of the head. Under the table, he kicked Chris's shoe.

After dinner, Chris offered to wash the dishes in the kitchen. Calliope led Jake into the sitting room, where the old cat spat at him as he attempted to sit down.

'Oh, just ignore her,' said Calliope. 'Her judgement isn't what it used to be, and she's had another litter of kittens. Her last, no doubt. She's feeling defensive.'

'How long have you had her?'

95

Calliope sat in the armchair and frowned thoughtfully at the fire. 'Many years now. She was a stray. We found her on the motorway when we first came up here. Jackie believed she was sent to protect us; a household guardian.'

'Protect you from what? Mice?'

'No one needs protecting from mice, Jake, but from wolves and sea-ghosts and the things of the night. From the demons we carry inside us. Jackie believed that black cats were kind witches in disguise. Jackie had a great many fears. She begged me to rescue the cat, and so, of course, I did.'

Calliope rummaged through her basket of knitting and wound up a ball of red wool. Jake eyed the miserable cat on the sofa beside him. He struggled to find anything to say to break the silence.

'What was Chris like when he was young?' Has he changed much?'

Calliope turned towards the hallway. The sounds of water and crockery echoed from the kitchen. Chris would be busy for a while yet. She brushed a loose strand of silver hair from her face and continued winding up the wool. In the half-lit room, the dark lines on her face seemed more pronounced, her skin more haggard. Jake had the eerie sensation that she was ageing as he watched. The illusion passed as quickly as it had come, and her face became clear and hard and majestic again.

'He had a strong will when he was a child. He still has it and, I think, he's now learnt how to use it. But there is more anger in him. And he is harder now.'

She cast her serious dark eyes on Jake.

'He has been waiting for you a long time, Jake. Perhaps all his life. He needs to be forgiven, you see. Not that he's done anything particularly wicked, but that's what he needs. Sometimes, when bad things happen to people, they feel guilty, responsible, especially if it's out of their hands. Chris feels responsible for the bad things that have happened to him. He needs absolution. I think you will be good for him. I think you are absolving him. Perhaps you have come just in time. You do understand, don't you?'

Jake did not understand, but before he could question her, Chris came back to the sitting room. Hecate closed her eyes and purred contentedly as he sat beside her.

'Anyone fancy a walk?' he asked, stroking the cat. 'It's not too late, is it?'

'I'm tired,' said Calliope, 'but you should take Jake to the abbey. Yes, you must take him to the abbey. It's spectacular at night. You might see a ghost.'

'You think I can go there?'

'Of course you can, darling.' Calliope took up a book and flicked absently through its pages. 'That was years ago. You get over your fears. Look at you now, all grown up. You can do anything now.'

The path to the abbey ran across the bridge over of the River Esk and up the steep sides of the cliff. The wind from the sea whistled down the empty streets, rattling the door knockers and shaking the window frames. As they climbed the steps to the abbey, Chris introduced Jake to Dracula.

'It was in this port that the vampire first landed in England. When we get to the graveyard, you'll see the harbour better.'

'But it was only a film, right?'

'A book, and because of that it's much more true.' Chris smiled, his teeth gleaming in the streetlights.

'Sometimes, Chris, I think that you think you're living in a book. Like tonight: you act like you're acting, not like real person at all.'

'Well, that's a head-fuck. What do you mean?'

'I don't mean it in a bad way. Just, like back there. You grinned like Dracula, like a demon or something. But you weren't being ironic. Or you were, but you didn't know you were.'

Chris considered this for some time before speaking. 'There's a theory that says we are all acting, all the time; that everything we say is always already scripted. In that sense, perhaps we are just acting like characters in a book. Perhaps you're just a myth: my personal myth. Or perhaps imagining that you're a character in a book is the only way to cope with the absurdity of life, with the divine comedy.'

'You are absurd, but your life's not so bad.'

'You're not wrong there.' Chris pulled Jake up the last few steps.

They reached the graveyard at the top of the cliff, where the wind blew so hard they had to link arms and lean against the tombstones. The broken ribs of the abbey arched into the moonless sky, illuminated by the distant lights of the streets below. Chris drew Jake's back against his chest, wrapped his arms around him and pointed at the harbour wall.

'That's where the townsfolk saw Dracula leap from his ship in the form of a wolf.'

'How did they know it was Dracula? Could have just been a wolf.'

'They thought it was at first. But then, one by one, people began to fall prey to his appetite. Corpses were found drained of all blood, with only two neat teeth marks in their necks. Soon, my mother, sister and I were the only ones left.'

Chris pressed his lips against Jake's neck and sucked loudly. Jake fell laughing to the grass and pulled Chris with him. They kissed in the shelter of a tombstone until Chris lifted his face and gazed with unexpected sadness into Jake's eyes.

'I love you,' Chris whispered, but the words were snatched by the pirate wind and carried away to the roaring sea.

Walking back through the deserted town, Jake made a decision to break the clumsy silence.

'Did you say it? Did you say the "love" word?' His hands were clenched deep into his pockets. Chris admitted that he did.

'Have we ever said it before?'

'No,' said Chris. 'It's not something I find easy to say.'

'I didn't think so.'

'Is that a problem?'

'Well.' Jake halted on the bridge over the river and looked down at the rushing water. 'Perhaps you should have said it before we exchanged vows. I mean, now I have to reconsider everything.'

Grinning broadly, he grabbed Chris's waist and pulled their cold bodies together.

'Better late than never.'

* * *

They spent the week toiling in Calliope's garden, undoing the damage of the winter storms. Calliope persevered with her garden wall, mixing small amounts of cement in a wooden kitchen bowl. Jake questioned her use of garlic in the mixture and received a withering look for his trouble.

On the third evening, the wind had calmed to a gentle breeze and the sea gleamed immaculately. Calliope rested her hands on her hips and nodded approvingly at the finished wall.

'That should keep him out,' she said, satisfied with her progress.

Jake glanced expectantly down the empty beach. 'Keep who out?'

'That devil of an ex-husband.'

'Chris's dad? I thought he lived down south.'

'He does, but that doesn't stop him sending his pathetic demons into my garden. You know, we've spent every night for the past ten years fighting each other, and he still hasn't surrendered. Some men never know when they're beaten.'

'You mean, you still stay in touch? By phone?'

She smiled patiently at Jake as though he were a sweet but simple child.

'No, *agapi mou*, most definitely not by phone. We battle among the highways of the stars. Hasn't Chris taught you anything?'

98

Jake felt obliged to laugh and earned himself a disapproving glare. Calliope called for Chris.

'Chrissy, darling. You remember that evening your father sent his devil the last night you lived here? Have you told Jake nothing of this?'

'Excellent craftsmanship,' he said, coming out of the house with two mugs of coffee. 'The Great Wall of Whitby is complete. The night of the Devil? No, I don't suppose I have. Is he still doing that sort of thing?'

Calliope took her mug and sat cross-legged upon the earth. Untying the red ribbon, she shook her head and released her silver hair in the breeze.

'The bastard never gives up. You know, in April last year he sent a gargoyle to uproot all my chives. It took three broomsticks and I almost lost my voice chasing it away.'

'You tried lavender, I assume? That usually works.'

'Used it all up. And Jackie was no help. She just locked herself in her bedroom and refused to believe it was out there. Said it was just a seagull. That girl can be so stubborn sometimes.'

'How is the little princess?' Chris sat on the ground beside his mother. 'Still terrified of the wolves in the woods?'

Calliope reached inside her jeans for her cigarettes. She offered the packet to Chris before lighting one for herself.

'She's doing okay. Moving on to university in the autumn. Then the last of my chicks will have flown the nest and I will be alone. I feel like Niobe: all my children gone. That's well. It suits me.'

'Come on, Calliope. Jackie will never be far away from you.'

'You know, she hates this house with all its noises and faces at the window. Doesn't believe it's all your father's doing.'

'She won't go back to him, will she?' Chris's lips tightened. He looked remarkably similar to his mother.

Calliope turned and looked earnestly into Chris's eyes. 'Jackie adores you, you know. She wants to do what you have done, to go where you have been. She writes to you – how often?'

'A few times a year.'

'More than that. And does she ever mention your father?'

Chris shrugged and looked down at his mug. 'If she does go to him, will you give her the same ultimatum you gave me?'

Calliope tossed her head back and frowned at the darkening sky. Her face became severe, a profile etched in walnut.

'If she wants to go back to him then, of course, that will be her choice. But she will know the consequences. And then, if she still wants to go, she'll have to live with that. I will have nothing to do with her while she is in contact with that man. She will be dead to me, as you were dead to me.'

Calliope rose to her feet and cast the remains of her coffee upon the seedbeds. She walked to the new wall and patted the drying cement.

'Good wall,' she said, more to herself than to anyone else. Then turning suddenly, 'Chris, you do understand now, don't you? You understood why I had to do what I did? Why I said what I had to say?'

Chris smiled reassuringly at his mother. 'I think I'm beginning to.'

That afternoon, Calliope went with Jake and Chris to the abbey. She walked between them, their arms linked firmly against the cold. As they climbed the steep path to the cliff top, she told them about her childhood in Greece, a story Chris had heard many times before. She was born in Missolonghi on the mainland, from solid Greek stock. Her father was a fisherman and republican soldier in Athens during the civil wars of the 1920s. After the military coup, her father gave up trying to save his country and returned to his fishing boats with a young comrade as his bride. They had eight daughters before Calliope was born in the 1940s. Her mother died giving birth to her.

'I met Chris's father after I came to England to study. He was very different back then. Maybe he wasn't. Maybe I didn't see what he was really like. It's hard to believe, but we actually met on a peace march in Paris. No, that's not quite how it was. I was on a peace march in Paris, and I thought he was too. But he was visiting a seminary for his training. He must have just got caught up in the demonstration. It was probably very irritating for him. I saw what I wanted to see, and he didn't tell me the truth until years later. I thought he was a pacifist when we met; he was actually just being very quiet.'

'What happened to him?'

'He turned into a demon,' she explained matter-of-factly. 'It was a slow transformation. It wasn't obvious in the beginning. It took time for me to acclimatise to your rotten English weather. And to the contorted way you English have of saying what you think, which is never what you mean. In the months after our over-hasty wedding, I realised that something essential was missing from the man. There was no electricity in his touch, no humanity in his dead eyes. It was not just because he was English, I realised. It was that he felt no love, only frustration and perhaps even shame. I can't imagine what he could have been ashamed of. Perhaps he was ashamed of not being a saint, who knows. And shame is the mother of all monsters, don't you think?'

They reached the graveyard beside the ruined abbey and gazed out at the black trawlers on the horizon. Calliope's long thin shadow stretched over the edge of the cliff, pointing towards a fishing boat that sailed into the harbour. She turned towards the bronze sun as it sunk behind the town.

'There, Chrissy, to the left of the setting sun. You know what planet that is?'

'I suppose it must be Venus, the Evening Star.'

Calliope pointed it out for Jake. 'If you ever lose your direction, Jake, follow the Evening Star. It will lead you wherever you need to be. I followed it the night we came to Whitby. There will no doubt be a day when you need to follow it, too.'

'Why?'

'How am I to know? You should follow it, though, when the time comes.'

Calliope sat beside a gravestone and lit a cigarette. She contemplated the scene, as dignified as a goddess surveying her world, breathing mist over the ebbing sea. Chris led Jake by the hand to the cliff-edge. They sat and watched the seagulls fight on the rocks beneath their feet.

'I haven't felt so at peace since I was a child.' Chris corrected himself. 'No, not even then. Things have never felt so auspicious.'

'How do you mean?'

'I mean we can do anything. It means that nothing will be impossible ever again. We could turn these graves to gold with a touch, spread wings and fly down to those rocks like seagulls, or rule the kingdoms of the earth from this high place. As long as we are together, everything is possible.'

'We should try that gold thing. We're getting short of money.'

Chris laughed and pressed his mouth against Jake's until they had to stop for breath. When they stood up to leave, Chris picked something up from the grass.

'It's not gold.' He put a grimy fifty pence piece into Jake's hand. 'But it's the best I could do at such short notice.'

Walking back through the quiet streets, Calliope sang the *Internationale* in Greek and cursed in English when she passed a church. As they crossed the bridge, she stopped singing and turned to her son.

'Chrissy, when was the last time you saw your father?'

Chris slowed his pace and looked thoughtfully at the harbour. 'About three years now. Probably more. Why?'

'You know he is rich. His family were very wealthy. Old money clings to a bloodline like congenital syphilis. And he kept all my money too. I left without a penny.'

Jake's ears pricked up at this turn in the conversation, but Calliope resumed her song and marched them back to the cottage. Chris and Calliope prepared vegetable stew in the kitchen, while Jake pulled faces at the cat in the lounge. Unimpressed, the cat hissed at him until he stopped. He walked around the room and inspected various ornaments – decorative plates, a small mandola, a bust of Karl Marx, a ram's horn. When he came to the kitchen door, he overheard Calliope continuing her conversation from earlier.

'Who do you think he will leave his money to when he dies?'

'The Church?' Chris shrugged. 'The Conservative Party? General Pinochet perhaps?'

'No, not the Church. The Church was a screen for him. It provided him with a respectable costume and a title, nothing more. He won't leave his money to the Church. He's even more vindictive than that.'

'To you, then?'

'Less likely. He knows I'm too clever to accept it. It would be a curse: hexed money. He knows me too well for that. So, who else?'

'Then to me and Jackie.'

'I think so. The most damage he could inflict is to leave it to you two. The sins of the father passed onto the next generation, handed down like a virus in the blood. If I tell Jackie what he is, what he has done, then I think she would choose not to accept it. But would you?'

Jake listened to the silence, which was broken only by the hard crack of Chris's knife on the chopping board.

'I could do a lot of good with it,' he said eventually. 'Undo the harm he has done. Take possession of the oast-house; transform it into something else. Reclaim a better future from the rotten past.'

'That would be your decision. But you would be tainted by him, beholden to him. And you know what it would mean?'

'You would never speak to me again. I'd be as dead as he will be.'

'You'd be polluted by him, *agapi mou*. Poisoned. Unclean. I couldn't see you. And think, what if his curse touches your love?'

Chris laughed genuinely. 'That would never happen. If nothing else, I know that our love is stronger than anything he can inflict. We're immune from all that.'

'But is Jake's will as strong as yours?'

Chris laughed again, less convincingly.

When they sat down for supper, Jake saw the dark lines reappear again on Calliope's face. She stared at her stew without appetite and never raised her glass. Chris ate in silence and turned to the window at the sound of the jeering seagulls.

'Niobe is a sad story,' said Calliope suddenly. 'You know it, Jake?'

Jake apologised that he had never heard of it.

'It's about a woman, a mother, who earned the resentment of the gods. You see, she dared to suggest that her own children were more beautiful, more perfect, than any of the offspring produced by the Olympians. She, Niobe was her name, instilled in her seven sons and seven daughters a boundless belief in their own fates, that they could touch the sun and run with the moon, that they were as good as any god. Better than any god. She watched her children grow and she became proud. I cannot blame her for that.

'But the gods are also proud. They trembled at the sound of Niobe's blasphemy. To avenge their reputations, they murdered all Niobe's children in front of her. They made her watch, unable to intervene, as child after child fell bleeding on the earth. One by one, she held their bodies and watched the light die in their eyes. Now they could never touch the sun or run with the moon. She could do nothing.

'Some say that the gods took pity on her and turned her to stone so she would feel no more pain. Others say that she weeps for eternity and her tears turn to crystals, that each crystal is a wish that her children were still alive. One day, when she has wept enough, she may gather up her crystals and cast them like missiles at the gods. Perhaps then, the gods will grow angry again and take her life as they took her children. But she would find that a relief.

'I do not like the gods. They are far too human.'

Throughout the story, Calliope's eyes had remained fixed on the food she had not eaten. When she finished her tale, Chris glanced briefly at her face and then to the window. Outside, the sea breeze shook the ribbons on the dream-tree.

The last days of their week in Whitby were unusually warm for the time of year. Chris and Jake walked along the beach beside Calliope's garden and tied seaweed tresses to the smooth branches of the dream-tree on the boundary of her land. On their final evening, Jake asked Chris to take another walk to the abbey. Calliope smiled to herself and flicked through the pages of the book she always kept by her side.

'Of course you should go,' she said. 'On a night such as this, you must go and touch the stars.'

The town was quiet as Chris followed his lover through the twilit streets and up the steps to the ruined abbey. They did not speak. Jake seemed mysteriously thoughtful as though biding his time before breaking his silence.

When they reached the top of the cliff, Jake knelt beside the gravestones that had sheltered them on their first evening at the abbey. He took out a knife and carved something into the stone. Chris peered closely to read the words etched deep into the red moss and granite. The glow of the setting sun lit up the fresh hieroglyphics.

'"Jake loves Chris forever,"' he read.

Jake knelt down among the lengthening shadows of the graves and unbuttoned Chris's jeans. The seagulls rose from the grass around them and soared among the early stars. Far beyond the harbour wall, the fishing fleet drifted out to sea. The cabin lamps flickered on the purple waves.

'I love you,' Jake said softly. He pulled Chris down to the darkness of the dewy grass. The sea breeze lifted over the edge of the cliff, passing like a cool breath over their shivering skin.

The next morning, as a parting gift, Calliope gave them a basket. Inside was the wide-eyed kitten.

'It's Circe,' she said. 'Hecate's seventh daughter. She's as black as her mother and promises to have just as big a personality. You'll need her around, I reckon. A household guardian is a useful friend.'

Calliope waved briefly from the station platform, but left before the train had pulled away. Chris kept the basket on his lap as they travelled northwards.

'How does it feel to be a father, Jake?' asked Chris.

'Daunting,' said Jake. He stared out of the window at the furrowed fields of the Yorkshire countryside.

* * *

Chris returned home from town as Jake was finishing his tale. He greeted the kitten before anyone else and tugged a woollen mouse across the carpet for her to kill.

Jake said he was going for a bath and left the room.

'I'll join you in a minute,' Chris called after him, teasing the cat with the mouse's tail.

When Jake's footsteps had faded upstairs, I asked Chris what had happened after Whitby.

'It was difficult at his parent's house,' he replied. 'I think he's still quite rattled about that.'

Chris sat beside me and watched the kitten kick the mouse into submission with her hind legs. After a while, he rubbed his tired eyes and told me what happened in Jake's home village.

He described Elliston was a bleak cluster of grey brick terraces that gathered around a single institution, the Working Men's Club. The village was overshadowed by the rusty iron towers of three dilapidated mineshafts. As he stared at the rusty giants from the back seat of the taxi, Jake advised him not to speak when they were in the street.

'Why not?'

'Don't let anyone hear your accent. They'll think you're a southern poof.'

'I am a southern poof.'

Jake pleaded with his earnest blue eyes. 'They'll kill you. I'm not joking; they will kill you. It's happened before. In fact, it's probably safer to run from the taxi to the front door so you're not seen.'

'You're kidding, aren't you? Seen by who?'

'I don't know. Scuffers. They don't like foreigners.'

'I'm not a foreigner, Jake.'

'You are if you're not from Elliston.'

The taxi pulled up beside a row of darkened houses. Jake exchanged a few words with the driver and told Chris to head for the front door of the nearest house. Obediently, Chris gathered the basket to his chest and ran up to the porch. Jake followed and pushed his shoulder against the doorbell. They looked up and down the empty street.

'You made it sound like Beirut. There's nobody around.'

'Better safe than sorry.'

'Is there someone in particular I'm to be hidden from?'

Before he could answer, Jake's mother opened the door and let them in. She glanced nervously in both directions before closing the door behind them.

'Did anyone see you, Jake? Did you see your da?'

'I don't think so.' He looked apologetic. 'Mam, this is Chris. Chris, this is my Mam.'

Jake's mother shook her head and attempted to smile at Chris. She was a large woman, with the same wide mouth and light blue eyes as Jake. She rubbed her fingers on her apron and reached out a soapy hand.

'Why, what's that there in that basket?' She withdrew her hand. 'A cat? Oh dear me, no. No, you can't have that thing in this house, Jake. What on earth were you thinking? Your da would never allow that. Put it outside before it pisses on the floor. Your da won't let a cat in the house.'

Jake pleaded with his mother and eventually persuaded her to let the basket be kept out of sight in his old bedroom. She busied herself laying newspapers on the floorboards. When she was done, she stood in the doorway of the lounge and looked uncertainly at her son.

'We've been staying in Whitby,' Jake said. 'With Chris's mam.'

'Oh, Whitby is a long way to go. Your da says it's a right dive. Are you from Whitby, Clive? Is that where you're from, pet?'

'Chris,' he corrected her gently. 'No, my mother moved there a few years ago. But she's from Greece.'

'From Greece, is she? Oh, Greece is a long way to come, pet.' She glanced at the door 'Your da will be home soon. How long you reckon you'll be staying?'

'We had thought about staying the night.' Jake exchanged a meaningful look with his lover. 'But we can get the bus back tonight, if that's a problem.'

'Oh no, no. Your da wouldn't want a stranger in the house overnight. He'd never allow that. He'll be home soon, but you'll be wanting some tea before you go, won't you?'

She went into the kitchen without waiting for an answer and filled the kettle. Through the open doorway, Chris watched her stand motionless beside the sink, waiting for the kettle to boil. She was clenching a fistful of apron.

'Sugar and milk, pet?' she called without turning. Chris watched her press a finger tip against the hot white plastic of the boiling kettle.

'I really think we should go,' he whispered to Jake. 'I think, maybe your mum's anxious about me meeting your dad?'

Jake nodded, relieved, and called through to the kitchen, 'Mam, we won't be staying for tea. We've to get the kitten home.'

'Jesus, the kitten,' she agreed.

Jake dialled for a taxi while his mother worried about it being late. When the car did pull up outside, she opened the front door and checked the street.

'Okay, off you go now. You come and see me soon, son.'

'I'm glad to have met you at last, Mrs Edlestone,' Chris said. 'Please come and visit us in Sunderland sometime.'

'Yes, yes, Clive. Now make sure the taxi doesn't leave without you. Bye, pet.' She kissed Jake's cheek and shoed them both outside.

* * *

'Why was Jake so agitated?' I asked.

Chris rested his head against the arm of the chair and closed his eyes.

'Because his worlds have collided. Because I was in his parent's home, where I should never have been. Because there are two Jakes – my lover, Jake, and his parents' son, Jake – and they were never supposed to meet. It's called cognitive dissonance.'

'You mean, his parents don't know about him?'

'I don't think either of the two Jakes have any idea about the existence of the other.'

Chris put the kitten on my lap and went upstairs to join Jake in the bathroom. Minutes later I heard the splash of water as they rolled around in the tub. Circe twitched her tiny ears and cocked her head at the rhythmic movement above our heads, the shrill squeak of wet skin against enamel bath. Outside, the wind rocked the dream-tree and rattled the crystals. The kitten rested her chin on my breast and purred. I closed my eyes and let my thoughts drift.

In my aimless daydreams, I imagined Calliope, not as I later came to know her as a real woman, but as a porcelain goddess weeping glass tears. I saw Chris standing on the Whitby cliffs, reaching for the sun and running with the moon. And I saw Jake's face smiling in the shadows of the abbey. Jake rolling stones across the sea towards the continent. Jake trying red ribbons to a dead driftwood tree. Jake kissing his mother goodbye on the doorstep of his home.

Sometimes, it is hard to remember Jake as he was in those early years.

VII
Daedalus and Icarus

Chris's Society of Heathens was founded in early May, the same time as the lupins and night-scented stock seedlings stretched above the rim of the window boxes. The early summer sunlight collected around the crystals, which twinkled like daytime stars from the branches of the dream-tree. I sat at the kitchen table and dreamily turned the pages of the university newspaper. I found Chris's article promoting his new society.

The Coven, as his Society became known, was to meet monthly at each full moon in the Yellow Room. Its purpose was to retell ancient stories inside a magic circle, to re-craft and make relevant the old myths in the present day, to mortalise the immortals. Once the circle had been cast, Chris would always start proceedings with a reading of Ovid's introduction to the *Metamorphoses* – "Of bodies changed to other forms, I tell," – and then a usually pagan tale would be re-told, re-invented, deconstructed and dissected by discourse until it disappeared in a drunken haze and reappeared in our dreams.

There was only ever a few of us, the regulars, at these story-telling gatherings. Sometimes a curious classics student or devil-worshipping Goth would turn up once, never to come back again because they never quite seemed to get the point. And at the time, I too wondered if there was any point to these unorthodox monthly sabbaths. Now I know that there was a purpose. We bound ourselves together with common archetypes and images, we cultivated a shared culture. We activated something approaching a collective unconscious.

As Conrad had forewarned, Chris's article in the college newspaper was a damning indictment of organised religion and a celebration of the world, the flesh and the pleasure principle. It was Chris's personal manifesto, a Promethean vision of anarchistic spirituality, and a red rag to the Christians.

For the first fortnight after the article was published, the Coven's mail-box in college was overflowing with complaints each morning. Most of the correspondence was from outraged Christian Unionists, damning the sodomites, Satanists and subversives that they presumed us to be. The Student Evangelical Movement, moved by a more fanatical spirit, went further and posted proclamations around the university, admonishing students to avoid all contact with our demon-possessed Coven. Chris was so delighted with this attention that he responded with a second, sardonic letter in the newspaper, grateful to each faction for their helpful publicity.

The article even came to the attention of Joseph, Chris's ex-partner, whose congregation consisted of some college students who lived in his parish. The jilted priest retaliated with his own tract in the university newspaper, warning against the fanciful flights of New Age rhetoric and urging the containment of unruly desires. Self-control and restraint were traditional English virtues. This was, he claimed, a Christian island after all. He painted a picture of a fanciful model village the size of a country, the plastic little people all obediently standing to attention. As I read the priest's article, I imagined him farting every word.

Thus, the summer months passed pleasantly on the north-east coast, with the battle lines marked in black and white print and the distant thunder resounding like war drums far across the unruffled North Sea.

By the Christmas vacation of our second year, the Coven was infamous throughout the university as a hive of licentious activity. Rumours abounded about our unconventional private lives, with some particularly amusing tales about Chris's sexual habits. It was commonly believed that he held a black mass each Sunday evening, at which he copulated with Satan who appeared in the form of a goat. Chris's responded with another letter in the college rag. He said that, although he liked his men to be hairy, he objected to woolly backs. He preferred his goats to be shaved.

This was to be Chris and Jake's first Christmas together, and they spent the last pennies of their overdrafts on preparations for the winter solstice. Day and I had agreed to forfeit the festive suffering of our respective family commitments for Yuletide with Chris. He was delighted even further by Conrad's promise to stay for the holiday.

The twenty-first of December was a cold day, even for north-eastern standards. The AGA refused to raise the temperature of the kitchen above a few degrees, and I struggled to light the fire in the Yellow Room. Circe licked her paws on Chris's vacant throne as Conrad reclined on the settee, smoking a joint and editing his response to the latest attacks in the college paper. We three each raised our heads as a loud thud echoed down the stairs.

'You alright, guys?' I called after a moment of ominous silence. Chris grunted something from the landing and the thumping continued. Conrad and I ventured curiously into the hallway to see what was happening. Circe remained behind, perhaps recalling what had killed the cat. Chris appeared at the top of the stairs, dragging his king-sized mattress into view. Jake poked his flushed face over the banisters and told us to move out of the way.

'We're kipping by the fire tonight,' he explained, wiping his brow. 'Move it. The mattress is coming down the stairs.'

'But it'll knock all the pictures off the wall,' I said. Jake was thinking with his muscles again.

'No, it'll be fine. Trust me.'

Chris shrugged and stepped back. Jake gave the mattress a shove with his shoulder and sent it tumbling down. It somersaulted slowly at first, gathering speed as it fell and knocking both Van Gogh prints from the wall as I had predicted.

Circe fled in panic as we dragged the saggy mattress into the Yellow Room and lay it down before the fire. Jake sprawled across it and stretched his legs until his dressing-gown fell open, exposing his soft but well-formed prick.

'I think you've just made Conrad's day,' I said, nudging Conrad in the ribs. Jake blushed and quickly covered himself.

'Sorry Jake, but I have seen better,' said Conrad with a sly glance at Chris.

'So, you have tasted some man-on-man action?' I asked.

'I don't know what you mean,' he said dismissively and returned to the business of writing his letter and smoking a joint.

That evening, the first of our three Yuletide visitors arrived. Day had spent the last of his student loan money on a bottle of superior whisky and was pouring each of us a glass. I remember that I was kneeling beside the fire with Jake, burning chestnuts on forks. Chris and Conrad lay on the mattress, discussing the myths they would tell at the next Coven meeting – which was basically the extent of the Society's activities. The scandalmongers would have been sorely disappointed had they known the reality of our activities.

'There's a girl in the same corridor as me in halls,' Conrad was saying. 'She writes a review in the society section of the paper. Says she's keen to write about our group.'

'A journalist?' Chris grinned. 'That could be useful. What's her name?'

'Anna Brisker. I've asked her to come this evening.' Conrad raised the spliff to his lips and squinted at me. 'She's very attractive, Cat. I might go so far as to say she's stunning.'

'Be careful, Conrad,' I warned. 'She may turn you straight.'

'Undoubtedly, she would. If I wasn't already.'

I dropped my chestnut in the fire and tried to rescue it with a fork. Conrad smiled and returned his full attention to Chris. As they spoke, I watched the smile fade from Conrad's face and a gentle sadness dim his eyes. Though you can never admit it, I thought, moved by

Conrad's expression, you have lost the one you adore. The act of storytelling has replaced the act of lovemaking. You can only share myths now, not kisses – if you ever got that far before the advent of Jake. It was an understanding that came to me suddenly, a secret radio wavelength that played briefly clear and desolate on my frequency. I wondered if Jake had also tuned in.

'Do you remember fire-gazing with me, Chris?' I interrupted again, abandoning the chestnut. 'It was about this time last year. You saw Jake in the flames, do you remember? Your moon-man. I reckon we should try it again tonight.'

Chris agreed instantly and set to sweeping a magical circle around the hearth with his hand and muttering something under his breath. When he had finished, he nominated Jake to go first. Resting his chin on Conrad's knees, Chris gazed into the flames and told Jake to do the same. Jake pouted, evidently unimpressed.

'Look deep into the fire,' said Chris. 'Search among the shadows, where the lights flicker and shapes move across the grate. There, tell us what you see.'

Jake frowned at the fire until his eyes watered. The coals shifted and a flock of sparks soared up the chimney. Jake shook his head.

'You know how fucking stupid this looks?' he said.

'Look again, love,' Chris urged him, but Jake glared at Conrad and turned his back on the hearth. He poured himself another glass of whiskey. 'It's only a game. Make something up if you can't see it.'

'I can see something,' Conrad said, seizing the awkward moment to tell his own vision. 'Down among the lowest embers, where the ashes glow like red eyes. It's like a furnace in there. If you listen carefully, you can hear the clash of hammer against steel. You hear it?'

We listened. The only sound I could hear in the room was the regular ticking of the clock on the mantelpiece. Conrad nodded in time with the rhythm of seconds, tapping his fingers against his knee.

Jake stood beside the door, clutching the handle as though he half intended to leave at any moment, but might miss something if he did. His face was pale; he looked miserable. When he noticed me watching him, his lips trembled slightly as though a whisker away from crying.

'This is fucking bollocks,' he said and left the room.

'No, it is there,' Conrad continued, leaning closer to the fire. 'The furnace is as hot as hell. There are blacksmiths at work, two of them labouring away. You can see their red bodies sweating in the heat. They're hammering like demons in an underworld cavern. Clink, clink, clink - all day and all night, for centuries on end.'

'What are they making?' Chris asked, lifting his chin from Conrad's knee. 'I can't make it out.'

'It's a suit, I think. Not a suit of armour, nor of chain-mail, but a suit made of feathers. Fiery feathers, such as the phoenix wears when it rises from the ashes. The smiths are Icarus and Daedalus, pounding the fire into freedom.'

I peered at the embers and forgot about Jake. I stared, but the vision was broken by the sound of the front doorbell. Chris swore and went into the hallway.

'It's probably that student journalist I was talking about, Anna,' said Conrad. He looked expectantly towards the door as Chris returned.

'Sorry, Conrad,' Chris said. 'You all know Father Cuthbert.'

The priest followed Chris into the Yellow Room. Unfeasibly tall, he had to bow his grey head to enter the doorway. He glanced disdainfully at each of our faces in turn.

'Oh dear, Christopher,' said Father Cuthbert, his mouth twisting into a grim smile. 'I do hope my house hasn't become a seedy commune for every low-life beatnik in town. I'd hate to think that those unsavoury rumours I've heard could possibly be true.'

'Do sit down, Cuthbert,' Chris said with a lame attempt at hospitality. 'We've just opened a bottle of whisky. I'm sure there's a glass somewhere.'

'I don't think so,' the priest said sharply, although he lowered himself into Chris's throne. He read the label on the bottle and winced as though he had been personally insulted. 'It would be ungracious of me to deprive you of such – luxuries. I think you will need as much Christmas cheer as you can afford, this year.'

He reached inside his cassock and produced a cigar with the swift manoeuvre of a magician. I was fascinated by his spindly movements. He worked with anticipation, holding the room in morbid suspense as we wondered what his next manifestation would be. Glancing coldly around, his fingers tickled the ridge of the brown cigar.

'You see,' he continued, in no particular haste, 'a parishioner of mine, an inexperienced youth who has the misfortune of attending the same polytechnic as you, suggested that I take a look at a series of juvenile articles in his student rag, written by a certain Christopher Mavrocordatos. Oddly enough, my young parishioner found much to amuse him in these scribblings, but he is particularly immature and I can forgive young men most things. However, I failed to find the humour in a letter entitled 'Church of the Poison Mind'. Do you recall that article, Christopher? I imagine you do. You wrote it.'

'Yes, I do,' Chris replied, dangerously calm. 'And, Father Cuthbert, I'm delighted by your appreciation of that letter. It was about abuses of power by the clergy. It wasn't intended to be humorous.'

'Then, perhaps, you may also like to know that two elderly ladies of my parish also happened upon it. Sadly, they were deeply offended by what was insinuated.'

'I imagine they were. The path to truth is littered with all sorts of people being offended by things they didn't want to hear.'

'Of course, my parishioners are one thing,' Father Cuthbert continued as though he could no longer hear Chris, 'but my bishop is quite another. He really is quite upset, and he is usually such a level-headed soul.'

'I never flattered myself to imagine that your bishop would ever read my scribblings.' Chris raised his chin and crossed his arms. Cuthbert held his gaze and tapped his cigar in irritation. I could not think why Chris was provoking the landlord in this way. At their last confrontation, Chris and Jake had seduced Father Cuthbert with soft words and shoulder massages. Tonight, Chris was taking no prisoners. Perhaps he had lost patience with the unflinching priest who exuded possession over all he saw. Perhaps he knew there was no other way of dealing with the gangling spider who was occupying his throne.

The two antagonists stared at each other without blinking for a moment, bracing themselves for the storm. At last, the cigar snapped in Cuthbert's fingers.

'You fucking little shit,' the priest hissed in an unexpectedly shrill voice. 'Who the hell do you think you are? Aleister Crowley? You are nobody, Christopher. You know nothing and you are nothing. If you were blessed with even the vaguest trace of intelligence, you would know I'm the last person you should have crossed. Shall I tell you why? Because now, you queer little fuck, you and your worthless, degenerate chums have just found yourselves homeless. Happy Christmas. Fucking. Little. Shit.'

Chris stepped ever so slightly forwards. The priest pounced to his feet, uncertain whether to clench his fists or make for the door. Perhaps it was this gesture, this sudden movement of air that caused the fire in the grate to flare up, illuminating Chris's features from below. His teeth looked unnaturally white in the sudden glare.

'I'm afraid you've made the mistake, Father Cuthbert,' he said so deathly quiet and intense that we spectators had to lean forward to catch his words. 'See, I'm the last person that you should have crossed. Let us be sure we understand each other perfectly.

'First, Cuthbert, you have never given me a contract, and I have never signed a tenancy agreement. As such, and as long as I continue to pay the rent I have been paying, I am entitled to live here, if that is my will. You can try to pursue this case through the courts, but that will be costly and will undoubtedly take many months, possibly years, before you reach an uncertain conclusion. That's the first thing I know.

'I also know what you do every Sunday night after Evensong. I know about your furtive visits to the toilets in Mowbray Park. I know about your guilty fumblings with young pricks in the cubicles. No one will give it to you for free, not to a bitter old man like you, will they? Clergy cash for Mackem cocks. It's got a scandalous ring to it, don't you agree? I wonder what your level-headed bishop will say about that? I wonder what your wife will say. I would ask her name, but I doubt even you can remember it.

'Finally, Cuthbert, let me remind me of the night you stayed here. I don't believe you'd want that visitor to take up residency in the sanctuary of your own vicarage, would you? Remember it, now. That face behind the curtains. That thing standing outside your bedroom door. But this is just a friendly warning, Cuthbert. I think we understand each other at last.'

The priest backed out through the door and into the hallway. He glanced up the stairs and rubbed the hairs on the back of his neck.

'Fucking little queer,' he said, and his voice was no longer shrill but unsteady, fragile. 'Do you think you'll get away with this?'

'But you are frightened now, aren't you, Cuthbert?' Chris walked him to the front door. Conrad, Day and I followed in mesmerised awe. 'Let's imagine that you caught something nasty in the toilets last Sunday. Let's imagine an infestation of something unpleasant. Let's imagine something with six little legs and sharp pincers crawled into your pubes when you fucked that young guy for twenty quid. Let's imagine you caught crabs, Cuthbert. What would that be like?'

Instinctively, Father Cuthbert reached a hand down to scratch his pubic mound, once, twice, a third protracted time. His fingers twitched, wanting to scratch lower. He restrained himself and twisted his body to contain the urge.

'I think you'll find a visit to the chemists is in order,' said Chris sympathetically.

The priest opened the front door and came face to face with a young woman wearing a neat tartan suit.

'Gracious,' she said, taken aback by the grimacing priest. 'I think I'm at the wrong house. I'm looking for Chris Mavrocordatos and the Coven?'

'It is the wrong house,' the priest said, pushing past the woman to get out as quickly as possible. 'Infernally wrong. And you'll find Satan himself is at home.'

We watched Father Cuthbert walk in obvious discomfort to his car, unable to restrain himself from scratching and cursing Chris as he went. Half-glancing back at the priest, the woman introduced herself politely to Chris as Conrad's reporter friend, Anna Brisker.

'Don't worry about him,' Chris said, waving Anna inside. 'We were debating how the Church can help alleviate the housing crisis. Father Cuthbert is more accommodating than you can possibly imagine.'

In the crowded hallway, Anna sought out Conrad's face. She smiled thinly as her eyes fixed on his smile. She was a short woman with a petite face, whose tense lips twitched with apprehension at the kind of the society she was about to enter.

I shook her small hand and complimented her on her smart outfit. She eyed my tie-dyed skirt sceptically, raised her over-plucked eyebrows and turned towards Conrad. He returned her smile and dug his fists deep inside his pockets. How the mighty have fallen, I thought, remembering how Chris had similarly lost his cool on the night he met Jake.

'How did you do that?' I asked Chris quietly, as Anna was led into the Yellow Room. 'With Cuthbert. How did you know all that stuff about him?'

'I have eyes and ears. Ask me another time. We have a new guest to interrogate.'

Chris handed Anna a large glass of whisky and offered her his throne. She sipped the drink, delicately as a wasp, and straightened her suit. Conrad knelt beside her sensible shoes and looked adoringly up at her. Her gaze passed critically over the objects of the room, assessing the value of the property and the people within.

'I smell a bitch,' I whispered to Day as he pressed his warm lips to my ear. 'She's evaluating everything. Perhaps she expected something more decadent. Lord Byron's mansion; a menagerie of peacocks, goats and Turkish rent boys.'

'Or the Marquis de Sade's harem,' he agreed. 'Maybe we should act up to her expectations?'

As though summoned by these bohemian thoughts, Jake came into the Yellow Room with a skimpy towel wrapped around his waist, his body still steaming from a hot bath. How apt, I thought as he strolled casually across the room and lay beside the fire, as sleek as some exotic pet. The room was filled with the scent of his perfumed body. He had emerged from the sauna of our desires.

'Anyone fancy a beer?' he asked, gazing absently at his clipped nails. 'There's a stash that needs to come out of the freezer.'

'You know, I would love a cup of tea,' said Anna, quickly rising to greet him. 'Earl Grey, if you have any?'

Jake turned to the stranger he had not noticed in the room. At the sight of the well-dressed woman, her sharp eyes evaluating his muscles, he lifted a hand to cover his nipples.

'Sugar and milk?' he asked, at a loss as to her identity. He pushed himself up from the carpet, his naked skin glowing in the light of the fire.

'Or lemon,' she replied. 'I can give you a hand.'

She followed the path of his scented body into the kitchen.

'Uptown girl,' I whispered to Day. 'Now she's looking for a backstreet guy.'

'Isn't she incredible?' Conrad asked Chris, his eyes wide and excitable.

'Oh, she's simply divine,' I replied for him. 'Isn't she? Isn't she the most divine thing you ever saw, Chris?'

'I don't expect you to get her,' said Conrad, 'not now you've switched to boys.'

'Can't say I really noticed her,' Chris shrugged and teasingly spoke instead of Jake's beauty beside the fire, the steam rising from his warm, downy skin and the seductive ease with which he moved. Conrad retaliated with a list of Anna's finer points: her style, intellect and acute sense of taste. Chris asked if she could play the piano as well as Jake, if at all.

Day rested his head on my lap. I stroked his brow and sipped my whisky. Chris and Conrad were like too old men in a Gentleman's Club, I thought in disgust: Henry Higgins and the Colonel playing homosocial tennis. Chris lounged on the settee and waxed lyrical about Jake; Conrad returned the serve with Anna's exceptional career prospects. Their voices rose, the testosterone pumped. Two cigars and a decanter of port would have completed the scene.

Chris used to say that the gods were transformed into beautiful things whenever they fell in love. He said that Zeus became an eagle, a swan or a shower of gold when he was overwhelmed by desire for particular mortals. Now it was Conrad's time to change, I thought, watching him gesticulate enthusiastically. Indeed, he was changing already. The aortic rhythm had altered, the electric flash had occurred. I even felt a pang of sorrow that Chris's silent adoring companion would never be the same again. Whether he and Anna ever consummated their desire or not, Conrad was transforming himself into something new before my very eyes.

In the brief pauses of their verbal contest, I caught the low murmur of Jake's voice in the kitchen and found myself wondering what Jake had to say to Anna. It was unusual for him to venture into conversation with a stranger, particularly with one of Conrad's crowd.

When Anna returned to the Yellow Room without a cup of Earl Grey, her lips were pursed and she refused to meet Conrad's gaze. Something had happened in the kitchen, I knew. Something had been said by Jake to freeze Anna's already frigid disposition. Some mischief had been made, but for what purpose I could not think.

Perched on the arm of the settee, she shifted awkwardly within the armour of her tartan suit. Tersely, she thanked Chris for his – she coughed – hospitality, and said she had to get home while it was safe, before the pubs closed and the drunks emptied out onto the streets. I saw the dejection spread over Conrad's face. Chris insisted that she stay for another drink, but she shook her head.

'I think it's appropriate that I leave now.'

'But what of the interview?' asked Chris. He spoke to Anna but his eyes remained on Conrad's devastated face. 'You haven't asked us anything about the Society of Heathens.'

'There will be no interview.' She stood up and walked firmly towards the door.

'Before you go,' I said, disentangling myself from Day's embrace, 'I need to give you something, a little information, in my room. It won't take a minute of your time.'

'That won't be necessary. I have everything I need. Tonight's been more of a fact-finding mission, thank you.'

'No, Anna. You will take this with you. I absolutely insist.'

Anna rolled her eyes and reluctantly followed me up the stairs. Raising the collar of her jacket, she queried the well-established belt of low temperature on the landing.

'It's always this cold,' I said as our breath condensed in the air. 'Jake says that the stairs are haunted, but Chris says that the only ghosts are the ones we carry around with us. He says that it's his own phantom protecting the bedrooms from unwelcome visitors.'

Anna stepped gingerly between the assorted ashtrays, odd socks and mould-filled mugs on my bedroom floor. I sat on my bed and searched among the books for a file of non-existent papers.

'Look, Catriona, you needn't get whatever you're pretending to look for. I can guess why you've brought me up here. It really is nothing to do with your coven, is it?'

I lay the books on the bed and sighed. 'No, it's not.'

'You want to find out why I'm leaving.'

'Anna, I know you'll think it's none of my business -'

'You're damn right there,' she laughed harshly. 'It is absolutely nothing to do with you.'

'If one of my friends is unhappy, then I'm afraid it is my business. We're like a family here, you see. When you arrived, you and Conrad couldn't keep your eyes off each other. Nothing was said, but there was never any doubt that something would happen between you two. It was blatantly obvious. But something went wrong while you were in the kitchen with Jake. What did he say to you?'

Anna sat on the bed beside me and played with her gloves.

'He urged me not to say anything.'

'About what?'

Anna sighed deeply and turned towards me, her cold brown eyes piercing mine. She reminded me of a squirrel: a neat, well-behaved, unblinking squirrel with her paws clutching a handbag of unshelled peanuts.

'Jake said he'd been talking to someone at some bar; Dane, I think he said. It seems that people are saying that Conrad is not entirely –'

'Straight?' I asked; she nodded.

'Jake was very sweet about it. He didn't mean to cause any trouble, I'm sure. But he thinks Conrad is only pretending to show interest in me because he doesn't want anyone to guess the truth. He suspects Conrad of being – or of having been – or of wanting to be – erotically entangled with Chris.'

Despite my own suspicions of what may have happened with Conrad in the past, the idea that Chris would cheat on Jake was too absurd. I thought of Conrad's love for Chris that would never be articulated, the loneliness he must feel every day as the gooseberry in our coven, and the look on his dejected face when Anna said she would leave. I wished for a remedy, something that would eclipse his loss. A strategy stirred in my mind, a sleeping snake that rose at my summons. I forced myself to laugh.

'What's so amusing?' Anna asked. 'What is it? Naturally, I'm mortified by all this nonsense, but hardly think it's a source of comedy.'

'But that's precisely what it is: nonsense. Has Conrad never told you that I tease him about his sexuality?'

Anna shook her head. She rested her chin on her knuckles and looked at me askance. She was going nowhere now I had her curiosity.

'I torment him about it all the time. That's what I do, Anna. It's a dialogue we have. He pretends to be in denial; I pretend to know the truth. The real truth is, of course, that he's the straightest among us. I wouldn't say he's a paragon of heterosexuality, nobody is. That's the beauty of the spectrum. But, honestly Anna, you have nothing to worry about with Conrad. He genuinely likes you.'

'But how can you be so certain?'

'Because it doesn't bother him when I tease him. If it did, then I'd have legitimate doubts. But he doesn't.'

Anna chewed a painted fingernail and blinked. I put my arm around her shoulders, thinking she was about to cry. Instead, she fell back upon the duvet and laughed strangely into her gloves. It was an odd, high-pitched hacking noise. I thought she was fitting, but she recovered almost instantly and sat bolt upright again, as though nothing had occurred.

'It's my own fault,' she said. 'There are so many rumours flying around college about this deviant house, it's hard not to listen to gossip. Though I do try. I suppose you think that I owe you all an apology.'

'No, it's Jake who owes you the apology. He nearly ruined your evening, and Conrad's. Surely he can't believe that Chris is – what was your expression? – erotically entangled with anyone.'

'Perhaps he listens to rumours, too.' She rose from the bed still clutching her handbag of peanuts and adjusted her skirt. She was steeling herself for the Yellow Room.

'There are always rumours about all sorts of things: goats and black masses and god knows what. But Chris is honest. If nothing else, he has that integrity. And his love for Jake is an absolute,' I exclaimed, more to the universe than to Anna. This unnoticed, unsuspected fissure in our home had disturbed me. I had not seen it coming. 'You can see it in his eyes, it burns like Greek fire. He says Jake's name like it's a spell. How can Jake doubt that?'

'Maybe he listens to all your talk of free love?' Anna was keen to go downstairs, to give the evening a second chance. 'Look, I really have no idea. Shall we?'

She left the bedroom without another word. I listened to her leather boots tap lightly down the stairs and turn into the Yellow Room. Conrad's voice echoed through the ceiling, highly delighted at her return. I stayed in my bedroom, disturbed by the cloud of uncertainty she had left behind. Her arrival had unearthed a rift in our community, a faultline that would grow steadily as the dark winter nights closed around the house.

* * *

The following morning, I was woken by the shrieking cries of gulls fighting outside my window. I lifted Day's heavy arm from my chest, gently so as not to wake him, and looked out of the window. The street was dark and empty. It could only have been about six o'clock as there was not even the promise of a winter sun on the horizon. Deep purple, bruised clouds hung over the tower blocks, weakly reflecting the orange glow of streetlights.

The gulls had clustered around something on the pavement. They fought viciously over the obscure shape with outstretched wings, defending, surrendering and then reclaiming their prize. Disturbed by the noise, I padded quietly down the stairs and opened the front door.

I tightened my dressing-gown against the chill morning breeze and shooed the gulls away. The birds cried aggressively and stood their ground. As I came closer to the object, some gulls pecked at my slippers while others flapped in my face. I punched the air indiscriminately, mostly missing but sometimes striking a warm feathery body.

Eventually, the birds withdrew to a safer distance, circling the street from above the rooftops. I looked at the object on the ground for some time before fully comprehending what it was.

The white thighbone of some animal jutted at an angle from a clump of red flesh. I covered my nose with my sleeve and peered closely. The meat, whatever it was, still seemed to be bleeding; a trail of dark blood trickled between the cracks in the paving. Black feathers clung to the sticky blood and trembled in the breeze. Perhaps because I thought this must be a dream, I poked a finger into the flesh. The tissue tightened at my touch.

The gulls circled lower, brushing my face with their wings. I picked up the bone from the pavement and the meat hung down like a heavy sponge. Opening the lid of the neighbour's bin, I buried the meat in a bag of rubbish. The seagulls hovered around, eyeing me sideways until I was back inside the house.

Washing my hands in the kitchen sink, I was surprised and relieved to see that it was not blood at all, but a kind of acrylic paint. I used turpentine and a brush to wash the dye from my fingers. Sitting beside the kitchen window in the dark, I watched the sky grow lighter and considered the mystery of the painted meat.

Anna was the first to join me in the kitchen. Wearing Conrad's favourite T-shirt of The Cure, she sat beside me and gazed at the sunrise. I smiled at her glossy eyes and turned to the pink sky. Through the window, the sunlight glistened on the tiers of broken glass that were cemented to the tops of garden walls. The whole city seemed on fire.

'Is Conrad asleep?' I asked.

'Absolutely. He's snoring as sweetly as a pussy cat, bless him.'

'I love it when they do that. The trick is to make them purr without waking them.'

'I came down to get him a saucer of milk, he looked so cute.'

After a few minutes of inane conversation, Chris strolled into the kitchen, holding his head in both hands. He slumped upon a stool and groaned painfully.

'How can a head hurt so much?' he asked. 'How can one man experience so much mental suffering?'

I patted his hand. 'And you'll never drink again, right?'

'Absolutely. How did you sleep?'

'I didn't sleep at all,' Anna replied. She grinned saucily. Chris's eyes flashed with interest and he sat upright.

'You've violated my unblemished friend, have you? Did you leave any remains?'

'He's in one piece, thank you very much.'

'And was it how you imagined? I want to hear everything.'

'He's spectacular, if that's what you want to hear,' she said, throwing her hair back and laughing wildly, so unlike the smothered squirrel noises she had made in my room. There was an air of spectacle about her, an artificial recklessness that she was perhaps trying out for the first time. Perhaps she believed it was what we expected from her, this faux high-school performance. 'Why are you so desperate to know everything? Doesn't Jake fulfil your nocturnal needs?'

'As spectacular as Conrad undoubtedly is, I wouldn't exchange Jake for the world.'

'Maybe if you'd had the night I've just had, you wouldn't be so sure?' She sipped her tea and then added, unnecessarily, without looking up: 'Naturally, we didn't do everything, but we did most things.'

'Wait till we have one of our legendary orgies,' I said, quite viciously, to shock her. 'I assure you there wouldn't be much left undone.'

By midday, the various sleepers had awoken and someone, probably Chris, suggested that we all set out on a walk to Penshaw Monument. Penshaw was a once a mining community to the south of Sunderland, but now lay abandoned like its erstwhile industry. Some Victorian aristocrat with a taste for the absurd had built a replica of the ancient Athenian Temple of Hephaestus on the hill behind the mining village. Thus today, the Penshaw Monument still overlooks the city, looming on the horizon like a colossal tombstone to a forgotten joke.

The wind worked against us as we struggled up the hill. Jake retold a muddled version of the legendary giant worm that lived under the hill. Someone, perhaps St George but Jake was not too sure, had slain the worm on this spot, which was why the hillside took the coiled shape of the monster's body.

Conrad held Anna's hand and supported her delicate progress up the steep bank to the monument. I watched Jake frown in confusion as the new lovers pulled their bodies together and kissed. Jake tugged his baseball cap over his brow and walked apart from the rest of us.

'I've decided to make a solemn vow, Conrad,' I shouted against the wind, paying close attention to Jake's reaction. 'It concerns you. I swear on this ancient hill, where dragons roamed and were slain by wicked Christian knights, I swear never again to tease you about your sexuality.'

'Why ever not?' Conrad cried back. 'It makes me sound much more interesting than I actually am.'

'Because some moron might take my banter at face value.'

Jake kick clumps of earth down the hillside. He thrust his hands deep in his pockets and skulked between the pillars of the monument. Anna looked sternly at me, at Jake's averted face and at the ground.

'Like who?' asked Conrad. 'The Christian fascists? Why would I care what they think? I'd be honoured if they did think that.'

'Congratulations, Bodhisattva,' I laughed. 'You've just passed another test on the road to enlightenment.'

Jake disappeared behind the black stonework colonnade. Day glanced quizzically at me.

'Don't know what that was all about,' he said quietly so no one else could hear, 'but Jake didn't seem to take it kindly.'

'You see too much, love. Don't you worry about it.'

Chris followed Jake among the pillars and found him perched on the edge of the precipice. I do not know how much Chris understood of what I had hinted, but he knew Jake well enough to guess something was wrong. They talked in tense sentences, exchanging deep glances and kicking their feet over the steep drop.

'On a clear day, we could almost touch the sun from up here,' Conrad said suddenly. 'If only it was a clear day.'

'Perhaps if Icarus had chosen a day like this to fly, he wouldn't have fallen,' I added, glancing at Chris's back as he gestured wildly with Jake. Whatever it was they were arguing about, their words swirled irritably through the grass and down to the fallow fields below.

We stood in silence between the pillars of the Victorian folly and looked out over the sprawling city. To oblige my thoughts, the sun broke through the lumbering clouds and sparkled on the distant sea.

* * *

Our third Yuletide visitor was waiting for us on the steps to the front door when we returned home. From a distance, I recognised his clerical collar and melancholic, bovine expression. The seagulls were still flapping around the neighbour's bin where I had dumped the strange offering of meat. Father Joseph sat among the birds, cringing from their commotion and seemingly at a loss as to why his displeased countenance had not brought them to order.

'Joseph,' Chris announced stoically. 'That's all I need.'

'Tell him to fuck off,' Jake mumbled, digging his hands deeper into his pockets. Evidently, his dispute with Chris had not been resolved.

'We're going to head back to halls,' said Conrad, swinging Anna's hand playfully and casting a last glance at Chris. 'We've seen enough fireworks for one day.'

As we approached the door, Joseph climbed painstakingly to his feet. He was in his late twenties at the time but, from the way he moved, could have been at least half a century older. The birds jeered as he attempted to wave them away.

'Hello Christopher,' he said with a wretched attempt at a smile. 'I am sorry to intrude, but I was hoping to have a few minutes of your time.'

'We have a busy afternoon ahead of us,' Chris lied. 'Since your letter about the Coven to the college paper, we've been inundated with requests for more information. Sadly, I can't spare the time.'

'You must be Jake,' said Joseph, reaching a hand towards the lover who had replaced him. 'I've come to see you in particular.'

'Me?' Jake smiled doubtfully, flattered by the unexpected attention.

'Yes you, Jake. I'm afraid our introduction has been long overdue. It's an oversight I'd like to rectify. I believe your first anniversary is coming up soon and congratulations are in order.'

'Right. Thank you.' Jake's eyes widened in naïve curiosity.

'Certainly. We both know that Christopher is hardly the most, shall we say, steadfast partner you could have fallen into bed with. You should be complimented for keeping his famous inconstancy in check for such a considerable time. Twelve months is something of a record, no?'

'Joseph, fuck right off,' said Chris. He stepped between the two figures, separating his past and his present.

'Come now, where's your sense of humour, Christopher? I don't come bearing any animosity. I've even brought an anniversary gift as a token of my goodwill. It is actually more for your boyfriend, though. I hear you are something of a musical prodigy, Jake.'

Jake blushed and lifted the baseball cap from his head. Running his fingers through his hair, he shrugged and lowered his gaze.

'Don't be so modest. I have it on good authority that you are a pianist of some promise. With the appropriate support, I imagine you could move onto greater things. Here,' he pushed a brown envelope into Jake's hands. 'Happy anniversary from me.'

Jake grinned and accepted the envelope. Joseph nodded at Day and appeared not to notice me as he left the front garden.

'I do hope to see you both soon. Oh, and I almost forgot. There's a vacancy for a pianist at my Sunday School class. I don't know how you feel about Church, Jake. But I would question other people's intentions if they laid obstacles in the way of this opportunity. I do hope you will consider it.'

The priest waved farewell and walked to his car. Jake fingered the envelope in his hands.

'There's something rotten out here,' Chris said, forcing his key into the lock. 'Even the seagulls can smell it.'

'That's the clergy for you,' Day concurred.

'That'll be the dainty offering I found on the step this morning,' I said. 'Someone left it to fester outside the front door. Probably a gift from Father Cuthbert's fan club. I threw it away.'

Chris turned abruptly. 'What offering?'

'An uncooked joint. I think it was a beef or pork, painted red. That's why the seagulls haven't left the house all morning. They know it's there in the bin.'

Chris pushed Jake roughly aside and opened the neighbour's bin. The stench from the decomposing meat was repugnant; it sent the birds into a frenzy of excitement. I covered my nose and retreated into the house.

Jake put his hands on his hips and glared at Chris. 'You don't like Joseph's offer, that's obvious, but don't ever push me like that again.'

'Fuck Joseph and fuck his fucking Sunday School,' Chris cursed, slamming the lid. 'Cat, I need some black cloth and nails and a mirror. Day, can you light the barbecue in the back yard?'

'You're not cooking that thing, are you?' I asked.

Chris did not reply.

* * *

The nauseous stench of burnt meat haunted the house well into the evening. Chris had closed all the windows and lit lavender incense sticks in each room. He was now sweeping ashes around the back garden with a broomstick made of twigs and singing quietly to himself. Day and I stood in the Yellow Room and watched through the window.

'What's going on in that curious head of his?' asked Day. Gently, he stroked his chin against my shoulder.

'I imagine he thinks the meat is some kind of curse. But you know what he's like. He'll never explain.'

'How did it get here?'

'He's made quite a few enemies in the last year. Still, I can't think of anyone who would do this. Perhaps someone from his past?'

Jake opened the back door and stood with his hands in his pockets. He glanced at the blackened bones in the smoking barbecue.

'Chris?' he said. 'I want to talk about Joseph's offer.'

Chris went on sweeping but he glared at his lover.

'What was in the envelope?'

'A music score. Something he wants me to play at a church concert next month. It's for a charity, not for the Church.'

Chris rested the broomstick against the wall. 'Will you do it?'

'It depends on how you feel about it.'

'No, it depends on you. It depends whether you can see the trouble that he's trying to stir up. You can do whatever you want. Just make sure you know what you're getting yourself into.'

Jake laughed defiantly. 'I won't be fucking bullied, Chris.'

'I'm not fucking bullying you. If your ego won't let you see what he's doing, then fine. Play your little piano for him. Good luck to you.'

Jake turned abruptly away and was about to slam the door, when his attention was drawn back to the embers in the barbecue. 'What the fuck was this all about?'

'Nothing. A Christmas present from my father. It's nothing.'

Day and I looked at each other. We knew next to nothing about Chris's father, but we did know that he lived in a vicarage in Sussex. He was unlikely to have delivered a slab of painted, rotting meat to our doorstep in Sunderland and gone home again without a word. We knew that Chris was being less than rational so we said nothing.

After Jake had left the garden, Chris took up his broomstick and resumed his song.

'*Hey dirla, dirladada, hey dirlada,*' he sang. '*Farewell, sir; it's over. Farewell to the child you're leaving too.*'

I heard Jake slam the door to the Green Room and lock it from the inside. The piano lid banged open and the first angry strains of a tune rumbled through the wall. It was something traditional by Benjamin Britten, I think, the sheet music that Joseph had given him. But Jake played it too fast, too heavily, and stumbled over the keys. He made indignant mistakes, halted and tried again from the beginning. Still the same mistakes, still he thumped the piano lid and tried again and again.

Outside, the dream-tree tinkled lightly. Chris was tying a new crystal onto the bough. A new spell, I thought. Something to counteract the curse that had arrived in the morning. Something to lighten the murk that had settled on the house. Perhaps something to restore the peace that had so suddenly been brought to an end.

VIII
Alcmene

January swept over the north coast in a wave of winter storms. For three days and nights, the sky poured ice relentlessly upon the city, burying the roads and houses in a deathly shroud. Electricity was in short supply and all reserves were directed towards the hospital. The telephone wires were also down and unlikely to be repaired until the roads had been cleared, and there was no knowing when that would be. True to its name, the city was sundered from the rest of the world.

The radio was our only channel to the outside world. When far-fetched stories of looting in the city centre were reported, Chris barricaded the doors and windows. Day thought this was pointless because the doors were already buried under snowdrifts, but Chris insisted. During those muffled days, Chris seemed less like himself than ever, shunting furniture against the entrance to his underground castle like a man possessed. In the evenings, we gathered around the fire in the Yellow Room and played Scrabble. We told the myths and prophecies that we pictured in the flames.

Sometimes at night, as the windows creaked with the weight of snow, I heard Chris utter strange sentences in his sleep. During the ice siege, the four of us slept together on the mattress in front of the fire, hugging closely for warmth. When Chris talked in his dreams, Jake covered his head with pillows and groaned, evidently familiar with this phenomenon. The words were fragmented and meaningless on their own, but they clustered in my unconscious to form mirages of snow giants and church gargoyles and sea-ghosts behind the curtains.

On the second night, Chris woke me with a howl. In the orange glow of the dying fire, I saw him sitting up in bed and pointing at the window. I looked, half-expecting to see a shape behind the curtains, but there was nothing.

'Not here,' he said, running his fingers through his wild black hair. 'Not him, not here.'

I stroked his hands and told him it was only a nightmare. Chris gabbled about the face at the window and reached his arms protectively around Jake.

'But not here,' he said, turning to me. 'Not him, not here.'

Now fully awake, I remembered Chris's lullaby.

'*Hey dirla, dirladada, hey,*' I sang softly, repeating the simple lines over again until he was soothed and mumbled the words with me. '*I have only one friend, the river. She goes dirla dirladada.*'

Within minutes he had buried his nose against Jake's shoulder and was breathing steadily. Troubled by Chris's nightmare, I crept to the window and looked outside. The garden was empty and the dream-tree echoed in chimes the tune we had been singing. The sky was filled with boundless flakes of snow, swirling in spirals over the houses. Sometimes I saw shapes in the blizzard, grey figures somersaulting from chimney to chimney, swinging on the aerials and pirouetting on the cars. Then the gale blew the figures into clouds of white dust that dispersed and settled against the windows and doorframes.

Early on the morning of the third day, there was a knocking at the front door. We must have had cabin fever by this point, as the noise spooked us all. Chris wrapped a blanket around his shoulders and went to the hallway.

'Who is it?' he called, waiting for an answer before he would remove the barricade. There was a mumbled reply and a soprano laugh. Chris shunted the wardrobe out of the way and opened the door.

'It's over,' I heard Anna's voice breeze airily through the hall. 'The roads have been cleared at last, and the phone in halls is up and working. Hurrah.'

Anna sashayed through the hallway and blinked into the darkness of the Yellow Room. Day and Jake lay slumped beneath the duvet, spooning each other. I hugged the cat to my chest and waved faintly from the throne.

'Dear me, poor creatures. You have let yourselves go, haven't you?' Anna laughed and hesitated at the door, reluctant to enter our animal den. 'Oh my, the stench. You really are Neanderthals.'

'We're hibernating,' I replied. 'We're the only survivors of the nuclear winter. Wake us up when the mutants have all eaten each other.'

'Well, Conrad has tried to ring you,' Anna said, seeming to accuse us of being responsible for the damaged phone lines. Partly repulsed, partly curious, she poked the duvet with her pointed black boot. Jake shifted beneath the covers, grunted and rolled over, revealing his smooth, sculptured chest. Anna seemed satisfied with this result.

Chris stood behind her and yawned. 'What did Conrad want?'

'To rescue you from the Great Freeze. His parents have gone abroad for a few weeks and their house in London is empty. I said you probably wouldn't want to come down with the two of us at such short notice, but he was most insistent, the silly boy. Naturally, I don't expect you've time to –'

'We're coming,' Chris and I said in unison.

'In that case,' Anna raised her button nose and sniffed the air. 'You do have hot water, don't you?'

Conrad's invitation came like the ending of a siege. Chris locked himself in the bathroom for two hours, leaving the rest of us to fight over a trickle of hot water in the twenty minutes that remained. When he reappeared, he bore no resemblance to the mangy wolf that had stalked up the stairs earlier that morning. Clean-shaven and fully dressed for the first time in days, he looked more like the Chris we knew, the one that had gone missing the day the meat-curse arrived on the doorstep.

'I'm ready for my public now,' he said, only half-joking. He stood at the door with his rucksack packed, wondering why we were running late.

The six of us travelled down by train and stayed at Conrad's parents' house, somewhere between Camden Town and King's Cross. The house was in a cramped and littered street, overshadowed by the broken shell of the railway depot, and shaken regularly by the rumble of trains. Anna was smitten with the humble chintz of Conrad's home. She commented upon the garish wallpaper, the nicotine-yellow ceilings, even the cheap prints of dogs playing cards that hung on the walls of the lounge. She tottered on her heels through the weed-infested garden to lean, poised and pre-Raphaelite, over the low wall and breathed deeply from the stench of the stagnant canal.

'So deliciously Dickensian, don't you agree?' she laughed carelessly. 'It's just so real. I never dreamed that such places still existed. Do you suppose they still have polio in this neighbourhood? And look, over there,' she pointed down the canal to where a skinhead was dragging a rusty bike from the icy sludge. 'A real Artful Dodger! How perfectly quaint. Oh, go fetch my camera, Conrad.'

Anna twittered like an excited canary throughout our time in King's Cross. She clapped and pointed out the china menagerie, plastic snowstorms and decorative plates that cluttered Conrad's childhood home, mementos from a lifetime of annual package holidays. She was the first to dress in the mornings, determined to find the best bargains of the January sales in the West End. At sunset, she returned with bags of designer clothes and complained about those "dreadfully common boys" who wolf-whistled as she passed the canal on her way home. As she said it, her eyes glittered with crystal satisfaction. She relished the thought of making those cockney cocks stiff with desire for her.

For us, London was as much a release from the winter siege of Sunderland as a liberation from the malaise that had fallen on our cloistered commune. Chris and Jake spent most of their time in bed, enthusiastically making up for the row they had had about Joseph's invitation. The quarrel, their first, had erupted abruptly and was quickly over but it was memorable for its vehemence. It had struck like lightning and left a perceptible disjuncture in their relationship for days afterward. London gave them the space for reconciliation. They spoke no more about the fight and made tactful, considerate eyes at each other whenever somebody raised the subject. On our last Friday in Kings Cross, Jake announced that he would rather never play the piano again than demean himself at Joseph's Sunday School, nor would he have time to rehearse for the concert if he wanted to get a good degree. Chris smiled and said we should all go out to a wine bar on Old Compton Street to celebrate. Jake spoke no more about it.

The wine bar was costly, but Chris insisted that we make our final night one to remember. I funded the evening, spending the dregs of my student loan on bottles of cava and sambuca shots. At some point, I lost sight of the expense and sunk further beneath the table. When last orders were called, Chris grew morbid and declared that tonight was the last night of our youth. He raised his glass and called for a toast.

'Care and vexation belong to tomorrow; tonight we are young and beautiful. To the end of the springtime of our lives, my friends.'

'And to the beginning of our glorious summer,' I rejoined.

I walked back to the house holding hands with Chris and Jake. Sometimes we danced, sometimes we staggered, often we swung our arms in a childlike way.

'There are never any stars in London,' said Chris, gazing at the clouds. 'I don't know how anyone finds their way home without them.'

'You sound like your mad old mother,' Jake laughed and stumbled off the kerb. 'I thought to myself, tonight, I thought how much you look like her. You do look like your mad old mother.'

Graciously, Chris bowed and took this as a compliment.

Conrad had been lurching ahead with Anna and Day. Struck with a sudden thought, Conrad turned and swayed unsteadily.

'Guys, hey guys,' he called back to us. 'Anyone know where the house has gone?'

'Come along, silly boy,' Anna said, taking his arm and leading him up the pavement. 'You can't even find your way home without me.'

Day lingered beside the lamppost with a meaningful grin. I knew exactly what he was thinking. I pursued the labyrinthine passages of his thoughts, the unlit bridges and Venetian tunnels of his meandering mind. Over the water, barely touching the surface, I followed the theme to its source. Day nodded and moved on.

'I think we should do something spectacular to commiserate the last night of our youth,' I said loudly enough for Day to hear. 'Chris, do you know any suitable games for such an occasion?'

Of course he did. Chris was a master of dubious drinking games, most of which ended in some form of nakedness. I believe he learned everything he knew at Joseph's theological college. In those days, the gin-swigging priests had used cards up their sleeves to swindle his clothes and forfeit his consent. Chris had learned every trick of survival and cunning from those vipers.

'Games,' he repeated, his eyes slowly focusing on mine. 'Oh, yes, I know some games.'

* * *

Sometimes nowadays, when the house is quiet and Lionheart is asleep, I sit beside the fire with a glass of whisky and remember the sensations of that night. Sometimes I thrill at the memory of that bedroom in King's Cross, the woodchip wallpaper, the dripping sink in the corner, the underground trains rumbling beneath the foundations. The window that would not close banging softly against the frame; the thin white curtains shuffling in the breeze. Sirens wailed longingly over the streets, far from the coast, far from the deadly rocks of the North Sea. The streetlight flickered pulsingly, teasing my imagination with precious glimpses of our bodies writhing over the blankets like six snakes coiling into one skin, like the blink of a pagan heaven.

Sometimes I close my eyes and feel the melting heat of strange flesh against familiar flesh, reach my hands into space and explore the oceans of skin. We became water in streams, weaving down the slopes of each other's parting waves, to dissolve in fountains and condense in tissue and bone. In my mind, I stretch my fingers across warm hair and fluid muscle, to sweep the tides of body over body, and touch again the fire of the Coven's last night together.

Sometimes I close my eyes.

* * *

When it was over, Jake was the first to speak.

'If we'd thought about it, we could have all shared the one bed this whole week,' he said.

He stood beside the window in unashamed beauty, the first glow of dawn lacing his pink outline. He walked to the sink in the corner of the room and washed his face in cold water.

Anna sat on the end of the bed and stared at the carpet.

'I need the bathroom,' she said at length, and walked out of the bedroom without looking back. 'Conrad, you joining me?'

We heard the water heater click as she stepped into the shower. Conrad kissed Chris's forehead twice and followed her out.

'Won't be any sleep now,' said Day, pulling a sweater over his head. 'Going to get breakfast from the all-night chippy. Anyone want anything?'

'I'll come,' said Jake, buttoning his jeans. He would not look at anyone. 'I need some fresh air.'

They closed the door quietly behind them. Chris took my hand and rubbed it between his fingers. He pulled the duvet over my naked body.

'Covering the shame of post-modern Eve?' I asked.

'Oh dear, Cat,' he grinned. 'What have we done?'

We did not speak on the train back to Sunderland. The night in King's Cross remained an unspoken deed, a thing of dreams and too much wine. Instead, we rested our heads on our sleeping partners' shoulders and reclaimed the bodies that had become common property for one night.

* * *

February was an anxious month for me. I waited for the period that never arrived. My fears were confirmed in March. I leaned over the kitchen sink with the pregnancy test and stared at the faint purple line that had delicately materialised in the plastic tube. It refused to go away.

'It could be a false positive. It could, though,' said Chris.

I winced at the sound of his voice. In the garden, the dream-tree hung silent and tense. The seagulls circled the clear blue sky: vultures anticipating my reply. The details of everything took on greater significance, distracting me from the faint purple line that would not go away. I stared at the lupins in the window-box. They had returned from the dark soil for a second spring. I wondered if they would flower this year too or whether the soil was too shallow. There was no hope for the night-scented stock which had been left to wither and die in the first frost.

'It could, but we both know it's not,' I said, forcing my attention back to the kitchen. I gave the plastic tube to Chris and cursed my earlier optimism. If I am honest, at that time I felt diseased with the thing inside me, infected by an unwelcome alien feeding off my body. I rinsed a cup under the tap and noticed that my hands were strangely steady. Even now, I thought, in every second, in every breath, the cells are dividing and multiplying.

I remembered the last time I had felt that way. I was twelve years old and visiting my cousin's house. He was a year younger than me and we were sharing a bedroom. On the last night of my visit, I climbed under his blankets and dared him to take off his pyjamas, which he eagerly did. We explored each other with dares.

My parents had never mentioned sex and at that time I knew no names for the parts. They called it innocence, but it was ignorance that caused me to lay awake when I went home to my own bed. I envisaged horrific scenarios of the secret birth that would inevitably follow from the touch of my cousin's cock. I imagined myself flushing the new born child down the toilet. Or hiding it in my wardrobe at home. Or keeping it in my rucksack and taking it to school each day. The choice confronting me now was not dissimilar.

'We can take another test,' said Chris. I registered his use of "we".

I filled the kettle and kept my back towards him. I could do a better job of it than my parents, I thought. I could raise him without any guilt or ignorance. I could raise a hero. I could do things differently.

Or I could get rid of it.

'I need to get away,' I said, stroking the handle of the kettle. 'I need to be somewhere else. To think. I can't go to my parents.'

Chris drummed his fingers on the table. I could feel him watching me, analysing my reaction.

'Have you ever been to Whitby?' he asked. 'It's lovely in the spring and I know of a quiet house beside the sea. You can walk along the shore; it's quite deserted. There's hardly anyone about this time of year. There's plenty of space to think.'

I carried my cup to the table and sat beside him. The seagulls settled on the garden wall and cried at our faces through the window.

'Would your mother mind?'

'She's not bad at this sort of thing,' he said, resting his hand on mine. I flinched at his words. *This sort of thing* – as though that faint purple line happened to Chris all the time. 'And I'd know you were safe there. She can be a clever woman, sometimes. She knows exactly what to do: how much space to give, when to speak, when to be silent. If nothing else, she taught me to have faith in my own decisions.'

The crystals on the dream-tree chimed a soft lullaby, soothing the seagulls into silence. The birds gave up their squawking and abandoned the garden altogether.

'Would you speak to my tutor for me? Tell her I'll be away for two weeks, at least. I guess she'll have to know the reason why.'

Chris nodded and smiled reassuringly. 'I'll let Calliope know you'll be with her this evening.'

'How quickly it's all happened,' I said. Circe walked into the kitchen and mewed at her empty bowl. She glanced up at me, aghast that I had not reached for her biscuits.

'I'm not sure I can go through with this,' I added, disturbed by the meow's resemblance to an infant's demanding cry. For a moment, the cat turned into a hairy baby walking on all fours and flicking its impatient tail.

'You know, you don't have to have it, Cat. But if you do, we'll all be here to help. More than that, we'll all be parents with you. What's that they say about it taking a whole village to raise a child?'

I stood up and looked down at my belly. I felt no sign of the stranger inside, no shift in the contours of my body.

'Isn't it odd, nobody's mentioned the night in Kings Cross since we came home. Conrad and Anna avoid us. The only contact we've had are brief, embarrassed nods in college. Jake doesn't know what to say to me anymore. He glares at you every time you mention Conrad's name. Day takes it all in his stride, of course. When I told him we've all become estranged, he just shrugged. I don't know how they're all going to react to "this sort of thing" – as you so delicately put it. What if they don't want anything to do with it? What if someone insists on being the father?'

I went to the sink and washed my hands in cold water. Still steady as anything, I thought. The cat mewed and brushed her fur against my bare legs. I dried my hands and walked towards the door.

'It doesn't matter who the father is,' said Chris, reaching a hand to hold my arm. 'What matters is we'll be with you when the time comes. If that's what you decide.'

'I have to pack,' I said and left the room.

* * *

Calliope was waiting for me at Whitby's empty station. She was wearing a red sarong and a knitted jumper. My first thought was how closely she resembled Chris. She glided across the platform, her long silk scarf sailing in her wake.

'Catriona,' she said. She reached out a hand in welcome and held my fingers. I noted the toughness of her palms. 'You've come at the best season. The daffodils are in bloom and your bedroom overlooks the garden. I think you like roses, yes, *fíli mou*?' She glanced sideways at me. 'Then you must certainly stay until the roses have blossomed.'

She carried my rucksack into the narrow street and pointed out the abbey on the cliff.

'Jake told me about this place,' I said, gazing at the ruined arches on the hill. Ahead of us, the harbour wall stretched out into the sea, shielding the fishing fleet from the vagaries of the open water. The seagulls seemed to have followed me from Sunderland; they swarmed around the little boats.

'I don't like those miserable birds either,' Calliope said, watching my face. 'By and large, they always seem to foreshadow misfortune.'

Abruptly, she turned away and led me down a cobbled lane of dilapidated wooden houses. One minute we were in shadows, hidden from the sun by the closely bunched shacks and ginnels, the next we were in blinding daylight. She strode like the captain of a ship through the winding streets of the harbour, past pastel cottages and black fisherman's huts. I quickened my pace to keep up with her.

'Over there, on the edge of the town, that's our home. You can see the red roof through the branches,' she said, pointing at a small dwelling that seemed to be built dangerously close to the high tide. A copse of trees surrounded the house like a wooden stockade.

'Jake never told me about all those trees.'

'He didn't see them when he was here. They're new. I had them planted last summer. Twelve trees for the twelve tree months of the year.'

'Tree months? I haven't heard of that before.'

Calliope laughed harshly, a smoker's cackle. She tied her grey hair back with a ribbon.

'While you are here, you will learn much you haven't heard before. Chris's sister, Jackie, she was always afraid of the things I'm talking about. She never wanted to learn, never listened. Chris doesn't suffer from that kind of fear. His imagination is too strong, his will too bold. I think you are more like Chris than Jackie. And now you are going to be a mother, you will need to learn about these things.'

'I haven't decided to keep it yet,' I said, trailing the woman through a crowd of burly fishmongers.

'Not it. *Him*,' she said confirming the vague suspicion I had had since that morning. She placed a hand firmly on my shoulder and peered intently into my eyes. 'I will only mention it now, this one time, and will never discuss it again. You can decide to keep him or not, that's your choice. But I have seen this son already. I saw him last night in a dream, hours before Chris told me about you, hours before you knew the result yourself. And I know that he will be loved.'

Her face relaxed into a smile and her brown eyes twinkled mischievously. 'And now I know what you are thinking. You are thinking I want you to have this child because he could be my only grandson. But I'll let you into a secret: it is not Chris's child. He is not

134

the father. Do not ask me how I know, I just do. Chris and Jackie will be the last in the long and distinguished line of Mavrocordatoses. When my children die, that will be the end of our genes.' Calliope shrugged and pulled an I-can-deal-with-that expression. 'But genes are not everything. In fact, they're hardly anything. What matters is the idea, you understand? The idea lives forever. I don't care that my particular genes aren't carried on. I care that infinitely more important things are.'

We had left the cobbled streets behind and come to a standstill beside the sandy beach. Calliope still held my gaze. She could see I did not understand what she was saying and she waited for me to ask.

'What idea?'

'Why, the idea of love, of course. Your son will be loved. Chris's love will continue. Jackie's love will continue. There, I've said what I've said. Let's speak about it no more.'

As Calliope had promised, her garden was aflame with daffodils. Rose bushes clustered against the white walls of the cottage, but she said I would have to return in June to see them in flower. She rested my rucksack against the gate and introduced me to each of the twelve trees surrounding her house.

'You must meet them before you enter,' she explained, 'so they know you are a friend. Otherwise, your stay will not be a restful one.'

'One day, I will have a garden just like this,' I said, stroking the bark of each tree. 'With a vegetable patch and a herb rockery. And wind chimes on the boughs. And mistletoe growing on the apple trees.'

'It's a pity Jackie isn't here to hear you talk so fondly of my whimsies. You might have been a good influence on her. But if you are still here in the autumn, you will perhaps meet her. You will meet her one day, I know it.'

'She's at college in York?'

'In Italy for the time being. An exchange something or other. She likes languages, just not the language that her mother uses. In the meantime, walk among the dryads,' she said, opening the unlocked door to her house. 'Smell the herbs, feel the leaves, stray down to the shore if you like. Don't hurry back. This house is your home while you are here. Supper will be ready whenever you return.'

I walked the cobbled path between lavender and thyme, savouring the scented air as I went. The pigeons cooed in Calliope's dovecote and the crystals chimed gently in the trees. I felt myself becoming enchanted in this wonderland, charmed by the magic of her garden. Each herb was planted with a purpose, each shrub for a reason, and behind every trunk and stem lurked a sprite, a boggart or a hobgoblin.

I leaned against the stone wall and gazed at the softly stirring tide. A wrinkled, leafless tree stood alone on the sand, cutting the sky like an inverted strike of lightning. Seaweed and ribbons dangled from the branches, waving in the salty breeze. This, I knew, was Calliope's own dream-tree.

The pungent smell of garlic rose from the stonework of the wall, keeping the gnats away from the garden. The seagulls, too, seemed to be offended by the scent and remained encamped beyond the sand dunes. I looked for the recognisable garlic stems among the leaves and stalks of the Calliope's garden, but found myself being watched by two fiercely amber eyes. Crouching in the grass, a black cat mewed and stared back at my face.

'Hello, little puss,' I called to Calliope's feline familiar. 'You must be Circe's mother. How do you do?'

Emboldened, the cat emerged from the grass and walked towards me in casual stages, pausing occasionally to lick her paws as she came. I waggled my fingers for the old black tiger to sniff. She approached them politely, having nothing better to do, and raised her nose to my hand.

'How could Jake dislike you? You're a big old softy.'

'Hecate approves of you,' Calliope said, watching me from an open upstairs window. 'She's a good judge of character. They say that dogs will lick the boot that kicks them. That's not so with cats. Enjoy the sunshine. The seagulls won't disturb you.'

When I returned, Calliope had laid sliced oranges and sandwiches on the dining-room table. She lifted the teapot to pour a curiously brown water into cups. The steam rose in a cinnamon cloud.

'This will strengthen your immune system,' she said, passing me a cup. 'The winter's gone, but people still get colds in the spring. You need to protect yourself.'

'And the baby,' I replied, not noticing that my decision had already been made, and tasted the warm water. Surely, I thought, she hasn't added garlic to the tea?

'You'll get used to it,' she nodded, taking my grimace as something she had expected. 'Living beside the sea is also good for warding off infections. It's the salt in the air, I think. Salt used to be our most precious possession, more valuable than gold. In the old times, the chiefs of hunter-gatherer tribes would give salt to wandering storytellers in return for a tale. Why salt? Because salt was precious to life, as precious as stories.'

'Is that why you live here, beside the sea?'

'The sea is my religion,' she said, gazing through the window at the shimmering water. 'It gives me my strength when I am at my weakest. It sings in the night when I have forgotten the old lullabies. It whispers stories from across the world when my imagination is exhausted. The sea is my mother. When the sea turns black and ceases to flow, I will also cease to be.

'You must find something that is your own religion, Catriona, something that feeds your imagination. When you are weak or needing comfort or inspiration, you must have something to nurture you. You will find something which gives you power. I wonder, what will it be?'

'I'm afraid I was never one for religions,' I replied cautiously. 'I'm not comfortable with any of that humility and deference.'

Calliope scoffed and rolled her eyes. 'Who said anything about humility and deference? I don't speak of priests or sin and bowing and scraping, but of power, genuine power, your own source of power. Eat up your cheese sandwiches, Catriona. You need the calcium. We go to the abbey after supper. We'll talk more then.'

She picked up a half-knitted sock and began to click the needles together. I glanced out of the window and watched the seagulls rise from the beach. The seaweed tree on the beach swayed like an old fisherwoman returning home as the evening fell. Calliope hummed a simple tune, a familiar tune that reminded me of Chris.

* * *

'In days when dragons roamed the earth, Chris once told me, they burrowed deep into the cliff-sides beside the sea, to lay their sacred eggs and hoard their stolen treasures,' I said. 'I think they must have built a sacred city beneath this hill.'

Calliope laughed and hugged her knees. Her grey hair streamed behind her in the breeze. 'I used to tell Chris and Jackie that all hills and mountains were the bodies of giants that had fallen during long-ago battles.'

'And now the Church builds abbeys and altars over their corpses.' I looked back at the stone arches behind us and leaned against a gravestone to shelter from the wind.

'But those churches are just corpses, too: ruins that people visit, like dinosaur bones at a museum. Like dead mummies. Deader. But we still have giants that live and walk the landscape.'

I smiled and rested a hand over my belly. A black cormorant hovered into view, lifted on an upsurge of air from the rocks below. The bird turned its dark eyes towards us and then fell again, hidden now beneath the ridge of the cliff.

'You don't believe me?' Calliope continued, 'but we do. I send armies of giants and dryads and harpies south by night. Chris's bastard father sends devils north in the air and we fight, we fight, we fight. One day, when the battle is done and we are both dead, all my giants will lie down to sleep on a flat terrain. The local people will wake one morning to find new hills and downs where there were just fields the night before.'

'And will they build abbeys on the sleeping bodies?' I asked, infatuated by her voice. She surveyed her sea kingdom like an ancient queen, her hard eyes glistening in the twilight.

'They are more likely to build superstores and shopping malls nowadays,' she said. 'Money is the new magic, bankers the new priests, debt the new bondage. There is always something to keep the people distracted and obedient, in their place. For centuries, the monks told us that only they could understand the mysteries of life and death, of the cosmos and of magic, that such things were far too complicated and we should leave the big questions to them, the big men. When I was a girl in Greece, we were told that the orthodox patriarchs would look after us, that only the Glücksburg kings could grapple with the complexities of state. Then we were told that the military junta would take care of things, that we shouldn't worry our silly little minds about politics. Democracy would only muddle us. And now there is a different caste of big men to pat us on the head and use big words like exchange rates and quotas and debt and deficit to confuse us. Go back to your superstores and shopping malls, say the new patriarchs in their new vestments, and leave the big things of the cosmos to us, the grand wizards of eternity. Fuck them all: money men, monarchs, military and monks.'

'Come the revolution?' I asked.

'Come the revolution, indeed, *fíli mou*.'

'Fuck them all,' I nodded. I waited for the right moment to ask the question I had been itching to ask since I first met Chris. Calliope sensed my hesitancy and turned, daring me to say the words.

'What did Chris's father do?' I asked slowly, struggling with the burden of the question. 'What did he do to Chris?'

'He hasn't told you, has he?' Calliope sighed. 'I didn't think he would. He imagines that he is strong enough to bear it all alone, which he probably can.'

'Sometimes he hints at things, strange things that went on at his father's house. Praying naked at night on stinging nettles and thistles. His father thrashing a choir boy over the altar. I don't know if these are real or if he's teasing.'

'It's no joke.' Calliope turned fiercely. She became a lioness defending her cubs. 'The priest is a twisted man. He has no love in his heart, no compassion. He has only guilt and shame – and we were to be his oblation, his offering. We had to be made as lowly and humble as worms to appease his God. A meet and right sacrifice for his salvation.

'It didn't begin at once. It took its ugly shape slowly over the years, growing with intensity as Chris and Jackie grew older. We were not allowed to sleep on Thursdays or Fridays. Sundays and saints' days were feast days when we could eat three meals. He locked the iron gates to the house so we couldn't leave. "I believe you can be saints," he whispered in the evenings, hugging us lovingly while we held our breaths with terror. "God wants you to be a light to the world, if you would only submit to his will." He gave the children razors to cut themselves in secret places. The flesh was evil and had to be subdued. He flagellated them with a wooden clothes brush, and I would beg him to beat me instead. He was most pleased when I asked him for this one little favour. You see, he wanted the sacrifice to be willing. It wouldn't mean anything if we weren't willing.

'Eventually, I made the kids sleep in my attic room, on the floorboards behind me. I laid myself down against the door. In the darkness of the night I told them stories from my homeland, sang them lullabies from the Peloponnese, listened for the weight of his boot on the creaking stairs. I told them of Prometheus rising up against the will of the jealous gods, stealing fire from the sun to give to the cold people of the earth. I told them of Icarus and Daedalus, who forged wings to escape from the prison tower of wicked king Minos. And I told them of their own powers of magic and cunning, of will and imagination with which they could touch the sun and run with the moon. These myths, these stories were our resistance.'

'Jackie would rest her head on Chris's lap and fall asleep as he stroked her hair. He listened to my lore, raising a hand to hush me if he heard a noise in the house. He still felt some loyalty to his father, or else he believed that we would never be free. The priest's omnipotence was all he had ever known. Every morning, I sent Jackie to the iron gates to pick the lock with a knitting needle. I never sent Chris because he didn't believe it would work. And, of course, it wouldn't work if he didn't believe it.

'One morning, the needle opened the lock. I told the kids to act normally all day, not to make their father suspicious. That night, the priest was at a parish meeting and we made our escape to Whitby. And that was the end of that chapter.'

Calliope gazed down at the labyrinthine streets of her town. The sun was setting behind the abbey and the fishing fleet sailed out to sea, their cabin lights rocking as they mounted the dark waves.

'Chris only lived here in Whitby for two years before he returned to his father's house.' Her voice was now low and sorrowful. 'I think he wanted protection from his devils, his desires. He thought the priest's god would cure him of being gay. Chris has never told me what happened when he went back. One day, he called me to say he'd moved to Sunderland. He said he would never return to his father's house.'

'What happened when he went back?' I asked, waking Calliope from her remote world of memories.

She shook her head and moved away from the cliff edge. 'I don't like to think. I simply send giants at night to fight the bastard. I will keep sending them until the day one of us dies. It's getting cold, Catriona.' She reached out a hand to help me stand up. 'We need to get you home. We've talked enough for one night.'

* * *

My fortnight break in Calliope's sanctuary grew organically and without discussion into a full seven months. The university was very understanding and arranged for me to continue my degree in the autumn semester. Day visited at weekends and was sometimes accompanied by Chris and Jake. I spent my mornings walking to the shore or to the abbey, and my afternoons listening to Calliope's lore. We sat beside the fire in the evenings weaving willow-twig spells and telling stories from the flames. She introduced me to the properties of herbs and trees, how to brew decoctions and infusions, which leaves and stones to sew inside medicine bags, which colours to cast in wax candles for healing or hexing. She taught me the alchemy of the mind, how to cast a glamour with a glance and how to change the body with different quantities of the four elements.

'Air for freedom,' she said, pointing at the quarters of her midnight circle on the sandy beach, 'fire for passion, water for purification, and earth to bury sins.'

One Sunday in August, I was sitting on the cliff-side with Day, watching the trawlers creep across the blue horizon. I fingered the rose he had nipped from Calliope's garden. We had not spoken for almost an hour, but basked in the golden silence of the afternoon sun.

'I worship these hills,' I said casually, watching the humming insects on the buttercups. 'They make me feel powerful, like a prince of all I can see. I don't think I've ever felt such peace.'

Day shifted uncomfortably beside the tombstone and waved the tormenting flies away from his face. He glanced at me and opened his mouth as though about to speak. Thinking better of it, he contemplated the sea instead.

'How are Chris and Jake?' I asked, trying to draw him into conversation. 'I thought Chris seemed subdued last time he came.'

'They're spending all the holiday in bed,' Day replied. 'The Coven hasn't met properly since you went away. Don't suppose it'll happen again till you come back, if ever again. And the Christians seem to have settled down. No articles in the college rag for months now.'

'Has Joseph tried to seduce Jake further into the Church with glamorous promises of Sunday School recitals?'

Day shook his head. 'Nobody's seen that priest since Chris told him where to go. Jake's trying to write a composition for his degree.'

Day paused, wanting to say more but holding back. After some time, I turned to find him weeping silently.

'Day, sweetheart, what's wrong? What is it?' I put an arm around his shoulder and dropped the rose onto the grass. He stared helplessly at his open hands.

'You've changed,' he whispered, almost inaudibly. 'You're different now. I want to be with you, I want to be part of the whole birth thing, but you don't need me anymore. You don't feel the same.'

He continued to weep, covering his face with his hands and sobbing quietly. I stroked his hair and watched the tears fall among the buttercups.

'Day, love. Day, listen. You're right in one way. I am different. No one stays the same forever, feeling the same things for the rest of their lives. People do change and that can be frightening. But my love for you hasn't died, it's only grown. I love you, Day, now and always. I don't need a hunter to bring home meat for his woman and her child. I just need friends to help me bring this boy up. Do you think you can help with that?'

'Just as a friend?'

'As a friend to my child and as an exquisite, golden-haired lover to me.'

'I thought I was losing you,' he said, smiling at last through the tears. 'I thought all this Whitby witchcraft had taken you away from me.'

'Nothing could take me away from you, not even the most potent of herbs,' I said, picking the rose from the ground. I took his hand and led him down the cliff-side steps into town.

We passed the fishmongers' stalls and white teashops on the seafront. As we crossed the bridge, Day dropped a penny into the water and watched it sink.

'What was that for?'

'For luck. Chris asked me to drop it in. He's had some weird shit from his dad recently. At least, he says it's from his dad. More meat on the doorstep, some letters written in Hebrew, I think. He's looking forward for your return, especially now that you know your spells.'

'Has anything happened in the house, anything – weird?'

'Like when Cuthbert stayed, you mean? No, nothing like that. There's been banging at the windows at night. And the jasmine was ripped up by its roots last week, but nothing inside.'

We walked back to Calliope's house in silence. I thought about Chris and his warfare with his father, but found it hard to see why the old man would leave meat on his son's doorstep. Imagining trolls and gargoyles was one thing; the rest was inexplicable. I could see myself being drawn into the conflict, enrolled in Calliope's army against the man who threatened her children. I had to get back for Chris's sake, I knew. I would go when the time was right.

* * *

I returned to Sunderland in mid-September, when the sea had turned as pale and pastel as the autumn sky. Chris met me at the station and carried my rucksack to the taxi rank.

'Jesus, Cat,' he said, staring at the size of my belly. 'Are you sure there's just the one in there? This will really get the Christians talking.'

'Thank you, Chris. If I didn't feel so attractive, I might develop a complex. It's not like I'm desperate to drop already, is it?'

'If I didn't know you so well, I wouldn't have said anything. But you do look magnificent.' He gave me a careful hug and a kiss on my cheek. 'How's Calliope? Did you meet Jackie?'

'Sadly, not. She flies back from Italy tomorrow. Your mother's as bewitching as ever and sends her special love. She's expecting you to visit when Jackie gets back.'

'I've had some postcards from her,' he said, lifting my cases into the taxi. 'She says she wants to visit my father.'

'What for? Why the fuck would she do that?' After everything I had heard, this news was alarming. Chris climbed in beside me and told the taxi driver our address.

'Because she wants to make up her own mind about him now, as an adult. She doesn't trust him or forgive him. She wants to work things out for herself, she said.'

'Perhaps that's why your mother wants you to go over when Jackie gets back. To tell her what happened to you.'

Chris threw me a warning glance and said nothing.

Now that the Coven had all but dissolved, the full moons were celebrated only in memory of Chris and Jake's first night. I rarely saw Conrad and never Anna. She was said to be so embarrassed about my pregnancy that she would not know what to say. As Chris had predicted, my obvious state caused whisperings among the white-blouse brigade at the front of the seminar room. Walking into a suitably named *Gothic Fiction* seminar, Chris and Conrad accompanied me to our row at the back. All eyes turned to ogle my belly. A rustling breeze of rumour swept across the tables, culminating with the definite word "slut" from the front of the class.

'I thought these people were supposed to be educated,' said Conrad.

'I could do the crabs thing on them,' said Chris. 'You remember, like with Father Cuthbert?'

'No need,' I said, drawing a banana from my shoulder-bag. Holding the fruit high, I peeled the skin slowly and sucked the white flesh between my lips. There was an audible gasp from the room, followed by an even louder hiss from the chief white-blouser: 'Shameful.'

'Okay, Chris,' I conceded. 'Do the crabs thing.'

* * *

Early on the last day of October, I had just rushed to the bathroom with an urgent need to pee when I felt the first contractions. I was already a very long week overdue, but the sensation still came as a shock. The house was quiet, except for the now-familiar sound of Chris talking through his disturbed dreams and the seagulls tapping against the window. I clutched the towel rail and felt the unmistakable tightening of muscles.

'Jesus Christ,' I cried, staring at the toilet bowl. I was aware that nobody had cleaned it for weeks. Dust and hair had settled around the rim.

Within seconds, both Day and Chris appeared naked and bleary-eyed in the doorway. The contraction had passed and my composure returned.

'No one ever cleans the fucking toilet in this house,' I said, covering myself with a towel.

'Has it started?' Day asked, rubbing his eyes and evidently confused. 'Should I call the midwife?'

'Call the stork. There's a baby on its way.'

I ordered the men around like drones. Jake emerged in his dressing gown and stared sleepily at the commotion.

'I'm producing a human being,' I explained, bracing myself for the next contraction.

'I know you are,' he yawned and wandered towards the bathroom.

The midwife arrived at the same time as the postman. Jake accepted the envelopes absent-mindedly from the latter and perched himself on the edge of my bed, oblivious to the situation.

The midwife, Mrs Millward, was a short, stocky woman with a broad Sunderland accent. She glanced disapprovingly at Jake and insisted that only the father should be present.

'They're all the father,' I said, counting the seconds of my contraction. 'They're staying put.'

The midwife rolled her god-help-us eyes and shook her head. We had already discussed this in previous consultations, but I knew she would try her luck now she had assumed command.

'No, my dear.' Mrs Millward picked Jake up by the collar of his dressing gown. 'They'll have to go. Baby doesn't want to be delivered under these conditions, does he?'

'Baby wants you to fuck off if you try it on again.'

'Are you having Baby now?' Jake asked, turning to stare for the first time at the bucket, plastic sheets and disposable pads around the bed. 'In here? Like, today?'

'I'm having him here, today, and with you three present. And if the midwife doesn't like it, we'll get a different one. Jake, sit.'

The midwife dropped Jake onto the bed and went downstairs to the kitchen, grumbling under her breath. Day cleared mugs and books from the floor and pulled the curtains against the seagulls gathering outside.

'There's a postcard from your sister, Chris,' Jake said, turning the card in his hands. 'She says she's visiting your father next week. And there's a letter here without a name on it. I guess it must be for me.'

He ripped the paper open and stared blankly at the message. Chris knelt beside the bed and held my hand.

'Tell me a story, Chris,' I said, panting with the increasing pain. 'Tell me something, anything. Just speak.'

'Have you heard the story about Alcmene and the birth of Heracles?' he asked, holding my gaze with his dark, calm eyes. The midwife returned with a bowl of hot water and knocked roughly against Chris's shoulder.

'Ignore Claire Rayner,' I said, glaring at the woman. 'Go on.'

'Alcmene was the mother of Heracles,' he began. 'She loved her mortal husband beyond all others, and she rejected the advances that the king of the gods, Zeus, kept making to her. Like all unreconstructed gods which have been formed in the image of unreconstructed men, Zeus was fascinated by her loyalty to her husband. He plotted to break her chastity. He came in every dazzling form to tempt her, appearing as fountains of gold, as a silver swan and as a bronze bull. Yet she still resisted him. It was only when Zeus appeared in the form of her husband that she succumbed to him.

'Alcmene became pregnant with Zeus's child. Like all unreconstructed men, he abandoned the woman after he'd bedded her and returned to his divine wife, Hera, with a bunch of roses. For nine months, Alcmene watched her belly wax full. When her time was ready, she lay upon her bed for seven days in agony. You see, the child was prevented from being born by Hera's jealous magic.'

'Shit,' I cursed, riding another wave of pain. 'Do I really want to hear this?'

'It gets better,' he said, trying to unclamp my fingers from his wrist. 'Hera sat at the door of Alcmene's chamber, crossing her legs and crossing her fingers, preventing the birth. Like all unreconstructed women, the goddess hated the mortal for being a victim of her husband's desires. Alcmene pushed and Hera clenched, and the child was locked somewhere in-between.

'On the seventh night, Alcmene's handmaid went outside for some fresh air and saw the goddess crossing her legs on the doorstep. The handmaid was a clever girl and realised that Hera's jealousy was the cause of this prolonged labour. So, the maid cried out to the goddess: "Congratulate our mistress: Alcmene has given birth to a boy!" Hera was so surprised that she uncrossed her legs. At that moment, the spell was broken. Alcmene pushed and Heracles was released from the womb.'

'Don't listen to that daft boy,' Mrs Millward growled, dabbing my sweating forehead. 'He knows diddly squat about childbirth. No one could survive seven days of labour. She would have died before then, long before then, no question about it.'

'It's only a fucking story,' I cried, straining my head from the pillow.

'Here, I think this one's for you,' said Jake, passing the letter he had opened to Chris. 'Is it from your da?'

'"If a man also lie with mankind, as he lieth with a woman,"' Chris read slowly from the paper, '"both of them have committed an abomination: they shall surely be put to death; their blood shall be upon them."'

'And this was in there too.' Jake handed Chris a tissue of clotted blood and hair.

'For fuck's sake,' Chris exploded, rising panic-stricken from the bedside. He grabbed the tissue from Jake's hands and ran outside. I listened to his footsteps echo down the stairs and into the back yard.

'Dear me,' Mrs Millward sighed, wiping her own sweaty brow. 'I'm not used to delivering under these conditions. I've never seen anything like it in all my years.'

The labour went on through the afternoon and into the evening. The midwife called the doctor, who insisted that I be moved to a hospital. Between panting for air and complaining about the state of the toilet seat, I told him that I was not going anywhere. Chris appeared occasionally to say he was helping in a different kind of way. I knew the substance of what he was saying and imagined it had something to do with the dream-tree. Still, I begged him to remain in the room and hold my hand.

'I can't,' he said, wiping ash from his fingers, 'but I'm doing what I can, you know I am.'

'Hearken to him, will you,' said Mrs Millward. 'The boy can't sit still for five minutes and says he's doing what he can.'

I would have cursed her again but another wave of contractions racked my body. Day's cheeks were wet with sweat and tears as he held my hand and stroked my forehead. Jake sat on my left, watching in horrified silence. His face was pale and whenever I screamed he patted my shoulder and promised to clean the toilet seat in the future.

Just before midnight, I gave birth to my child. A boy, as both Calliope and I had predicted. I held his warm body to my breast and closed my eyes. I felt Day's hot breath close to my face as he leaned over to kiss my cheek.

'He's got hair,' Jake said. He stood up and stared at the baby.

'Aye, many babies are born with hair,' Mrs Millward explained, removing her plastic gloves. 'It means you must have had terrible heartburn when you were carrying him, isn't that so?'

'But he's got white hair,' Jake continued, his voice cracking.

'It's just a little white streak on the top,' said the midwife. 'Just like his father. Well, just like one of them at any rate.'

'I know what to call him,' I said, opening my eyes and looking at Day. 'He's definitely a Richard.'

'Richard?'

'Definitely. At least, until he's old enough to choose his own name.'

Chris appeared in the doorway, panting heavily. His face was streaked with dirt and white chalk. He stumbled into the bedroom and lay beside me on the bed.

'Hello, little man,' he said, smiling at Richard.   'Hello, little princeling.'

'You look tired,' I said to him. 'Tough night for you, was it?'

Chris dropped his head upon the pillow.

'Exhausting,' he whispered, still smiling at Richard. 'I've just killed my father.'

The baby struggled in my arms and began to cry.

IX
Echo

23rd December 1999

Kneeling beside the fire, Catriona paused in her long tale to poke the embers. Through the window, I watched a flock of wood pigeons circle the oast-house and settle in the leafless oak trees. The winter sky was already darkening, although it was only half-past two. The windows of the old vicarage glistened pink with the reflection of the setting sun.

'Chris killed his father?' I asked. 'My father?'

Catriona turned with a look of intense sorrow and laid the poker to rest on the hearth. Before she could answer, Lionheart kicked the door open and ran towards me. He was grinning wickedly.

'Jackie, Jackie,' he cried. 'He's here, he's here. Chris is back for Yule. He's just parked in the driveway.'

Lionheart paused, seeming to hear silent footsteps approach the house. I, too, raised my eyes and counted the seconds before the knock on the door.

'Wait here,' Catriona said to me, rising from the fireside. 'I'll bring him in.'

Catriona followed her son into the hallway. I listened as the front door opened and Lionheart roared with delight.

'Hello, Man-Cub,' said the voice I barely recognised. 'There's a Solstice present for you in the car. I guess it could also be a late birthday present. You decide which it is.'

'Can I see it?' Lionheart asked. Without waiting for an answer, he skipped down the path to the car. That boy is an enigma, I thought, listening to his trainers kick the gravel. Outside the house, he smoked and cursed and sprayed the local Conservative Club with obscene but accurate graffiti. Inside, he yelped and played like the household puppy. I wondered if Catriona imagined half of the adventures her son got up to.

'It's been a hell of a journey,' Chris said in the hallway. 'You look more gorgeous than ever, Cat, if that's possible.'

'Give me a hug,' she replied, 'and then I want to introduce you to someone special.'

I waited beside the fire, nervously playing with the silver ring on my little finger. My mother had given it to me the day before she died. She said she wanted me to have something to remember her by, as if she knew that she was soon to go. It was one of her tricks, that constant prophesying. Perhaps I only remember the ones that came true.

'I don't need anything to remember you by,' I had said at the time, dropping the ring back into her palm. 'You're not going anywhere. You'll always be here, freaking me out with cryptic utterances.'

My mother just shook her head and placed the ring on the table.

'Sometimes, Jackie, I can feel what's coming. Sometimes I know the right things to say at the right time. Something's coming now and I need to tell you this.'

'Stop it,' I said, angrily. 'Stop doing this. Do you know how much I hate this bullshit? It's all so absurd, so deranged. It's like the stories you used to tell us when we were children. You've come to believe in them yourself, haven't you? You think they're true.'

'I know you don't like to listen, Jackie. But this time you must.'

'No.' I fled to the window and pressed my hands against the glass. It was late afternoon, almost twilight, and the trees in the garden were shedding their autumn leaves. Out at sea, a trawler pitched the rising waves on the horizon. I counted the flashes of its red cabin light. Once, twice, three times... They don't usually flash like that, I thought, watching the rapid pulse of the beacon. My mother came to the window and stood beside me. She laid a gentle hand on my shoulder.

'Little Jacks,' she said softly. 'Do you remember the time I gave you the last knitting needle in my sewing case? Do you remember what you said?'

I smiled with the memory and closed my eyes. 'It was a thin metal needle, cold against the skin. You acted as though you were giving me a sword. I felt like a warrior. You told me that the last needle is always the magic one. You said that when we've tried everything else, the last try is the one that works. I remember seeing you smiling in the attic window.'

'And what did you say?'

'I said that I believed you.'

My mother lifted her hand to stroke my cheek. Even now, I can smell the cinnamon and nicotine of her fingers.

'You see, Little Jacks, I gave you the needle and you opened the lock. You did it because you believed. When did you stop believing?'

I fixed my eyes on the trawler's red beacon and counted the flashes from the beginning again. One, two, three...

'When did you stop believing, *agapi mou*?' Her words came to me from across the waves, a distant signal from a ship in distress.

'When I didn't need to anymore,' I said, tapping the windowsill like a message in Morse Code. 'When I couldn't stand the hope it gave me. When Chris went back to the vicarage. Perhaps earlier.'

'Listen,' she said so quietly that perhaps I imagined her voice. 'Listen to the night. Don't speak, don't be afraid anymore. Just listen.'

The beacon on the trawler grew faint and disappeared as the ship was engulfed by a rolling wave of mist. The cloud swept towards the shore, swallowing the rocks and seagulls with a ruthless inevitability. Fathom by fathom, it galloped over the face of the water, a grey mass of sea-wolves, an apocalypse of fog.

The wall of mist reached the coast in seconds and streamed over the sand dunes. It smothered my mother's dream-tree so completely that I could no longer hear the wet slap of seaweed against wood. I watched the stone wall dissolve and the trees melt as the cloud surged into the garden. Not the lavender, I thought as I watched the herbs disappear. There must be something left; leave the lavender. I counted the last herbs down: three, two, one. And then the mist took everything.

In the silence that followed, I felt nothing.

* * *

Something was watching me from the doorway.

'Jackie?' He spoke my name cautiously. I felt like a ghost that had been seen. I lifted my gaze from the fire and blinked at him.

'Chris?' He crept into the room like a suspicious animal, wary of my human presence. I stood up and looked into his face, but he avoided my eyes and circled the chair.

If he resembled Chris, it was only as his shadow, a pale phantom of the brother I once knew. His eyes were darker than I remembered. His skin seemed translucent as he stood beside the fire. I could almost see the flames behind his body as he reached inside his jeans for a packet of cigarettes. He glanced at my face. Our eyes connected for a moment. With that one look, a chill stole over my skin, a foreboding as heady as if I were standing on the brink of an arctic abyss.

'I knew someone would be here, waiting for me,' he said, lifting a match to his cigarette. He breathed a cloud of blue smoke towards the ceiling and watched the patterns unfold slowly in the air.

'I hardly recognise you,' I said. 'You look so different, so changed.'

He laughed and revealed those large white teeth I remembered from childhood. A wolf, I thought, grinning spitefully in a copse of trees on the South Downs. I retreated into the wide arms of the chair.

'You expected me to be the same, after all these years?'

'I didn't think you would have altered so much.'

'Altered?'

'You look much older.'

'On the brink of the grave, you mean.'

'I suppose we've both aged a lot since we last saw each other.' I heard Catriona fill the kettle in the kitchen. She's giving us time, I thought, cursing her for her consideration.

'You look just the same,' he said, walking towards the window. The purple clouds had lowered over the Downs and the wind rattled the wood-chimes. I heard the weathervane on the oast-house creak its evening song. 'You haven't changed at all since I saw you in York.'

I mumbled an apology for my reaction to his coming out, the last time we met.

'We don't need to talk about that.' He dismissed the past with an wave of his hand. 'How was Calliope's funeral?'

'Quiet,' I replied. Empty would have been a better description. I was the only one to attend the ceremony in Whitby. She wanted to be cremated and her ashes scattered from the cliff. I collected the urn from the crematorium the following week and climbed to the abbey in my black graduation dress. Over the boiling North Sea and above the eastern horizon, the red clouds had seethed. I had felt a warm, unseasonal breeze on my face. The threat of the coming hurricane breathed against my skin. Around me, the seagulls circled the ruins, silent, expectant.

I lifted the lid from the urn and freed the contents over the edge. The gulls dived among the windblown remains, as though I were scattering crumbs for their dinner. The ashes drifted far out to sea, flying down to the black water where the trawler had sunk beneath the waves. The oil slick from the accident still smothered the water, reflecting the sky like a dark scrying mirror.

When all the ashes had touched the sea, I turned to leave. Hovering between the arches of the abbey, I saw the Evening Star shine more brightly than I had ever seen before. Venus, I thought as I climbed down the steps of the cliff. The star that she followed throughout her life. That is where she watches me now.

Nobody else came to the funeral, nor to the scattering of the ashes. Nobody was waiting for me when I returned home. The summer had passed and now the autumn winds stripped the leaves from the twelve trees in her garden. The lavender drooped across the cobbled path as I entered the gate. Even the smell of garlic from the cement in the garden wall seemed fainter than usual. Everything was wilting. I needed something to hold on to. When the wild gale arrived, I drove south.

I fingered my mother's silver ring. Chris was watching me. His dark eyes softened with sympathy and his lips relaxed into an attempt at kindness. Failing that, he turned towards the fireplace and lit another cigarette.

'She told me not to go,' he said, answering my thoughts. 'To her funeral. The last time we spoke, over ten years ago. She said that when she died, she didn't want me to go to the funeral. Those were her words.'

'Do you honestly think she meant it?'

'What does that signify? It's what she said.'

'Ten years ago?'

Chris spat into the flames. There dwelt an indescribable emotion in those eyes, I thought, something I could not identify. It was neither hope nor despair that raged within, but something beyond, abandonment perhaps. He lowered his face and stared at the flames.

'If you're trying to make me feel guilty about not being there, you're wasting your time. I don't need you to make me feel that.'

'I'm not trying to make you feel guilty,' I said. 'There's so much I don't understand, so much I need to know.'

Chris inhaled deeply from his cigarette. The smoke poured like a mist between his lips.

'Then ask me,' he said simply.

'I don't know where to begin. I thought I knew you. I thought there would be something of a link between us, a blood thing, in spite of all these years of separation. But now, seeing you again, seeing how changed you are, I don't know anymore. What happened to you? Was it Jake?'

At the sound of the name, something savage flickered across Chris's face. He half-turned away, but I saw him grimace. A raw frown carved his brow. In the red glow of the fire, I thought for an instant that a demon was standing before me.

'Don't,' he whispered so quietly and with such menace that I had to lean closer to hear the words. 'Just don't.'

He knelt down to stir the embers. Grabbing the shuttle, he rattled more coal into the fire. His breathing became calm again and he regained his composure.

'I don't want to hear it spoken.'

Without warning, the door crashed open and Lionheart ran inside, clutching something small and black to his chest. He peered blindly into the darkened room, until his eyes became accustomed to the gloom.

'Chris, she's lovely, she's so sweet. Is it a she or a he? Does it have a name? It's so cute.'

'It's a she and her name's Medea,' Chris replied, smiling now with love for the boy. 'Isn't she beautiful? She's the granddaughter of a cat I used to have at college. I picked her up from Conrad's house.'

'I love her,' Lionheart said, lifting the tiny creature to his face. Could this be the same gargoyle-boy who told me to fuck off when he first saw me all those months ago?

After dinner, I strayed into the garden to give Chris some catch-up time with Catriona and Day. While we had been eating, the conversation was confined to their college days and to absent friends. I gathered from Chris's face that I was superfluous to his evening, so I said I needed some air and left them to their memories. He smiled kindly at me for the first time since the afternoon.

The clouds had passed beyond the Downs and now the sky was clear with crisp stars. The oast-house loomed silently beyond the wall, its windows shining in the warm glow from Catriona's cottage. I leaned against the hard bark of Eurydice, my favourite tree, and lit a cigarette.

'Give us a light,' Lionheart said from the dark boughs above my head. He dropped to the grass, a monkey in combat trousers, and nodded towards the cottage. 'They'll be busy for hours. Come on, Jacks.'

'I've told you before, I'm not supposed to encourage you.'

'It's not that I need any smokes, I've got my own. I just need a light.' He held out a crumpled pack. 'Or I can just go to Kevin's and shoot up a line of ecstasy with him.'

I was going to say that I didn't think anyone shoots up a line of ecstasy, but I passed him the lighter instead. Lionheart lit his cigarette and climbed back into his tree.

'Do you still think you know Chris?' he asked.

'I don't want to talk about it tonight, Lionheart. Let it go.'

He nodded thoughtfully and kicked the bough. 'He's only here for one night. He's leaving in the morning.'

'Where to?'

'Conrad and Anna's posh pad in London. Then back to Greece. He'll stay there until the spring.'

'What does he do over there?'

Lionheart breathed smoke at the stars and shrugged. 'Looking for something. Some old house, I think.'

I heard the back door of the cottage open and someone step into the garden. Lionheart dropped his cigarette into the dewy grass and climbed higher among the branches. Instinctively, I withdrew behind the line of shadowy trees.

'Are you hiding from me, Jackie?' Chris lit a cigarette and walked casually towards me. Ashamed, I stepped out onto the open lawn.

'I just needed a fag.'

'You can smoke inside the house, you know. Cat pretends not to approve, but all ex-smokers are the same. She's easily corrupted.'

He stood beside me and gazed at the South Downs. A fox padded cautiously beside the length of the garden wall, flinching at the sounds of the cottage. Its bright eyes reflected the lamplight as it turned towards Chris and lifted its nose. The garden was dark, but I was able to see Chris twitch his lips into a smile. Alarmed, the fox bolted from view and disappeared among the shrubs.

'You haven't lost your natural charm,' I said when Chris's laugh had died down. 'That smile used to terrify me when we were young. I know how the poor fox feels.'

'You used to enjoy my stories, Jackie. Do you remember the one about the faceless monk that haunted the vicarage? Or the Old Woman of the Downs swinging from the guttering?'

'They weren't just stories for me, Chris, they became real. I remember lying awake in the attic, listening to the weathervane creak in the wind. I was even convinced that one time I saw her face grinning through the curtains, mouthing my name.' I shuddered at the memory and pulled my coat tighter for warmth.

'Family ghost stories. Childhood fears. But I suppose,' he paused to look at the weathervane. 'I suppose they do become as real as anything, after a time.'

'Like the sea-ghosts in Whitby. You told me about them too, before you left. Why did you leave us, Chris? I was too young to really understand it back then.'

Chris walked towards the stone benches and I followed him across the damp grass. The sound of Catriona's laughter drifted from the cottage through the cold night air. The fox rustled in the undergrowth and then careered across the lawn, a flash of red lightning. I sat beside Chris on the bench and watched the creature glance over its shoulder with terrified white eyes.

'I was young then as well,' said Chris, 'and trying to come to terms with many things: what our father did, the separation, my sexuality. I still heard his voice at night, you know, in the wind during those long winter evenings. He whispered awful things, hell and damnation – real damnation – in my ear as I slept. Sometimes I would wake to find him watching me through the window, or disappearing through the bedroom door. Sometimes he said he loved me, that he could help me. At other times, he simply shook his head with shame and turned his back. I didn't believe that we had escaped him, or that we ever could. He was always watching. Always.

'I thought that if I could sacrifice something to him and his hungry god, then you and Calliope would be safe, that I would be safe. I thought that if I gave up the one thing that I wanted passionately, the thing I secretly dreamed about in my frustrated adolescence, then all would be well. I went back to him to renounce my teenage sexuality. Perhaps I even thought that my sexuality was the cause of all our troubles. I was like Jonah returning to Nineveh. You remember that story? There was no getting away from it.

'Of course, Calliope tried to convince me to stay, but she allowed me to make my own decisions. It took me many years to understand how she could have let me go. Now I realise that she let us make our own mistakes. She gave us a sense of our own power, our own responsibility. She was the best parent we could have wished for.'

'What happened when you went back to him?' I had been watching his face intently as he stared down at his own hands. He lifted his face and I saw that his eyes were glistening with tears.

'You don't need to know.' Chris stood up and walked towards the tall garden wall. The oast-house towered into the moonless sky, eclipsing the stars. He stood still and looked at the weathervane.

'Chris, I need to ask you something. You don't have to answer if you don't want to, but I need to know.'

I paused, awed by the weight of the question I was trying to form. He waited patiently for me to go on.

'Did you kill him?'

At first, he did not move. When he did, it seemed to be in slow, deliberate stages. He lowered his head into his hands. I thought he was weeping and was moved to comfort him, to lay a reassuring hand on his shoulder. But before I could reach him, he turned abruptly and the lights from the cottage fell over his grinning face.

'Is that all you need to know, Jackie? Just that?' He raised his head and barked a short, spiteful laugh. 'After everything he did to Calliope and me. After all the years of torment we went through. After all the evil he could imagine doing and saying. Yes, Jackie, I killed him.'

I flinched at the sharpness in his voice. The stars became unfixed in the sky and danced around each other, as they had the night we travelled to Whitby in the car. I thought I heard my mother's voice asking if I could see Venus. I laid a hand on the cold stone bench and stared at the sky. It must be there, I thought, searching for the Evening Star, but nowhere could I find it.

'Jackie?' Chris touched my hand and peered into my eyes. His face grew kinder, his voice concerned. 'Sit down. I'll get you something to drink.'

I sat alone on the bench and rubbed heat into my arms. When Chris had safely disappeared into the cottage, Lionheart shifted among the leaves of his tree and dropped to the damp earth.

'Fucking hell, Jackie, he's a bit hard on you, isn't he? Are you alright? You need a fag?'

He dropped a cigarette into my open palms and glanced back towards the house. 'You got a light?'

He took the lighter from my hand and was soon blowing smoke into the air.

'Thanks, Jacks,' he said, planting a wet kiss on my cheek. By the time Chris emerged from the back door of the cottage, Lionheart had already returned to his hidden roost among the dark branches.

Chris placed a demijohn of Day's ale on the paving slabs and handed me a glass. I took a sip and immediately felt the effects of the powerful homebrew.

'Not bad, is it?' said Chris. He smiled reassuringly. 'I shouldn't have shocked you like that.'

'How did you do it? How did you kill him?'

'With a dose of his own medicine. He had been sending me little gifts through the post, sometimes in person. The usual messages of fatherly hate and damnation, occasional curses. On the day that Catriona gave birth to Lionheart, I received his final curse. Your letter, the one that said you were going to visit him, it arrived on the same day. I had to do something to stop him.

'I knew he'd been coming closer to the house all summer. Seagulls attacked my dream-tree in the back yard, pulling off the crystals that I'd hung from the branches. There was a definite something, a threat in the air. The flowers that we'd planted in the window boxes never blossomed. Things began to move around the house at night: chairs in different rooms, knives in patterns on the kitchen floor. It became a routine. I would get up early and put the house to rights before anyone saw what was going on.

'And the old dreams came back. I heard whispering in the night. In the morning, I watched him slither out of the room, smirking with satisfaction. On the day that Lionheart was born, I woke to find him sitting cross-legged at the end of my bed. He was twiddling his thumbs as though waiting for something. I tried to kick him off the blankets, but I couldn't move my legs. I tried to strike him, but I couldn't do anything. I was paralysed under the covers, terrified as his fingers twitched closer to my face. He leaned his mouth to my ear and gave his curse. I heard him say it as clearly as I hear my own voice now. "Vengeance is mine". Just that. And then I heard Cat scream and that broke the vision. I leapt out of bed and found her standing in the bathroom, recovering from her first contractions.

'The message he'd sent me in the post was that old quote from Leviticus. You know the one. If a man sleeps with another man, they should be put to death. After I'd read it, I knew his revenge was coming. There was sulphur in every room, like there was on that evening the

Devil came to us in Whitby, you remember? I took his letter into the back yard and tore it up. As I was doing that, the seagulls took flight from the dream-tree and circled the house. They had ripped all the crystals from the tree. Nothing remained but the loose strands of string.

'Throughout the day, I listened to Cat's screams as she lay in labour and couldn't give birth. Outside in the garden, I poured petrol on the pieces of his letter and burnt it. That sent the gulls into a frenzy, but I still felt his presence spreading throughout the house. I cast every spell I knew using herbs and rags and candles to protect us.

'As twilight fell, I felt the old scars on my arms and legs tingle. Do you remember the razors, Jackie? Do you remember when he gave them to us and said we would be saved if we suffered. Do you have any memory of that? After all that time, those scars opened and the blood seeped through my shirt.'

Chris stood up and moved to the opposite bench. He lit another cigarette with trembling fingers and closed his eyes with the memory. I stared at the familiar marks on my own wrists. There was so much I had blocked out and much I was too young to remember. Only the giants in the landscape and the scars on my skin remained, signposts to the past.

'Speak to me, Chris. Tell me everything.'

Chris turned to me with wild eyes. 'She came, Jackie. I didn't know what else to do. I had to fight him somehow. I had to summon her, and so she came. The Old Woman of the Downs. She came when I called her.'

I listened to his voice rise and fall as he spoke of spells and planetary sigils, protective circles around the dream-tree and the elemental guardians of the four quarters. On the night of Lionheart's birth, he said he painted the back yard with geometric signs from lost civilizations, symbols from the days when dragons stalked the South Downs and myths lived side-by-side with mortals. Sweeping the ground with a broom of twigs, he had whispered her name to the tune of the wind.

The wood creaked slightly at first, as though touched by an invisible finger. Chris spoke her name again and again, raising her breath from the dust of the garden. The autumn leaves danced around the circle, climbing higher into the disturbed air. The dream-tree rocked as he sang, his voice merging with Catriona's birthing cries from the bedroom upstairs. As he swept the yard, the blood trickled down his wrists from the long-sealed scars of his father's razor.

The church clocks had struck eleven when, exhausted with his vigorous sweeping, he laid the broom against the tree. He slouched against the wooden pole and closed his eyes. The tree was still creaking, although there was no wind now and the leaves lay still.

At the sound of a footfall, he glanced around the empty yard. The streetlamps cast an orange glow over the wall, illuminating the garden in an otherworldly light. The back door remained closed and the curtains were drawn. Catriona's rising screams echoed within the walls of the house; the dream-tree continued to rock from side to side. All else was quiet. Again, he distinctly heard footsteps approach the circle and halt at the white paint of his markings.

'Who's there?' he said, standing and looking into the thick air. 'Who is it?'

The dry leaves rustled in the guttering, though he felt no breeze on his face. Holding onto the wood, he leaned over the line of the circle. The crackling of leaves grew louder until he realised that it was not the leaves at all, but a familiar, rasping laugh.

He said he saw her poised upon the roof of the coal-shed. Her face was so creased with age that her features had sunk beneath the wrinkles. The grey hair had clotted like sun-bleached seaweed, slapping against her rotten skin as she rocked. Chris clung to the dream-tree and stared in horror as the creature's tongue twitched over her lipless mouth.

And then the roof was empty. Chris sat beneath the tree and counted the heart-beats that thundered in his ears. The church clocks struck eleven-fifteen. Everything was still except the creaking wood and rustling leaves.

'Chrissy,' she wheezed behind his ear. Chris spun around in dread and stared into her face. She clung to the window box with her toes, her grotesque smile flickering in the orange light.

'Who are you?'

The leaves crackled in the guttering. The banshee tilted her face sideways. Deep within the folds of her skin, Chris saw the shadowy sockets where eyes had once been.

'I am. You called: I am.'

'You came? From the oast-house? From the weathervane?'

'Weathervane?' She tilted her head the other way and leaned towards him. 'From you.'

The rustling leaves fell silent. Chris pressed his back against the wood and rubbed his eyes. Catriona's cries rose within the house.

'Jesus-fucking-Christ,' he mumbled.

'Fucking-Christ, yes,' she grinned and rocked on her hands and feet. Her talons dug deep into the window box, splintering the wood.

'Can you stop him?'

'I can do what you will.'

'If I will what?'

'What you will.' The creature threw back her hair and laughed.

'Do it, then. Stop him. Make it end.'

'How, make it end? How, stop him?'

'I don't need to say it,' said Chris, recoiling from the vacuum of her eyes. 'You know what I will.'

'Say your will, Chrissy. Say your will.'

'I will you to kill him.'

'Say who to kill, Chrissy. Say who.'

'Kill my father.'

'Fucking will, fucking will,' she gibbered and then she paused, slyly. 'And then?'

'Then you go back where you came from.'

She pointed at his chest and grimaced. 'Where I came from.'

The clock struck eleven-thirty. Catriona's screams resounded through the walls of the house. Chris felt the blood trickle down his wrists, dropping onto the concrete at his feet.

'Bargain, Chrissy, bargain,' she curdled with delight and rocked to the sound of the creaking gutter.

'Just do it.'

'Need something.'

She glanced with keen interest at the blood on the concrete and then she looked at Chris, coyly. He knew what she wanted. He held his arm over the line of the circle. The Old Woman jumped to the ground and raised her mouth to his skin.

'Bargain.' She pressed her lips to his scars and suckered. Chris felt the tongue flicker over his hairs, licking the sides of the open wound. She held his eyes for a moment and then she was gone.

The church clock struck midnight. He sat dazed and light-headed on the cold ground. The empty yard flickered and went black as the streetlight lost its power. Somewhere out at sea, a fog horn moaned. Sirens wailed over the roofs of the houses. He became aware that Catriona's screams had ceased.

Standing among the white sigils and symbols of the circle, he looked in vain for the blood stains on the concrete. He searched his arms, but found no sign of the seepage on his skin or clothes. The scars were as sealed as they had ever been, his old wounds healed.

He stumbled out of the circle and entered the house. As he closed the back door, he heard the dry leaves rustle in the guttering, sibilating his name in the breeze.

'The police came around next evening,' Chris concluded. 'They said a fire had broken out in my father's chapel. He'd managed to smash his way through the stained-glass window, but the flames had weakened the rafters and tiles on the roof. The parishioners found his body on the lawn. Apparently, the weathervane had snapped in the heat and fallen to the earth. The iron arrow pierced his chest. It went straight through his heart.'

Chris drained his glass and placed it on the bench beside him. His face had grown softer and melancholy during his recollections. Now he had finished, his expression hardened to the present. He raised his dark eyes from the ground and stared into my face.

'Is there anything else you would like to know, Jackie?'

* * *

In the morning, Lionheart ran into the bedroom still clutching the kitten in his arms. He stroked my nose with the kitten's paw to rouse me from my sleep and laughed when I opened my eyes. Day stood at the sink in his boxer shorts, splashing cold water onto his unshaven face. I lifted Catriona's arm from around my waist and blinked in the morning sunlight.

'Get up, Jackie,' pleaded Lionheart. 'He's heading off now. You have to say goodbye.'

'He's going already? What time is it?'

'It's late. It's nearly half-eight. Come on, get up. You'll miss him.'

I grabbed a long T-shirt from the floor and dressed hurriedly. Day followed me down the stairs. Lionheart stayed to torment Catriona into consciousness.

Chris's suitcase was waiting beside the front door. Day padded into the kitchen, his golden hair shining in the light that streamed through the windows. I sat on the bottom step and rubbed the sleep from my eyes.

'Did you ever wonder how weird it would be for me?' Chris said as he descended the stairs. 'My sister and my best friends in a *ménage à trois*. I would never, absolutely never, have imagined that.'

'I thought Catriona would have told you.'

'She likes surprises, does Cat. I suppose I'll have to get used to it.'

'That's very gracious of you.' I moved aside so he could get past. He picked up his suitcase and turned towards me with a flicker of kindness in his eye.

'I'm even quite proud of you. It's a good thing, you know, to be in love.'

Perhaps because of his condescension, perhaps because I felt embarrassed, I wanted to hit back. How would you know? – I wanted to bite, but I held my tongue and glanced at the oast-house.

'Because I was in love once, too,' he said, answering my thoughts.

Before I could say anything, Catriona bounded down the stairs, flapping her hands like an overgrown child.

'Don't you dare leave without a goodbye kiss,' she said, hugging him tightly. Day emerged from the kitchen with a glass of cold milk. He passed it into my hand and joined in the communal hugging.

I watched from the doorstep as Lionheart loaded Chris's suitcase into the car. They said their goodbyes and Chris climbed into the driver's seat.

'You'll still be here in the spring, won't you, Jackie?' he asked.

I nodded and waved farewell. The car turned out of the drive and disappeared up the lane.

'Bloody freezing, bloody freezing,' Day sang, as he hopped in his underwear through the front door. Lionheart remained in the garden, staring down the lane with the kitten in his hands.

I walked to the kitchen and filled the kettle. Catriona dropped some sausages in the frying pan and hummed a tune under her breath. The house creaked with the sudden emptiness of Chris's departure.

'It's bloody freezing,' Day repeated after breakfast.

'Get some clothes on,' Lionheart said through a mouthful of toast.

Day nodded and wandered to the bedroom.

'Where will Chris be now?' Lionheart asked. 'It's been an hour.'

'Nearing London. Go and look at a map.' Catriona sipped her coffee and waited for her son to leave the table. She turned to me when we were alone.

'You haven't said much since last night.'

'No.'

'What did he tell you?'

'Too much. Not enough. A myth.'

'You were out there for quite some time.'

I looked down at my hands and played with the silver ring. She shrugged and collected the plates. Outside the window, I watched the pigeons circle the white tip of the oast-house.

'Catriona, what happened the morning after Lionheart was born?' I asked. 'Did Chris seem different?'

'Not especially.' She dropped the plates into the sink and ran the hot water. 'He was relieved the birth had gone well. He looked tired, but we all were. Some more than others.'

'Tell me more. Tell me what happened afterwards.'

Catriona smiled and turned off the hot water tap. The steam clouded the window like a sea mist, veiling the Downs from view. The last thing I saw before the steam smothered the glass were the pigeons settling in the dovecote, seemingly seduced by the sound of Catriona's voice.

X
Venus and Adonis

The winter of Richard's first year was memorable for its mildness. None of us had forgotten the previous year, in which we had been snowed into the house for three days. We dreaded the thought of another such season. Fortunately, the cold sky remained clear for endless weeks and I looked forward to a glorious summer when I could take Richard for picnics on the beach. I dreamed of the salty breeze on my skin, of making seaweed trees and pebble gardens with my son, as I myself had done as a child with my parents.

Day and Chris were marvellous with the baby. They took turns to rock him when he cried in the night, to change the truly unpleasant nappies, and to sit with him at meal times. Jake watched everything Richard did with his own childlike wonder. At first, he seemed troubled by Richard's arrival, eyeing the baby suspiciously as a usurper to Chris's affections. But Jake's wide grin inspired Richard's first smile and Jake was smitten from that moment. I said it was just wind, but Jake insisted that it was a real smile.

Jake never acknowledged his parentage of the child, though it was clear for all to see from the child's straw-coloured hair and distinctive white streak. I believe that it was this unspoken fact that caused Chris to love Richard as his own.

I spent all my time with Richard and struggled to catch up with my reading list and essays. I was too busy to attend the final handful of Coven moots. Likewise, Chris spared less time for the group and so the last days of the Society of Heathens passed under Anna's stewardship. When we heard that Anna wanted the group to engage in an ecumenical dialogue with the Christian Union, Chris abandoned it altogether. No more letters were written to the college newspaper and no more stories were told. The Coven went out with a whimper.

The season of finals passed like a heavy cloud of late-night smoke through the house. I still trailed a full semester behind the others and observed their stress from a safe distance. Some nights, when Richard woke me with teething pains, I could hear Chris typing his essays in the bedroom next door, or rattling coal into the stove to escape from the tedium of academic sentence structures, or begging the universe for 'another word for "ostensible"'. Other nights, I would try to sing lullabies to distract Richard from the pain in his gums, but it was only the repetitive bars of Jake's final composition echoing through the floorboards that soothed him to sleep. May blossomed, June ripened, and the results fell in early July.

Chris's triumphant First Class degree was overshadowed by the catastrophe of Jake's Two-Two without honours. On the morning that the results came in the post, Jake walked into the Green Room and closed the lid of his piano for the final time.

'No point playing now,' he said as he turned the key in the lock. 'I've been making a fool of myself for years. In front of people, too.'

Chris took Jake's hands and tried to draw him into an embrace, but Jake's arms fell listlessly to his side.

'Love, of course you can play. You're a virtuoso. When you touch the keys, you make the world a better place, a place I want to be. When you get inspired, you inspire me. Of course you can play. They just haven't got the ears to hear.' And so on.

'Bullshit,' said Jake, and pulled himself out of Chris's reach. 'So tell me, how does it feel to get a First?'

The piano was never unlocked. Even after the fire that later ravaged the house, the lid remained firmly sealed.

The lupins flowered for the first time in early August when Richard was barely nine months old. They came into blossom on the same morning that Day taught him his first word. Day had been reading a book about existentialism with Richard on his lap. When Day reads particularly complicated texts, he has the habit of mouthing words as his eyes trail across the sentences. I was in the garden when he came running outside with the baby in his arms.

'He's just said his first word, Cat. I've taught him his first word. He listened to what I was reading and repeated it.'

'What did he say? Was it Day-Day?'

'Much more advanced than that. He said, "Nietzsche"'.

Richard's ears pricked at the word. 'Nichey,' he repeated.

'Thus spake the philosopher's pupil,' I said, ruffling Richard's hair. 'Have we created a monster?'

'No, Cat. We've created the *Übermensch*.'

Richard repeated his favourite word endlessly for the next eighteen months. We had shown him such attention for this accomplishment that he would not let it drop.

When the first chill wind of September rattled the crystals on the dream-tree, I realised that I had not taken Richard for a summer picnic on the beach. It was something I had looked forward to throughout my pregnancy. Now the season of mists was upon us, it was too late to take a bucket and spade to the sands of the harbour. Too late to feel the salty breeze on bare skin and make seaweed trees in pebble gardens as I had done as a child. His first year had passed too soon.

Instead of the shore, I decided to take Richard for a pushchair ride through Mowbray Park. The trees were awesome in their autumn splendour as we strolled in the afternoon sunlight. I lifted the fallen leaves to his face and whispered their names into his ear.

'Chestnut,' I said, stroking his nose with the leaf. 'Chest. Nut. Good for the whooping cough, but don't you go eating the nuts. And this is hazel. Hazel, the tree of wisdom. You can eat these nuts, but only when you're older. And there, oh there are roses. Look, Richard.'

As Calliope had once guessed, roses were my perennial favourite. I loved the story of how they grew from the blood of Venus when she was wounded with mortal desire for Adonis. I hastened towards the flowerbed, forgetting entirely about the summer picnic on the beach that had never happened. Richard laughed and turned his blue eyes to see if I was laughing with him. But when we reached the flowerbed, I saw that the roses had been stripped by the autumn winds, most of their petals lay scattered among the ground ivy. A single red bud nodded above the rest, its petals curled against the coming cold. I nipped the bud from its thorny stem and lay the flower on Richard's blanket. He stared at the gift and searched my face for a smile.

'Nichey?' he asked unsurely.

'I saw that,' said a voice behind me. Though I had not heard her speak for three years, the tone was unmistakable. I turned to face my one-time girlfriend.

'Gail. How pleasant to see you again.'

'You remember me then, Cat? I couldn't miss you from behind.'

'Well, quite. All I ever showed you was my back.' We laughed briefly. 'And you're still in Sunderland? Surely even you must have graduated by now?'

'Still here. Living with Dane now. You remember Dane, don't you?'

'Indeed, how could I forget him?' I said, smiling as best I could. My face was beginning to ache.

'You know, me and Dane, we were talking about your little accident just the other day.' She glanced down at Richard.

'My little accident?'

'You know: too much gin, not enough johnnies. Or else you were all too stoned. I forget the gruesome details. And there've been that many versions. You've had your three minutes of fame, believe me. Such a shame, isn't it?'

'Shame?'

'That you sold out, of course.' She grimaced unpleasantly. 'That you turned out to be a breeder. And then to have it right in the middle of your degree, talk about bad timing. I mean, it must really have pissed on your chances of ever finishing the sodding thing. Especially as you don't know which one is the father. Though I could make a guess from the colour of its hair. But it's not like you'd ever get Jake to pay any subsidence, could you?'

'No, but they're all helping with the maintenance. So nice to see you haven't changed at all, Gail,' I said, turning to leave. 'Richard can be so cantankerous when he's bored.'

'I don't have the time either. We're out with Jake again this evening, talk of the devil.'

'Jake?' I paused and waited for the wind to die down among the rustling chestnut leaves. 'Chris's Jake?'

'Chris's Jake? How sweet that you still call him that. But I guess you would. He really lets his hair down when he's not in Chris's shadow, don't you think? Just like in the old days.'

I walked slowly back to the house against the wind. The dusk was falling and I felt a growing apprehension at Gail's insinuation. It was Freshers' Week again. As I pushed the pram though the crowds of undergraduates, I remembered my own first Freshers' Ball at Wearmouth Hall. It was three years since I first saw Chris standing there on those steps, staring moodily at the swarm of bright young things, a cigarette hanging from his lips. That stranger then was one of the fathers of my son now. I felt ancient.

Passing the building, I saw him again standing there in the same spot in the same pose, one hand in his pocket and the other holding a cigarette. He appeared as though summoned from my memory, a trick of the past returned to tease more cynical eyes.

'Chris,' I called. 'What's that dirty thing in your hand?'

'My old friend, Signor Nicotine. Haven't seen him for years. I know, I know; he's a stubborn little bugger.'

'So, why's he back now?'

'He comes and goes.' He shrugged indifferently and threw it away. 'I had a letter from Jackie this morning. She told me what I'd already guessed: Calliope's cut me off. There's to be an absolute communication shutdown.'

Chris walked with us back to the house and related the details of the letter. The inquest into his father's death had uncynically determined the cause to have been an "act of god". Since the contents of the priest's last will and testament had been revealed, Chris was undecided whether he should accept the fortune of which he alone was the beneficiary. He had telephoned Calliope several times about sharing the inheritance, but she steadfastly refused to touch the money.

'Why not share it?' he said to me as we headed up the hill towards home. 'There's no reason not to. You simply don't turn your nose up at thousands of pounds. Hundreds of thousands. She could plant a lavender farm, if she wanted. She could sow a forest of dream-trees. She could recruit her own fucking international brigade and take on the armies of the patriarch.'

'She won't accept any of it?'

'Not a penny. It's cursed, she says, infected by my father's memory. She says I'll be dead to her if I have anything to do with him. Of course, there's now a weathervane running through his heart and he's an all-you-can-eat feast for the worms, but that makes no difference. The war's over but she's still fighting.'

'What will you do with it all?' I asked after a pause.

'It'll be for all of us, Cat. Especially you, Prince Nichey,' he said, poking Richard on the nose. The baby laughed and kicked his legs. Chris smiled briefly and then turned his face away. 'For fuck's sake, it should be all over. It is all over. Why isn't it all over?'

'I'll speak to your mother,' I said as we reached the front door. 'Maybe she'll listen to me.'

Chris helped me lift the pushchair over the front door step and into the dark hallway. 'No, she won't. She won't talk to any of us. We're all tainted with the old bastard's blood money, even you now. She's told Jackie some of what had happened in the vicarage, the things my sister blocked out. Now Jackie won't accept any of the money either. Doesn't want to get involved. She won't risk losing Calliope.'

Later that evening, after Richard had been put to bed, I decided to telephone Calliope. Jake and Day had not come home, so we ate dinner without them. Afterwards, Chris knelt beside the crib in the bedroom, playing with the rose and whispering the myth of Proserpine's journey to the underworld. I listened to his voice from the doorway.

'He's too young for that,' I interrupted. 'It'll give him nightmares.'

'No one's ever too young for this story, Cat. It'll help him cope with loss when he's older. We're all have to deal with loss one day.'

'Yes, but people don't generally come back from the underworld, do they? Besides, he doesn't understand a single word you're saying. Don't tell him about Proserpine yet.'

'Pospin?' asked Richard. Chris laughed and the delighted child repeated the name again.

Frustrated, I left the room and shivered at the familiar chill on the stairs. Chris's ghost, we fondly called it, having no better explanation for the odd phenomenon. Chris insisted that it was his own thought-form guarding the stairs. Glad of the protection, we accepted the legend as a just another member of the household.

Alone in the Yellow Room, I lay the phone on my lap and dialled Calliope's number. She answered it almost immediately.

'Catriona, *fili mou*,' she said before I had spoken a word. 'I've been waiting for you to call.'

'One day, Calliope, you'll learn to answer the phone like a normal person.'

'The day I do anything like a "normal" person is the day I cease to be me. You talked to Chris today, didn't you? Of course you'd call. He's accepted his father's inheritance. We can never speak again. That is all.'

The problem of speaking with Calliope was that she was always one step ahead, knowing beforehand what one was about to say. I had learned to be as direct with her as she was with me.

'That is not all, Calliope. Far from it. You're abandoning Chris all over again. He's not thirteen anymore, but he needs you as much as he ever did then. He's too proud to say how much it hurts because you're both as tough and hard-skinned as each other, but he does. And it's all over of a dead man – a man who's won for all time if he succeeds in separating a mother from her son. But you know all this already.'

'If you make a bargain with the Devil, you pay the price.'

'There was no bargain with the Devil. Chris's father was only a man. A twisted fuck-up of a priest, maybe, but still a man. How dead does he have to be before it's all over?'

'He still lives, Catriona. This is what you don't understand about people. He lives and breathes in the pain he has left behind.'

'Then get over it,' I cried, moved to tears by the steeliness of her resolve. 'How can you cut Chris out of your life over money? You've lost, surely, if you let that happen. Do you hate his father more than you love Chris? Or Richard. Or me, for that matter?'

'You don't understand, *agapi mou*,' she said, more kindly. 'One day you will see why I have to do this thing. I've spent so long fighting, so long defending the ones I love from that monster that I can't give ground. And now, once again, Chris takes the Devil's hand and accepts the poisoned gift he left behind. I cannot change, not now.'

'Of course you can change. You taught me that much.'

'You are so young, Catriona. To you everything seems possible, and to you it probably is. My mind, like yours, was once as fluid as water. I could melt and then condense again into any form I willed, even stream between the bars of my husband's prison. But now, after all these years standing watch and waiting at the walls of my acre of land, the relentless sun has baked me into clay. I'm as tough as old pottery.'

'You taught me that people are always capable of being different,' I said, 'that the elements shift and the body transforms. You told me nobody is ever fixed. If you have the will to fight, you have the will to be different.'

Calliope sighed and clicked her tongue. I felt the break in her breathing, the pain of our separation before she spoke the final words she would ever say to me.

'There is a fire in this ancient stone body of mine, sweetheart. It pounds in my head like a fever at night, like a river in my blood. It has shaped me, made me what I am today. I can change? No, love. It's too late for that now.'

And she put the receiver down.

I sat for an hour, maybe more, with the dead tone ringing in my ears. I laid the phone to rest on the carpet and glanced at the clock. Eight o'clock. Day will be home soon. I went to the fireplace to stir the embers.

Chris came downstairs at nine and found me curled beside the hearth, still weeping.

Richard woke me in the night, crying in distress at his teething pains. I tried to feed him but he would not eat, so I carried him around the bedroom and sang Calliope's lullaby:

'Farewell to the child you're leaving too. I have only one friend, the river. She goes dirla dirladada.'

The bedroom door opened softly and Chris entered, still fully dressed. He took the baby and sat on the edge of the bed, rocking him.

'Behold, the king of heathens,' he said. Richard grew quiet and closed his eyes. 'This princeling has taken over all our lives.'

'How late is it?'

'After five. Jake's still not home.'

'Neither's Day.' We exchanged an uneasy glance. 'And they've not phoned?'

Chris shook his head and smiled at the baby. 'We'll make them suffer in the morning, won't we, Prince Nichey? We'll have real teething pains when they want to sleep, won't we? Yes, we will.'

'Day always calls,' I said, and then remembered my conversation with Gail in the park. The ending with Calliope had wiped it clean from my mind. 'Chris, does Jake ever see Dane or Grim Gail anymore?'

'Never. Absolutely not. Not as far as I know. Not since I chucked Dane out of the house in our first year. Why do you ask?'

'Because of something Gail said this afternoon. I met Her Grimness in the park. She said that she and Dane were seeing Jake tonight.'

'Highly improbable.' Chris's eyes flashed. 'Definitely not. Jake would have told me. He would have. Why wouldn't he have told me?'

I took the rose I had left on the crib and looked at its petals. Without water and in the heat of the house it was already beginning to wilt.

'He would have told me, wouldn't he?' Chris repeated.

'I'm sure he would.'

'And besides, he has to be with Day. Day would never fraternise with the enemy, would he?'

'Absolutely not.'

I unpicked the petals of the rose. Hidden among the crimson anthers and white filaments, I saw movement. Something yellow and alive curled around the stamens and raised its tiny blind face towards me. Repelled, I threw the rose into the bin.

Chris looked up and Richard began to cry.

We sat in the bedroom until Richard was soothed to sleep by Chris's song and then, sleepless ourselves, we crept downstairs. I listened to the faint tinkling of the crystals outside in the wind. Chris opened a bottle of wine and poured out two glasses.

'Apparently patience is a virtue,' he said. The clock on the mantelpiece struck six as we clinked glasses.

'So is saying if you're going to be out all night.'

At seven, there was a key in the lock. The front door opened with a long, slow creak, pushed with the unmistakable effort of someone who was trying to make as little noise as possible.

'Shit,' we heard Jake say. 'Light's on. They're still up.'

Day's hushed voice told Jake to keep quiet. As their footsteps gingerly approached the Yellow Room, Chris uncorked our second bottle of wine.

'Hey, love,' Jake whispered to Chris, creeping into the room as though entering a hospital ward. He spoke with the exaggerated condescension of the pissed. 'What are you guys still doing up?'

'We couldn't sleep,' Chris replied coldly. He poured himself another glass.

'Are we a little late?' Jake grinned. He fell backwards onto the sofa and gawked, bewildered, at me and Chris.

'I guess you are a little.'

'What are you still doing up, babe?' Jake repeated. He kicked off his shoes and began to unbutton his jeans. Outside, the dream-tree creaked.

Day raised his eyebrows and nodded up towards our bedroom. I took the hint and said my goodnights. Day followed me upstairs.

'I hope you two behaved yourselves,' I said in the privacy of our bedroom. Day put his finger to his lips and closed the door.

'We did. Well, I did. I was catching up with Conrad in Diana's Bar. Just an afternoon drink. It went on a little longer than we anticipated.'

'And there's not a single phone box in town, of course.'

'I couldn't call. I had to keep an eye on Jake all night. He showed up at the bar around eight. You won't guess who he was with.'

'I'll take a wild stab at Dane and Grim Gail.'

'See you've been fire-gazing tonight.' Day looked impressed with my foresight. 'You should have seen Jake's face when he clocked me and Conrad in the bar. Think he pretended not to notice us.'

Richard stirred in his cot. I blew at the dangling mobile of over his head and sent the silver moons into a spin. Richard reached his hands out and tried to catch them.

Day spoke quietly about the events of the night, his voice soothing the child to sleep. He spoke of how Dane had flounced into the bar with his usual inelegant flair, hogging an imagined limelight. Grim Gail followed in his wake and Jake trailed behind, tensing his pectorals and pouting with attitude. They went to the bar and arranged themselves against the counter.

'Oh, girlfriend, you look delicious,' Dane had said, puckering his lips at Cyane the barmaid. The nymph recoiled from the threatened kiss. 'What? No smooch for the best dressed boy in town?'

'What's your poison tonight, Dane?' she asked. Her butterfly wings twitched disdainfully over her shoulders. 'Hemlock on the rocks?'

'You are such a tease, darling. Pina Colada for me, of course.' He turned to Gail. 'And, pour vous, princess?'

'Pint, ta, and a bag of cheese'n'onion.'

'Oh, princess,' Dane gasped in shock disbelief. 'You'll never keep your fabulous figure that way. We did notice, it was already something of a squeeze getting you down those stairs, wasn't it?'

While they were squabbling, Jake gazed around the room with cool detachment. He paused to eye a Mediterranean man smoking alone in a shadowy alcove. The man held Jake's eyes momentarily, but Jake's confidence slipped and he lowered his gaze. It was then he noticed Conrad and Day sitting at a nearby table. Shifting uncomfortably, he whispered something into Gail's ear. She turned and laughed ostentatiously.

'What's that? Doris Day is here?' Dane waved at Day. 'Hey, girls. How sweet of you to save us a table. I'm about ready to drop.'

Dane sashayed swiftly towards Day's table. Jake followed and, sitting sheepishly close to Day, leaned over to whisper:

171

'I just ran into them in the street, honestly. They dragged me along. You know what he's like. I didn't have a choice.'

'I'm sure you didn't,' Day said unconvincingly and sipped his drink.

'That's right, darling,' Dane cackled. 'You had no choice whatsoever. And you resisted so fiercely when I told you Gary would be along later tonight too, didn't you? You randy little mare.'

Day frowned, trying to place the familiar name. In some muddy field of his subconscious, a buried memory stirred. It trembled on the edge of his recognition, a relic from an obsolete age.

'Of course, Chris knows who you're here with, doesn't he, Jake?' Conrad muttered disapprovingly.

Jake shrugged and stared into his glass. Absently, he reached for Gail's crisps. Without looking, she pulled the packet away from his fingers. Day tapped the table and repeated the name that Dane had spoken.

'Gary,' cried Dane blithely. He leaped to his feet and waved his arms loosely in the air. 'Over here, you gormless hunk.'

Beneath the stone arch of the entrance, in the green mist of the underground strobe lighting, stood Gary. Wearing a tight white T-shirt over a chiselled body, he was clearly of the same fashion genus as Jake, although a good few years older. His face was unknown to Day.

'My word, pumpkin,' said Dane as Gary approached the table. 'Someone's been popping the steroids like boiled sweeties, haven't they? Gravity won't be kind to those adorable abs when you're sixty-four, you know. And I don't care what they say: man-tits will never be in vogue.'

'Go fuck yourself with a razor blade, Darlena,' Gary replied. He sat down heavily on the other side of Jake and laid a firm hand on his knee. When he moved in for a kiss, Jake shifted uneasily.

'Call me astute,' Conrad said, staring at the hand that groped Jake's thigh, 'but do you two happen to know each other already?'

'Who wants to know?' said Gary. 'Who let the nerds in?'

'Jake and his boyfriend, Chris, have been my friends for years. We're incredibly close. You'll have met Chris? Chris is Jake's boyfriend.'

Realisation came slowly to Gary. He removed his hand from Jake's knee and reached instinctively for Gail's crisps.

'You and Jake are forever on the scrounge,' she hissed. 'Go buy your own for a fucking change.'

Jake leaned closer to Day and explained that Gary was an old flame he had not seen in years, except for a few unplanned meetings in the same gym they shared.

'I can see it in your face,' Jake continued, 'you think it looks odd. It does look odd, but there's nothing more to it than that. Honestly.'

'And I'm sure Chris is *au fait* with all of this,' Conrad said, pulling on his coat. 'Look, I have to go home else Anna will have her own questions to ask. Day, will you keep an eye on things?'

'No one needs to keep an eye on anything.' Jake laughed, but was beginning to sound frustrated.

'So, naughty little Jake can't come out to play with the cool kids without his babysitters?' said Gary, staring blankly at Day. Day flinched and lowered his eyes.

'Suppose I may as well stay.' Day searched in the depths of his glass for courage and drained what little he could find. 'Sounds like fun.'

The evening lurched from one spiteful shard of sarcasm and insinuation to another. The cavernous lungs of the club dripped with body sweat and a rich mist of whatever poignant aftershave was all the rage at that time. Day shifted uncomfortably in his seat, wiping the moisture from his brow. At closing time, when Dane cooed and invited everyone back to his flat for drinks, Jake accepted and drunkenly persuaded Day to join them.

As Jake passed through the stone arch to the stairwell, he glanced once more at the solitary Mediterranean man in the smoky alcove. The man returned the stare without a flicker of interest and lit another cigarette.

'*Et voila, mon beau château,*' Dane said, reaching inside his sequin jacket for the key to his flat. 'Abandon hope all you who enter. *Apres vous.*'

The brown paint of Dane's back door was scratched and peeling. The threshold reeked of urine and perhaps worse. Stepping inside the gloomy hallway, Day was aware that the smell was even sharper. Covering his nose with his sleeve, he followed the trail of abandoned clothes up the stairs and imagined what multitudes of hungover souls had fled down these steps in the shamefaced glow of countless dawns, not one of them pausing to retrieve their lost socks or mislaid dignity.

Gail disappeared into her bedroom without a word and slammed the door. Dane led his guests into a low-lit lounge that was draped with Japanese-style throws and cluttered with chinoiserie.

'As you can see, I'm something of an Orientalist, sweethearts,' he said with a sweep of his arms. 'I consume and exude only the exotic. On my menu tonight we have tequila, advocaat, Malibu or Martini. What juices can I tickle your tonsils with?'

'Beer for me and the boy,' Gary said, stretching out on a sofa. He grabbed Jake's wrist and pulled him down between his legs.

'Gary, you're such a predictable prole,' cried Dane. 'Why down the same old diesel when what I am offering you is nectar?'

'Beers,' he repeated, kissing the white streak in Jake's hair. Jake pulled himself free and retreated to the opposite end of the sofa.

'Behave, Gary,' said Jake with a contrite glance at Day. 'Chris wouldn't like it. Bad Gary, bad.'

'Chris who? Fuck Chris. Fuck me. You want me to talk porn?' Gary laughed and, leaning closer, growled in an American accent. 'You want this, bitch? You want this big hot cock up your tight little ass?'

Day perched on the edge of a chair and watched the melodramatics unfold. Dane returned to the room wearing a Japanese silk kimono and bearing a silver tray of plastic cocktail glasses. He perched himself between Gary and Jake, and pawed their thighs.

'Come now, girls; we must keep the chatter down or we'll wake the whale. She's already sulking because she's fat and has no friends. Try this: I call it the Darlena Colada.' He passed a blue, faintly steaming glass to Jake. 'You know you want it, *ma chérie*.'

Jake sipped the concoction and spluttered. 'It's disgusting.'

'It's indecent is what it is. Take it like a man, Jacob. Down the happy hatch it goes. Down in one, two, three.'

Jake obeyed and slammed the empty glass on the tray. He rolled his eyes and within seconds dropped his head upon the cushions. He was out cold. Gary leaned over and pressed his nose against Jake's unconscious face.

'That's more like it,' Gary murmured.

'Well, thanks for a fun evening,' said Day, gathering their coats and standing to leave. 'I suppose I ought to take Jake home now.'

'Oh no, no, no, darling.' Dane pushed a glass into his hands. 'The party's just getting started. I couldn't forgive myself if you left so criminally sober. All this is tame compared to the fun you heathens have, surely?'

'Give or take the issue of consent.' Day made towards the door, but Dane draped his arms around his neck.

'Now, you just try and get away from me. Just try, I dare you.'

'Well,' Day looked around the room for an escape route. 'Suppose I could have one more glass, if we all have a round together.'

'A toast,' cried Dane, delighted. He released Day from his embrace and handed the glasses around. 'How very splendid. *Bonne chance*, girls.'

They each downed their drinks and slammed the glasses on the tray. Gary's head was the first to droop. Dane smiled impishly, but his head pitched like a floundering balloon.

'Oh, sweetheart,' he said and his face plunged into Gary's shoulder.

Day spat what liquid he had not swallowed back into the glass and hauled Jake's body from beneath Gary's sprawling limbs. He twice slapped Jake's face and poured water over his head without effect. Jake grunted and reached an unconscious hand down his own trousers.

'Jake, I think you ought to wake up,' Day said, dragging the insensible body towards the window. He unclasped the rusty latch and lifted Jake's head into the chill morning air. The window overlooked a small wooded park, dimly lit by streetlights. The branches shifted in the breeze, scattering dry leaves upon the pavement. Day thought he heard a voice whispering in the wind, and a swift movement among the leaves caught his eye. He stared among the shadows of the nodding boughs, but saw nothing more. Just his watery eyes making shapes in the shadows, he thought.

Dane slipped serpentine from the sofa and rolled on the floor, his flinty teeth gleaming in the amber streetlight. Day shook Jake's shoulders and repeated his name without success.

'But why didn't you telephone me, love?' I asked quietly so as not to wake Richard. Day raised his tired eyes and shook his head.

'Couldn't find a phone anywhere in Dane's flat. You wouldn't believe how cluttered it was, filled with all kinds of chintzy shit. I waited in that dingy room for hours, listening to Dane grind his teeth and Gary snore. Jake finally woke up around six. He was still barely conscious and gabbled on about something outside, someone trying to bite his arms. He wanted the window closed and wouldn't walk home. I carried him down the stairs and into the street. Maybe it was just the wind in the trees, but he said someone was whispering his name. We walked home through Mowbray Park. Every time a tree creaked, he clung to me. Once, a falling leaf touched his face and he screamed. I mean, he really screamed. It was probably just the poison Dane gave him, but he ran right through the bushes calling Chris's name. His clothes got ripped on the thorns.

'I spent half an hour searching for him in the trees. I was just about to give up altogether and come home, see if he wasn't here already, when he leapt out onto the path in front of me. Didn't speak, just grabbed my arm. Pulled me most of the way home. My shoulder still aches.'

Day rubbed his arm and looked tired and miserable. I stroked his golden hair and kissed his shoulder.

'Poor love. I hope Jake appreciates you as much as I do.'

* * *

Neither Day nor Jake stirred from their beds until the following evening. I sat beside the fire, feeding Richard and watching Chris flick through the tattered pages of a book. Since the Coven had dissolved, Chris now spent much of his time reading on his own.

'What's this one?' I asked, as he folded a page down and hid the battered paperback behind his chair.

'The Greek myths as re-imagined by a Roman.'

'The *Metamorphoses*, yet again. You should try reading something else. You're becoming a pagan fundamentalist.'

'Very funny, Cat. I don't think you get many pagan fundamentalists. In monotheistic religions, there's only one god, one holy book, one way to think and do things. My god is god, everyone else's is a devil: let's go on crusade and slaughter the unbelievers.' He spoke without interest, as though a script had landed on his lap and he was going through the motions of reading it. His mind was elsewhere, but he continued nonetheless. 'In polytheism, there's a lot more tolerance going around. Diana co-exists with Dionysus, Adonis with Aphrodite, and so on. Much more civilised.'

'Marginally. Olympus is still a patriarchy. Zeus heads his royal household as jealously as Jehovah rules his harem of dull, harp-playing angels. Both are templates for order on earth, don't you think?'

Chris did not want to play this game; his thoughts were on the events of the previous night. He shrugged and stared absent-mindedly out of the window. I tried a different tack.

'Your *Metamorphoses* looks as old as Noah. Is it a first edition?'

'That?' Chris did not smile. I knew he was barely hearing me. 'Oh, Calliope gave me that copy when we moved to Whitby.'

'Which chapter are you on?'

'Adonis and Venus. The goddess is giving up her place in heaven because she's in love with a mortal man.'

'Silly bitch,' I laughed and startled Richard. The fire hissed and released a cloud of sparks up the chimney. Somewhere in the house we heard movement.

'The Kraken wakes,' I mused and listened to the footsteps descend the stairs. Jake entered the room wearing nothing but his tight white underwear. The white streak in his hair protruded like a unicorn's horn.

'I can't remember a thing about last night,' he said, resting his head on Chris's lap. 'I must have been bad. Very bad. Don't suppose I'll ever be forgiven, will I?'

'It's under consideration. You'll have to make it up to me.' Chris stroked spirals on Jake's bare chest and played with the blonde hairs under his arm. 'Actually, there's one thing you can do to be absolved.'

Jake cocked his head, terrier-like. 'What?'

'You're coming to Diana's Bar with me and Cat tonight. Day can babysit.'

'Why?' Jake asked. He had not expected this.

'To mend the damage you did last night. To reassure the underworld that all is well with Chris and Jake. To restore order in the universe. You owe it to me.'

Jake groaned and buried his face into Chris's neck. Richard laughed and gurgled something nonsensical.

'Did you hear that?' Chris said, staring at the child. 'I do believe he said, "gutted".'

* * *

Diana's Bar was still the murky red dragon's lair I remembered from our first year. Chris led us down the dripping stairwell and into the mirrored disco room, where all those questing warriors from past generations had drowned their failures in one of Cyane's perilous cocktails. Here, lurking within the many alcoves of the rock catacombs, knights had abandoned lifelong causes and slowly disappeared into the despairing smog of age and bitterness. Sometimes, when the infernal strobe lights flashed and the gin was flowing, I caught the lost glances of ruined lovers fleeting across the mirrored shields of the dance floor. Lost within these walls, there was no return for the witless wanderer.

'Chrissy,' the barmaid hailed from her eternal seat among the shimmering mirage of bottles. 'Long time, no see. How goes the revolution? Are all the kings' heads on spikes yet?'

'I'm working on it, Cyane,' he replied, shaking her hand. 'Swings and roundabouts at the moment.'

'Nothing ever happens, does it? I haven't been above ground for thousands of years and still nothing changes up there,' the barmaid winked at me. 'Much safer down here. Call me when it all kicks off.'

'You'll be Minister of Pleasure in the new earth republic, I promise.'

'Everyone will be Minister of Pleasure,' she corrected him.

Chris ordered the drinks and we looked for an empty table.

'There's an empty bench over there,' Chris pointed towards a smoky alcove. 'He won't mind if we join him.'

Within the flashing smog of the recess, I saw a man, possibly of Mediterranean appearance, sitting alone and scowling at the sweaty, wide-eyed dancers. Jake blushed and suggested that we stand at the bar.

'He won't bite,' Chris said, leading the path through the bodies on the dance floor. 'And if he does, I'll bite back even harder.'

The man glanced over our faces and then turned back to the dancers, indifferent to our arrival.

'Yes, I suppose there could be some room for you there,' he said in a lush Greek accent, although we had already begun to sit down.

Chris's eyes sparkled. '*Kalispera, filos mou. Ti Kánete?*'

The man shrugged and lit the cigarette that had been dangling loosely from his lips since we arrived. He stared in boredom at the dancers, manifestly unimpressed.

'You learned Greek from very bad books. Your accent is very poor, very poor.'

'*Mitéra mou,*' Chris said, sitting beside him. Struggling with his forgotten Greek, he gave it up. 'My mother was from Missolonghi.'

'*Entaxi*, then that explains your terrible grammar.'

Chris laughed and asked where he was born. The Greek's dark eyes flickered, mildly amused. 'Missolonghi, of course.'

Jake shifted along the bench towards the Greek until their thighs were touching. He looked at Jake as a sated spider might eye up yet another desperate fly.

'What is your name?' Jake asked, speaking loudly – almost shouting – so the Greek could understand him. 'I mean, what is it you are called?'

'I am not short of hearing,' the Greek replied disdainfully. 'I am Kassios. Kassi to my many friends. Did you get it? Say it: Kass-i-os.'

Abashed, Jake bit his lip and looked down at his hands. I felt a pang of sympathy at his humiliation and an instant aversion to Kassios.

'Don't be sorry,' Kassios stroked Jake's hands. 'My bark is louder than my teeth. And, God knows, my teeth are not very loud.'

Jake's blue eyes gleamed as absolution washed over his flushed face. Both he and Chris laughed emphatically at the bad joke. Chris moved closer to his compatriot and asked what he was doing in England. In shameless competition, Jake shifted closer on the other side until the handsome curio was crowded by their attentions.

As Kassios talked about his early release from military conscription and the exchange programme from Athens University to Sunderland, I lost interest and grew fascinated by the convulsive movement of the thin moustache on his upper lip. It was infinitely more compelling than his conversation. He was attractive, I conceded, in an Errol Flynn type of way: a young chevalier, a Count Vronsky or an aristocratic cavalier – but he was so self-satisfied with his own good looks that it bored him. As he spoke, I improvised an alternative monologue: *Yes, I am – how do you say – exquisite, but I suffer from existentialist ennui. It is too much to bear. Everything is boring. This place bores me. You bore me. I bore myself.*

'It is very much like anything, really,' he went on, his words slothfully lumbering back into my consciousness. He had been speaking for as long as I could remember and is probably speaking now. He talked without deviating from the same horizontal tone, without conviction in whatever was being said, but as certain of Chris and Jake's attentiveness as a pampered pasha would be of his indulgent, adoring court. 'I give as an example your English fascination with fag hags. So odd, so peculiar. Like you want your own little mummies, your – how do you say it? substitute? – surrogate? – mummies following you around the room or wherever you go, laughing at whatever you say, wiping your little bottoms for you. And all the time, you pretend she is not in love with you. Like your woman here, this one. I don't know her name and she don't know mine. Is she interested in what I am saying? Not at all. She has her eyes on you, Cristophe. She wants to keep her little boy to herself. It is the English way. Peculiar.'

He blew smoke into the air, casually and the same time dramatically, as though exhaling my presence from the room.

'Don't be offended – Kassios, is it?' I leant across the table. 'It's just, I find the game that my friends are playing somewhat tedious.'

'Please, I am not offended. Of course I know that they both want to fuck with me.' He shrugged. Evidently, this was nothing new to him. 'And, most probably, they will both fuck with me tonight.'

Chris laughed loudly, trying to catch the Greek's eye. Jake supplemented his own treacherous giggle and stroked Kassios's thigh. Bastards, I thought. Backstabbing bastards, renegades and traitors. The faintest scent of a cock and they were off and away in pursuit of the quarry. There was, however, a recklessness in Chris's behaviour tonight. His desire to return to Diana's Bar, to this place where he had met Jake a lifetime ago, was out of character. I had thought it an ominous attempt to recharge his connection with Jake, to restore an element that had perhaps become fragile. Maybe their attentions to the Greek were part of that plan, but I suspected something more desperate was going on.

'Okay, that's me done,' I said, gathering my coat. 'You can play stroke-the-ego with your charming friend here as much as you like. I'd prefer not to watch you flatter this narcissist any more than he already flatters himself.'

'Come on, Cat.' Chris grinned and reached a hand for me to stay.

'Fuck off,' I said and abandoned the smoky lair. The mirrors reflected the frenetic lights, the momentary flashes of bare-skin dancers and, it seemed, the gaping faces of legions of lost souls. There's two more for your halls tonight, I thought, and climbed the stairwell into the free, salty air.

* * *

'Kassi is an Olympian,' said Chris the next evening. It was the first time we had spoken since Diana's Bar, since I had left them to savour their treat alone. Standing in the Yellow Room, he stroked the air as though painting the curves of Kassios's exquisite figure with his fingertips, manifesting the body before our eyes. 'He is actually a Greek god, an Adonis. Don't you think so, Jake? Ripe as an olive. Riper, in fact.'

'I'd eat olives if they tasted like that,' Jake replied, holding Richard in his arms. He was staring blankly at the fireplace, perhaps with fatigue, perhaps with indifference. He was difficult to read.

'But your olive is hardly extra virgin,' Conrad sighed. He glanced at me and his eyes were cold. He was disappointed, I thought; resentful, even jealous. Jealous for what, of whom?

'We're touching the sun, Jake,' Chris continued, oblivious to the reaction of his audience. He was staring at Jake with an intensity that was uncomfortable for everyone present. 'Running with the moon. There's an article just waiting to be written for the college rag: "The Art of Trigamy", or "Three Men in a Bed". It would so piss the Christian Union off.'

Conrad stirred. 'I think it would so piss Anna off, too.'

'As if that worries me,' Chris laughed. 'Father Cuthbert would turn in his day-time coffin. It was all so phenomenally rude.'

'Just like Byron's orgies on Lake Geneva, I imagine,' Conrad said flatly, repeating Chris's words from earlier.

'Yes, yes. Exactly like that.'

'Well, you are so very Shelley,' I added, returning Conrad's look.

'The Modern Prometheus,' said Jake to our amazement; it was the only time any of us could remember him making a literary allusion. 'I suppose that makes me Mary Shelley. We've created a monster, Dr Frankenstein. It's alive. It's alive.'

'That's enough for tonight, guys,' I said, taking Richard from his arms, 'it's bedtime for baby and me. I don't want you Romantics corrupting him with any more wild talk of natural philosophy or free love and orgies.'

'Really?' Chris asked, lounging in his throne. 'It was, after all, how Richard was conceived.'

In the silence that followed, Conrad coughed and Jake scratched his arms. Kings Cross was one thing, I thought, an exceptional night of comradeship and empathy that did not – and would not – compare with whatever animal desperation was prompting Chris's current ménage. I glared at his smirking face and wanted to smash it. Fuck you, I thought. Fuck you and your conceited Adonis. I hope he brings you to ruin.

180

Chris and Jake's infatuation with Kassios infected the house as the September leaves decayed in the guttering. When a bleary October sun dawned over the city, it cast giant shadows between the high-rise monoliths. During the day, I would take Richard to the library and smile flirtatiously at the librarians. I hid among the bookshelves and waited for the inevitable attendant to pass the aisle, muttering "tramp" loudly enough for me to hear.

'Fuckwit,' I said, flicking through the pages of Marlowe's *Faustus*.

'Fuck-it,' Richard repeated. When I laughed, my collaborator shouted it again with a jubilant grin. 'Fuck-it!'

Laying the books on the counter, I produced my identity card for the librarian to check. She glared over the sharp edge of her glasses. I noticed the gold crucifix winking behind the crimped collar of her spotless blouse.

'The library is a quiet place,' she said without looking up. 'We consider the child to be inappropriate in this environment.'

'Fuck-it!' Richard screamed, his cheeks dimpling sweetly. I smiled innocently and pushed the books into my bag.

At night, the seagulls circled the house. As Richard's first birthday approached, there seemed to be more birds at the window than ever, tapping their beaks against the glass. Their cruel voices seemed to bawl Jake's name.

Sometimes, I could hear Kassios's monotonous tones murmuring through the bedroom wall. He rarely came to the house, usually insisting that – if they wanted a threesome – Chris and Jake would have to pay court at his flat. I had also made it clear that I did not want the sloth in the house. Richard always cried when he heard Kassios's voice.

The night before Richard's birthday, I was awoken by an inhuman howl. In his cot, Richard whimpered in his sleep but did not wake. I listened to the sounds of the house and counted the passing seconds. Downstairs, Circe's eerie mew rose like a siren. Through the wall, I heard Jake moan in the midst of a bad dream.

Somewhere in the house, floorboards creaked with the weight of a body walking. I sat up in bed and stared around the room. Through the curtains, the streetlamp streaked the cluttered floor, revealing the details of my familiar things in an uncanny light: the dressing-gown draped over the chair, the books piled on the desk. Everything was in its usual place, but was steeped in this preternatural glow, as though the house had been plunged into an amber netherworld.

The footsteps paused at my bedroom door. The silver moons hanging above Richard's cot shifted and casted dancing silhouettes over the wall. I waited for several heartbeats before the handle turned and the door creaked open.

Chris stood in the doorway. His eyes were open but they were entirely white. The balls had turned inwards to gaze inside their sockets. His damp fringe clung to his brow and his body glistened with sweat. Standing in a shaft of streetlight, he was submerged in lurid orange.

'It's here,' he said simply, without explanation. 'It's back.'

Richard whined a feverish song of fear in his sleep. I rose from the bed and approached Chris. He stared without sight at my face. I took both his hands and found them cold to the touch.

'Come on, love,' I said. 'Let's get you back to bed.'

Circe was still mewing as I led Chris into his room. The window had been pulled wide open and the curtains shuffled in the autumn breeze. The black heap of Jake's unmoving body lay on the blankets. In the deep gloom of the unlit bedroom, my eyes caught fleeting shapes on the air. I waited for my eyes to grow accustomed to the dark and it was then, for a terrifying instant, I saw her face over the bed.

Perhaps my tired eyes were playing tricks with the darkness. Perhaps my imagination had fed on all that talk of monsters and banshees to conjure this particular chimera. But I did see her, Jackie, as plainly as I see you now. I saw her face creased in grim delight, her eyes buried within the folds of white, withered skin. A quick tongue flicked over her lips as she pawed Jake's throat. The phantasm lingered for only a moment, but I saw it.

I screamed at the thing and beat the empty air with my fists. When I opened my eyes, the cackling face had gone and the curtains were rising higher, lapping the ceiling in the breeze. Jake was gasping for air. His spine was arched and his chest rose and fell with the sudden in-breath. I jumped when Chris touched my shoulder.

'Cat?' he asked, blinking in the darkness.

I put a hand over my mouth and calmed my breathing.

'You've been sleep-walking,' I said, not knowing what else to say. 'Go to bed. Jake needs you.'

Obediently, Chris lay on the mattress beside his lover. He gazed sadly at Jake's sleeping face and stroked the golden contours of his back.

'*Hey dirla, dirladada*,' he whispered, as I closed the door.

* * *

Kassios came among us like a plague. He observed our petty conflicts and growing strife with mild indifference, teasing disorder out of long-established friendships. He entered the house as a jaded prince, come to witness – and to accelerate for his own amusement – our declining empire. He occupied Chris's throne and sighed wearily when he had to light his own cigarette. Jake jumped to his aid and lifted the flame to his idol, an adoring acolyte beneath the beautific monstrance of his hero's face.

'You have no respect in yourself, Jake,' Kassios said, stroking Jakes' cheek and smiling benignly. 'I am humiliated for you.'

Jake retreated to his position at the pasha's feet and blushed.

'How tiresome it must be for you,' I said, 'having two such beautiful men fawning over your every whim.'

'I do not understand what this woman is always talking about,' Kassios said to the air. 'And now there is an ache between my eyes.'

Instinctively, Chris reached to massage the bridge of Kassios's nose.

'Not like that, Cristophe. You do it wrongly. It's like so.' He demonstrated the correct method of massaging his own nose. 'This is much better.'

'*Yes, Cristophe,*' I mimicked. '*This is good. Now I am – how do you say – humiliated for you. You have no self-respect. Now kiss my bottom.*'

'What now is this woman saying?' Kassios asked dismissively.

'This woman is saying that you're a bigger baby than Richard; you're a spoilt child. Worse than that, you're a spoilt adult. You make me feel embarrassed for my friends. And the sooner Chris stops fantasising that he's Byron in some drama set on the Adriatic coast and sees what a detestable snake you are, the better for everyone.'

'Fuck off, Cat,' said Chris, laying a protective hand over his prince's knee. 'Kassi is a guest in my house. How dare you speak to him like that?'

'Is this what things have come to?' We stared at each other, but Chris did not see me. He saw a heretic, a dissenter, an enemy of his vision. I was a threat to the monstrous replica of the Coven he thought he had created.

'Is that why Conrad won't enter this house anymore?' I carried on, too incensed to hold back. 'Because no-one's allowed to tell the truth? Because everyone's banned from saying that the emperor has no clothes and looks ridiculous? I hate to burst your self-indulgent fantasy, Chris, but you are looking ridiculous. He,' I pointed at Kassios, 'makes you look ridiculous.'

'Or maybe Conrad's embarrassed by you,' Chris roared. It was the first time we had ever shouted at each other. He paused for a heartbeat with a look of horror on his face. Even the house seemed to hold its breath, waiting to see if more thunder would follow. For a moment, he hesitated on the brink of backing down, but he could feel Kassios's eyes on him, watching what he would do next. He knew he had gone too far to stop now. 'Maybe Conrad won't set foot in this house because he and Anna are embarrassed by some old tramp and her fatherless bastard. Did you ever think of that?'

In the time it took for his words to settle on my skin, something long-suffering within me shrivelled and died. In all our years together, Chris had never uttered anything that could have cut as deep, or so cracked my heart, as this. Jake shifted uneasily and glanced at Kassios. The Greek sucked his cigarette and admired his manicured nails.

'Again, this peculiar thing of the English,' he mused.

Silently, I left the Yellow Room. As I climbed the stairs, I was vaguely aware that something was different. There was a conspicuous absence. The air felt vacant, as though an explosion had gone off in the house and my ears were deafened by the blast. I knew, as soon as I reached my room, that the presence which had lingered along the stairway, the spirit that guarded us while we slept, was gone. Chris's ghost, we had called it, but now I wondered if it was ever his at all or if somehow together we each had contributed an element to it. Some unquantifiable part of me had died and now the stairs were empty. Chris called after me, but it was too late. The cracks in the house had become insurmountably wide. Phaethon was falling, fast as a meteor. The vultures had gathered over the mountains in the West.

Richard babbled with delight when I entered the bedroom. I took him from the cot and sat on the edge of the bed.

'Nichey?' he asked expectantly and gazed into my eyes. I looked at the untidy room: the mugs cluttered on the carpet, the books piled high on the desk. Outside, the leaves whispered in the gutter. The autumn wind sighed against the window. All around, the world was drained of colour.

'This house is damned,' I said. The gleam in Richard's eye faded and he struggled to free himself from my hands. 'Where shall we go, my love? Where can we go? Tell me the place and there we'll go.'

I heard footsteps on the landing. Hesitantly, Jake entered the room. The resemblance between father and son had never been more apparent, nor would it ever be so again. He smiled weakly and reached out to hold Richard, but I affected not to see the gesture.

'I'm so sorry, Cat,' he said, digging his hands deep into his pocket. 'Can I come in? I need to talk.'

I nodded towards the empty chair at the desk. Jake stepped carefully between the debris on the floor and perched on the seat.

'What's up with Nichey?' he asked. The child struggled quietly in my arms, boxing the air but making no sound.

'He's out of sorts. What do you have to say?'

Jake did not reply. He fidgeted and hung his head.

'You want to talk about Kassios.'

He nodded. 'Things are different. Chris has changed.'

'You think he's in love with that reptile downstairs.'

'Oh no, not that,' Jake broke into a smile. 'It's all a game to him. Free love and trigamy. None of it's real; it's just a fantasy, a story from a book. Like something people will read about in years to come.'

'Like someone "abandoning heaven for the love of a mere mortal,"' I quoted. 'But you're going to tell me that it is real for you.'

Jake glanced towards the door at the sound of Chris's laughter downstairs. We both flinched as though we had heard a gunshot.

'I think I've fallen for Kassi,' he whispered. 'I had a dream about him last night. Don't know if it means anything; you might be able to tell me. I saw Kassi skulking in the corner of the garden. At least, I thought it was him, but when I got closer I saw his face was really old. Like, really old. His skin was all wrinkled and it looked like he didn't have any eyes. In spite of that, I knew that I loved him. I couldn't help myself. I tried to comfort him for growing so old, but he just laughed and looked away.

'And then I remember that the sun was really weird. It was bright red and crackling. I could actually hear it in the garden. Chris was standing on the roof, trying to touch it. Sound familiar? He jumped and strained to reach it, but it was too high. Everything – the house, the back yard, even the sky – was covered in this strange red glow. Does that mean something, Cat, if you dream in colours?'

I shrugged and began to fold Richard's clothes. To be honest, I was barely listening to him. In my heart, I had already left the house and its bad dreams behind. Jake continued, oblivious to my coldness.

'Kassi – or the old thing I thought was Kassi – laughed at Chris and grabbed my hand. His fingers were cold as ice. He took me into the coke-shed and down a tunnel in the coal. It was like a secret mine beneath the house, with crystals and jewels in the walls. I looked back at the entrance and called for Chris, but I knew he was still trying to touch the sun. He couldn't hear me, or else he wouldn't listen. We went down into the earth and seemed to be walking for days. Then the tunnel opened out into an enormous cave, like a marble palace with pillars and mirrors around the walls. Icicles hung like chandeliers from the ceiling, and the floor was white with frost. I had to rub my arms, even in my sleep, to keep warm. I looked for Kassi, but he'd gone. There was no tunnel anymore and no way back. I spent the rest of the dream wandering around the palace, searching among the mirrors for a way out, back to Chris. All I saw was my own reflection, wherever I looked. My hair was white with frost.'

Jake paused and played with the ring on his finger, the one Chris had given him on the night they exchanged vows by the lighthouse. Their hand-fasting had become a thing of legend, retold so often that it had taken on a mythological status. Yet here was the same ring from that pre-historic night, a relic from the days when dragons roamed the earth.

'Do you still love him?' I asked, moved by the memory of those early days. 'I mean Chris. Do you still love Chris?'

'I can't imagine not loving him. But this thing with Kassi is different. It's like, I want him to care for me. I want to please him and I want him to want me back. I want him to turn and see me, really see me. They talk in Greek a lot – or he does and Chris tries to, badly – and they barely notice me. I just watch and listen.'

'But you're falling in love with him?'

There was another burst of laughter from downstairs. It came from Chris because the pasha never expressed himself so exuberantly.

'Maybe. Sometimes I find them kissing on the settee or talking about Greece in bed, and I think that they don't want me there, that I'm an accessory to their main show. So I do things to make them notice me.'

'Like walking around in your underwear?'

'Like walking around in my pants, or else I'll start having sex with them. It's only then that they notice me.'

'Why did you come to me,' I asked softly, taking his hand in mine.

'Who else can I talk to?' He lifted his face and the warm tears streaked down his cheeks and fell on our hands. 'Who else will listen?'

'What advice can I give you? We both know you won't take it.'

'But I don't know what I can do.'

'Then tell Kassios to fuck off,' I said. 'Tell him to leave, to get out of the house and go far away from you and Chris. He doesn't care for either of you. At best, he's entertained by your attention. He's an incubus in your relationship, sucking the love from both of you. Once he's finished, he'll move onto other victims, leaving you broken and loveless. There'll be nothing left of you and Chris at the end. Tell him to fuck off.'

Jake dried his eyes and stared at the floor. He raised himself slowly from the chair and moved towards the door.

'No. I don't think I can do that, Cat,' he said quietly and left the room. As his footsteps descended the stairs, I heard the monotonous drone of Kassios's voice rumbling through the floorboards.

I lay Richard in his cot and tucked the blanket around the edges. The curtains lifted in a sly draught that gently turned the mobile of silver moons over his head. Outside, the wind was picking up and the clouds swept low, consuming the coastline. Somewhere along the harbour, the foghorn moaned a warning of the treacherous mist that smothered the sea. I pulled the suitcase out of my wardrobe and began to pack our clothes and what few belongings we owned.

XI
Orpheus

The first of November was a clear day, a cruel day. The evening gale had ripped the last leaves from the cemetery trees and now I could see the sunlit gravestones from my bedroom window. I looked over the city for the last time and pointed landmarks out to Richard. The sea glistened beyond the high-rise flats and great white clouds lumbered like steam on the horizon. The details of the world were etched in clear lines and bright colours. All I could think was that Richard's first birthday had passed uncelebrated.

As I descended the stairs, I saw Jake lurking outside the Yellow Room. He was eavesdropping on the voices behind the door and did not notice me. I paused and listened to the words being carelessly discarded inside the room.

'The trouble with Jake,' Chris was saying, 'is that he doesn't aspire to anything anymore. He's lost some quality he used to have, something I loved about him.'

'And this matters because what?' asked Kassios.

'I mean, he doesn't play the piano now. He thinks that us, the threesome, is just about sex. He doesn't imagine – he can't imagine – that it's more radical than that, more political.' Chris paused. 'Kassi, you have fucking beautiful legs.'

'So you are often telling me.'

Jake stepped back from the door and was startled by my presence on the stairs. He put his fingers to his lips and approached the banisters.

'Spying on heaven, are you?' I asked.

'Just listening. You know what Kassi said? He said I was "funny-looking". He said, "Cristophe, your boy is funny-looking". What does that mean? Did he mean my face? Is there something wrong with my face?'

'He's just jealous of your beauty, darling. It's classic of you not to think of that.' I rested my suitcase on the carpet. Jake stared incomprehensibly at it. He would never have made a great sleuth.

'I'm leaving,' I explained. 'I'm getting as far away from this house as I can. Chris will be too entangled in his three-manned sexual revolution to notice my absence immediately. He'd try to prevent me if he knew. You won't tell him until after I've gone.'

'You can't,' he faltered, wide-eyed in disbelief. 'We need you now more than ever. I need you.'

'How predictable of you to think of yourself,' I said. Jake flinched and I softened my tone. 'Look, this is my time now. Mine and Richard's. I've saved some money. We'll find somewhere to rent in the West Country. You can tell Chris I'll call him when we get there – wherever there is. And you can always call us, Jake. We'll always be there for you.'

'But why?' He took my hand and held it to his chest.

'Because it's over. The thing we had, our coven, our heathen society, it's broken.' I glanced up the empty stairs. 'Camelot has turned sour. You can taste the rot in the air.'

Jake turned towards the closed door of the Yellow Room, to the sound of Chris's voice rising again.

'In fact, none of them aspire to anything anymore,' Chris continued. 'It's like they all woke up one morning to find they'd aged overnight, that the possibilities had diminished. What happened to touching the sun?'

'Jake,' I whispered, leaning close to his ear. 'Help me get my suitcase to Day's flat. I can't manage it alone.'

'You can't leave, Cat. I don't want you to. I know Chris is really sorry for what he said last night. You just need to speak to him.'

'Will you help me or not?'

Silently, I unlocked the front door and stepped out into the cold new world. Jake helped me lift the pushchair over the threshold and into the front garden. Richard winced at the November air but refused to cry.

'Thank you, Man-Cub,' I said, grateful for his silence. Jake carried the suitcase onto the street and discreetly closed the front door.

'They didn't hear,' he said. 'Too busy talking about themselves.'

I nodded and took one last look at the house. The seagulls were perched in a row along the roof, watching my departure with satisfaction. A late white moon lay on its side in the sky just above the chimney. Below the tiles, the guttering sagged under the weight of wet leaves. The windows were shrouded with curtains, blind to my final farewell. I kissed the front door and let the tears well in my eyes. I pushed the buggy through the gate and did not look back. It was the last time I would ever see that house.

I had telephoned Day the previous evening to tell him my plans. He accepted everything stoically, as has always been his policy, and said he intended to join me in the West Country as soon as he could.

'No jobs left up here, anyway,' he said. 'Ancient Wessex is as good a place as any to start from scratch.'

He agreed to spend the first few nights with me in the hotel I had booked in Marlborough. After I found somewhere to live, he would return to settle his affairs in Sunderland before moving in with me. He did tentatively ask why I had chosen the West Country as my place of refuge. All I could say was that it was a place I used to come for my summer holidays when I was a child. My parents would rent a room in the great white hotel in Marlborough, or sometimes a bed-and-breakfast in Salisbury, even once a caravan in Dorchester. Most days, we would drive south to the Dorset coast to make sea-gardens on the shore with cuttlebone and starfish and pebbles. In my mind, Wessex remained an unchanging and eternal summer country.

My parents were of a near-extinct generation and lived in a country that had, thankfully, all but disappeared. They did not consent to the twentieth century, much less to anything beyond that. They had become increasingly bewildered at the outlandish words they heard on the BBC. They quietly stopped using their beloved local library when it continued to stock Germaine Greer's *Female Eunuch* in the 1970s, despite their anonymous letters of (surprisingly vulgar) complaint. If they could have cut their cherished Rutland adrift from the rest of the world, they would gladly have done so – even if it meant suffocating in some dark, airless corner of space.

In my early days at Sunderland, they had stared with silent incomprehension at the telephone receiver as I gave them a censored version of my unconventional lifestyle. After Richard was born, the phone calls had stopped altogether. There was no blame-laying fuss, no hand-wringing fracas, just a dignified retreat on both our parts. They had awoken one morning to find that both their daughter and the world they thought they knew were neither what they imagined, nor to their liking. Like the faeries, they disappeared discreetly into the landscape.

I agreed with Day: Wessex was as good a place as anywhere to start our lives from scratch.

At Sunderland station, Jake planted an awkward goodbye kiss on my cheek. He tried to speak, but nothing came. We had nothing more to say to each other. I ruffled his hair and climbed onto the waiting train. Day lifted my suitcase aboard and we sat beside the window.

'Richard, say goodbye to Jake,' I said, lifting the child's unwilling hand into a farewell wave. 'Say goodbye.'

From the platform, Jake returned the gesture and began to cry.

* * *

Even in winter, Wiltshire was a land of incandescent green hills and fertile pastures that contrasted vividly with the salt-and-pepper city we had left behind. Richard loved the milder climate and our daily walks beside the River Kennet. In the evenings, the starlings gathered on the treetops outside the old hotel and delighted him with their churlish cacophony. We would sit for hours on the park bench, watching the flock in erratic, organic flight until the twilight fell and the birds roosted in their bickering nests.

Day was reluctant to return to Sunderland, but he had to serve notice on his tenancy and arrange for his substantial collection of books to be brought down. Although I spoke to him daily, I was relieved that Richard and I had time to explore the countryside by ourselves. Each morning, we took a local bus and discovered another ancient hill fort or Neolithic stone circle, or followed an ancient trackway as far as we dared. I recovered something of that power and peace I had experienced during my months of pregnancy in Whitby, learning Calliope's lore.

One morning, I decided to visit a site in the countryside to the west of the town. The dawn was dank and murky, and the sunlight struggled to pierce the heavy mist over the fields. I had taken to carrying Richard in a papoose harnessed to my chest. It was infinitely more suitable for outdoor adventures than the inconvenient pram. As the seven o'clock bus arrived, Richard babbled cheerfully at the now familiar sound of the engine.

Together, we gazed through the window at the passing landscape. As we travelled through the mist, I recalled the telephone conversation I had had with Chris on my first night in Marlborough. He had apologised for his unforgivable outburst the previous evening but could not understand why I had abandoned our home.

'Was it because of what I said? I know it was unfair –'

'It was more than unfair, Chris,' I interrupted, ready to put the phone down. 'It was fucking inexcusable. I don't have the words to respond to it. It wasn't worthy of you. But there's more to it than that, obviously.'

'You mean Kassios? So, he's the crux of all our problems. Is that really why you ran away?'

'Kassi-gate,' I said lightly. An argument now was the last thing either of us needed. 'He's merely symptomatic. Things were amiss before he turned up. Maybe that's how he got a toehold so easily.'

'But you believed in free love as much as anyone of us. Why the sudden moral high-ground over Kassi?'

'The difference is that we had a community, Chris. We had a fidelity to each other. We had an integrity that is beyond comparison to your hollow *ménage à trois*. We were equals that night in Kings Cross. No, something had already gone wrong. You must be able to sense it, even you. It smells like decay. It hangs over the house like a shadow. I don't know what it is, but it's there. I had to get Richard out.'

'That's the kind of bunk I'd expect from Calliope,' Chris said, becoming exasperated, 'not from you. What, did you feel it in your waters?'

'No. I watched it as your relationship with Jake disintegrated.'

He was quiet for a few moments. Whether he was thinking about my words or contemplating a rebuttal, I could not tell.

'Look, you've made your point,' he said at length. 'You left as dramatically as you could. Now come back and finish your degree. We can reform the Coven. It will be just like before. Naturally, Anna can fuck off and die. You talk of loyalty, but where was hers when Richard was born?'

'Where was yours when you called him a fatherless bastard?'

'Touché.' He began to apologise again but I cut him short.

'Chris, it's finished,' I said, finding myself in the quarrel I had tried to avoid. 'Things have turned rancid and that's why I've gone. You've lost all sense of perspective if you can't see that.'

Chris fell silent, sensing the determination in my voice.

'I'll send you some money,' he said, finally accepting my resolve. 'For you and Richard. You'll be able to find a place, somewhere to live. I'll visit when I can, if you'll let me.'

'No, Chris; not the inheritance. It'd be like raiding your father's tomb. All we need is Tutankhamen coming after us.'

'Too late for that,' he said carelessly. 'I broke into it months ago. Now you really are beginning to sound like Calliope.'

'Maybe Calliope was right about the money. Nothing good has happened since you accepted it.'

'Take it anyhow. Call it belated loyalty. Or an apology.'

The following day, I received a substantial cheque in the post. Inside the envelope, Chris had also enclosed a photograph for Richard. It was of himself and Jake standing on the harbour wall, the lighthouse behind them. Inscribed on the back was a quote: *"It is true: we love life not because we are used to living, but because we are used to loving."*

How self-indulgent, I thought, passing it to Richard.

'Nichey?' he asked, waving the photograph without looking at it.

I nodded. 'You're getting good at this, darling.'

Richard's laughter brought me back to the present. I peered through the bus window into the thick mist. The dense moisture in the air was saturated with sunlight. It drowned the landscape around us, and yet within the cloud I could still discern the dim mass of ambiguous shapes. A shadow that I thought could be a far-away mountain or tor would suddenly materialise as a tree branch or a post box. Pterodactyls on the wing were transformed as they approached the window into blackbirds. This was Ovid's dreamscape, where the surface tension of all things was thin and fluid.

As the bus trailed slowly down the country lane, a colossal outline emerged on the roadside. It rose from the grass like an upturned bowl, a gargantuan teacup that an ogre had perhaps once used to drink the blood of Christian men, now cast carelessly aside. Instinctively, I pressed the stop-button and strapped Richard to my chest.

'Come on, sweetheart,' I said, climbing down the steps. 'Here, we walk with titans.'

The driver smiled knowingly through the closing door, and then the vehicle disappeared into the mist. Within seconds, it was if there had never been such a thing as buses or combustion engines. I had never felt so absolutely alone. In the silence of the deserted countryside and the eerie yellow dawn, I felt that we had passed back in time to the very first morning. Behind a thin line of bare trees, loomed the monstrous shadow that had caught our attention. Richard laughed and pointed at the giant.

'Okay, love.' I said, taking a deep breath. 'I'll take you to her.'

Trudging through the dank grass, I found a chalk path that led down an intensely steep slope. The giant became more solid as we approached; it towered beyond sight into the dense mist. I came across a wooden fence that was tethered with barbwire. A warning sign in white paint announced: "National Trust, Keep out".

'Fuck that,' I said, dismayed by this rude reminder of the modern. Taking Richard from his papoose, I sat him on the grass beside my haversack and fractured a weak seam in the fence with a well-aimed kick. The wood splintered and broke, allowing us enough space to crawl through.

Silbury Hill rose before us. I clambered on my hands and knees up the well-worn chalk steps. Richard gaped at the grassy beast we were climbing and stretched his fingers in awe. As we climbed higher, the mist began to clear and I caught my first glimpse of the blue sky above our heads.

Time and distance, which had become meaningless in the misty cloud, now broke over us in blinding sunlight. I turned towards the sublime scene that rolled around the hilltop.

The old world had been washed away and only the crest of Silbury Hill and a handful of distant ridges survived. We stared at the expansive ocean of mist, the deluge that stretched as far as the archipelago of the Marlborough Downs in the north. Nothing besides remained. No sound carried through the vapour; nothing stirred. I released Richard from his harness and we sat upon the grassy summit, bathed in the golden light.

'The earth is being reformed,' I said, watching this nebulous new world forging itself in the swirling mist.

I remembered Calliope's dictum to me during the pregnancy, that I should find my religion. A communion to fire my will, she said; a lightning rod for my imagination.

'This is it,' I said, folding Richard's hands in my own. 'It's here on this hilltop. I've found it, Man-Cub. This is it.'

We ate a breakfast picnic on the hill as the cloud dissipated in the heat of the rising sun. Gradually, through the haze, we watched the formation of a new landscape. The burial chamber at West Kennet appeared first in the south, followed by Windmill Hill in the north. Trees became manifest where there had only been void. We listened to the chorus of first birds as the sunlight reached their nests. The spell of silence was broken. The world evolved before our eyes.

I will lose many things throughout the years. Emotions that were all-consuming at the time will pass from memory, and those I once loved or despised will be forgotten. But as long as I live, that vision of the new earth will always remain. It is my religion. It gives me the faith to wonder.

We descended the hill after breakfast and crawled through the hole in the fence. Patches of mist lingered on the lower ground, but I could see much further ahead than before. We walked along the damp verge and then turned down a footpath through a kissing-gate. Occasionally, we were startled by the contemplative presence of a huge megalith that seemed to lumber out of the residual mist. Like femurs and tibiae of long-extinct dinosaurs, the stones jutted out of the grass and pointed us onwards. Richard babbled and pointed at the dreadful shapes.

'Here be dragons,' I whispered and followed the labyrinthine path to a wide field at the heart of the settlement. Here, the great stone bodies formed a ring that stretched so far into the wispy fog that we could only imagine the circumference of the circle.

I discovered a village in the midst of the stones, and a fairytale tea-shop where we rested. The last of the mist dispersed as I read a guide to the ancient stone circle of Avebury and sipped a mug of fresh coffee. Richard slept in my arms and chirruped in his dreams. We both felt the sense of peace that had been absent for so very long.

The morning slipped easily away as we drifted in a quiet daydream of contentment. Occasional figures popped into the tea-shop to buy one of the curiously spiced soul-cakes, or investigate the display of dream-catchers, ceramic goddesses and homemade jewellery for sale. As each figure walked through the quaint little door, they nodded and smiled amicably at us, as though they knew – how obvious it was – that we should make our home in this magical village. In the afternoon, we explored the notice board in the post office window and followed an advert to one of the local pubs.

The hefty landlady at the Black Dragon, Maggie, rented rooms and accepted us as long-term tenants. She cheerfully complained that business was slow at this time of year and queried whether Richard's father would be joining us.

'Possibly,' I said. 'Although two of them are living as lovers up north. But my partner will be coming down in about a month.'

'Quite so, my dear,' she agreed, as though it was the most common thing in the world. 'And what does your girlfriend do?'

'He's a philosophy graduate,' I explained.

'You know, I never get it quite right,' she laughed and raised a hand to her peachy cheek. 'We get all sorts in here, which makes for a merry old world. You can never be too different, that's what I've always said. It takes all kinds to make the world go round.'

'I'm sure that's true, most of the time,' I replied.

She heated some milk for Richard and pumped me a pint of local ale. On the house, she added with a wink.

'I'll be looking for work,' I admitted. 'We've got savings, but I don't want to touch it, if it can be helped. Do you know of any vacancies in the village?'

'Not much call for anything here. There's only the post office and tea-shop, couple of pubs.' She stroked her chin and pouted impressively for some considerable time. 'Though, there may be one position, my sweet, if you've ever done any bar work. The seasonal workers who come for the summer solstice and whatnot, they've all packed up and gone south for the winter, so to speak. We're a tad short behind the bar.'

'I'm sure I'd be delighted to step in,' I said. Maggie grinned toothily and raised her glass to mine.

* * *

The Black Dragon became my sanctuary during the chill winter evenings in Wiltshire. Maggie's teenage daughter babysat Richard upstairs, while I pulled pints behind the bar. The termination of Day's tenancy agreement was in dispute, so I was waiting for him to join me throughout December.

Chris telephoned at the winter solstice to wish us a Merry Yule. I had been looking forward to a catch-up with him, but a few minutes of his conversation was enough to demoralise me. He was jittery, disturbed, and it was clear that things had not improved in the house.

He spoke nostalgically about the Coven and blamed Anna for sabotaging his friendship with Conrad.

'On those oh-so-rare occasions when I am allowed to speak to Conrad,' he said, 'it has to be by phone. And she's always there, sitting beside him so she can pry and interrupt. She's even got him moving to London with her. More desertions from the Coven, Cat.'

'That sounds a little paranoid, Chris, if you don't mind me saying. How is everything in the house?'

'You mean with Kassi?' he laughed briefly, without humour or feeling. 'No matter what we're talking about, you won't let him alone, will you?'

'Correct me if I'm wrong, but I don't think I mentioned his name.'

'He's fine, thanks for asking. In fact, the three of us are going strong. Couldn't be better.'

'Listen, I haven't got long,' I lied. 'Is Jake around? I haven't spoken to him in weeks.'

Chris muttered a distracted farewell and called for Jake.

'No pleasantries, Jake,' I said as soon as he came to the phone. 'What's wrong with Chris? Tell me what's going on.'

'You were right,' he replied quietly so he would not be overheard. 'Something's here. You sensed it before you left.'

'What is it?' I had felt disheartened talking to Chris, but Jake's voice broke my heart.

'It happened the day Chris sent you the cheque. We came home to find the house turned upside down. I thought we'd been burgled, but all the doors were locked. There was a kitchen knife stuck in the wall and Chris said it was no burglar. He wouldn't say any more.

'It gets worse at night, after sunset. We lie in bed and listen to things move downstairs. We came down one morning last week and found rips all over Chris's chair. It was like an animal had torn it. It couldn't have been the cat. She never comes inside now.'

I saw the house as he described it, the cutlery emptied over the kitchen floor, the shredded furniture, the atmosphere of despair. I had to ask what had been on my mind since the morning I found the meat-curse on the doorstep.

'All this weird shit has happened since things started going wrong between you two,' I said, carefully choosing my words. 'We both know that Chris has a wild imagination, and we both know some of the things that have happened to him in the past. Calliope says he has a strong will, but what about all the other stuff that he buries, the bad stuff he can't face? Is it him, Jake? Do you think that Chris can be doing all these things?'

'I did wonder – but,' Jake's voice grew so quiet I strained to catch his words. 'I've seen it, in the darkness, this thing. I can't make out the face. I know there is a face, but to be honest I can't look at it. It's something that you feel coming towards you in the night, crouching on the bed or hanging from the ceiling. I've shaken Chris, but he won't wake. I've felt it pawing at the blankets. I've even smelt it and, like you said, it's rotten. You knew it was coming; you told me on the day you went away. Well, it's here now, Cat, and I don't know what to do.'

He fell silent. I tried to think of the right words to soothe him, to give him the strength to fight Chris's demons, but I knew it was too late.

'You have to get out, Jake, both of you. You have to leave that house and start from fresh somewhere else. What about Kassi's flat?'

'Kassi?' Jake asked, plainly taken aback by the suggestion. 'We haven't seen Kassi for weeks. Didn't Chris tell you?'

'No. He told me – something very different.'

'The day you went away, I told Chris I didn't want us seeing Kassi anymore. We argued for hours. He said we could work it out. The usual stuff, you know, about revolutionary relationships, the evolution of society, radical stuff and things. I said, either Kassi goes or I go. So Kassi went. It's just the two of us now.'

'No, he didn't tell me any of that,' I said. Chris had lied to me about Kassios, but I could not understand why. He knew how much I detested the Greek, and the feeling was blatantly mutual, but what purpose did it serve not telling me he was out of the picture? Either he was embarrassed by the collapse of his brave new Coven, or he was humiliated by his bad judgement. In any case, Chris did not do shame well.

'Is there nowhere else you can go?' I asked at length. 'Anywhere, just to get out of that house. You can't live there anymore, Jake. Not with that thing.' I remembered the face of the chimera I had seen crouching over Jake's sleeping body and I shuddered.

'But what if it's not in the house? What if it's in him.'

I sat at the window for a long time after we had said our goodbyes and lost track of time. At some point, Maggie bustled into my bedroom, drying her plump fingers on her apron.

'Cat, pumpkin, it's nine o'clock,' she chirped pleasantly. 'Pub's packed with all kinds of kooks from the midwinter ceremony. I need your burly muscles behind the bar, my sweet. A barmaid at nine, finishes on time, that's what I always say.'

* * *

December aged ungraciously over the next few days. The grey clouds froze to a standstill over the chalk banks of the earthwork henge. Even the birds seemed to stop singing. I took Richard each morning to Silbury Hill to watch the world reform anew. He loved the climb up the steep slopes, particularly the crawl through the vandalised fence. Sometimes we met travellers on the summit who talked about their lives on the road, moving from site to ancient site like nomads migrating with the seasons. We exchanged joints and messages from the druids who frequented the stone circles, passing on news for the next gathering.

On Christmas morning, I excused myself from Maggie's family celebrations at the Black Dragon and trudged to Silbury Hill to meet Suede and her daughter. Suede was a Scandinavian traveller in her early thirties who had strayed into the pub on the night of the Winter Solstice. Her daughter, Amber, was born on the same day as Richard, and we bonded over this coincidence as much as a shared loathing of Christmas.

'The Festival of Contrived Alienation,' she had termed it. 'Right, sister. We're spending it together. No excuses. It's my last day in Avebury before I head off. Meet me on Silbury Hill at sunrise. We'll have pickled herring and figgy pudding for breakfast and a flask of mulled wine. Then back to The Visitation for a party.'

The Visitation was the name of her Volkswagen campervan. She belonged, loosely, to a mobile collective of militant environmentalists that was on constant manoeuvres from one frontline confrontation with bulldozers to another. She never travelled in a convoy with the others, but always on her own route and according to her own schedule. She distrusted the herd instinct and consulted her pack of Tarot cards for the way to her next battle.

As we approached the hill, I saw the lonely pink campervan parked unevenly on the grass verge. Suede had smashed a wider breach in the National Trust fence, making it easier for Richard and I to climb through.

'Merry meet, Cat,' she said as we reached her on the summit. 'Happy Saturnalia.'

'Happy what?'

'Saturnalia: the true festival which those fuckwit Christians stole. I did think about saying "Merry Anti-Christmas", but Saturnalia sounds so much more positive, don't you think? It's about turning the patriarchal world order upside-down. Beggars become kings, women are considered wise. Just for a day, mind you. No wonder the fuckwit evangelists misappropriated it.'

'You should meet my friend, Chris. I think that's one man you wouldn't disapprove of.'

'Is he straight?'

'Mostly not.'

'Well, perhaps. It's still a risk, no matter where on the spectrum they sit.'

We toasted our flasks of mulled wine and listened to the church bells ring across the world below. I asked Suede about her name. I assumed it was because she always dressed in brown leather.

'Suits me, don't you think? It's weathered well,' she said with dignity. 'Suede the Swede; tough as old rawhide. Tougher. What about Cat? Where does she come from?'

'Catriona,' I said. 'After a grandmother. Parents' choice.'

'Your fucking parents? What, aren't you old enough to have your own name yet?'

I laughed and gave Suede her present: a walnut cake I had made in the night.

'Gifts?' she queried. 'Do we give gifts at Saturnalia?'

'If it's homemade, it doesn't count as consumerist.'

She rummaged in her rucksack and produced a pack of Tarot cards. Laying a silk scarf on the grass, she apologised that it was the best she could offer at such short notice.

'Shuffle them, Cat, and think of some question you want answered. It can be about anyone or anything at all. Just don't tell me what it is.'

I accepted the well-worn cards and admired the colour designs.

'Painted them all myself,' she said. 'Fucking masterpiece.'

I agreed and wondered what question I should ask. For Richard and myself, I was content. There was nothing I needed to know for ourselves, but Chris came to my mind like a ghost in the shadows. Ever since my conversation with Jake, I had worried about the thing that haunted him.

Suede split the cards and laid them in a circle on the scarf. When the circle was complete, she frowned and chewed her short nails.

'This man you're fretting about is the Knight of Swords,' she began. 'He's wilful, tempestuous, foolhardy. He aspires to high ideals and follows his quest wherever it leads. His crusade is the Sun card in this position above, the source of his strength and his heart-home. It is his religion.

'The Knight is surrounded by three foes, waiting in ambush like a pack of wolves. The first wolf is Hubris, falling off his horse. Hubris waits for his moment to act, brooding in silence below the scene. The second is Lust, the card of cold delight. Lust is without care or conscience, and sharpens his razor sharp phallus. The third is Envy, the bull behind the fence, mooing with discontent. He covets the greener grass on the other side.

'Two ambiguous cards accompany the Knight. The Man in the Moon is his constant companion, his ally and his betrayer. He is romance and deception, love and treason. He rides the white unicorn of purity, yet bears the fated chalice of poison.

'The Washer at the Ford also accompanies the Knight. She wears a gown of autumn leaves and laughs with the gaping mouth of hell. She does not move from his side. She is the corrupt glory of summer, grown old and indolent. She sucks the Knight's energy. She is the guilt of all his crimes, the end of his empire, the waiter at the gates of death.

'And this last card is the imminent future. The Man in the Moon and the Washer at the Ford lead your Knight to this unspeakable place.' The final card in the circle, the only card without colour, was The Underworld.

'Take one more,' she ordered, placing the deck in my hands. 'Choose one from anywhere in the pack.'

I selected a card from the heart of the deck and laid it in the vacant space that remained. Suede sighed with relief and rolled her eyes.

'At last, a ray of fucking sunlight. It's the Lion, the card of true power. The Lion brings harmony where there is strife. He is the king of the deck, champion of the underworld and conqueror of she who guards the gates. He bears resolution.'

Suede collected the cards together and sucked her teeth.

'Most enlightening,' I said, after a suitable pause. 'Do I get an interpretation?'

'I've given you enough,' she said, wrapping the cards in the scarf. 'Now, go make up your own meaning out of that load of old bollocks.'

* * *

The sky remained frozen and bleak for the last few days of the month. On New Year's Day, I awoke to a shaft of sunlight streaming through the curtains. I stood at the window and gazed at the green banks of the grassy henge. The long shadows of the megaliths stretched across the circle and pointed towards the centre of the village.

I reached into the cot to show Richard the bright new year and found him weeping. He lips remained closed and he made no sound, but the tears were rolling down his cheeks. I lifted him into the light and studied his features. Something was wrong, I thought, searching his face. He looked different, changed, as though a faerie had visited in the night and swapped my child for a changeling. I rocked him in my arms and tried to soothe him with a lullaby, but he continued to cry.

Over breakfast, I spooned the parsnip soup between his downturned lips and shook my head. Something had surely altered in the night. I decided to take him to the doctor for a check-up, to put my fears to rest.

Maggie bustled into the kitchen, carrying two skinned rabbits in each mighty hand.

'No time to talk, my lemon,' she hollered. 'The watched pot never stops boiling in this house.' And yet she did stop to stare at Richard. 'Gracious me, Cat. What in heaven's name have you done to his hair?'

I looked at his brow and was startled by the absence I had failed to notice all morning. The straw-coloured fringe drooped over his eyes, but the white streak had vanished. I ran my fingers through the fringe. There was not a trace of the white he had inherited from Jake. The flash of moonlight had disappeared overnight.

'Still, I'm sure there's a sensible reason why you did it,' Maggie continued, hanging the rabbits from a hook above the oven. 'For one thing, people won't stare at him anymore. Just a normal little poppet now, like any other handsome baby boy.'

* * *

It was Twelfth Night before Day finally settled the dispute over his tenancy agreement and arrived at the Black Dragon. I was working behind the bar in the afternoon when he walked in, lugging a suitcase behind him. He brushed the long, golden hair out of his eyes and leaned across the counter for a kiss.

'I'm not alone,' he said, glancing furtively back at the doorway. 'I'm seriously hoping I haven't made a blunder.'

I looked at the entrance and saw a man lurking on the threshold.

'Can I come in?' he asked, rubbing his cold hands together. His head was bowed and his shoulders hunched, so I could not see his face.

'Sure, come into the warmth. Any friend of Day's is welcome in this place.'

'What about a friend of yours, Cat?' he asked and stepped into the light.

Chris had altered beyond recognition. His eyes were ringed with dark, sleepless circles and his cheekbones looked sharper than usual. He appeared like a pale apparition in the dim afternoon light, a skeleton from a mediaeval doom painting.

'You do still consider me a friend, don't you, Cat?'

'How could you possibly doubt that?' I said and ran to hug him. 'What's happened to you? You look half-dead.'

His neck was cold against my check and he winced as I stroked his back. Gently, he pushed me away.

'It hurts. It's healing slowly, but it still hurts.'

He slumped onto the stool and rubbed his bones to keep warm. Maggie took one glance at him and instantly gave me the night off work. I wrapped an arm around his waist and led him up the stairs to my bedroom. He had to pause between floors for breath.

'It's nothing,' he said, smiling at his pathetic progress. 'Something, probably the fucking cat, scratched me in the night. It's bad, but it'll heal.'

'We both know it was no cat,' I said as I led him into the bedroom. His face contorted as I helped him lie down on the mattress. He exhaled deeply and lay still. 'So, she finally got you.'

Chris glanced at me, gauging how much I suspected, and then turned to the wall. He could hold my eyes for no more than a brief moment.

'I talked to Jake at the Solstice,' I said. 'And I've seen her myself.'

Outside, the barn owl that lived in the church tower cut the night with her cry. Moving towards the window, I gazed at the long shadows of the moonlit stones.

'It's a full moon,' I said, listening to the hungry owl. 'But you would know that already.'

Chris didn't make a sound. In the dimly lit room, he lay on his side and I saw his cheek glisten with tears. A fallen Pierrot, his strings severed.

'Speak to me, Chris,' I whispered. 'Tell me what happened. You're safe here. Believe that you're safe. The stone circle surrounds the village. Speak to me.' I knelt beside his enervated body and wiped his cheek with my sleeve. He lay silently on the bed and stared as the white moon rolled behind the cusp of the horizon.

Downstairs, Day was leaning against the bar and talking to Maggie.

'Is Richard's daddy asleep now?' she asked, shaking her head. 'Best thing for him, poor pumpkin.'

'He won't sleep,' said Day without looking up from his pint.

'He will tonight from the looks of him, treacle.'

'No,' Day persisted. 'He never sleeps. He's been awake for days. He won't even close his eyes.'

'What has he told you?' I asked. Maggie leaned closer, intrigued by the mystery of the strange man upstairs and eager to catch a hint of any dark gossip.

'Barely anything,' Day replied. 'I went to see them on New Year's Day. They hadn't been answering their phone. Chris was just as you see him now. All he said was that Jake had left. He'd disappeared, gone. He wouldn't say where. That's as much as I know.'

'What do you mean, gone?'

'Just that.' Day sipped his pint. 'No Jake.'

'You read about this type of thing in the papers all the time,' the landlady said cryptically. 'It's not to do with drugs, is it?'

'No, Maggie, it's not to do with drugs.'

'It does make you think though, doesn't it?' she carried on, warily eyeing the ceiling and weighing up the potential glamour of being indirectly involved in a scandal of some kind.

* * *

Day and I laid our blankets on the floor and listened to Chris breathing feverishly in the bed. I slept fitfully and dreamed that a pack of dogs were barking in the fields, just beyond the stone circle. I woke at sunrise and heard the barn owl cry a dawn reveille.

They say that the screech of the midnight owl is an omen of death, but to hear it after the sun has risen foreshadows something worse. I lay in the early dawn light and listened to the night-bird's cry echo between the banks of the grassy henge. Day turned in his sleep and spread a heavy arm across my back. Richard whined a dreamy imitation of the owl and kicked his feet. The house creaked softly in the morning breeze and lay still. It was then that I felt the fear of silence.

During the darker hours, Chris's erratic breathing had kept pace with my own unsettled thoughts. Now that the sunlight crept over the walls, I realised that his breathing had stopped altogether.

I knelt against the bed and stared at his face. His eyelids remained open but the balls had turned inwards, as they had that night he came sleepwalking into my bedroom. I held my palm over his mouth to feel the movement of air, but there was nothing.

I said his name, quietly at first. His lips remained slightly parted, but deathly dry and still. I called his name again, more urgently, and slapped his face. Startled by the noise, Day woke from his sleep and knelt beside me.

'He's not breathing,' I think I said. I may have said, 'he's gone.'

Day shook Chris's shoulders and thumped him in the chest repeatedly. I pressed my mouth to his lifeless blue lips and forced air into the empty lungs. At some point, after an eternity of panic, Chris gasped painfully at his resuscitation, choking as the life flooded back into his body.

I stared into his wild eyes and saw something I did not understand in the dark pupils. Besides the horror of the threshold of death and the pain of resurrection, I saw disappointment.

'It's okay,' I said, clutching his cold hand. 'It's over, love. You're all right now. You're breathing again.'

He closed his eyes and rasped something inaudible. I leaned forward and caught the odour of death from between his teeth.

'He's gone,' he whispered. 'There's no need to breathe.'

* * *

Chris's recovery was hampered by his refusal to accept any professional medical treatment. Despite my insistence on a home-visit from the doctor, Chris refused to see anyone. The only compromise he made was to take my own soporific herbal teas at night and a poultice of soothing comfrey leaves for his lacerated back. The marks were deep. The skin around the wounds had seemingly been cauterised. I hung lavender bags around the room to cleanse the air of nightmares, and burned thyme and eucalyptus oils to help his respiration. This was Calliope's lore; it was what she had prepared me for, and I was having to use it alone. I tried to call her in the first few weeks but she refused to answer the telephone. It was too late for her to change, she'd said, and I had to accept her decision.

March was a month of severe gales and clean skies. Inside the Black Dragon, Chris sat at the old village well, now a table in the lounge bar, and rocked Richard in his arms. To the child's delight, he told the tale of Orpheus, the poet who went to the underworld in search of his beloved wife, Eurydice. His voice echoed down the brick hole into the caverns of the earth.

Maggie served him lunch and retreated hastily behind the bar.

'That one will never get fit and well again until he starts eating meat,' she complained, eyeing him suspiciously. 'But maybe he's already eaten too much meat, if you get my meaning. I take it they haven't found the body yet?'

'Maggie, it's honestly not murder most foul,' I explained for the twentieth time. 'Jake's left him, that's all.'

'Told you that himself, did he?'

'He will do, when he's ready to talk.'

The missing pieces of Chris's last weeks in Sunderland were not easy to find. He turned away when I raised the subject and refused to speak. I was so concerned by his emaciated condition that I had to ask if he had played safe with Kassios. Don't forget, this was at the tail-end of the gay-plague frenzy. Only a few years earlier, we had all seen the pictures of successive body bags being carried out of quarantined hospices by medics in protective clothing, fearful lest they catch the unknown virus from touching the infected. Even now, there was no treatment. Even now, there were those who were given just months to live after their first diagnosis. Love in the time of AIDS is hazardous; in its heyday, it took courage.

'We hedged our bets,' said Chris, laughing for the first time in weeks. 'Of all the things that will finish me off, I can't bank on that one.'

It was only at the end of the evenings, when I rang the last-orders bell and collected the empties, that he hinted at what had happened. Holed up in some dark corner, he lowered his guard and talked to the dregs of his glass. I gathered the loose fragments of his tale when the travellers were no longer listening and he thought he was alone. He made no distinction between the real world and his nightmares, so neither will I.

Jake was not at home the night the creature, the Old Woman of the Downs he called her, had come for him. The last thing he remembered was falling asleep in his armchair in the Yellow Room. When he awoke hours later, he was rolling in torment on the floor. The back of his shirt and the skin beneath had been repeatedly scored by something – a talon, Chris said – as sharp as a scalpel. Beneath his body, the blood had seeped into the yellow carpet, leaving a moth-shaped stain where he had reeled from side to side. Jake was on his knees beside him, shaking him back to consciousness.

'She's come for her dues,' he replied to Jake's panicked questions. 'It was the bargain she made.'

Jake helped him climb the stairs to the bathroom, where he inexpertly bound the wounds with bandages. After he had settled Chris into bed, he made sure all the doors and windows were locked and then swept the house clean, singing the few familiar lines of Chris's lullaby that he knew.

Throughout the following day, neither of them left the house. They stayed in the bedroom as though it was under siege. Whenever Chris woke, he found Jake sitting beside the bed, watching him with a puzzled frown.

'I need to know how this happened,' Jake asked in a low voice, leaning forward so Chris could hear him. 'I need you to tell me.'

Chris turned his face to the wall and said nothing. Jake sighed and sat back in his chair. Beyond that, there was no sound. The house was deadly quiet. No cars travelled down the deserted street and no wind rocked the dream-tree. Even the seagulls on the roof were mute.

All things were in suspense, anticipating the night that would inevitably follow.

When evening came, Chris grew restless and asked Jake to help him into the bathroom. Awkwardly, they washed the flayed skin of his back over the sink and redressed the wound with fresh bandages. Returning to the bedroom, Chris asked Jake to cast a circle of salt around their bed. He said it simply as though it were a commonplace request, as though he were asking for the washing-up to be done or the bins to be put out.

'What good will that do?'

Chris eased himself beneath the covers and did not reply. Perhaps Jake would not have gone through the motions of scattering the salt if the dream-tree had not, at that moment, begun to stir and rasp against its concrete foundations, although there was no wind.

It was a long December night. Chris lay awake and listened until his ears were ringing with concentration. The distant noises of the city sounded as close as the occasional loosened spring in his mattress. By three o'clock, the only disturbance had been the fitful rattle of the dream-tree in the garden. Circe padded the blankets. Jake breathed quietly and murmured in his dreams. Chris stroked invisible spirals on his lover's golden skin and waited. Somewhere along the coast, a dog howled at the late moon. The church clock struck four.

It is now that the borderland between the world of solid objects and the subterranean realm of dreams is contested. It is here that the subconscious encroaches on the physical. I do not know what happened that night. There are many eyes, says Nietzsche; even the Sphinx has eyes and, consequently, there are many truths. And maybe there is no truth, literal or otherwise. I do not know. All I can do is retell what was told to me, the remnants of a fractured memory muttered darkly into a glass at closing time.

'Christopher.'

The voice came faintly at first, soft as a whisper in a bottle. Chris raised his head and stared at the flickering streetlight on the wall. Perhaps it was simply the wind in the eaves, although the night was still. Circe hissed at the darkness and retreated beneath the bed.

'Christopher.' This time, the voice was unmistakable. The words unfolded in the air like smoke from a cigar, like sickly incense from a thurible. 'Christopher. Christopher.'

'You are not welcome here,' Chris whispered. He held Jake's sleeping body closely against his own.

He knew the voice. It was the voice that had seeped into his childhood and poisoned his dreams at their source. It was the voice of the creaking staircase in the oast-house night. The sound was as dry as a holy man's lips, as clipped and cutting as the serrated weathervane on the old vicarage roof.

"'There is no health in my flesh because of thy displeasure,'" it said weakly, reciting an old familiar psalm from the darkness. He spoke with a stifled laugh, a contrived fusion of devotion and derision, mockery and sincerity. "'Nor is there any soundness in my bones.'"

Chris opened his eyes and looked at his father. The dead priest was seated in the corner chair, still wearing his black cassock and silver-rimmed spectacles, still bald but for the ridge of wispy grey hair that fringed the back of his skull. His legs were crossed and his hands rested limply on his knees. The old man smiled tightly. His eyes remained deathly cold.

"'The sacrifice of God is a troubled spirit,'" he continued, raising his eyebrows as though expecting Chris to complete the phrase. "'A broken and a contrite heart.'"

'You are not welcome here,' said Chris. 'You have no power now.'

"'For my loins burn with a sore disease.'" His father giggled and patted his knees. "'And there is no whole part in my body.'"

'I won't engage with you, dead man.' Chris tightened his grip around Jake's chest. As he did so, the scars on his back ripped softly open.

'You dear boy,' said the priest, leaning forward to rest his chin on his knuckles, affecting parental concern. 'I see your creature, your Old Woman has been kinder to you than she was with me, but she was your innovation after all. I do suffer from some appalling twinges in my chest, thank you for asking. Though I imagine that's to be expected when a weathervane has pierced straight through one's heart.'

'We both know you're not here.' Chris pressed his cheek against Jake's back.

'Well, that is a relief,' the old man laughed. 'Imagine how awkward it would be if I were.'

'Why come now? Was hell too liberal for your tastes?'

'It is somewhat permissive,' his father shrugged innocently, 'my son lying with another man as with a woman. Doesn't it seem so to you?'

'What do you want?'

'Let's call it paternal pride. I like to keep an eye on my progeny. Did you honestly suppose I would ever abandon you?'

'Why wait so long for this family reunion?'

'I've been otherwise occupied. What was it Denmark's ghost said to Hamlet? Ah, yes: "Doomed for a certain term to walk the night, and for the day confined to fast in fires". As you can see, I've had time these past few months to catch up on some reading. Your library is surprisingly extensive.' The dead priest rose from his chair and paced contemplatively to the window. 'But to return to your question: why. Your creature, the Old Woman, performed her side of your bargain most diligently, didn't she? Shake hands with the Devil and she will undoubtedly take her dues. I recognise her bloody signature written on your spine, my lamb. Her handwriting is clumsy, but she is your product after all. From you she emerged: to you she has returned. "Dust thou art, and unto dust thou shalt return". How very poetic. I trust it's not a burden, this debt you have to bear?'

'Is there any particular purpose to this hallucination?' Chris asked. 'Or is it simply to remind myself how much you loved hearing your own sermons when you were alive?'

'Before you killed me, to be precise,' the ghost corrected him. He glanced at the brightening horizon through the window. 'Your creature performed her task most effectively. Now she has returned to her heart-home. She will sup from you until she is sated, as and when she likes: that was your bargain. But where are my dues, Christopher? What of my compensation? Isn't parricide a sin that cries out to heaven?'

'My cries were ignored for years. Heaven is deaf.'

'*Non facias malum ut inde fiat bonum.*' The priest pulled the curtains against the dawn. 'Were my crimes any worse than yours?'

'Yes.'

'Honestly?'

'Yes, they were.'

The dead priest sighed. 'Time is against me; I will be brief. If I begin to sound like Marley's ghost, humour me. You, my son, will lose your dear friend, there. Such a terrible loss. You will indeed be horribly grief-stricken but, "the sacrifice of God is a troubled spirit, a broken and a contrite heart," is it not? That will be enough for me, Christopher. I will accept that as my due.'

'Get out of my house,' Chris said, quietly but firmly. He closed his eyes and cradled Jake's head against his chest. Gradually, the sun rose.

* * *

Jake woke at eight and struggled to extricate himself from Chris's possessive embrace.

'Let me breathe,' he said. 'You're suffocating me.'

Chris opened his arms. Jake stretched, yawned and sat on the edge of the bed in his white underwear. He was bathed in a shaft of golden sunlight that kissed his stubble, the soft blonde fur on his arms.

After a few minutes, he walked to the door and kicked a break in the salt circle with his bare feet. He looked at the breach and turned to his lover.

'I love you,' said Chris.

Jake left the bedroom.

* * *

A week later, on New Year's Eve, Chris was sitting on a bench in Mowbray Park. He watched children throw broken bricks into the frozen lake, but was only half conscious of their gleeful cries.

'Gracious, girl,' said a familiar voice behind him. 'You're looking positively consumptive. How have the mighty fallen?'

'Fuck off,' Chris said with a brief glance at Dane. 'I can still bite.'

'But, darling, I've heard you'd lost all your teeth. Word on the scene is that things aren't going well and now you're a complete pussy. Mind if I join you?'

Dane perched himself delicately beside Chris and gazed at his reflection in a compact mirror.

'You know, this cold weather plays havoc with my complexion. The girl at the make-up counter says the same. Says she never leaves the pharmacy between September and March. Says the winter wind murders her skin. I said to her, where do you sleep? She said, in the sun-bed department. Girlfriend, I said, it shows.'

'What do you want, Dane?'

'Charming,' Dane said, putting his compact away. 'There was me doing the charitable thing, passing the time of day with an old chum. And aren't you looking old, Chrissy? Father Time has been unkind to you. Would you just look at those crow's feet. Thought you may be in need of a little consolation at this sad time, but I see the gesture's not appreciated.'

Chris lit a cigarette and stared at the tops of the leafless trees.

'Come on, *ma chérie*,' Dane continued, with a tentative pat of Chris's knee. 'No need to play the strong silent type with me. I know all about it. Gary told me this morning. I told him, no, Jake would never leave Chris. Whatever life throws in their path, those birds of paradise will be together forever. Oh no, Darlena, he says, this time it's definitely over. Strange things are occurring in that household. Unnatural things that go bump in the night. I said, maybe it's a ghost? No, he says, I reckon they're fighting because Jake ain't ever going back again. Then Gary winked at me like the dirty little bugger he is. I know, he says, because I fucked Jake up his tight little ass last night. Those were his exact words, I swear. I fucked Jake up his tight little ass last night and Jake is never going back. How sad, I said. Chris will be upset.'

Chris stood up and stared at the pond.

'You're lying,' he said after a long pause. 'You live on these lies. You get off on the misery you make. You're poison, Dane. Nothing true, nothing wholesome has ever passed your lips.'

'I'm as devastated as you, I swear.' Dane sighed and gathered his cosmetics together. He glanced nervously at Chris and then left the bench. He was heading to the park entrance when Chris called him back.

'Wait. When did you say this happened?'

'Last night. Between nine and ten. In Gary's car. At the seafront in Seaham. Darling, I do feel awful, being the bearer of such ill-tidings.'

Chris turned back to the frozen lake. 'Now, fuck off.'

Chris walked slowly homewards. His head was pounding with sleeplessness and the echo of Dane's words. Last night, he thought. Between nine and ten. At the seafront in Seaham.

As he approached the front gate of his house, he hesitated. The window boxes were empty and the curtains were all closed. To him, it seemed abandoned. The seagulls were perched in a line on the roof. Every once in a while, one of the birds would cry a mocking parody of Jake's name.

In Gary's car. Last night.

Chris turned his back on the house. He walked down the littered streets, crossing roads and cutting through parks. He walked aimlessly, like a body without purpose, following the invisible ball of wool to a house he had not visited in weeks.

Kassios was sitting by his bedroom window. He looked up from what he was doing and saw the familiar figure cross the street. Chris waved and pointed at the front door.

'It is open,' Kassios called down through the window.

'Can I come up?'

'I have said it is open, for crying aloud,' Kassios sighed.

Chris unlatched the door and entered the darkened hallway. Somewhere in the house he heard the soft trickling of running water. Hushed voices whispered in one of the downstairs rooms. He glanced one last time at the early evening sky, to where Venus hesitated over the sea. The streets were drained of colour, blanched by the glare of the setting midwinter sun. The windless cold had stolen his sight and now the world blazed white and without form through his tears. A passing siren sliced the icy air. Vacantly, he closed the door and approached the unlit stairs.

XII
Eurydice

Half way along the steep path to the summit of Silbury Hill, I stopped to search the spring-green landscape for a pink campervan. Chris followed slowly in my wake with Richard harnessed to his chest. Breathless, he glanced at me and asked what I was looking for.

'The Visitation,' I replied, shielding the sun from my eyes. 'Suede said she would return earlier than usual this year in time for the Equinox. I can't imagine what you'll make of her. Her daughter was born the same day as Richard.'

'So, two devils were born on the same Halloween, were they?' Chris ruffled Richard's hair and cooed at the child. He tramped ahead, abandoning the path for the un-trodden slopes of the hill. I watched him bend slowly to the steep rise, clutching the grass for support.

'Is it your back?' I asked. 'Let me carry Richard for you.'

He struggled onwards to the level plateau of the summit and crouched exhausted beside the edge. I sat next to him and surveyed the land of folklore faeries and white horses in the hills. High above the fields, hovering motionlessly in the cloudless blue, a skylark filled the air with a song of spring's return. Chris chewed a dandelion stem and eyed the bird.

'Why sing to nobody, so far above the earth?' he asked, screwing his face up at the blinding sky.

'Wouldn't you, if you could, if you were glad winter was over?'

'Maybe she's in love. Must be love. It is springtime, isn't it? I thought all creatures were supposed to be in love at this time of year.'

'That myth's long since been dispelled.' I lay an arm over his shoulder, still mindful of the scars. He closed his eyes and breathed deeply. The skylark dived towards the ground, levelling out at the very last moment.

'You're still in love with Day, aren't you?' he asked.

'What do you think?'

'It took time with you two, didn't it? It wasn't all fireworks on the first night. You drifted towards each other like a tendency, an awakening. I think it makes your roots deeper.' He took another heavy breath and brushed the hair out of his eyes. 'It is spring, isn't it?'

'I think we can safely assume it is.'

'Then tell me how it feels.'

'Chris, where are you going with this?'

'I want to know. Tell me what it's like to feel him lying beside you in the night. Do you still look at each other when you turn off the

211

lamp, so the last thing you see is his face? Do you hold that picture in your eyes, even though it's too dark to see? Tell me, Cat. How does it feel?'

'Don't do this to yourself. It's not kind to either of us.' I took my arm off his shoulder and plucked the grass between my bare toes. 'Besides, you know what it's like.'

'No, Cat. I'm not in love.' He spat the dandelion sap onto the grass. The skylark rose again from the field, reaching higher into the firmament than before. I watched the small black figure poise amid the turbulence of air. 'Surely, there's a difference between loving someone and actually being in love. To be in love would imply that Jake is equally in love with me. Which he isn't. All I can do is to love him on my own. It's like emotional masturbation. He is always in my eyes, whether the light is on or off.

'You know, I think there must be a moment at death, at the instant your mind ceases to be, when it will be too dark to see anything but his face.' As Chris spoke, there was a light the shape of a dancing lark in his pupils, but his eyes were no longer seeing mine. 'At that moment, it must all come back at once. All those times you marvelled at him, all those times you watched him sleep, all those times you turned off the light as you looked at his face: it must all come back in that instant. And everything you ever felt – everything – all that must come back too. And you must find yourself thinking, even at the last, that you never knew it amounted to so much. You never guessed it.'

Chris stood up with difficulty and turned to another horizon, towards the White Horse Hills in the east. I was unsure if he had finished speaking or there was more to come. I waited without moving.

'Each time he kissed you or said he loved you,' he continued quietly, 'or maybe he said nothing but smiled, and you thought that was all there could be to love. You thought, it's inconceivable that there can be anything greater. But you're wrong, for at the end it must all coalesce in one hellish flash: his voice, his skin, his warmth, his moods, but most of all his love. It must all come back in one blinding snap-shot of his face, as if you'd just switched off the light to make sure he's the last thing you see of the day. Dust to dust with him in your eyes. It must be the last thing there is.'

Chris lowered his head. I pulled my boots on and walked a few steps down the slope.

'Don't talk of death, Chris,' I said, searching the skies for the missing bird, 'not here. This hill, I like to think of it as a place of life. It's why I brought you here.'

Chris laughed. 'It will take us all someday, whether we're ready or not. Me, I'd like to take the moment when it's ripe, when there's nothing more for me to do. We think the stars own us. We think the span of our lives is preordained. It isn't. We can cheat the universe of its last laugh. That's what makes us gods.'

Don't speak like that here, Chris, I thought. Please, not here. I kicked the loose chalk down the hill. Chris had just revealed more of his feelings at this moment than he had in all the months since he had arrived. I longed to descend the hill, to walk as far as the burial chambers at West Kennet, to carry this hexed melancholy from Silbury to the distant stones of the long barrow. But Chris had spoken and he might say more.

'Let's go to West Kennet,' I said decisively. 'It's more fitting.'

'More fitting for what?'

'For all your talk of death.'

I followed Chris's slow descent down the hill. As we crawled through the broken fence, Chris gave Richard back to me. The baby was babbling constantly and ended each sentence with the word 'Kith'.

'What's that, Man-Cub,' said Chris.

'I think he's saying your name. He's talking to you, Kith.'

'We haven't heard that before, have we, Prince Nichey?'

'Perhaps you haven't been listening. You certainly haven't been saying much. Except to the bottom of your glass at closing time.'

Chris fell silent as we entered the kissing gate and followed the river through fields of furrowed earth. We left the main path behind and skirted the edge of the seeded field beside a budding hawthorn and blackthorn hedge. The ground rose gently towards the burial chamber on the ridge. In the autumn, I thought, I shall return here to gather blackberries and sloes for a Samhain feast. Suede had said the roots of these brambles drank deeply from the bones of warrior queens. To taste such fruit was to become a blood sister of Proserpine. We would have to wait until September for that communion.

Chris passed beneath the shadows of the great monoliths in the forecourt of the prehistoric chamber. He raised a hand to the warm stone and closed his eyes, listening to a voice within.

'It's like a row of teeth,' I said, pressing my cheek against the rock. 'Look, this one's a canine, that's an incisor and those must be the molars.'

'The mouth of the underworld. Let's go in.'

I peered into the darkness of the chamber and felt a chill pass over my skin. Richard had stopped his babbling. He craned his neck to stare in awe at the otherworldly gloom.

'I think we'll stay out here,' I said.

'Abandon hope, all you who enter.' Chris smiled kindly and reached a hand for me to take. 'Come on, Cat. It's time I talked of Jake.'

213

'Tell me out here, love. I'm not ready to abandon hope just yet.'

'Come with me. You were right: it is more fitting in the tomb.'

Chris passed between the mossy bones at the entrance of the burial chamber and hummed the tune of his Greek lullaby. Reluctantly, I followed.

The smooth earth of the barrow floor echoed our footsteps against the cold stone walls. The air was as musty and stale as a damp cellar or disused chapel. I felt we were being watched from the darkened catacombs, as though four thousand years of dead eyes were glaring jealously at my living presence. I felt unwelcome.

'Stay close to me,' Chris said, recognising my unease. 'They sense me as one of their own. They're not hostile, just curious. The dead take their identities from the living, like mirrors or pools of water.'

'Chris,' I said, folding my arms protectively around Richard's papoose. 'Don't speak of death. It doesn't feel safe.'

'You're wrong, Cat.' Chris walked deeper into the barrow. 'It is safe to talk of it here. Especially in here. You yourself said so.'

I followed his silhouette to the stone heart of the chamber. The walls were illuminated by the glow of a dozen votive candles nestling in niches between the slate slabs. Chris knelt on the smooth earth and wrote letters with his finger in the dust. The shadows crept closer to catch the unwonted words that fell from his lips.

He spoke only of things after New Year's Eve, as though Year Zero had struck at midnight and everything before that was unrecorded history. Memories of the earlier life were mere fragments of a half-remembered dream, to be muttered at closing time when he thought no one was listening.

'I was lying in Kassi's bedroom,' he began, scratching patterns in the dust. 'There was a lava lamp on the floor. It cast red and yellow shadows on the wall. The patterns shifted like amoeba over our limbs. We were both sweating in the heat. It was so hot it felt like a swamp.

'After Kassi's spasms had died down, he released my wrists and slid from my back. He reached over the edge of the bed and let his condom slop to the floor. "I am sorry," he said. "My bed is my bed. There is not the space for two persons to sleep here."'

Chris paused and stared at the words he had scrawled on the floor. He stretched his palm over the writing and closed his eyes, feeling the heat of the letters. His voice echoed softly from the walls and carried between the chambers like the whisperings of ghosts.

Idly, Kassios repeated his dismissal and pulled the sheets over his shaved legs. He nudged Chris away with his knee and rolled over. Chris rose tortuously from the mattress and faltered towards the window. He could feel the bruises beginning to spread like a throbbing rash over his neck and down his arms. The lacerations on his back wept for the pain they were giving him. Kassi snored quietly and scratched his pubes.

Outside, the church bells had stopped pealing but people were still calling out New Year greetings in the street. The last of the fireworks exploded above the tower blocks; the embers fell like volcanic ash to the houses below. Pompeii knew a night such as this, thought Chris, pulling his T-shirt over his head. The shirt clung to his wounds and blood seeped through the fabric like a rose unfolding.

'Take off the rose,' he said absently, 'and set a blister there.'

The ash continued to settle on the town. It stroked the windowpane, spiralled in the breeze and blended with the snow that was now falling. Chris stared at the high-rise canyons of the frozen cityscape. The waxing moon emerged through the ragged clouds, lighting the entire sky with phosphorescent snow.

'It can do that,' he said aloud, gazing at the sparkling sky. 'It can snow when the moon is out.'

Kassios moaned in his sleep and stretched beneath the sheets. Painfully, Chris dressed himself and lowered his face over the Greek.

'Goodbye Kassi,' he muttered quietly, so as not to wake him. He reached inside his T-shirt and fingered the wounds that had been unsealed. Lifting his hand in the light of the lava lamp, Chris watched the blood trickle around his hand-fasting ring and down the creases in his palm.

'I leave this with you,' he said, drawing a symbol on Kassios's forehead. 'You will never touch anyone again. You will never be touched again. So be it.'

The street was deserted when Chris emerged from Kassi's house. The pavement, the muted terraces and the scattering of roadside trees were smothered in a clean blanket of unsullied snow. In the morning, he thought, the city will be buried. In the morning, no one will wake. Tonight, a white spell has been cast and the world is blanched.

Chris walked through the abandoned city towards his house. The intense episodes of the past twelve hours had cascaded at such a pace that it took a considerable effort of will to think of anything. Several times, he found himself turning down a dead end or standing at a junction he did not recognise. The revelation of Jake's infidelity seemed like a distant memory now, kicked into the past by his own betrayal. He could not think why he had found himself lying on Kassios's bed, confessing secrets about his lover to a man who loved nothing.

The Greek had plucked a condom from the bedside cabinet and slipped it onto himself in one seamless movement.

'I don't want to fuck tonight, Kassi,' Chris had apologised.

'You are not going to, Cristophe. This is my fuck.'

Chris was unprepared when Kassios rolled him onto his stomach and locked his wrists in a grasp beneath the pillow. He struggled to release himself from the grip, but the rough stubble on Kassios's chest grated against his scars. Their sweaty skin adhered together and then pulled apart.

'Kassi, I'm serious. I said I don't want to fuck.'

'Hush, Christopher.' The voice was no longer Kassios's. The sound fell in beads of cold, immaculately clipped English. It slipped like a sleek needle through his heart and blunted his resistance.

Chris tried to shout, but the abrasive bristles on Kassios's chest pierced the cuts and took his breath away. His muscles clenched painfully as Kassios pushed inside him with one pitiless lunge.

'Hush, dear boy. Be still,' said the unmistakable voice against his ear. 'It would be unbecoming to make a scene, don't you agree?'

Chris winced as the weight of the body grinded against his opening scars. Kassios pressed the ridge of his chin into the back of Chris's neck, pushing his face harder against the pillow with each heave, hollowing him out from every angle.

'"For the sacrifice of God is a troubled spirit,"' the voice continued. '"a broken and contrite heart."'

Kassios's sour cologne seemed to fade with each violent movement, to be replaced by a miasma of incense. Chris twisted his face from the pillow and stared at the wall. In the delicate light of the lamp, the red and yellow lava dripped from the surface of the wallpaper. The colours seeped away with each fluid revolution in the oil, dissolving the wall in a rapid conflagration of layers to expose another, older grey stone wall behind. Towards the ceiling, he was aware of a stained-glass window. Although he could not see it, the window bathed his face with the illuminated outline of a familiar St Paul, his right hand raised in perfunctory blessing.

'Take, eat; this is my body,' his father's voice came from between Kassios's lips. 'Do this in remembrance of me.'

The mattress was hard now, as hard and cruel as an altar stone against his cheek bone. Chris closed his eyes and played a lullaby in his mind. He waited for the seeping glow of the lava lamp to return.

* * *

Chris turned the last corner to his own street and walked towards his home. The curtains of the darkened windows had been drawn tightly against the falling snow and there was no smoke rising from the chimney. He stepped through the gate and pressed his key to the lock. Something had changed, he thought. Something was missing from the garden. He stared at the vacant space where the window box had been. Jake must have removed it. The night-scented stock had never flowered anyway and the soil was too shallow for the lupins to thrive. Still, it was unusual for Jake to concern himself with the garden.

The key would not slide into the lock. He pushed it harder against the hole, but it refused to fit. Gradually he understood that the lock had been changed. He stared at the gleaming steel face where the old lock had been. He lifted the letterbox and called for Jake. Nothing stirred in the unlit house. He whistled for Circe, but there was still no movement. All life had been suspended. Only the dead shells of empty houses remained. The world was as hollow as the zero inside him.

He left the garden and walked towards Roker. His earlier footprints had already been smothered by the new snow and endlessly falling ash. Now, no trace of his previous movements remained. He too was being erased.

Diana's Bar had an all-night licence for New Year's Eve. It was the place he and Jake had arranged to spend their anniversary, barely twelve hours before the volcano had erupted. Buried deep within the burrows of the cliff, there was a chance it may have survived the apocalypse of snow.

Chris entered the silent body fields of the graveyard. The cemetery was unlit by streetlights, but the ground glistened in the bright glare of the moon. He could see the shattered walls of the old chapel standing among the graves: a ruined giant surrounded by her midget tombstones. He walked alongside the chapel and down the aisles of broken stones. The foghorn bawled a single warning from the coast and then fell silent.

He emerged from the gates at the lower end of the cemetery and followed the seafront towards the underground club. The sea lapped against the edge of the promenade, spraying the road with icy water. Chris pulled his coat tighter and felt the wounds on his back stick to his shirt.

Deep beneath the surface of the pavement, he heard the steady rhythm of the underground music. The rainbow lights from the entrance sign spread across the road and retreated, an ebbing tide of colour – the last in this blanched world. He stepped over the threshold and descended the stairwell to the dragon's lair.

The chessboard dance floor was filled with naked torsos of varying shapes and sizes, each one celebrating the end of the world in a carnival of desperate energy. Chris pushed a path through the crowd and made his way to the bar. Cyane waved at his approach and leaned over the counter.

'Evening, comrade,' she said, kissing his cheek. 'Thought the last stragglers came in at midnight. Dread to think what you've been up to.'

She poured him a glass of dark rum and told him some anecdotes about the more eccentric clients she had served that evening. Chris sipped his drink and glanced vacantly around the smoky alcoves.

'You looking for your man?' she said. 'The Muscle with Attitude? He's right over there. Had a right night, he has.'

She pointed towards a table in the corner. The alcove was partially obscured by the bodies on the dance floor.

'Take care, lover,' said Cyane, patting his hand. 'You don't look well and the wolves are out tonight. Be careful.'

Chris nodded and walked towards Jake's table. The mirrors reflected every watchful pair of white eyes in the chamber. He crossed the chessboard and felt the faces follow his movements. He flinched at the damp hands that stroked his back and the lips that mouthed kisses as he passed.

The white stripe in Jake's fringe gleamed in the flashing strobe light and drew Chris towards the table. Jake was laughing. He laid a hand on Dane's shoulder and grinned until the dimples showed in his cheeks. Dane pawed Jake's arm and pressed his lips close to those dimples. Jake glanced up and met Chris's eyes.

'*Quelle surprise*, Chrissy-baby,' Dane cried. 'Who'd have thought it? Must say I, for one, didn't expect to see your rugged face tonight. Thought you'd have your hands full elsewhere. Folk never cease to astonish me. Have my seat, honey. Methinks I need another tipple.'

Dane flounced to the bar, leaving Chris to occupy his seat.

'How's Kassi?' Jake asked, smiling unnaturally. It was an expression Chris had never seen on him before.

'Sleeping, I believe. How's Gary?'

'How would I know? I haven't seen him for weeks.'

'Can't have been that memorable for you, last night's fuck in the back of his car.' Chris turned to the convulsing dance floor. 'Didn't know Seaham was such a romantic spot.' He could barely believe what he was saying. This was not what he wanted. These words were not of his choosing. They were flung from the remote whirlpool where his feelings had been relegated.

'What the fuck are you talking about? I was here with Gail. If I say I haven't seen Gary for weeks, then I haven't seen him for weeks.'

'Of course, you would say that.'

'You're right; I would.' Jake laughed spitefully and sipped his drink. 'And I guess, you would say you didn't fuck Kassi tonight, though Dane saw you nip into his house. Good fuck, was it? Is that your radical way of celebrating our anniversary? Guess, I'm not political enough to understand.'

'Dane's a puppet-master.' Chris glared at the bar. 'He's playing with us both.'

'I asked you to stop seeing him.' Jake's anger had slipped and now his eyes filled with tears. He ran his fingers through his hair and gasped at the ceiling. 'I begged and you agreed. You did, Chris. You promised.'

The full realisation of Dane's string-pulling dawned on Chris. From the insinuations about Gary at the Iunniversary party in their first year to the unqualified lie in Mowbray Park, Dane had been gnawing away for years. Chris listened to Jake in silence, his back smarting in shame. The horror of the last few months slowly dawned on him. Until that moment, he had not known how much he had taken for granted, how far he had fallen.

'You remember the morning Cat went away?' Jake asked. The words that had been dammed behind months of frustration now spilled out in furious condemnation. 'I stood outside the room and listened to you and Kassi talking. He said I was "funny-looking" and you laughed. You laughed and said that I had lost something, some quality that you used to love. Truth is, it was you who'd lost something.'

'I told him you were the most beautiful man I'd ever seen,' Chris said quietly, his eyes fixed on the table. 'I told him how much I loved you.'

'And then you laughed, Chris. You fucking laughed. I listened to you say those things and I knew I'd lost you. Cat saw through Kassi. She saw immediately that he was trouble, but I didn't want to spoil your vision. I couldn't stand up to you. I've never been able to stand up to you. It's always been your will, Chris, your utopia, your private party. I've been in your orbit for so long that I don't even know what I think anymore. I've lost myself. You've lost me.'

Jake scowled at the dance floor and wiped his eyes. The strobe lighting cast an icy paleness over his skin, freezing his features forever in that underground cave. He sat cold and motionless. For a moment, Chris felt as though Jake were no longer flesh and blood, but cold white marble, transformed by his sorrow into loveless stone.

'After listening to you and Kassi talk,' Jake went on, cracking the illusion of stone, 'I helped Cat get to the station and I watched them leave. Then I went to the lighthouse where we had exchanged vows – do you remember that time? – and I thought about ending it. I thought about throwing myself into the sea because there was nothing left of me. I'd become a reflection of what you wanted me to be. I didn't even know if I loved you anymore. Your feelings were all I knew. I had none left of my own.

'Instead, I caught a bus to my mum's and watched TV with them. I haven't done that in years; I haven't even seen them in months. But sitting there, not talking, just watching the soaps that I would never have watched with you, I remembered that I'd come from there, that I had an existence outside of yours. That same evening I went for a drink with Dane and Gail, and I realised that I knew people other than your friends, people who aren't literary or political, who aren't always looking for a fight with the system or whatever. People who don't make me feel inferior. Nobody asked why I didn't play the piano anymore. And you know what? That was okay. I didn't have to think. I could just relax.'

'If this is all true, how could you bear to live with me for so long?' Chris asked in the pause. 'How could you have ever loved me?'

'Of course I still love you, Chris. But I wanted things to change, on my terms. Kassi was making me unhappy and I asked you to ditch him. But you were so wrapped up in your fantasy that you wanted him to stay. It was killing me. And, then tonight, on our anniversary, you were fucking him.'

Chris looked down at his hands and opened his lips. He could have said anything. He could have explained about Dane's lies or Kassios's violence. He could have poured out his emotions like music, charming even the stone walls to weep for the love that was passing away. He could have said that he had no vision left, no utopia, only his love. Instead of speaking, his tongue set against his teeth and he stared at his spellbound hands.

'I thought so,' said Jake. 'So, I guess you won't have been back home yet?'

Chris glanced up. 'I couldn't get in.'

'That's because the locks have been changed. Father Cuthbert's there now. He's taken the house back. Had the locksmiths in and the solicitors. He's evicted us. You would have been there, but you were too busy fucking Kassi. After what you did to Cuthbert last time, I guess he had no option. He despises you, that's what he said this afternoon. He cut your dream-tree down, chucked the pieces in the AGA and burnt it. You do make a strong impression on people, Chris.'

'You saw him do this?'

'Saw him?' Jake cried with that same, strange smile. 'I rang the bastard and invited him over. I told him that you were out and wouldn't be home till at least tomorrow. He was there in seconds.' Jake lowered his eyes and turned the glass in his hand. 'Dane told me where you were. Said he watched you undress at the window. Don't try to guilt-trip me, Chris. You're the one who's fucked up.'

Chris dropped his face into his hands. The mirrored walls closed in around him. The cavern felt suffocating under the weight of settling snow.

'Jake?' he asked softly. 'Where are you staying tonight?'

'Somewhere you're not. For the first time in years, I won't be cuddling up to you.'

'I know. I just think we should talk somewhere that's not here.'

'What's wrong with here? We can talk here. I can ask you questions about Kassi. You want to talk? Then tell me, Chris, what did you talk about? What did you laugh about? Did you talk about how funny I look? Did he fuck you good and hard?'

'I'm going to the bar.' Chris stood up and walked towards Cyane.

'I said, did he fuck you good and hard?' Jake shouted over the music.

Chris laid his money on the stone counter and waited for the barmaid to notice him. From the shadows of the dragon's lair, he felt the white eyes in the mirrors boring into his soul.

He returned to find Jake had disappeared. He put the drinks on the table and scoured the emptying room. The hour was late and the brass shutters around the bar were being drawn down. The rhythm still pumped from the speakers that were perched on the stalagmite pillars, but the lights were dimming. He caught sight of Gail leaning against the far end of the bar.

'He's scarpered, hasn't he?' she said as he approached her.

'I just need to know where he's staying tonight.'

'Sorry, mate. Nothing doing.'

'Is he with Dane?'

Gail snorted and looked away.

'I'll buy you something from the bar if you like.' He gestured towards Cyane but the barmaid shook her head. 'Look, I'll pay you to tell me where he is.'

'Heard you were in the money now.' She contemplated him with her enormous brown eyes for some time. 'Take a look at me, Chris. You think you can buy me? Gail, Gail, big fat whale: that's what they call me. That's all I am to you, you and your precious Cat. You think I can be bought?'

'I know you cared about her, Gail.' For the first time he saw a flicker of vulnerability in her dull eyes, a glint of confusion, maybe even tenderness. He realised, despite all their scorn, that Gail's heart had been broken in that first year at college and that she had never been the same since. 'I know you loved Cat, more than she ever guessed. More than any of us ever guessed.'

'You and Cat are no better than the rest of us.' She turned away and watched the last dancers leave the floor. 'You acted like you were all so high and mighty, like you were untouchable. You wouldn't have wiped your shoes on me. I know what you all thought of me.'

'I know you would have paid any price to get Cat back, if you could have. I know you loved her.' Chris leant against the counter but she avoided his gaze. 'Three years ago, you would have sold your soul to be where I am now, begging someone for one last chance to speak to her. You would have done anything before you lost her.'

Gail sighed and rattled the ice in her glass. 'Elliston. Jake's gone back to Elliston tonight. He's staying at his parents.'

'Thank you.' Chris opened his wallet and pressed a clutch of banknotes in her palm. 'Now, treat yourself to all the calories in the bar.'

Chris left Diana's Bar without a backward glance. As he emerged into the heavy snow, a taxi pulled away from the kerb and disappeared into the blizzard. The street was empty. He turned back and saw a scrawny figure sheltering beneath the arched doorway.

'Chrissy, darling,' Dane smiled and pulled the collar of his jacket up against the cold. 'It's all kicking off tonight, isn't it. Jake was really down in the dumps. But I assure you I did my utmost to console him. Still, probably all for the best, isn't it. *Que sera, sera*, as Doris would say.'

'Don't think you can play this game with me,' said Chris, stepping dangerously close to Dane. He grabbed Dane's slender wrist and twisted it until the weasel crumpled in pain to the pavement.

'Sweetness,' Dane whined. 'There's really no need for this scene.'

'We understand each other then.' Chris left him rocking in the shadows of the archway and followed the coastal road to the cemetery. The moon had long since disappeared and now the world was perishing in a gentle apocalypse of white down. The foghorn boomed regularly from the coast, but all else was silent.

Chris entered the graveyard and found shelter beneath the fallen rafters of the ruined chapel. Through the tumbled pillars of the aisle, he watched the snow erase the fields. Somewhere in the broken tower, a barn owl screeched its night-time lay. Chris waited for the clouds to break, for a glimpse of Venus, for a hint of the moon.

The snow stopped falling at sunrise, when the sky over the North Sea blushed cerise and colour returned to the world. Chris rose painfully cold from his vigil and stumbled towards the bus station. He bought a pack of cigarettes from the newsagents, where the shopkeeper reminded him that it was New Year's Day and no buses were operating.

'Still?' Chris looked blankly at the man.

'Still New Year's Day? Yes,' the shopkeeper laughed. 'You've had one hell of night, by the looks of it. First-footing went on a bit, did it?'

Chris flagged down a taxi and directed the driver to Elliston. Light-headed and cold to the bones, he gazed at the landscape and watched the impeccably white fields speed past. Somewhere in the back of his mind, he heard a voice whispering caution. This was the world of Jake's origins, the land before Chris. Here, he was neither invited nor welcome.

Penshaw Monument loomed black against the snow-laden hills. The giant snake of the hillside lay smothered in ice. This was the country where men killed dragons, where good and evil were defined by a sword, where right and wrong was carved in stone. He had found a man once, in a dragon's cave deep within the earth. Now he was travelling to the dragon-slayer's country to fight for that man, armed with nothing but his shame. This is the site of hopeless perseverance, he thought. This is the point when the sun turns and begins its long uphill haul back to crown the heavens.

The taxi driver slowed down at the outskirts of the village and asked which street Chris wanted.

'I don't know,' Chris replied, digging in his pocket for change. 'I'll find my own way from here.'

He stepped out onto the street and felt his boots sink deep into the snow. The pavement was as untouched by footsteps as the road was by tyre marks. He stared at the houses without recognition and walked towards one of the three derelict mining towers that surrounded the town.

'Felpham Avenue', he said, reading a street sign with a flicker of recognition. This was the street of Jake's first home, the house where he had been born. Chris remembered because it was also the name of the town where William Blake had lived. He had once seen a photograph, the only one from Jake's childhood, in which the dimpled imp with the white streak in his hair had run down this very pavement in his father's slippers. Jake's grin had not changed in twenty years and neither had those blue eyes.

Chris turned a corner and followed an alley towards the rusting pit frame. He remembered this construction from his last visit and knew the street lay somewhere close by, buried beneath the snow. He turned another bend and saw the house where Jake's mother had peered through the window for her husband's return. This was Jake's sanctuary and he was not wanted.

The curtains were open and somebody was moving in the kitchen. Chris stood on the kerb and looked at Jake's mother. Within a blink, she had felt him watching her and glared back defensively. She froze when she recognised him. Dismay passed over her features, dulling the face that so closely resembled Jake's. She put a hand to her mouth and let a plate slip to the kitchen floor. Chris took a deep breath and approached the front door.

It opened the instant he pressed the bell. A large man with ruddy skin and a bulbous nose stood in the doorway, breathing heavily. The original white streak in Jake's father's hair had been lost in the advancing grey. He looked every part the giant that Chris had imagined, squinting pugnaciously at the southern poof on his doorstep. He grumbled something incoherent and frowned.

'Good morning, Mr Edlestone,' Chris said, as politely as he could through his exhaustion. 'I'm a friend of Jake's from university. He left something at the bar last night. I've come to return it.'

Jake's father nodded and held out his palm. Chris reached to shake the great hand, but the man withdrew it.

'No, son,' he growled. 'The thing, whatever it is. Give it me.'

'It's best I give it to him myself. Gail, the girl at the bar last night, made me promise to pass it onto him. She said it's personal.'

The man's face slowly spread into a grin. He nodded again and moved aside to allow Chris into the house.

Jake's mother stood beside the sink, clutching her apron. She smiled weakly but her eyes were afraid. The man staggered back to his armchair and thumbed the direction to Jake's room. Chris walked towards the bedroom door, conscious that the mother's gaze never lifted from him.

Jake's old bedroom was now used as a storeroom for his parents' gardening tools. Only the small bed and a shelf stacked with toy cars and mangy teddy bears remained of his childhood. Chris stepped over a pair of shears and approached the gently breathing body under the duvet. He sat on the edge of the bed and stroked spirals on Jake's shoulders. Jake smiled without waking and murmured Chris's name.

'I love you,' Chris whispered.

'Love you, more,' Jake replied in his sleep.

Jake's straw-coloured hair looked golden in the shaft of midwinter sun. His face was sheltered within the concave of his pillow and his lips twitched with the memory of words.

'*Hey dirla, dirladada, hey dirlada*,' Chris sang quietly, running his fingers through Jake's streak. '*I have only one friend, the river. She goes dirla dirladada.*'

Jake stirred as the first tear fell and splashed on his shoulder. Startled, he opened his eyes and pulled the sheets around his bare chest.

'Chris?' he cried. 'How the fuck did you get in here?'

Chris pressed a finger to his lips and glanced at the door. He listened to the old man rise from the armchair and tread heavily towards the bedroom.

'You alright in there, son?'

'Yeah, Da,' Jake said, still staring at Chris. 'I'm fine.'

'Then watch your fucking language in my house, you hear?'

The footsteps returned to the armchair and Chris relaxed. Jake pulled his clothes on and glared indignantly at Chris.

'What did you say to them?'

'I told them you left something at the bar last night. And you did, you left me. Don't worry, I don't expect a hero's welcome.'

'Good. You won't be disappointed.' He sat beside Chris on the bed and tried to flatten the wayward tufts of his hair. 'I said all there is to say last night. There's nothing else.'

'There is everything else. There's us.' Chris took Jake's hand in his own and pressed it to his lips. 'Do you imagine we have anything without each other? Last night, you'd only pieced together some of the story; you didn't know everything. You didn't know that Dane has been telling me tales about you and Gary. He found me in the park yesterday. He said you'd been shagging Gary in his car. He told me pure lies, with times and places, and I believed him. I shouldn't have, but I did.

'After that, I was in pieces. I wasn't thinking properly. I wasn't thinking at all. When I got to Kassi's – it wasn't what you think.'

Jake slipped his hand away and folded his arms. They could hear movement in the bungalow. Jake's mother was vigorously stirring a teacup, his father was barking at the TV.

'I won't let you go,' Chris said quietly so his voice would not carry through the walls. 'I know I've let you down. I've failed us both. But what we have to overcome is not insurmountable. Moving back here to this house, it's like you've given up. I won't let you accept defeat. I'd rather die than let you accept defeat.'

'You've defeated us already. Besides, I'm not living here for long. Father Cuthbert's asked me to move back to the house.'

Chris mouthed the words he had just heard, repeating them in his head in an effort to grasp their meaning.

'As his lodger,' Jake explained, trying to help Chris understand. 'He says he wants someone there that he can trust. Guess I've proved he can trust me.'

'You've gone over to the enemy?'

'There is no enemy.' Jake turned to the window and looked out at the winter desert beyond. The sound of a police helicopter hummed low over the rooftops. 'You're your own enemy.'

Chris wanted to speak. He considered all the words he could have used in the bar last night, the words he should be using now, but they would not come. There was a strange, previously unseen look in Jake's eye. A change had come over him. It was new, but Chris did not want to encourage it by saying the wrong thing, by saying anything. They sat in silence until a battered car roared down the street and passed the bungalow.

'I want you to go now.'

Chris did not move. He looked at the threadbare toys on the shelf: a faded koala, a towelling frog, a teddy bear that had been stitched back together after countless mishaps. He breathed in the warm, comforting, intimate smells of Jake's bedroom. He had never been so conscious of Jake's body so close to him before.

'I want you to go now,' Jake repeated.

'Tell me, is it hopeless?'

'Yes. No. I don't know. I need time to make sense of everything. I don't know how long. Perhaps I'll call you in a couple of months. Perhaps I won't. I don't know. I want you to leave now.'

Chris picked up his coat and followed Jake into the hallway. In the lounge, his father was still in his armchair, snoring now beneath a newspaper. His mother was nowhere to be seen. Jake pointed to the back door. It would make less noise, he indicated. Chris nodded and left the house. He did not look back at Jake's face. He did not want to remember him that way.

In the back garden, Jake's mother was standing on the lawn in her slippers, dusting the snow from the washing-line. She turned at his approach and glanced behind him at the house.

'Don't come back here no more,' she said quietly, drying her hands on her apron. 'Please, son. Don't. And leave our Jakey alone. He doesn't want to see you again. He's not like you, see. Please, son, listen to me now. Don't come here again.'

'I love him. Though I know you can't understand that. I love him.'

'Please, son,' she said urgently, stepping ankle-deep through the snow. 'Don't come back here.'

Chris opened his mouth to speak, but stopped himself. For an instant he imagined it was Calliope standing before him, head raised and fists planted firmly on her hips in defence of her children, and he understood.

'I promise,' he replied. 'Not here.'

* * *

Chris leaned against the long barrow's wall and gazed at the words he had written in the dust. The shadows, which had been seduced by his voice, retreated into the catacombs as he fell quiet. One by one, the flickering candles grew dim and the burial chamber grew dark.

'I see his face in everything,' he said after some time. 'In the moss on these walls, in the clouds around the moon. Mostly, I see him in Richard. They have the same smile, have you noticed? I sometimes think he's watching me through Richard's eyes, waiting for me to be ready before he calls me back.'

'What happened to Circe?' I asked, lifting Richard into my arms.

'She was meowing outside the house when I went back to get my things. I called Father Cuthbert to arrange a time to pick them up. He'd left everything outside the door in bin bags. Circe sat beside them like a sphinx guarding her hoard. I've given her to Conrad and Anna. They're looking for a house in London. Said they'd take her with them.'

Chris rummaged in his pocket and produced a bag of tea lights. He planted each one between the slates of the wall and lit the wicks with his lighter.

'I come here every day, Cat. Forty-two candles for forty-two full moons. There was a time before Year Zero, but it was measured by the cycle of moons: half, full and quarter. I try to keep that moon-time alive. I have to keep it ticking.'

In his papoose, Richard craned his neck to watch the twinkling lights. I watched and waited for Chris to end his confession.

'Do you remember the full moons?' he asked when all the candles had been lit. 'They say that in convents or covens when the mother priestess has her period, all the other women are pulled into her cycle. I suppose that's sort of what happened with us. We celebrated every full moon religiously and we were all pulled in: you, me, Jake, Day, Conrad, Anna. We measured time by the moon. Now we've dispersed, we each measure time in different ways. The rhythms have changed. I want to keep this way alive, measuring the cycle, each half, full and quarter.'

Chris lit a cigarette. He leaned against the wall and closed his eyes, breathing smoke through his teeth. I leaned forward to read the words he had scrawled in the dust, but a shadow fell across the entrance, eclipsing the fading light of the sun.

'Merry meet, sister,' a voice echoed through the chamber. 'You been hibernating here all the winter? Don't you know it's spring already?'

Suede climbed between the stones of the entrance, passing the haunted catacombs without a glance. She opened her arms wide in greeting. I hugged her and kissed her cheek, comforted by the warm human contact. Amber smiled from her papoose and pointed at Richard.

'Who's the guy?' She peered down her nose at Chris.

'This is the one I told you about. Suede, this is Chris.'

'This, the Knight of Swords?' She laughed and leaned close to his face. 'Smells of the grave, looks like death.'

'You'll find him acceptable, I'm sure.'

'We'll see,' she mused. 'Amber's hungry and I need a pint. Let's head down to the Dragon. I haven't had a slash since Southampton.'

Chris seemed exhausted after his monologue. Tamely, he followed Suede into the late afternoon light. Before I left, I glanced at the writing in the dust. The earth was scratched with Jake's name, etched repeatedly in one continuous spiral, without beginning and without end. I turned my back on the chamber and pursued Chris through the stone teeth of the entrance.

'I've been thinking about you, mister,' Suede announced to Chris, as they walked beside the blossoming blackthorn trees.

'Don't flatter me,' he said dryly. 'We've never met before.'

'But I have encountered you before, through Cat. She talks about you a great deal. And she worries about you. I read your cards.'

I followed them through the kissing gate and listened to their voices blend with the song of the trickling river. Chris asked if Suede's reading had given her nightmares.

'Now, you don't go flattering yourself,' she laughed. 'There's enough in my own past to give me nightmares without taking on your monsters. I said I'd been thinking of you, not dreaming about you. I remember you were surrounded by wolves, all of them waiting for your fall. The only route lay to the underworld. The cards were packed so tightly. I couldn't see a way out. There was no way out.'

'Well, that does fill me with comfort.'

'Patience, mister. Listen, there were no gaps between the cards: they were numbered against you like a line of infantry. Then I thought, perhaps you could turn these wolves against each other. Perhaps you could set the antagonists together. Like two negatives cancel each other out, don't they?'

'How?'

'Cat says you see things. She says that you project your emotions into the ether and they return as things, phantoms, ghosts, hallucinations.'

'Oh, yes. I keep forgetting that Cat's a part-time psychologist.' He glanced over his shoulder and frowned inquisitively at me.

'No, dick-for-brains, she's far wiser than that. She's a goddess. And she's seen your ghosts too. All that shit you've got following you, I can't think why she bothers with you. Then again, I've never understood alliances that bridge the gender trenches. I tell you, I don't know what I would have done if Amber were born with that useless piece of flesh that your kind are so proud of.' Suede laughed and laid a reassuring hand on Chris's shoulder. 'Just messing. Anyhow, have you tried rearranging your wolves, bringing them into the same plane and turning them against each other? Maybe then the cards will shift, a gap will open. You could make a new path through the infantry. Depends how powerful your will is.'

'I don't know.' He gazed at the crest of Silbury in the distance. 'Maybe I deserve my ghosts.'

We halted at the road and waited for the cars to pass. Richard reached out his hand and slapped Amber's face. She returned the insult and soon they were scratching and howling at each other.

'See,' said Suede. 'The eternal war. It's innate.'

I took Chris's arm in my own and walked him across the road. High above the hill, the skylark's song ended abruptly as the bird plunged down to the shelter of trees, waiting for the screaming infants to pass. The sun dipped beyond the sanctuary stones. It threw giant shadows over the furrowed fields. Chris pressed my hand absently between his fingers and glanced back at the mouth of the burial chamber. His look lingered for some time.

XIII
The Fall of Troy

Day woke me early in the morning of the first of May, when the sky was still dark and the blackbirds were just beginning to sing in the oak trees. Richard smiled when I lifted him from the cot and told him what day it was.

'Bel-tane,' he repeated and laughed.

Maggie and Suede sat hunched at the kitchen table, drinking black coffee and holding their heads. Amber roared with delight when she saw Richard and flapped her hands expectantly.

'Traitor,' Suede muttered, scowling at the wilful child.

'Me or Amber?' I asked, pouring myself a mug of sugary coffee.

'Both of you. How could you do it, Cat? On a sacred day like today. You're betraying the sisterhood, girl. You've gone over to the dark side.'

'Well, you know what they say,' said Maggie, smiling through her hangover. 'Marriage is a profession. You're unemployed without it.'

'Yeah, no different from prostitution,' Suede shouted and thumped the table. 'Who in their right mind says that bullshit?'

'It's only a saying, pumpkin. I didn't mean anything by it.'

'Hey,' I said, massaging Suede's neck. 'No one's getting married. It's a hand-fasting, that's all. It lasts a year and a day, or so long as our love shall last. It's a commitment. It most definitely is not a marriage.'

'Listen, kiddo,' Suede whispered into Amber's ear. 'You ignore your auntie Cat today. She's sold out to patriarchy.'

'Patri-chy,' Amber repeated, slashing the air with her plastic fork.

Chris entered the kitchen wearing a blanket over his shoulders. He lowered himself onto a stool, graceful as an ageing Caesar.

'That was, undoubtedly, the last hen party I shall ever attend,' he said to the room at large. 'You killed me last night, Suede. I am undone.'

'If only,' she smirked. 'How's the groom this morning?'

'He's alive and well, thank you for asking,' Cat interrupted. 'I warned him about your homebrew last night. He didn't touch a drop.'

'Then I'm out of schemes,' said Suede, hanging her head. 'Guess there's nothing left but to wish you both all the best in hand-fasted life. Fucking sell-out.'

* * *

Day and I walked together up the avenue of stones as the sun rose above the cusp of the henge. Chris stood at the portal stones with

Richard in his arms. Suede and Maggie knelt in the damp grass beside the ring stone.

'I did something really stupid last night,' I admitted as we entered the field. Day raised his eyebrows. 'When I was pissed, I rang Jake.'

'Oh dear,' Day whispered. He glanced ahead at Chris.

'I asked him to come to the hand-fasting today. I said we all missed him, especially Chris. I said Chris mourns for him every day.'

'Oh dear.'

'He said, he didn't think it was appropriate to come today, but that he missed Chris and would ring him soon. He said he'll ask Chris to visit him in Sunderland.'

'There,' Day nodded sagely. 'It could have been worse,'

We entered the stone circle and walked towards the ring stone. I do not remember much of the ritual. The litany I had composed over the spring months and the words I learned by heart have shifted over time, ripening full, growing refined in the intervening years. What stays with me is the sun on Day's face as he shyly said his words, his golden hair blowing across his eyes. I believed Chris when he said that the last thing you see before you die is the face of the one you loved most in your life. Sometimes at night, when I listen to Day's quiet breathing, I turn the light on to watch him sleep and I remember how he looked on that May Day amid the Avebury stones. It comes back to me like lightning, his green eyes glistening with so much love, his lips trembling with the gentle magic of his words.

I know it was something that Chris was never able to do, to stand amongst friends in an open space and declare his commitment to Jake. Their hand-fasting was a secret ritual, whispered in the shadow of an unlit lighthouse, the sea raging beneath the harbour wall. Their vows were made in winter with only the mocking seagulls to hear. Mine were made in a warmer season, with the sunlight blinking through the trees on Day's face. And then I turn off the lamp, his smiling face still shining in my mind. It is the last thing I see before I fall asleep.

I remember Chris was leaning against the portal stone with Richard in his arms. He kissed Richard's hair and looked sorrowfully at me. We smiled at each other and winked, but the sadness remained in his dark eyes.

After the ritual, Suede strummed a Scandinavian air on her guitar and Richard rattled the tambourine that Chris had bought him for the occasion. We ambled slowly back to the Black Dragon, just as the travellers were gathering for the Beltane rites. Suede stayed behind to talk to some old comrades in dreadlocks that had fought beside her in some conflict with the Corporation, either the Battle of Newbury or Twyford Rising. I forget which of the ancient woodlands she has defended from the bulldozers. When she joined us in the bar, she was clutching something to her chest.

'Do you accept gifts from strangers, sugar?' she asked me.

'So long as it's given in kindness.'

'It is.' She laid a wooden dragon, the size of a hen's egg, on the counter. 'Minerva carved it from fir-wood for you.'

'Minerva?' I laughed. 'How sweet of the goddess to visit you.'

'Not that Minerva. This one's an Amazon from Greenham Common. We chained ourselves together at the Blue Gate. We were cell-buddies too. Anyhow, she makes dragons. Merry hand-fasting, Cat.'

I lifted the dragon in the morning light and studied the scales and feathers of the creature's body. One talon was curled beneath his breast, covering a wound. The other stretched out and upwards

'What art,' I said, moved by the expression on the beast's crude face. 'Are you absolutely sure it wasn't the goddess?'

Suede shrugged. 'It's a wishing-dragon. You hold it to your lips and make your wish. Minerva swears it'll come true within a day. She sees things: gargoyles in the cemetery, griffins on the cliffs. She says she can hear the feelings of trees and stones. She has a powerful imagination. Not unlike Chris in that sense.'

'Or his mother. Where is this Minerva? I want to thank her.'

'Talking to Chris,' Suede nodded towards the corner table. 'I knew it wouldn't take them long to get acquainted.'

Three female travellers in red batik dresses had gathered around the stone well in the lounge bar. They leaned over the iron grate and laughed like bawdy banshees, their cries echoing down the dark tunnel. A fourth had broken away from the group and was speaking to Chris. I approached but neither she nor Chris noticed me.

'There is a man,' she said quietly, 'a dangerous man lurking behind you, standing just there to your left. Do you see him?'

'No one else sees him,' Chris said, gazing into the curious woman's face. 'I see him every time I look in the mirror. I've tried salt over the shoulder, but he just blinks.'

'And here, your shadow,' she nodded towards the wall. 'The old woman rocking to soothe her conscience. Do they follow you everywhere?'

'Incessantly. But they can't touch me here. Not in the stone circle.'

Minerva knelt beside Chris and stroked his palm. She raised a hand to his cheek and looked sadly into his face.

'The nine circles of Hell ring your eyes,' she said. 'You look at me from two burning coals, yet there is hope in that fire. What is it you desire?'

'A word from the north. Forgiveness.'

'And if you leave the sanctuary of the stone circle, these ghosts of yours, they will torture you?'

'They will.'

Minerva glanced through the window and watched the travellers returning from the Beltane ritual. The morning sun blazed through the coloured glass, painting the floor with a prism of colours.

'Come with me to the long barrow,' she whispered, almost inaudibly. 'Tonight at sunset. They'll come for you in the darkness beyond the stone circle. We'll be waiting for them.'

'We?'

Minerva waved towards her accomplices at the well. 'My sisters and I. We'll bring your shadows together. We'll help you tame them.'

I returned to the bar and ordered another drink. Suede was amused by my anxious fidgeting.

'Relax, sister,' she said, downing her gin. 'Chris is in very capable hands.'

'They look like extras from an am-dram production of Macbeth.'

'They're Dianists, followers of Diana,' Suede explained, resting a reassuring hand on my shoulder. 'They've renounced the love of men for free love with each other. I call them the Four Mythical Lesbians, but I have no idea what they get up to in bed. I told them about Chris this morning. Fear not, Catriona. Your friend will be well looked after.'

The four women moved towards Chris with a grace that was almost a dance. They perched themselves elegantly around the table and listened to Minerva speak. Occasionally, one threw back her head to laugh raucously.

The sunlight travelled gently across the wooden floorboards. In the afternoon, I walked with Day around the stone circle and watched the drifting dandelion seeds disperse over the henge, soft as armies of windblown sprites. We sat beneath the cool shadow of the beech trees and ate Maggie's hand-fasting cake. Day gazed over the fields and whistled between his teeth.

'You're waiting to ask me, aren't you?' he said unexpectedly.

'Ask you what?'

'To go north with Chris. When Jake rings. To keep an eye on him.'

'You never cease to amaze me.' I cupped his chin in my palms. 'He will need someone to look after him. Would you think about it?'

Day sighed and lifted a golden buttercup under my chin.

'One week. Just a week. No longer.'

'And if he stays for two?'

'Ten days, no more,' he compromised. 'Then I'm coming home.'

We clinked our glasses of Suede's homemade mead and lay within the dappled shade of the trees. The travellers in the circle drummed a

May-dance on tambours and bodhráns. A woman in green stretched across a fallen stone and sang a Gaelic air. The wind from the south-west brushed over our faces as we listened to her voice, full of yearning and desire. I closed my eyes and imagined myself on a beach, making gardens in the sand with pebbles and seaweed. The rhythm of the drums pulsed through my body, rallying a war-dance in my blood. I felt Day's warm breath as he leaned near and whispered a vision close to my ear. The wind is on the sea, he said, stroking my brow. The sails of a thousand ships are lifting in the breeze. The shore is twinkling with the lights of the fires, more fires than there are stars in the sky. We've waited through the long winter months, the hardest winter these islands have ever seen. And now the south-west wind has arrived to bless our voyage. The waiting is over.

The soft hum of Day's voice carried me off to an evening coast. I wandered among the naked soldiers crouching beside their fires. The drums echoed across the purple waves, drowning the sighs of the sirens. I stroked the muscled backs and glistening skins of the men, passing silently among them as stealthy as a goddess. I felt the breeze, tender as Day's words, breathe life into the sails of the creaking ships. Time to cast off, he whispered.

It was dark when I opened my eyes, but the travellers' drums still beat within my blood. The figures were dancing around the inner stone circle, their wild silhouettes flickered through the flames of a bonfire. The woman in green lay silently across the fallen stone, her eyes shining in the light. Day snored quietly beside me, an empty bottle of Suede's homebrew nestling between his knees.

'Sleeping Beauty awakes,' a voice said above me. I stared into the branches of the beech and saw Chris straddling the lowest bough. Richard waved from the papoose around his chest.

'Chris, is that you?' I asked. 'I thought maybe it was a tree-goblin.'

'You were expecting one, perhaps?' he laughed. 'It's almost midnight. We've only just got back.'

I pushed myself up from the damp grass. The wind was blowing freely from the south-west now. It tasted of salt and the Atlantic.

'Got back from where?'

'The long barrow. Minerva and her sisters took me over there.'

'Tell me that you didn't take Richard.'

'He wouldn't have missed it for the world. I think he's learned a useful thing or two.'

Chris swung down from the branches and I took the child from him. We paused uncertainly when the barn owl in the church tower began to hoot.

'What happened at the barrow?' I asked. 'Has it ended?'

'No, Cat. It's just beginning. I leave for Sunderland in the morning. Jake called tonight. He said he's ready to see me.'

He nodded goodbye and walked across the fire-lit field towards the Black Dragon. The wind tousled his hair affectionately and drove him towards the glowing windows of the pub. At the turn-sty, he pointed at a bright star that burned brightly over the henge.

'Venus,' he called back, smiling like a child. 'You see it?'

I waved and watched him enter the pub. Above him, the sign of the great black dragon lifted in the breeze and swung as the door closed. The rhythm of the bodhráns beat within the earth, echoing through the empty mines that Proserpine had left behind.

* * *

The south-west wind swept thin clouds from the Celtic Sea overnight, screening the morning sun with a pink mist. I woke to the sound of Day packing his rucksack, rummaging for socks in the washing basket.

'Middle shelf on the left,' I directed. 'Don't take any of my knickers.'

Day laughed and stuffed the socks in his bag. He said the taxi was coming in ten minutes to take him and Chris to the station at Swindon.

'Think Chris is secretly pleased I'm going with him,' Day mused. 'He seemed to know before I even told him.'

As though waiting for this mention of his name, Chris nudged the door open and sat on the bed. He smiled in a way I had almost forgotten.

'I've come for my goodbye kiss,' he said, 'and I'm not leaving without it.'

'Here's something a little more to your taste.' I reached for Minerva's wooden dragon on the bedside table. 'Let's hope it brings you some luck.'

Chris accepted the dragon and stole his kiss.

'Look after the little prince while we're gone,' he said looking over Richard's cot. 'And open any post for me. I'm expecting something this week. We'll be staying at Conrad's, that's if Anna doesn't kick us out.'

I stood on the doorstep in my dressing gown and waved as the taxi took them away. The wind chased the morning clouds to the east and soon the field of stones was bathed in a hazy light.

Suede joined me for breakfast in the courtyard of the Black Dragon. She dropped the mail on the table and slouched despondently on the bench. Richard and Amber glared at each other, sensing another parting.

'We'll be off tomorrow, sister,' she declared without ceremony. I nodded and accepted the envelopes. I had been expecting this announcement for days; it came as no surprise. 'See, I feel like I'm sprouting roots in this place. That's not something I want.'

'Where to next?' I asked, opening an official letter addressed to Chris.

'Gothenburg.' She gave a brief itinerary of her journey north without explaining why she had to go to Gothenburg. I flicked through the documents in my hands.

'The sly, scheming little wretch,' I said, interrupting Suede. I reread the sentences in the letter that made the least sense.

'What's that, sugar?'

'Chris. He's bought a house. Two houses, in fact.'

'Who has done what?' Suede grabbed the paper from my hand.

'Chris. A vicarage – a fucking vicarage. And a tenant's cottage.'

'Balwick,' Suede muttered, reading the name of the village.

'A vicarage,' I repeated, 'of all things.'

'Fucking *jäkel*,' said Suede, slipping into vulgar Swedish as no other language would suffice. '*Borgerlig svin*. Fucking *skitstövel*. Fucking capitalist plutocrat. You know plutocrat, Cat?'

'Yes, Suede. It's also an English word.'

'And you've seen the price? How can he afford this?'

'His inheritance. The legacy he said he wouldn't touch.'

We sat in silence and sipped our coffee, though it now tasted bitter. I glared at the photograph of the oast-house and wondered why he had kept it secret. Guilt, I thought. He's ashamed of leaving us behind.

'Such dark thoughts,' said a voice that startled me. Gracefully, Minerva entered the courtyard and sat on the bench beside me. Without asking, she picked up my half-eaten toast and chewed on it. 'So much resentment in the air. I wonder, should I leave?'

'How did it go at the long barrow,' asked Suede, 'with the baron?'

'The baron?' Minerva looked blankly at her friend.

'The lord of the manor. *Herre magnat*. Chris.'

Minerva closed her eyes. 'They came, when summoned, his ghosts.'

'Did you tame them?' I asked.

'We cast a circle on the hill and guarded the four quarters. Chris held the child in the centre, keeping him close. Don't fret, your son was quite safe. At sunset, the shadows crept around us. Chris called them, his priest and his Old Woman, his guilt and his vengeance. And, yes, they came.'

'Did you tame them?' I asked again.

'Chris willed them together into the same plane. They resisted, of course. There was a fight, flames, defiance. But he tied them together into one form.'

'He put them to rest? And they're gone?'

'No, my friend,' Minerva smiled, playfully swinging the toast in the air. 'No, he brought them into the same plane, two spirits twisting in one shape. It makes them easier to control. He bound them as one and cast them north on the breeze. And that was the last we saw of them.'

'Fuck him,' I said, slapping the table. 'He's done it again.'

Richard glared at me over his porridge and shook his head.

'What?' I said, staring back into his blue eyes. 'You know what happened last time he dabbled in this shit. It doesn't end well.'

Richard giggled and drummed the table with his spoon.

* * *

I telephoned Chris at Conrad's house later that week. He said he had seen Jake several times and would tell me everything when he came home.

'Home? Balwick, you mean?' I spoke as casually as I could. 'Yes, I suppose you could call me when you've moved into your new estate. I look forward to hearing all about it.'

'So, the solicitors have written, have they?' he asked excitedly. 'What do you reckon to the house?'

'Houses plural, Chris. Don't forget the cottage next door. I'm sure you'll be blissfully happy there with all your money to keep you company.'

'You didn't think I'd go anywhere without you, did you?'

'I didn't think anything because I wasn't told anything. You expect us to come when you whistle? What are we, your camp followers?'

'Come on, Cat,' he laughed. 'I know you're content to live in the Dragon and wash glasses for the rest of your life, but think about it. We could live in our own community. We can have our own little patch of earth. Richard could grow up in his own castle, in the land he'll inherit.'

'Reaching for the sun again, are we? Was this a vision in the fire?'

'At least consider it, Cat. Don't decide until you've seen the place.'

'Oh, and I suppose you have seen this house already?'

'Of course I have.' He sounded surprised. 'It's where I grew up.'

At first I thought I had misheard him. I ran through the few solid facts I knew about Chris's childhood, the sparse pins on the map of his hidden past. There was Whitby, of course, and there was his father's house in Sussex. Understanding dawned cautiously, a strange sun rising over a stranger landscape. Where Chris grew up: the old oast-house in

Balwick, with iron gates, an old chapel in the garden and a tenant's cottage next door. But why? Why return to the prison of his youth, the house of childhood monsters? Bleak secrets lurked in the dusty corners of the halls, stalking the rooms like the ghouls that still tormented him.

'Why?' I asked. 'How can you bear to be there again?'

'To conquer my father's kingdom. To slay the ogre. It's what I learned at the long barrow. I can't run forever. I have to reclaim the past, change it into something harmless, something benevolent. It will always haunt me if I don't.'

'Chris, you know I've never asked you what happened there.'

'No, Cat, you haven't. Listen, I have to go now. I'm seeing Jake tonight. I'll talk to you later.'

He ended the call abruptly, a habit he inherited from his mother. One day, I thought, he will tell me everything. One day, he will lay the ghosts to rest by speaking to me.

Calliope used to say that the walls of the oast-house absorbed the secrets they witnessed. She said that the floorboards creaked with the words that were chanted in the dead of night, and the bleak deeds that were done. The house breathed the pain it had sheltered. Phantoms lurked in its rafters.

Day called me later that evening to tell me the things that Chris had been withholding. They were both staying with Conrad and Anna, and so he filled in me with news of our old friends.

'They're moving to London soon,' he said. 'Anna's applied for publishing jobs in the city. She hasn't changed, still dominates Conrad. Bit like old times, I suppose, except you're not here.'

When I asked after Chris, Day's voice lowered to a whisper.

'He's different. When we went back to the house on Monday, he was like his old self again. It's like he's been hibernating all winter. Now he's back.'

Day described their visit to our old house as a foray into occupied territory. Father Cuthbert had opened the door to them and scowled from behind his sunglasses.

'If you've come to clean the windows,' he said dismissively, 'I've had my house-boy do that already. Good afternoon to you.'

Chris stopped the door from closing with his boot.

'Hello, Cuthbert,' he grinned. 'Managed to shake the crabs yet?'

The priest removed his sunglasses and smiled thinly. Since their last encounter, Cuthbert had developed something of a nervous tic in his left eye. It twitched periodically as he glared at Chris.

'Oh, I do apologise, I mistook you for a street peddler,' said the priest, folding his arms and leaning against the doorframe. 'So, the prodigal tart returns. Thought we'd seen the last of you, although they do say a dog returns to its vomit. And what can we do for you?'

'As ever, there's nothing you can do for me. I've come for Jake.'

'What a pity you've wasted your time.' Cuthbert replaced his glasses and reached for the door. 'I can tell you that, come hell or high water, Jake never wants to see you again. You really have treated that poor boy abominably. You see, we've had many a heart-to-heart about your catalogue of transgressions. We've become rather close, you know. He is awfully empathetic. Well, the upshot is, you're not welcome here. Now, run along and stop wasting my time.'

Chris checked the closing door with his foot and pushed his way into the hall. Fingering his dog-collar, the priest retreated from the one-time master of the house and backed into the Yellow Room. Day followed uneasily behind. Chris glanced around the old room, which was now lined with brown flocked wallpaper. The carpet had been replaced with an ostentatious Persian-style monstrosity. It looked like a gentleman's club.

'I must warn you, Christopher,' said Cuthbert, his left eye winking erratically. 'I will call the police if you do not leave. This is my property.'

'This was my home,' Chris replied quietly. He seemed to grow in stature, drawing strength from the house he loved. The fire crackled in the hearth as it had on that December morning he was last here. The same mirror still hung on the wall and the same yellow curtains lifted in the breeze.

'Perhaps I should make some tea,' said Cuthbert, completely at a loss.

'This wasn't here before.' Chris took a wooden crucifix from the mantelpiece and examined it. Unimpressed, he casually dropped it into the fire. Cuthbert gasped and shoved Chris aside to rescue for his idol. Several times he almost reached it, but he balked at touching the flames.

'How dare you?' the priest cried, giving up his wooden god.

'Oh, I do dare, Cuthbert.' Chris glanced through the window to the hole where the dream-tree used to stand. The pots and window boxes had been cleared away. Now a black BMW dominated the small back yard.

'I once planted a tree in that garden, a tree of dreams. Wherever I lived, in whichever part of the country, I would plant that tree and make the same wish. I didn't know who it would be, what his name was or what he'd look like, but I knew he'd come. It was the only wish I ever made. And, you know, he did come. Eventually. Three years ago, when the moon was full and the snow was falling, he came.

'You will never know how that feels, Cuthbert. You will never see your own face reflected in the eyes of one you love. You will never listen to his breathing as he sleeps, while the wind-chimes ring in the silent night. You, who lie beside your resentful wife, hating her because you don't desire her. You, who finger adolescent boys in the broken toilets behind Mowbray Park. How could you possibly know how it feels?'

Chris crouched beside the fire and continued in a quieter tone. 'There is something between me and Jake that you will never fathom. It's more real than your god, Cuthbert, more alive than that piece of wood in the fire. Even though you burned the dream-tree, even though you breathe poison in Jake's ear, we will always have it. We could take on your whole army of saints and angels, even your god himself, and leave them broken in the morning mist. I dare. I dare to fight for this one most important thing.'

The priest rose from his chair and fiddled with his rosary.

'As God is my witness,' he said, clutching the beads to his chest. 'Jake will never have you back.'

Chris smiled and stared at his reflection in the mirror, his eyes glistening in the firelight. 'Swear it, Cuthbert. Swear it on your holy book.'

'May God strike me down,' the priest said, reaching for a Bible on the bookshelf, 'if Jake still loves you.'

'So be it,' said Chris. He turned to Cuthbert and raised his hand, stretching his first and fourth fingers into the Devil's salute, centimetres from the priest's eyes. Cuthbert retreated towards the door, clutching his Bible. Chris stood motionless, his fingers spread in the space between their faces.

'Get out of my house, Christopher. Get out now.'

Chris smirked and reached inside his coat pocket for the wishing-dragon.

'A little something for you, Cuthbert,' he said, laying the creature on the mantelpiece. 'Think of it as a farewell gift.'

Day followed Chris out of the room with one last glance at Cuthbert's pale face. The priest knelt beside the fire and ineffectually attempted to retrieve the charred body of his saviour from the flames.

Chris opened the front door and stopped when saw the familiar figure standing on the sun-baked pavement. Jake smiled broadly, his dimples creasing in uninhibited delight.

'You came,' Jake said simply. He was wearing a suit and carrying a leather brief case. The sun glittered on the broken glass that lined the garden walls, painting his face with light as from the reflection of a sunlit pool. Chris stepped towards him and opened his arms in admiration.

'Look at you, all dressed up,' he said. 'Could you be any more handsome?'

'Got a job working at the university,' Jake said with self-importance. 'In the admin office. Pays the rent.'

Their eyes met and were held in a moment of uncertainty. Chris opened his mouth and then closed it, lapsing into an embarrassed smile.

'I don't know what to say,' said Jake. He broke into a wide grin and pulled Chris to his chest.

'I missed you,' Chris whispered. 'I've missed you every day.'

Day stood on the doorstep and glanced uncomfortably down the street as they embraced. The curtains of the neighbourhood twitched. Jake pulled away.

'I would ask you inside, but –'

'We know, it would be difficult. We've seen Cuthbert.'

'Come with me,' Jake said, suddenly inspired and pulling Chris by the hand. 'We'll go to the lighthouse. The tide's in, but we can walk along the harbour wall.'

Jake led Chris away down the deserted street. The curtains stopped shifting, but the shadowy figures of suburban espionage could still be observed lurking behind the nets.

Day meandered through the littered back alleys towards Conrad's house. The seagulls lifted on currents of warm air, circling the city with sated stomachs and irascible cries. The Bank Holiday had brought noisy children to the coast and now the promenades were strewn with melted ice-creams and the curling crusts of half-eaten sandwiches. The rusting crown of the gas-works dominated the beach like a seaside citadel and out at sea a fleet of trawlers loitered on the horizon, basking in the glorious blue haze.

Day walked up to Conrad's house and rang the doorbell. He listened to Anna's purposeful steps echo down the stairs before she seized the handle.

'Day,' she cried, commandeering him into the cool hallway. 'I need your judgement on a job application. The covering letter is outstanding, but I do want your honest approval. Obviously, they've already invited me for an interview, but I do respect your opinion.'

She thrust the manuscript into his hands and drove him up the stairs. Conrad was standing at the sink, his hands sunk in a soapy wok. He grinned at Day's docile submission to Anna's will and dried his hands. Anna kissed his cheek and explained that she must buy a new suit for her interview at the publishing house.

'There's an adorable little black number in the market, complete with tie and cufflinks. It's so post-fem. I'll see you boys later. Behave yourselves.'

'She'll be shopping for hours,' Conrad said as the front door slammed. He opened the window to the balcony and breathed in the sea breeze. 'Fancy a beer?'

In the liberty that came with Anna's absence, they climbed through the window and dangled their legs over the edge of the porch. Day pulled the ring of his can and sprayed the dry street below with a stream of froth. The seagulls cried in disgust and fled from the roof. They flew towards the towering iron arch of Wearmouth Bridge in the distance.

'I suppose Anna will get the job in London,' Day said, sipping from his can.

'Undoubtedly she will,' Conrad nodded. 'She's already found a flat in Notting Hill. Nowhere else is quite right, she says.'

'Well, blatantly.'

'They even deliver organic veg. Almost daily.'

'Almost? Goodness, the problems of the First World.'

They sat in the afternoon sun and watched the trawlers creep past the harbour. The tower blocks cast their long shadows towards the shore, laying dark paths to the horizon. As the church bells chimed eight, Day pointed toward the first star of the evening, shining above the distant monument at Penshaw.

'Chris would know which one that is,' he said, but Conrad was not listening. He had turned towards the city and lifted his hand for silence.

'Sirens,' he said. 'Coming this way.'

They listened to the rising scream of fire engines racing urgently through the streets. Conrad pointed as the red trucks flashed between the shops, heading towards the cemetery. A pillar of black smoke rose from the graveside houses, leaning westward with the evening breeze.

Conrad and Day glanced at each other and climbed through the pile of empty cans to the window. As the sirens passed, Anna exploded into the apartment, flushed with excitement at the news she carried.

'Boys, boys.' She jettisoned her bags of new clothes onto the sofa. 'The house, Chris's old house, it's on fire. You can see the smoke from the city centre. Come and see.'

They followed her rapid steps through the evening streets, tasting ash in the air as the fallout drifted in the breeze. They heard the roar of the fire from the cemetery as Anna scuttled ahead through the graves. Turning into the old street, the windows of every house flickered with red flames, reflecting the fury of the blaze. A crowd had gathered behind the police barriers. There were whispered rumours about the priest's wife. They said she had lost her mind.

Anna caught sight of Chris and Jake leaning across the barricades. Chris turned when he heard Anna calling and waved over at us. The firelight glinted in his eyes. Clouds of black smoke rolled through the shattered windows, surging into the evening sky. Day noticed Cuthbert's wife standing beside the neighbour's wall in her dressing gown, her arms folded. A policewoman locked the impassive woman's wrists in a pair of handcuffs and led her, unresisting, to a police van. As her head was lowered through the door, she glanced sideways towards Chris and smiled bitterly, knowingly. Chris returned the smile.

'Tell me what happened,' Anna demanded, tapping the back of Chris's head. 'You must know something.'

'Constance found out about Cuthbert's trips to the toilets,' Jake cried excitedly, holding back his tears. 'Somehow she found out. She poured petrol over everything: the curtains, the bed, even Cuthbert himself. He's in a bad way. Really bad. They took him to intensive care. They think he'll survive, but –'

'God willing,' said Chris. 'We should get some food. I'm ravenous.'

'I'm fucking homeless, Chris.' Jake shook his head and ran his fingers through his hair. 'Where am I going to live? I've lost everything.'

'Stay at Conrad's until something else turns up. I promise you, something will turn up. Sooner than you think. They've got a spare room.'

'I'm not sure that's a terribly sensible suggestion,' Anna said a little too quickly. She turned to Conrad. 'What? I'm just saying: I've got the interview and we won't be there much longer. It's not terribly sensible.'

'What is it?' Chris asked her. 'What are you afraid of? What could happen if we're all together in the same house again?'

'Things got awfully confusing before.' She touched Conrad's shoulder and refused to look at Chris. 'It confused all of us. I'm not saying anything contentious, am I?'

'It did,' Conrad muttered, laying a reassuring hand on Anna's arm.

'We behaved like heathens,' she agreed. 'Least said, soonest mended.'

'We are heathens,' Chris laughed. 'Well, some of us are. You sold out, Anna. You bought a radical ideal for the kudos, then you sold out for the unimaginative life. The respectable life.'

'There are worst things than respectability, Chris. The Coven was just a college thing. It was puerile. That was then, and this is now.'

'The promethean society,' Jake muttered, staring at the fire fighters hosing the flames. 'That's what you mean, isn't it, Chris? Your ideal was King's Cross, Kassios, a house in flames, a burnt priest. All very radical. You haven't changed.'

Jake took one last glance at the smouldering house and walked into the crowd. Chris cast a venomous look back at Anna and pursued Jake through the spectators.

The house continued to smoke throughout the night. Day walked beside Anna as they returned to her house, nodding agreeably to her lengthy description of the suit she had bought. Conrad lingered silently behind, turning occasionally towards the dispersing crowd.

'Keep up, darling,' Anna called sharply as she climbed the steps to their house. 'You'll turn into a pillar of salt if you're not careful.'

Day slept fitfully on Conrad's sofa, disturbed by dreams of a city in flames. He was relieved when the first pale strains of dawn crept gingerly over the carpet, ending his nightmares. The church bells had barely tolled six when a resounding clink from the window startled him.

Chris was loitering on the pavement below, his hand poised for another well-aimed coin at the window. Day waved through the curtains and pointed downstairs, indicating he would open the door. He wrapped a fleece around his shoulders and slipped downstairs.

Chris sat on the lowest step, lighting a cigarette within the shelter of his hands. Day crouched beside him and glanced at the lurid clouds over the sea.

'Like my dream,' he muttered, tugging the fleece around his shins. 'A sky on fire.'

'I haven't slept all night either,' said Chris. 'Walked along the beach with Jake for hours, waiting for the sunrise. It takes forever when you wait for it.'

He reached into the pocket of his jacket and produced a handful of crystals. The glass reflected the dawn like a cluster of jewels on his palm. He held them up to Day.

'Jake rescued them from the dream-tree,' he said. 'We went to the lighthouse yesterday afternoon and he gave them to me. Said he's been keeping them on his bedroom windowsill so they would catch the moonlight. He said he often lay awake with the curtains open, watching them shine in the darkness. He's been waiting for me to return all this time.'

'Where is he now?'

'I left him on the beach.' Chris put the crystals in his pocket and frowned at the sunrise. He described how he had followed Jake away from the burning house and down to the shoreline.

'We talked and talked. He said he couldn't forget what I did with Kassi. He accused me of causing the fire. He said I burnt the house down.'

'Did you?'

Chris turned to Day and smiled faintly.

'I did go to the house, on Sunday night, the night before last.'

'On your own?'

Chris nodded and closed his eyes. He spoke quietly of the events of that night as though to a fellow conspirator.

When darkness had fallen, he used his old garage keys to get into Cuthbert's garden and stood beside the coal-shed. Looking up at the lamp-lit glow of Jake's bedroom window, he caught the fleeting glimpse of a pale face. It was a face he hadn't seen in five months, a face that rose like moonfire in his memory. As transient as a shooting star, Jake disappeared. He tugged the curtains and closed the fortress to Chris's secret siege.

Taking a box of matches from his pocket, Chris lit a cigarette and lingered in the shadows beneath the building. The sky was littered with stars, each familiar constellation mapping the heavens with his mother's legends. He knelt on the cool concrete and followed the line of the shifting myths: Cygnus the swan, diving to the underworld; Hercules triumphing over Draco, the dragon writhing beneath his feet. Prompted by this reminder, Chris reached inside his jacket and felt the warm wood of Minerva's gift nesting within the lining. He retrieved the wishing-dragon and held it to his lips.

The leaves rustled softly in the guttering as he breathed his wish into the ears of the wooden monster. A slight breeze circled the yard, a dry voice whispering through the leaves. Chris looked towards the house as the guttering creaked.

'Chrissy, Chrissy,' the leaves spoke. He peered into the shadows and caught a movement in the shades. The shifting darkness seemed to gather and disperse again, as though the air was a breathing fabric that whispered his name.

He struck a match and almost dropped it instantly as the door to the coal-shed creaked open and a body emerged. Her pale skin gleamed in the light. Her unforgiving smile and cold eyes were lit by his flame.

The match flared a final time and died, but Chris recognised the sickly face of Cuthbert's wife from years ago. Constance approached him slowly. Her thin arms looked bone-thin in the starlight. Without a word, she reached her fingers towards Chris and briefly touched the wishing-dragon. With her other hand she took his box of matches. At the back door of the house, she turned to look at him coldly one more time before she disappeared into the unlit passage.

'What was your wish?' Day asked when the story was over. 'What did you whisper to the dragon?'

Chris said nothing and stared at the red sea. Suspended above the water, the rising sun drew water from his eyes. Day shifted uncomfortably and suggested that they move inside the house. Upstairs,

Chris lay on the sofa and dozed until Anna emerged from the bedroom in her suit and talked loudly about her interview.

'Now, you boys will be all right when we've gone, won't you? There's some couscous in the fridge, and don't forget to feed Circe.'

'You're both going?' Chris asked.

Anna nodded tactfully as if to say, you know what Conrad's like; I have to keep an eye on him.

'Pity,' Chris sighed, closing his eyes. 'I intended to rip his clothes off, the minute you left the house.'

Anna froze at the breakfast counter, the milk jug poised over her cup of tea.

'Just kidding.'

Day stood on the doorstep and waved Anna and Conrad off down the street. The sunlight sparkled on the sea. He searched the horizon for ships but the coast was empty. As he turned to enter the house, Jake appeared at the corner of the road.

'Is he inside?' Jake cried, almost running up to him. His face was streaked with tears and he looked ready for a fight. 'For fuck's sake, Day, tell me. Is he inside?'

Before Day could answer, Jake had bounded up the stairs and into the apartment. Day took a deep breath and followed him inside. Chris had risen from the sofa, startled by Jake's frenzied entrance.

'A couple of days,' he said. 'You've been back just a couple of days, and already you've fucked up my life. There's nothing left now, nowhere for me to go. You've fucked it all up as only you can. You're a fucking curse.'

Chris moved towards Jake, reaching for his shoulders.

'Don't touch me. Don't come anywhere near me.' Jake thumped Chris on the chest and pushed him away. 'You're a fucking plague.'

'Love, what is it?' Chris tried to calm him. 'What's happened?'

'You,' he cried, digging inside his pocket for something. 'You happened. You know because it was you. The fire, it was you.'

He waved the charred wishing-dragon close to Chris's face, wielding it like a knife. Chris knocked the creature to the floor and took Jake's hand.

'I found it on the doorstep,' Jake continued. 'It's you, Chris. I know it is. It's because of you and all that shit in your head that this happened. Cuthbert's in hospital – he's burnt beyond recognition. He could die, and it's because of you.'

'I did not set fire to Cuthbert's house,' Chris grabbed Jake's shoulders and held him firmly. 'The dragon is mine. I gave it to him, but I lit no fire.'

'But you come back and then this happens?'

'Listen to me. Constance lit the fire. Constance poured petrol over everything. Constance struck the match.'

'But you come back and then the fire.'

Jake slouched into a chair and held his stomach. Chris laid an arm around his shoulder as Jake wept quietly against his neck. They sat like that for hours. The tears slipped between their faces until the sun had risen high above the rooftops. Eventually, Day boiled the kettle and brought them each a mug of coffee.

'What's happening?' Jake asked, calmly wiping his eyes as though the violent scene had never taken place. 'What's happening to me? In one night, I've lost everything.'

Chris stroked Jake's unkempt hair and stared at the window.

'You haven't lost everything,' Chris whispered. 'Listen, I'm going away for a while. I'm going south, to a house I've bought. It's in the Downs. It's the house where I was born. I'm going back to live there.'

'Where?'

'Follow the morning star until it disappears over the edge of the horizon. The hills are softer there and the sun is warmer. The oast-house is surrounded on all sides by the arms of sleeping giants. If you follow the Downs southward, you come at last to a steep cliff-face rising over the sea. That's where magic happens. That's where dragons fly. From there, when there's no sea fog, you can see the whole world, a new world, stretching across the horizon. On a clear day, you can even touch the sun.'

Jake opened his mouth but said nothing.

'Come with me,' said Chris.

Jake disentangled himself from Chris's arms and moved towards the window. Day could see the houses outside steaming in the afternoon heat. The surface of the city shimmered, intangible as a vision in the fire. Jake laid his palms on the windowsill and hung his head.

'I need time to think,' he said without turning. 'So much has happened. I can't take it in all at once. I've lost so many things. Moving south would mean giving up the rest.'

'It would be a new life, somewhere completely different. This place is full of death.'

'This place is where I was born. I'd be giving up my home for yours. I need time to think. I need somewhere to stay.' He returned to the sofa and sipped his coffee thoughtfully.

'I don't know anyone else in Sunderland,' Jake continued, his tone no longer pitiful, but unexpectedly cold and rational. 'I would need your help, Chris. I need your connections. Who can I stay with?'

'There is no one. Not if you discount Conrad and Anna.'

'Over Anna's dead body.' Jake smiled tamely. 'And, no, that's not a suggestion. There must be somewhere else.'

'Please tell me, you're not thinking of Dane?'

'No,' Jake chewed this over. 'I guess Dane would be a bad idea. Every night would be Tequila night. I'd need a lock on my bedroom door. No, I was actually wondering about Joseph, your ex?'

This time Chris laughed loudly and dismissed the idea as a joke.

'Why not? He offered to help me once,' Jake insisted. 'Don't you remember that disagreement we had over the church concert? He'd do anything to see you again. I don't think he ever got over you, not completely. I can empathise with that.'

'Well, he is human,' Chris smiled. 'But he's also divisive. He'd use any opportunity to cause trouble. You'd be courting disaster.'

'I imagine my rent would be cheap, if he could see you in return.'

'Your rent would be free if you'd come with me.'

'I need time,' Jake said, staring seriously into Chris's eyes. 'I need somewhere to stay, to think about what I want, not just what you want. I won't consider anything without that. I won't.'

'Stalemate,' Chris closed his eyes and sighed. Day watched his fists clench with the dilemma of his next move. 'Okay. I'll call Joseph.'

* * *

Joseph arrived to collect Jake after Evensong in his silver Saab. Jake had no belongings after the fire in Cuthbert's house, no clothes but for the suit he wore on the night it happened. He hugged Chris in the cool evening air and smiled.

'Give me a few weeks, Chris, and I'll come.' He said this as if his mind were already made up. 'Make the house ready for us. By the next full moon, I'll be there.'

'I'll paint a room yellow,' Chris said, opening the car door for Jake to climb inside. 'Complete with a fireplace, mirror and a throne.'

'Don't forget the Green Room too.'

'There'll be a grand piano waiting for you.'

'Don't go getting any crazy ideas.' Jake paused before climbing into the passenger seat. 'Maybe an upright piano.'

Chris closed the door and pressed his hand against the window. Joseph rested his chin upon the roof of the car and gazed like a melancholy bull at Chris.

'I envy you that, Christopher,' he said. 'It is something I always wanted for myself.'

Chris lifted his gaze from Jake's blue eyes and looked at Joseph.

'That emotion, it's written all over your face,' the priest continued, 'and those words. Perhaps the circumstances were simply not right for us. Perhaps it wasn't our time.'

He opened the door and climbed into the driver's seat. Chris stepped back from the kerb and stood beside Day. Joseph unwound the window and invited Chris to visit his vicarage whenever he wanted.

'I do mean it,' he said. 'Whether Jake is at home or not.'

Chris remained on the pavement long after the silver car had disappeared down the coastal road. Day brought two cold cans of lager down from the apartment and the two of them sat on the kerb in the warm evening. Silently, they watched the seafront lights dance reflectively on the waves. Sometimes, when the droning city fell quiet, Day heard the tide draw the pebbles back down the beach. Sometimes, he heard Chris whistle his familiar lullaby between his teeth. The tune sailed away like a memory on the breeze.

XIV
Glaucus

Day returned to Avebury, as he had promised, on the tenth morning of his wanderings. I was sitting in the shade of an immense standing stone while Richard careered in circles around the giant rock, his eyes gleaming beneath a white cloth sun-hat. A cluster of travellers had gathered within the inner circle of the field and were drumming quietly, as they had been on the day that Day left.

The taxi pulled up in the lane beside my stone and Day emerged smiling bashfully in the sunlight. He climbed over the fence and grinned at Richard's progress.

'He's learnt to run,' Day said as the child hurtled towards him.

'Suede would say that's the first thing men learn. But she called last week to say that Amber had started running too, the very same day.'

We lay together in the cool of the sheltering rock and watched Richard pour grass over his own face. The rhythm of the drums pulsed through the warm stone. At midday, we moved to the dark shade of the trees, where the grass was still damp and cold against the skin. Richard cocked his head, listening to the blackbirds in the trees and tried to climb the twisted roots to the trunk.

Day told me about Anna's successful interview at the publishing house in London and of her imminent departure for London. He said that Conrad looked uneasy at the thought of moving to the capital and often spoke wistfully of the hippie life he imagined we led in Avebury. Anna would quickly interrupt with a list of terrible reasons for living in the countryside, and convinced him that it was much more sensible to live in the city. Besides, she laughed, what kind of life would he have without her?

'And what of Jake?' I asked, platting Day's golden hair. 'Is he thinking with his head or with his arse?'

'Difficult to tell,' Day replied. 'He sees Chris every day. They walk up to Penshaw Monument and sit on the edge of the temple, watching the city for hours until the stars come out. Chris tells him stories from his mother's country; Jake rests his head on Chris's lap and joins the constellations up. Sometimes, the planets and the stories match perfectly. Mostly, they don't.'

'But does your tale have a happy ending? Are they back together?'

'Depends on what Jake's thinking at any time. When he looks at his watch, he says he needs more time. When he looks at the stars, he says he's ready to run with Chris to the end of the Downs.'

And Chris, I wondered, was he ready to return? I did not understand how he could consider returning to that house. I remember once in Sunderland, the night before I took the pregnancy test, he led me into the garden and tied a crystal to the dream tree. When I asked what it was for, he linked his arm through mine and smiled.

'It's for you, my lovely,' he said, 'so that, whatever happens tomorrow, whatever colour the test turns, it will all turn out well in the end.'

'The end? Fuck the ending, Chris. What about the here and now?'

He leaned against the dream-tree and turned to the night sky. The clouds were a murky orange, reflecting the glare of the city lights. Not a single star burned through the haze.

'How many crystals are on that tree, Cat?'

'I don't know. Thirty? Forty? What does it matter?'

'There's seventy-seven. I know what each wish is for. I know when I put it there and what I felt at the time. Do you see the lowest one, that piece of glass, the one nearest the ground? That was the first one I made. I was thirteen years old. I'd only just returned to my father's house. He called me into his study and ordered me to take my clothes off. He didn't look up from his papers, just carried on reading and expected me to strip. It was his will. So I did.'

I stared in horror at Chris's face, dreading the revelation that would follow. He kept his eyes turned towards the sky and continued.

'I placed my clothes in a pile beside the heater, folded neatly so he wouldn't complain, and waited for him to finish reading. After an hour or more, he put the letters to one side and took a woollen glove from a drawer. He pulled it tightly over his fingers and stared impassively at me.

'"Christopher, my love," he said. He always spoke kindly, sincerely, impeccably. "It grieves me to think how your mother led you astray. What a joy it is that your good sense and God's grace have combined to see you home safely again. Still, I see the mark of Cain on your skin, my poor lamb. As indelible as if the Devil himself had kissed you with his sin. My son, my own beloved son." And with that, he began to weep.

'He stood up from his desk, drying his eyes with the sleeve of his cassock. Reaching for a clothes brush, a smooth, polished wooden clothes brush that he kept on the mantelpiece, he approached me slowly until he stood centimetres from my face.

'"Christopher," he said, all compassion now. "I know that this may appear somewhat brutal, if not downright unpleasant. But it is

God's will, and in that we must take some comfort. We should be joyful. The Lord makes his face to shine upon our suffering."

'I closed my eyes, Cat, and didn't make a sound. I didn't even breathe. When he had finished, I went to the back door, feeling my way along the corridor in the darkness. In the garden, I stared into the night, comforted by the shadows that concealed my disgusting, hideous body. Shivering, I crept towards a single rose bush, the only life in that barren field, and curled myself under its branches. I didn't cry. I simply waited on that damp earth for the pain to recede.

'Eventually, after the stars had all shifted westwards beyond the spire of the house, the aching passed and in its place I felt a sharp stabbing in my thigh. Between my side and the soil, I found a lump of broken glass, like a hard tumour pressing against my skin. It hadn't cut my thigh, so I did it myself, grazing the flesh with the blunt edge until the blood flowed.

'There was a piece of string hanging from the rose bush, perhaps where the name of the variety had once hung. I tied the string around the glass and watched it swing, reflecting the little light from the house.

'And that was my first wish, Cat. I wished for someone to come, a boy like myself, someone to stroke my aching body while I slept, someone to keep watch until morning. It wasn't a wish for the here and now, for the moment, because I knew that the pain would last for years. It was a wish for the ending, for everything to work out all right when the world closed, regardless of what was happening in that moment. I watched the glass swing like a pendulum on the branch. It counted time as I tied more glass dreams to the tree. I took them with me wherever I went in the country. Seventy-seven crystals later and I'm here and Jake's asleep in the house, and everything's fine. There's a crystal for you, Cat. Not for tomorrow or the day after, but for the ending.'

Chris fell silent and turned towards me. I remember his face smiling benignly in the glow of the streetlamps, his eyes shining with confidence. That's something I remember well, his confidence.

Day shifted beside me in the shade of the trees, disconcerted by my silence.

'Is he ready to go back there,' I asked, 'to his father's house?'

'Well, he's going tomorrow.' Day thoughtfully chewed a blade of grass. 'He's leaving in the morning. He's got a huge white van. Can't imagine what he's taking in it.'

'He can't have bought the house already. Surely it takes months?'

'Apparently the Church wants to rush the sale through. Couldn't wait to wash their hands of it. They've had three vicars and one Diocesan Director living there, all supposedly driven away by flying cutlery and a disembodied glove. The last vicar's wife said she watched a troll trample the rose bed in the night. Pulled up all her perennials. A visiting deacon said he found garlic cloves stuffed up his exhaust pipe. No one will live there.'

One by one, the travellers ceased their drumming and drifted towards the Black Dragon. I glanced at my watch and sighed. The lunch hour shift was about to begin and I was due behind the bar. Maggie would be waiting with another tedious proverb.

'I hate glasses,' I said, lifting Day's sleepy head from my lap. 'I hate drip-trays and ash-trays, and not knowing the difference between any of the real ales. Most of all I hate the pumps and all those comedians asking me if I've pulled tonight.'

'You wouldn't have to do any of those things again, I suppose. Not if we moved to some old, tumbledown house in the South Downs.'

'Sure, and were driven straight back out by a flock of gargoyles.'

'Chris isn't worried.' Day picked Richard up and ruffled his hair. 'He says the gargoyles are more afraid of him.'

Maggie was waiting for me behind the bar, her fists wedged on her mighty hips. She pursed her lips and rolled her great brown eyes.

'A stitch in time, Cat,' she said.

'Spoils the broth,' I replied. 'I know, Maggs. And a busy bee has no time for sorrow. I'm sorry, but I was making hay while the sun shone.'

Maggie frowned and slung a couple of plucked chickens over her shoulder. She ducked beneath the low kitchen door and entered the cloud of steam that bellowed from pans of boiling potatoes.

'Then perhaps Catriona ought to look for a career in the open air,' her voice echoed through the mist. 'The foxes have holes and the birds have nests, but where is Catriona's lot in life, I ask myself?'

Day leaned against the bar and smiled smugly.

'Prudence is an old ugly maid courted by incapacity,' he quoted.

'Fuck off, William Blake,' I said. 'Okay. I'll speak to Chris when he rings. We'll take a look at the house. I'm not promising anything, mind.'

* * *

I did not hear from Chris for several weeks. The days grew ever longer and warmer as May hastened into June. The fresh south-west wind fell sick and died, and the dandelion seeds hung suspended like daystars in the humid air. I spent the mornings walking down the avenue of stones with Richard and Day, saddened by the sight of the wild-flowers wilting in the heat. I pacified Maggie with my punctuality, arriving for work on time or earlier, while secretly anticipating the phone call from Chris that would summon me to the South Downs.

When it came, the call that I had imagined would promise hope filled me instead with trepidation. Chris's words fell as empty sounds from lifeless lips. He spoke like a ghost, echoing the language of a previous life, a language that now lacked significance.

I told him that, after weeks of deliberation, I had decided to join him in Balwick without delay. In the silence that ensued, I heard him flick a lighter and exhale smoke. I repeated myself and waited for his response.

'Cat?' he said. 'You there?'

'Of course, I'm here. Did you hear what I said?'

'Something, what was that?'

'I said, we're coming to Balwick to join you.'

'There is that,' he said absently. 'Balwick.'

'Chris, are you okay? Is Jake there?'

'Is Jake where? Cat, is that you?'

'Yes, it's me,' I cried, becoming more afraid the less sense he made. 'What is it? Have you taken something? What have you taken?'

'Jake?' His tone changed, the vacancy replaced by an urgency.

'It's me, it's Cat. I'm coming today. I'm coming now. Chris, please don't take anything else.'

It didn't take long to pack our few belongings in one suitcase. Richard sat on the unmade bed and watched my frantic movements with mild curiosity.

'Not Kith,' he stated wisely, shaking his head.

'What do you mean, not Chris?' I snapped. 'It is Chris. Of course it's Chris. We're going to see him again. He's expecting us.'

'Not Kith,' he repeated miserably and turned to look at the skylark that hovered in the sky. I closed the window and took one last view of the stones that had marked the boundary of my sanctuary for the past three seasons. The travellers had moved on to another site, leaving the inner circle deserted. They would return next week, I thought with a flash of regret. When the sun seemed close enough to touch, when it lingered a finger's breadth beneath the evening horizon, they would return. But, by then, I would be gone.

'Taxi's here,' Day said, collecting our suitcase from the bed. 'We'll catch the one o'clock train, but only if the driver breaks the speed limit.'

'He will, or I'll skin him alive.'

Maggie waved from the doorstep, her face shining with relief.

'You'll find a replacement in no time,' I called out through the car window. 'It is summer after all.'

'Who could ever replace you, my dear,' she said, drying a crocodile tear, 'or the little poppet. Now remember, the Black Dragon will always be your home.'

'And there's no place like it. I know, Maggs. Goodbye.'

We managed to catch the one o'clock train from Swindon, to the relief of the taxi-driver who flinched at each of my threats. As the train pulled away from the station, I sat beside the window with Richard on my lap and tried to think calmly. Day smiled reassuringly, which did more to unsettle me than anything. The vales of Wiltshire turned into the manicured landscapes of Berkshire, which became the narrow suburbs of London. After changing trains in the city, we headed for the salty air of the Sussex coast.

* * *

Balwick station was empty when we stepped from the train. The concrete platform steamed in the sultry glare of the sun. The village was circled on all sides by the Downs. I felt entrapped immediately.

Day approached an elderly man who was resting on a bench beneath the cool shade of the Victorian station roof. The man wore a white suit and straw hat, and smoked a thin cigar. His eyes were closed against the blinding sunlight that came refracted through the windows. His lips were pressed tightly together as though hating the unbearable glare.

'You wouldn't happen to know which way the old vicarage is?' Day asked hesitantly, uncertain as to whether the old man could hear him or not.

A grim smile spread across the man's face. He did not open his eyes, but tilted his head backwards until his hat touched the wall. I was astonished by the shape of his monumental nose, the light gleaming down its sharp ridge. He looked like a great white bird of prey, spreading his arms ready to take flight. Day repeated his question.

'Are you taunting me, my son?' the man asked with a soft Irish accent. He opened his small, bead-like eyes and glared at Day. At any moment, I feared this human albatross would soar into the rafters of the old station and swoop down to strike his prey. Day retreated.

'Leave the old bird alone, darling,' I said. 'We'll ask someone else.'

'You are serious?' the man asked, rising to his feet. 'You want to visit the vicarage? Really? That house?'

'Very possibly,' I said, 'although we might just be taunting you.'

'A much safer option,' he said, regaining his composure. 'You wouldn't survive an hour in that house, not if you were in earnest. I apologise for my gruffness. I mistook your naiveté for impudence.'

'Why?' I asked curiously.

The old man breathed smoke through the nostrils of his magnificent beak and smiled thinly.

'Because, my dear, the Devil himself lives in that house.'

'Why would you think that?'

He stepped towards the entrance of the station and removed his hat. Wiping his brow, he blinked into the sunlight and pointed down the high street to the tiled spire of the oast-house

'I was the third to live there in two years. There was a fourth, but he will not speak of what he went through. I should have wondered when none of the parishioners would come to the house. They knew. All of those prattling old bags knew. But they didn't say a word. Not a single word.'

'You're a priest?' I asked.

'Indeed. Father Virgil Donoghue. How do you do?'

He took my hand and bowed slightly.

'What happened at the oast-house? Why did you all leave?'

'Why?' he laughed weakly. 'Now, let me see. Was it the wolf with burning eyes that crept through the hallways at night? Or, maybe, it was the faceless monk who loomed over my bed, grim as the reaper come for my soul? No, my dear. It must have been the carving knife that barely missed my face when it flung itself across the kitchen, slicing the hair from my chinny-chin-chin. That must have been it. Yes, my dear,' he concluded, almost absent-mindedly. 'I was a priest once.'

Richard shifted in my arms and strained to see the spire of the oast-house over the terraces. I indicated to Day that we should leave.

'Go along the road you have to go,' the old man sighed. 'But, my dear, if you take my advice, you'll avoid that place altogether. The wolf is never satisfied and the monk moves ever closer. Go another way than this. Indeed, get the next train out while you can. I've been waiting months for my carriage, months I say. My son keeps saying he'll take me home to Dublin when the summer comes. The summer's here, but where's the train? I'm beginning to lose faith that it will ever turn up.'

He returned unsteadily to his bench and rested his head against the wall. Closing his eyes, he dropped his cigar butt to the floor and laid a weightless white shoe upon it.

'I was a priest once,' he whispered, his Irish accent fading as we left the cool interior of the building.

Stepping out into sun-baked street, we almost collided with a tall, handsome man in a grey suit who was looking anxiously about him. His eyes were as piercing as the old man's had been.

'Excuse me,' he said in the same soft accent we had just been listening to. 'I seem to have lost someone. Man in a white suit, straw hat. I don't suppose you've seen him?'

'Father Donoghue?' I asked. 'He's inside. He said he's waiting for a train. He does seem a little confused.'

'He's just getting on,' the man replied, laying a large hand on my shoulder and moving me aside. 'It will happen to the best of us.'

Day carried the suitcase behind me and glanced back briefly to watch the old man being ushered by his patient son out of the station. I led the way down the high street, between the rows of thatched cottages and Tudor pubs, towards the towering bulk of the old oast-house.

The great ornamental gates to the house were hanging from their hinges. The garden was, as Chris had described, an ugly field of brown grass, overgrown and buzzing with dragonflies and wasps. The windows gaped in the heat, revealing the dark emptiness of the interior. Richard stared in wonder and pointed at the open front door, daring us to enter.

'You go first,' said Day. 'I'll bring up the rear.'

'Most gallant of you,' I replied. I stepped through the sun-dried thistles on the drive and approached the house. Leaning against the wall, like a rusting iron arrow, lay the battered weathervane. It was larger than I had expected it to be: at least a metre in length, perhaps more. The figure of a bowed woman stood at the crossroads of the four compass points. Irresistibly, I touched the face of the rusty figure. The iron flaked at the contact.

'Is that the – implement – that did it?' Day whispered.

I nodded and wiped the red dust onto my jeans. The weathervane shifted on the gravel and swung harmlessly in the sunlight.

The cool darkness of the hallway blinded me as I passed over the threshold. I blinked in the gloomy entrance as the objects of the room gradually came into view. Day loitered apprehensively on the doorstep.

'What can you see?' he asked, holding the suitcase before him as a shield. 'Is he in there?'

'No,' I replied, stepping deeper into the house. The hallway was stacked with cardboard boxes, filled with books and papers. There were neither carpets on the bare floorboards, nor furniture against the stone walls. A few metres ahead of me, the corridor broke into two distinct passageways, seeming to encircle a central room. I approached an oak door which was positioned at the junction of the diverging corridors. I could not ignore the deep gashes scratched into the wood.

'Take Richard,' I said, passing the child into Day's arms.

'Sure. We'd better check he's not in the garden?'

'If you can brave it.' We smiled at each other briefly.

I waited until Day had disappeared into the daylight and his steps had echoed around the side of the house. Turning, I searched the door for a means of entrance. The handle had been removed, probably during the redecorating process, I thought, as the house reeked reassuringly of new paint and turpentine. I fingered the hole where the handle had been and pushed the wood until it yielded.

There have been few moments in my life like this one, where I lost the power to think and doubted my own senses and the solidity of the real world. It was the awe of entering the otherworld, a fairytale hall where the world is stripped of signifiers. It was the terror of approaching the elf-king's court, the burning cavern where Phaethon plummeted. It was the tomb of Icarus, the shrine of promethean fire. These things come to me now, in retrospect, as I try to conjure the experience. But not then. Then, I could not think.

Most of all, I felt the heat. Sunlit colours through stained-glass windows poured like a hot gale against my face. The air was thick with luminous dust as though the room had drowned in syrup, as though a shower of particles had been released from the immeasurably high ceiling and now floated in the ether, suspended without gravity by the magic of dreams.

The walls had been painted a brilliant yellow which reflected the intense sunlight in all directions. It seemed that light emanated from the stone itself. Three mirrors hung in bronze frames against the walls, the largest and most ornate of which rested above a fireplace. The pine floorboards stretched across the great room, drawing me towards the tinted windows that spanned an entire width of the house.

Seated in an old yellow armchair beneath the window, Chris sat sprawled across the arms. A dark brown coat hung loosely over his shoulders. The chair was surrounded with a circle of cigarette ash and butts, and a black antique telephone provided his footstool. He did not open his eyes but breathed smoke through his dry lips and flicked ash to the floor.

'Chris?' I whispered. 'We're here now. Day's outside with Richard. Can you hear me, Chris?'

He shifted slightly at my voice and brought the dead cigarette to his lips. Gradually, painfully, he opened his eyes against the light and peered at my face. His skin was pale and anaemic-looking, as though the last of his blood had set within his eyes. He smiled dreadfully as I approached. Was this, I thought, once the desire of the Durham diocese, the whiskered panther that had prowled into adoring seminars, the same Christopher Mavrocordatos I had known and loved since we shared a bath in our first year?

'Cat?' he asked, distrusting his own eyes. The voice broke thickly as though it had never been used. 'What are you doing here?'

'You called,' I said, kneeling beside the chair and touching his hand. 'You called and I came. Don't you remember?'

'I did?' He stared at the mirror above the fireplace. 'I don't recall.'

He pushed himself up from the chair with difficulty and wrapped his coat around his body. Unsteadily, he stepped towards the fireplace and considered his own ghastly reflection.

'"Of bodies changed to other forms, I tell,"' he muttered, smiling weakly. 'I didn't die, then. Not completely. Can you figure that out?'

'What happened? Didn't Jake come with you in the end?'

'In the end?' Chris glanced expectantly around the room. 'No, in the end, I suppose he didn't. Of course he didn't. He would have come. He was going to come when I signed the papers. I told him I'd build a Yellow Room in the heart of the South Downs. I said I'd build a Green Room too, with a grand piano. I've built it all, that's what I've done.'

Chris walked towards the coloured windows and shielded his eyes from the sunlight. He wiped a pane of blue glass with the sleeve of his coat and shivered.

'Do you know anything about Van Gogh?' he asked, turning towards me. Confused, I shook my head. 'He also built a castle once upon a time, in the South of France. He was waiting for Gauguin to come and live with him. He called it the Yellow House and painted only yellow pictures. Yellow for hope. Day after day, week after week, he waited for the man he loved, painting yellow: yellow sunflowers, citrus chairs and beds and floorboards, lemon wallpaper, canary skies. Always yellow.'

'Did Gauguin come?'

'He did, for two months, but Gauguin hated it. He didn't want to be there. He didn't love Van Gogh. He found the Dutchman too intense. Van Gogh cut off his ear for love and Gauguin fled. The coward never went back to the Yellow House, never returned to that castle of dreams in the South of France. Without yellow, Van Gogh abandoned hope.'

'Is that really what happened?'

'What does that matter?' Chris returned to his chair exhausted and lit another cigarette. For the first time, I spied an empty plastic wrapper next to the telephone, a ten-pound note rolled next to it. Chris followed my gaze.

'Best I could get at such short notice,' he shrugged.

'Not good, Chris.'

'No, probably not.'

'Love, tell me what happened? Where is Jake?'

Chris rested his head against the arm of the chair and sighed. He spoke gently, reluctantly, as though breaking a confidence, his breath barely disturbing the golden air. He spoke so quietly, a lullaby for the sinking sun, his words as soft as the fallow dust that settled on his face.

He had lain beside Jake, he said, in the cool shadow of Penshaw Monument. It was his last night in the city before he returned to Balwick to sign the completion papers for the oast-house. Jake stared at the darkening North Sea, his face relaxed in a contented smile. He looked like his old self again, from the age before Kassios.

'Tell me a story, Chris,' he said. 'Tell me a story about the sea.'

'What shall I tell you about? Lovers or monsters?'

'Both. Are they particularly different?'

Chris gazed thoughtfully at the water beyond the tower blocks. The evening heat had summoned midges from the shallow ponds. They swarmed in dark pillars above the ground. He stroked Jake's white streak with a blade of grass and bent down to kiss his brow.

'Have I ever told the tale of Glaucus and Scylla?'

'Are they a constellation?' Jake asked, lying back to stare at the faint stars. 'Because if they are, you probably have.'

'I don't think so. Glaucus was a lonely fisherman on the coast of the Aegean. He wandered along the secret beaches of Greece before any other settlers had reached those shores, casting nets by day and hauling in vast quantities of fish. At night, he sat beside a driftwood fire, eating his catch and dreaming of a lover to share the oceans with. And so he lived, imprisoned in his loneliness on the empty coast for many years.

'One day in his wanderings he stumbled across the greenest meadow he had ever seen, nestling beside the shore. The meadow had never been trodden by man nor woman nor grazing herds, nor touched by midge or bee. He was the first to approach those elysian fields.

'Spreading out his catch on the grass of that virgin meadow, he was astounded to see the dead fish twitch and blink and flip in the air. His entire catch danced back into the foaming sea and he wondered at their resurrection. Had he been transported into a fairy-tale where such magical things could happen? Or was it some natural enchantment of the meadow that gave immortality to those who touched the grass? Taking a deep breath, he knelt upon the meadow, plucked a fat blade of grass and sucked it.

'The juice tasted strange on his tongue, sweet and not unpleasant. Almost as soon as the liquid passed down his throat, he felt his body twitch and flip as immortality came upon him. He somersaulted down the grass and dived into the sea. As he touched the water, he found his limbs stroked by a thousand sea-nymphs, each welcoming him into their deathless fellowship and dragging him deeper into the brine to cleanse him of his mortal essence.

'When he finally burst through the waves into the sunlight, he found to his horror that his body had been transformed. His legs curved down to form a fish's tail and his spine was ridged with fins. Horrified at his new shape, he dived beneath the waters to wash away the scales. But immortality is a blessing as much as a curse and he soon learned to love his freedom in the depths, and to swim to the ends of the world where the mermaids sing and Leviathan roars.'

'I thought this was a love story?' said Jake, rising in the twilight.

'It is. He hasn't met Scylla yet.'

'Tell me the rest another time. Tell me when you come back. It'll be something else for me to look forward to.'

They walked down the steep slopes of the serpent hill in darkness, the lights of the city twinkling beyond the trees. Above them, the monument loomed in the cloudless sky, a silent deserted pantheon.

'While the gods are away,' Chris muttered to himself and glanced back towards the temple. 'Jake, do you know what night it is tonight?'

'Thursday?'

'That too, but it's our last together until I come back for you.'

'What can you possibly be proposing, Mr Mavrocordatos?'

'Something that neither of us will forget.'

Jake grinned and ran his fingers through his hair. His teeth gleamed white in the darkness. He reached through the night and felt the heat of Chris's chest, his touch lingering over the quickening heartbeat. A breeze rustled the grass. Jake dropped his hand.

'I'm glad we came here tonight,' Jake whispered. 'Joseph says he'd feel uncomfortable if you stayed there with me. Not under his roof, he said.'

Chris halted on the path, his face suddenly fierce in the dusk.

'He said what?'

'It's not such a problem, I guess. It doesn't change tonight. It just means we can't do anything in his house. He's worried what the parishioners would think. Not that there's any way they could know what goes on inside his vicarage, of course.'

'So that's why he did it.' Chris turned back to the monument and kicked loose pebbles on the path. 'That cunning bastard. He said he only wanted to help, Jake. He said I could visit whenever I wanted, but not for you. He wants me there for himself. You're merely the bait. He's coerced us into chastity. He's supervising our abstinence. Cunning bastard.'

'There's always his church,' Jake smiled in the darkness. 'Maybe, if we crept there in the dead of night he wouldn't catch us?'

'You can't trust a priest. It would turn probably him on.'

'Not all priests are your father, love.'

He knelt down in the grass and drew Chris down with him, rocking him gently to the sound of the wind in the grass. He hummed a tune, an old tune of magic properties until Chris grew still and listened.

'See that star over there?' Jake lifted Chris's face toward the bright planet between the trees. 'I think it's telling us to stray from the path. I think we should follow it.'

'What can you be suggesting, Mr Edlestone?'

'Unsupervised fornication,' he replied, stroking the stubble on Chris's cheek.

* * *

Chris hired a removal van to transport his belongings to Balwick the following morning. Anna stood in the street, holding an enraged Circe against her chest and promising to look after the cat until such time as Chris was able to have her back. He nodded and glanced once more down the street, hoping beyond all probability that a muscular figure with a white streak in his hair would appear for a final kiss farewell. Jake said he would be at work, but Chris had believed he would still turn up. Resigning himself to the empty pavement, he told the driver to leave.

They journeyed south all day, as the summer heat cast an illusion of water on the dry land. The cornfields wilted in the blaze of the relentless sun and the cows retreated beneath the cool shelter of trees. Chris basked in the fast air of the open window and closed his eyes.

'My father used to say that the land suffers drought when his god was angry with sinners. See, he never enjoyed the summer.'

The driver nodded thoughtfully, although Chris knew he could not have heard a word.

'He used to say that the days grow longer and the sun gets hotter because his god enjoys chastising human flesh. He said the modern world needs to be cleansed with suffering, upbraided by fire. He was waiting for the apocalypse until his death. He died a disappointed man.'

The driver turned the radio on and ended their conversation with a blast of static. Chris smiled and gazed at the smooth ridge of rolling hills on the horizon. The evening sun flashed between the roadside trees as they passed over the crest of the North Downs and descended into the Weald. Pointing above the low thatched roofs of Balwick, the white tip of the oast-house glinted in the sunset.

The house was just as he remembered it, an ageing beast gasping its final breath in an overgrown field. The weathervane rested against the wall, having been extracted from the heart of his father and returned to the property after the post-mortem examination. As if, thought Chris, there could have been any doubt about the cause of death.

Seated on the doorstep, a tall man in a grey suit dozed in the evening heat. Chris approached the sleeping figure and knelt beside him. The man clutched a briefcase to his chest and rested his head against the wall, breathing deeply. His brows lowered over his eyes, as though troubled by unpleasant dreams. Chris reached a hand towards the man's shoulder and touched it gently.

'Away,' the man cried in a deep Irish accent, opening his startled eyes in terror. Chris backed off as he was bid and smiled an apology.

'Mr Mavrocordatos, I presume?' the man asked, collecting his wits and wiping the sleep from his eyes. 'I must apologise. It's been a very long day and I've been expecting you for some hours. I'm Martin Donoghue of Locke, Stock and Walkworth Solicitors. I just need you to sign these documents, then the house and its grounds are all yours.'

Chris accepted the papers and glanced through the details. Martin Donoghue stretched his legs and scraped his neat black hair flat with a comb.

'It must have been a pleasant change for you,' Chris said, glancing at the attractive young solicitor, 'to sit in the sunshine rather than in a dusty office all afternoon.'

'I have been waiting for four hours, Mr Mavrocordatos,' the Irishman replied coldly. 'Four hours. It has most definitely not been a comfortable experience. I would be grateful if you could sign the papers so we can both get on with our busy lives.'

'Certainly.' Chris handed the signed documents to the frowning solicitor and reached to shake his hand. Martin glared at the gesture.

'Do you know, Mr Mavrocordatos, my father lived in this house for six months,' the solicitor said quietly, refusing to take Chris's hand. 'He was the priest here after your father died. It wrecked his mind. It wrecked his faith. This place is cursed. No one is more relieved to see it off the Church's hands, and out of our lives, than me.'

'It is my home,' Chris replied, looking curiously into Martin's eyes. 'I was born here. Now I've come back. It's no longer cursed.'

'As you wish.' The solicitor folded the letters into his briefcase and turned to leave. 'Good day, Mr Mavrocordatos.'

Chris watched the tall man walk carefully between the thistles on the drive and slip between the iron gates. He listened to the steady footsteps echo down the street and fade into the dusk.

The driver took the boxes from the van and carried them into the dismal hallway. Chris walked around the garden and knelt beside an ancient dog-rose tree. When the driver had been paid and driven away, Chris stepped up to the darkened entrance. In the silent hush of twilight, when all but the last few birds had ended their evensongs, he stepped over the threshold and entered the room that had once been his father's study.

The vast stained-glass window, which had once cast colours over his father's desk, was lit dimly against the sunless sky. The bureau where the priest had brooded over his scriptures, poring over the painful words of his god, now lay empty and disused. Chris approached the leather chair where the old man used to sit with his grey head bowed to the psalms he recited:

"'Have mercy upon me, O God, after thy great goodness: according to the multitude of thy mercies do away with my offences'".

Chris laid a hand upon the chair and closed his eyes. The smell of the pine floor drew long-buried words from the dark places of his mind. Here, among the gin and rosaries, the lamp-lit books and letters written in his father's hard hands, Chris had waited like a statue for the priest to turn.

"'Thou shalt purge me with hyssop, and I shall be clean: thou shalt wash me, and I shall be whiter than snow.'"

There, on the mantelpiece, used to stand a black antique clock, crowned with an iron eagle that stretched his wings above the glass face of frozen time. Chris listened to the seconds of a dispassionate pulse. His father rubbed the bridge of his nose and turned a page.

"'Deliver me from blood-guiltiness, O God, thou that art the God of my health: and my tongue shall sing of thy righteousness.'"

Chris sensed the heat of the electric fire against his bare calves, singeing the adolescent hairs of his young body. The last slim ray of the setting sun dwindled on the wall, flickering before it died. He felt his testicles clench with fear, the sickness yawn in his stomach as the priest uttered the final line of his psalm.

"'Then shalt thou be pleased with the sacrifice of righteousness, with the burnt offerings and oblations: then shall they offer young bullocks upon thine altar.'"

His father closed the book and pressed his palms to his balding head as though he too were in pain. He breathed deeply of the night air, composing himself before removing a black woollen glove from a drawer and pulling it tightly onto his fingers. He turned to his son.

'Christopher, my love. I do hope you are quite decent.'

Despite the heat from the electric bars, Chris shivered. He bit his lip and stared at the cracks between the floorboards.

'What, my darling? No amen tonight? No, "Lord have mercy upon us"? No humility? Nothing? Oh, my lamb, how I weep for you.'

Taking up his weapon, the smooth, polished wooden clothes brush from the mantelpiece, the old man approached Chris slowly and smiled, his nose almost touching his son's ear. Chris lowered his hands to his genitals, covering himself shamefully from the old man's gaze. The priest glanced into Chris's face, searching for the meaning of this unexpected resistance.

'Christopher.' He laid the gloved hand upon his son's neck. 'I would ask the cause of this disobedience, but I fear I won't receive a reply.'

Chris turned away from the priest and looked at the mirror hanging over the fireplace. He caught his own eyes gleaming brightly in the lamplight, and thought how much his straight Greek nose and dark eyebrows resembled Calliope's. He lifted his chin in the light and admired his profile.

'And now, you turn your face from me,' the old man whispered, his features twisting grotesquely, tortured in the reflection. 'Christ is bleeding for your sins, my son, and yet you turn away? You dare to turn away from your father?'

'I do.'

'What was that, my darling? I don't think I quite caught it.'

His father pursed his dry lips and stepped towards Chris until the rough cassock grazed his son's bare skin. With menacing gentleness, the gloved hand stroked Chris's hair.

'I dare,' said Chris. He turned abruptly from his own reflection and went for the wooden brush in his father's grasp. There was a struggle, the priest opened his mouth and made a choking sound as he grappled with both hands, but Chris had taken the instrument. With one quick movement, he struck it against the priest's face. The smack of wood against cheekbone echoed across the room. The priest clutched his face and howled.

'You strike your father?' he cried. The old man bared his teeth and grabbed his son's wrist. Chris pulled himself free and brought the wooden handle crashing again upon his father's neck, cracking the air with the blow. The priest cowered back to the bureau and gasped for breath. He flickered weakly, a fading reel of imagery, a dying myth in the dim lamplight.

'My son,' he said faintly, staring at Chris. 'My darling boy, what drives you to this? What devil possesses you?'

'Jake,' Chris said, casting the clothes brush with all his might at the cringing man. 'His name is Jake.'

The air erupted at the contact, scattering glass across the floorboards. The fragments chimed against the walls and resounded into the endless night.

When silence eventually fell, Chris opened his eyes and peered blindly into the darkness of the empty room. It took time for his eyes to grow accustomed to the gloom, time for the vision to fade. Reaching into his pocket, he found his lighter and lightened the room with the flame. He kindled a fire in the hearth with newspapers and turned towards the window.

He had not imagined the explosion of glass. Three coloured panes had been smashed and the floor twinkled with fragments. He searched the debris for the clothes brush, but found nothing. The brush, the phantom and the fear had all gone. His father was gone. Leaning against the windowsill, Chris looked through the broken frames and surveyed the empty lawn outside. He listened to the night.

The leaves whispered in the garden, seeming to utter his name without a breeze. A chill spread over his skin as though a sigh had entered the window and passed through his body. He stepped back from the broken glass, recoiling from the stench of decaying foliage. He felt her eyes on him, watching from the shadows. When he turned around, he was not prepared for the sight of her crouching beside the hearth.

'Chrissy,' the Old Woman wheezed, her thin tongue licking the locks of her clotted hair. Deep in the creases of her face, Chris saw the black marbles of her eyes blink with delight. She raised a finger towards his chest and cackled.

'Bargain, Chrissy,' she smiled obsequiously. 'Bargain.'

Chris retreated behind the bureau and covered his nose. She watched his every movement, keenly and curiously.

'Old Woman free. Free from old man.' She grinned and nodded towards the shards of the broken window where the clothes brush had been thrown. 'Free from him. Back to where I come from.'

She chewed on a strand of hair and kept her eyes on him. Chris glanced at the open door, a few steps away. The Old Woman watched where his eyes moved, licking the air as though tasting his thoughts. When he sprinted for the door, she flickered momentarily and appeared beside him in an instant. She dug her sharp nails between his ribs and bent her face towards his chest, hungrily lapping his skin. Chris wrenched her away and flung her body against the fireplace. The creature howled in pain and disappeared.

Pressing his hands against his bloody shirt, Chris stepped tentatively towards the fire. He looked around the hearth to the place where she had vanished and peered at the flames. A dry cackling echoed between the rafters of the hall, far above his head.

'Bargain,' she jeered. 'Old Woman return. Where I come from.'

'Not now, not ever,' he shouted, turning to the ceiling. He stared into the deep shadows of the roof that lay untouched by the low blaze of the fire and sought her face among the beams.

'My son,' she called from her hidden perch, imitating the higher range of his father's voice, the words he had heard or had imagined hearing so recently. 'Darling boy, what drives you to this? What devil possesses you?'

He listened in fear, in cold realisation, as the Old Woman's voice changed again. No longer mocking his father, she now turned her art to Chris's voice.

'Jake,' she said, simply and knowingly. 'His name is Jake.'

For an instant, he saw her sitting on a rafter, swinging her legs over the edge of the beam. She cast her hand feebly as though throwing an object at Chris, a parody of his own exorcism, and then she was gone.

Chris stared desperately into the darkness of the ceiling. The stench of rotting leaves had lifted and the whispering trees fell silent. He crouched beside the fire and listened to the house creak with the weight of its own emptiness.

The first blackbirds began to sing before the dawn. When the earliest strain of sunlight glistened through the broken glass, Chris rose from his vigil and went into the hallway. Delving into the cardboard boxes, he returned to the room with two tins of yellow emulsion. He prised the lids open and stirred the paint with a brush. As the last embers in the fireplace flickered and died, Chris lifted the paintbrush to the wall.

'*Hey dirla, dirladada, hey dirlada,*' he sang, covering the stones with brilliant yellow. He tilted his head sideways and admired the colour. Like sunflowers, he thought. Like hope. He dipped his brush in the tin and painted the bright dawn.

XV
Scylla

They say that the path of the full moon leads sleepers to madness if they lie too long in its enchanted wake. They say that the man in the moon, cursed for gathering firewood on the Sabbath, seduces the wandering minds of dreamers away from their bodies with a trail of silver thorns. Sleep in the moonlight and you will stray among the stars. Sleep in the moonlight and your mind will be lost on the Milky Way.

Chris woke the following evening with the full moon in his eyes. Calliope used to sleep with the curtains open on a night such as this, so she could tiptoe to the nearest constellations. Chris said that he had learned the technique from her.

He pushed himself up from the floorboards and stared around the moonlit room. The row of empty paint tins cast long shadows over the floor. Chris reached behind the silver ladder that reached to the rafters and turned on the lights.

The Yellow Room had been completed. Two old chandeliers hung from the ceiling, lighting the bare stage of the scene that would become his court. Here, he thought, nestling beside the fireplace would stand two armchairs for the two new princes of this house. He went to the window and gazed through the broken panes. The barren field of his kingdom stretched towards the remote boundary wall. There, where the heavy dog-rose tree drooped with the weight of summer blooms, he would build a new dream-tree and tie wish-crystals on each branch. This world, he thought, this realm is now ours, mine and Jake's.

The full moon skimmed the tops of the silent oaks. Give me time, Jake had said. I need time to think before I follow you. Give me time, and I will come. Time for the moon-man to follow his own trail of silver thorns back to the face of this sleeper, thought Chris. Time for the constellations to shift westward until Venus dances beyond the Downs. Chris closed his eyes and basked in the fading moonlight.

* * *

They say that Diana bathed each night in a midnight pool, washing the scars of the chase from her immortal skin. They say that Actaeon strayed innocently upon her midnight lake and was mesmerised by the goddess's awesome beauty, her blue-grey eyes shining across the water. Perhaps he had lingered too long in the full moon's wake and his mind had wandered too far along the Milky Way. Perhaps the gods are capricious and raise a wrathful hand when mortals dare to stand on their hind legs and stare into the face of the naked divine.

Beneath the creaking boughs of aged oaks, among the blind slugs and lice of rotting leaves, Actaeon was torn to pieces by his own loyal hounds. But, Chris wondered as he watched the first rosy glow of dawn kiss the eastern clouds, perhaps the hunter had smiled as the moonstruck dogs laid into his flesh. Perhaps he had laughed one last bark of defiance as the goddess raged in his dying eyes. He had seen the gods in their full nakedness and no other had seen such beauty. What matter if he died? He would always be victorious.

Chris locked the front door to the oast-house and took a morning walk around the garden. The dog rose rocked in the morning breeze, her leaves rustling like the dry rags on a witch's tree. The brown grass cowered beneath the early onslaught of another scorching day. Such a summer, such a merciless sun was unknown to him, even this far south. Chris wiped his sweating brow and stole a final glance at his land. The rose tree nodded farewell and fell still, waiting for the prince to return with his lover.

The empty carriage of his northbound train sweltered in the morning sun. Without interest, he watched the flatlands of East Anglia pass by. The fields burned beneath the fiery sky and the smoking towers of power-stations rose like turrets from the plains. He looked for the murmur of a cloud and counted time by the stations of the sun.

Sunderland station sucked in the breeze from the North Sea and chilled it in underground darkness. Chris emerged from the train and shivered in the sudden shade, his shirt clinging uncomfortably cold to his chest. He climbed the stairs to the outside world and was pushed to one side by a crowd of schoolchildren in brown blazers. He pressed his body against the station wall and waited for them to pass.

In the midst of the flashing blazers, he felt a pair of eyes holding his own, a lipless mouth that curled as he waited. He stared into the crowd for her face, but it was gone. A train screamed through the station and sent the litter rustling in circles on the stairs. Above the roar of the rails, he heard – or thought he heard – the dry cackle of a laugh echoing down the tunnel. But the tribe passed, the litter fell silent and he stood alone on the stairwell.

Chris surfaced from the station into the sun-baked street. I remember the stories he used to tell us at night, sipping wine beside the fireplace before Richard was born. I remember watching Phaethon fall through the sky, his chariot blazing with the fire of the sun. Sometimes the chariot singed the earth with its wide sweeping arc; sometimes it shattered at the point of impact, leaving the soil as ash. Such was the heat of the sun-god's fall, such were the streets on this day.

Chris walked through the graveyard beneath the sheltering plane trees. The air hummed with a thousand insects that drifted close to his body for a taste of the moisture on his skin. He passed under the ruined arch of the old chapel and followed the winding path through the graves. Once, when the air was still and the insects hushed, he caught the whisper of a voice shifting through the leaves. He turned to stare into the branches, but saw only the sunlight flashing through the green. The insects lifted from the grass again and the air was filled with their murmurs. The leaves fell silent and Chris walked on towards the northern gate.

Joseph's vicarage was a detached house, removed from the road and concealed behind a military row of upright holly trees. Chris walked over the freshly mowed lawn toward the red brick building. Joseph's head appeared at the window, nodding sadly as he unlocked the door.

'Jake's still at work,' he said, holding the door open for Chris. 'He wasn't expecting you so early in the afternoon, Christopher. Neither of us were, but I am pleased to see you. Very pleased.'

Chris entered the bare hallway and noticed the familiar, all-pervading incense in the air. A crucifix hung above the kitchen door. The lifeless Christ gazed sadly over the austere furnishings of Joseph's house. As if being crucified wasn't bad enough.

'I haven't stepped foot in here for years,' Chris said, walking into the sitting room that still looked as though it had never been lived in. He seated himself on an unforgiving wicker armchair. Joseph perched on the edge of his desk and gazed over the rim of his glasses at Chris's damp shirt.

'It is rather close today,' the priest noticed. 'You can change your clothes, if you're feeling clammy. There are clean shirts in my bedroom.'

'Thank you, Joe, but I'll change into something of Jake's.'

'He may be quite some time. I believe he's seeing some friends later. It's unlikely he'll be home before nine at the earliest, knowing him as I do. He does enjoy his drink rather too much, does our Jake. It makes him forgetful. Which reminds me,' Joseph reached into his desk and passed an envelope to Chris. 'This was delivered to Father Cuthbert's. All your mail is redirected here, of course. It's probably someone who doesn't know you've moved. I suggest you inform them of your new address. It would be less bothersome for everybody.'

'It's from Jackie, my sister,' said Chris, glancing at the content. 'She wants to meet up sometime this week.'

'You're welcome to use my telephone, if you don't take too long. Incidentally, where are you staying tonight?'

'Wouldn't your parishioners be outraged if I stayed here?' Chris glanced at the priest's lips, always parted in dour surprise and drooping at the edges. Joseph stroked the edge of the desk with his ponderous fingers. He thought for some time before replying.

'Christopher, do you remember that holiday in Devon during our first summer together? Do you remember what I said to you?'

'Hardly, it was a lifetime ago. Was that when I walked in on you fucking the local deacon in the kitchen or was that the second holiday?'

'There's no call for vulgarity.' Joseph cleaned the lens of his glasses on his black shirt. 'Do you remember what I said to you?'

'You'll have to remind me, Joe. So many more significant things have happened since that time. It must have slipped my memory.'

'We sat on the cliffs overlooking Hele Bay. It was sunset. You dropped stones over the edge into the high tide. You said that each stone was a year that you would love me, Christopher. Do you recall that conversation?'

'Then it must have been before you fucked the deacon.'

'That is irrelevant,' said Joseph, his voice sharp with irritation. He tried his best to regain composure. 'I gathered a handful of sand and cast it over the edge. You asked why I did it. I said that each grain was a year I would love you in return.'

'I don't remember that at all. You're quite sure it happened?'

'Quite sure.' The priest replaced his glasses and walked to his virtually empty bookcase. He clicked his teeth thoughtfully, removed a Bible from the shelf and flicked through the pages.

'And this Bible, I presume you don't remember this either?'

Chris shook his head and apologised. Joseph lifted a letter from between the pages and handed it to Chris.

'You wrote this to me on the day you left your father's house. I was waiting outside in my car. I had that little Hillman Imp, do you remember? You ran out of the house looking so happy. You had only just turned seventeen. We were both so much younger then. I hadn't even started at theological college. I suppose, in retrospect, we were both unbearably naïve.'

Chris eyed the letter suspiciously. His handwriting was small and cramped within the centre of the page. The words seemed strange, almost unreal, written by a stranger in a far-away age. Still, he did remember the letter.

For Joe,
With all my heart and soul for all you've done and will do.
Yours forever, in the steadfast love of God,
Christopher.

'Do you remember this Bible, Christopher?' Joseph offered the book that Chris had given him. 'It's the only one I ever use. You see, it's all I have left of you.'

Joseph turned to the window and gazed outside. A blackbird scratched at the hardened earth, hopelessly searching for life in the parched lawn. The holly trees gleamed in the sunlight, rustling slightly in the breeze. The priest pressed his palm against the window and took a deep breath.

'You could stay here tonight,' he said so quietly that Chris had to lean forward to hear. 'I appreciate that you may require some quality time with Jake. I'm not entirely insensible to what you have with him. But please understand that it would be difficult for me, very painful considering our past. I would allow you to sleep with him – under my roof – if you could spare me a little consolation.'

'Consolation?'

'A small thing to ask.'

'Consolation is such an equivocal word,' Chris said, frowning at the priest's down-turned face. 'Some might accuse you of bribery.'

'Nothing so crude. I just – I miss being held. I long to be touched.'

'Touched?' Chris laughed. 'So, you'll graciously allow me to sleep with my lover if I submit to a quick fuck with you?'

'Would that be so preposterous?' Joseph asked icily. 'You fucked every other priest in this diocese when we were together. I don't see that you've changed so very much under Jake's influence. He told me of that Greek boy, for one.'

'Joe, when you and I were together, you fucked the odd priest in the diocese. The even ones were mine. What Jake and I have is beyond comparison.'

'I think not, Christopher. Is there any price you wouldn't pay to have him back? Or that I wouldn't pay to be held again? I see no disparity.'

'Have you stooped so low?' Chris rose from the wicker chair. 'Did you actually think this web of yours would work?'

'Please, don't underrate me,' Joseph said, returning the Bible to the shelf. 'I don't doubt your current feelings for Jake. And, in your present state, I don't doubt that your skin crawls at the thought of touching me. But we have both felt such loneliness as would make angels weep. Sometimes I can't bear the thought of another day alone. It was such a small thing to ask of you. Forgive me for raising it.'

'Forget it, Joe.' Chris walked towards the door. 'Conrad has a sofa I can crash on.'

'Wait, please.' Joseph moved hesitantly towards the doorway and then halted. Shaking his head, he turned back to the window and sat at the desk. 'You know how hopeless I am when it comes to expressing myself. It's not something I've ever been encouraged to do – at school or in the Church. If I tried to describe the pain of having you sleep with another man in my house, I would only fail. If I tried to say how lonely it's been all these years without you, you wouldn't listen. No one can really understand the loneliness of another human being, no matter how kind they pretend to be.'

'I'm not a particularly kind man,' Chris said at length, feeling a surge of compassion for the man he once loved. 'But I do understand.'

'You used to be kind to me. We used to be kind to each other.' Joseph pressed his face into the palms of his hands. 'You spoke of sex: I did not. I see now how different you are to that lost boy I picked up from his father's house in my car all those years ago. That Chris would never have been so callous, so crude. He would have known that just to be held for a moment, to be understood and safe in someone's arms, is enough to sustain a person through a lifetime of loneliness.'

'I do know how that feels. It's all I crave of Jake.' Chris leaned against the bookshelf and folded his arms. 'You were his forerunner, you know, Joe. If I hadn't passed through you, I may not have been ready for Jake when he came along.'

'Well, as long as I provided some use for you.'

They shared a brief, sad smile and then the priest hung his head.

'Joe, what can I do?'

'Just some human contact,' Joseph said, glancing up over the rim of his glasses. He pouted with anticipated rejection. 'I knew it would be too much to ask.' He removed his glasses and wiped his tired eyes.

'What are you asking of me?'

'I ask nothing of you.'

'Joe, what do you want?'

'Would it be so very wrong for you to hold me one last time?' he asked quickly, afraid of his own question. 'To go upstairs and be held by you for a short while? Yes, of course, I know. It would be too much.'

'I can hug you down here.'

'The parishioners, the curtains – '

'Of course. The parishioners. And that would be all?'

'It's all I need.'

Chris crossed the hallway and stood at the foot of the stairs.

'I haven't forgotten the way,' he said as he began to climb. Without a word, Joseph followed.

The musty smell of Joseph's den rose to meet Chris as he entered the bedroom. The socks on the chair, the underpants on the floor, the stack of model village magazines on the bedside table: icons from a love that could never have lived.

The priest closed the curtains and unbuttoned his black shirt.

'What do you think you're doing?'

'Such a little thing to ask,' Joseph replied. His arms fell limply at his side and he hung his head. He was a heart-beat away from crying. 'I know it means nothing to you.'

'Just to be held, you said. There was no talk of undressing.'

'Just to be touched, that's all. As you will be held tonight and every night hereafter by the one that you love. All I have is a handful of hoped-for moments to last me into retirement.'

Joseph dropped his shirt and white collar to the floor, and fingered the belt buckle beneath the folds of his stomach. His skin gleamed pale and hairless in the curtained light. He slipped his trousers to the floor and smiled sadly. Standing naked amid his discarded garments, he raised his arms towards his lost lover.

'Christopher,' he whispered softly. 'Please. Just one last time.'

Chris closed his eyes as the priest approached him. He felt the arms close around his body, the jaw press against his shoulder and the wet, downturned lips press against his neck. He remembered the rank odour of that familiar cologne and sweat, the flakes of white skin in that thinning hair. Joseph pushed him firmly to the bed and lowered his weight over him.

'Kiss me,' he said, as his tears dropped onto Chris's eyelids. 'I know you're confused, Christopher. You don't know what you want. Kiss me as you used to. It's okay. Everything is better now.'

Chris clenched his teeth and turned his face away. He listened to the steady rhythm of a clock counting time on the mantelpiece, the hum of an electric fire heating his calves. A thin stream of sunlight broke through the closed curtains and blinded him with colour. Somewhere in the bedroom, the model village magazines flapped in the breeze as though shuffled by light, curious fingers. He felt Joseph's hardness against his thigh, pushing against his jeans.

'Christopher,' Joseph wheezed, reaching between Chris's legs. 'Kiss me like you used to. Do this in remembrance of me.'

Chris felt the iron springs press hard as an altar stone against his spine. Somewhere above the murmuring insects in the garden, somewhere above the rustling leaves of the holly trees, the church bells chimed five. Time for Evensong.

'Open your mouth.' Joseph was panting now. He heaved himself up the bed, pitching his stale-smelling erection towards Chris's face. 'Do it, Christopher. Open your mouth.'

The bed springs creaked as Chris's shoulders were crushed beneath the priest's overweight thighs. His arms were held down by the pressure; he could not have moved if he tried. The curtains rasped in the breeze, whispering memories in the sultry bedroom air. The sentences came of their own volition, instinctively, inevitably, like ants to an injured animal, like Furies to their feast:

Deliver me from blood-guiltiness, O God, thou that art the God of my health: and my tongue shall sing of thy righteousness. Thou shalt open my lips, O Lord: and my mouth shall shew forth thy praise.

They say that Prometheus was chained for eternity to the mountains as a punishment for defying the gods. They say that an eagle tormented him each day, tearing at his flesh and eating his liver. At night, his liver would grow back, only to be torn and eaten again at dawn by the relentless eagle. At sunset, the bird returned to his eyrie and waited for the darkness to lift, for the dawn to reveal the body of his prey. Ixion's wheel turned, the stars shifted ever westward, and Prometheus opened his weary eyes upon yet another sunrise.

Then shalt thou be pleased with the sacrifice of righteousness, with the burnt offerings and oblations: then shall they offer young bullocks upon thine altar.

Chris felt the childhood scars on his forearms twitch and tear. He felt the fabric of skin unravel and the blood seep freely between his hairs. As the first drop unfurled like a petal on the white sheet, he knew that she was crouching in the corner of the room, watching him.

'Chrissy,' the Old Woman said, as though announcing herself.

Joseph held the back of Chris's head and pulled him closer.

'Open your mouth, Christopher,' he said. 'For God's sake, open your mouth.'

Chris only half-heard the priest's words. His eyes shifted towards the withered face of the Old Woman. Beneath her grey tresses, her quick tongue licked the stifling air. She smiled blindly and then stood up, her crooked figure rising behind Joseph's arched spine.

'Bargain, Chrissy,' she said. 'Remember bargain.'

For I acknowledge my faults and my sin is ever before me.

She grinned and clasped her leaf-and-bone fingers around Joseph's throat.

Chris heard the tendons in her wrist creak, the bones grind in her shoulder socket as she flung Joseph across the bedroom in one swift, effortless movement.

'Open wide,' she said, her ghastly eyes glaring at Chris's chest. 'Open wide for Jake-his-name-is-Jake.'

And then she was gone. The last victorious glint of her marble-black eyes faded from view and in her place, standing in the doorway as though summoned by her words, stood Jake.

Chris rose slowly from the bed and blinked uncertainly at the pale face. Jake's mouth was fixed firmly into a tight smile. He did not speak but looked at Chris and then at the naked priest on his knees.

'Damn you, Christopher,' Joseph choked, clutching his neck. 'That really was too rough. You know I don't like it rough.'

Chris made a move towards the doorway. Jake stood for a moment in the thin stream of sunlight, his white streak shining in the cool darkness, as it had done years before in the underground cavern of a dragon's lair. Chris closed his eyes and held the contours of his lover's face in his mind: the smooth line of his jaw and the faint mole on one eyelid. He held the image jealously, although Jake's steps had already echoed down the stairs and out to the front lawn. Only the blackbirds sang in the holly trees as the footsteps faded and the cut grass withered beneath the sun.

* * *

The Yellow Room was in darkness when Chris finished speaking. I watched his shadow walk towards the mantelpiece and hold a lighter against the wick of a black candle. The flame gave little relief to the gloom of the chamber, although it cast a sparse light on his insensible features. He returned to his throne and stared at the hearth.

'Did you go after him?' I asked.

Chris laughed quietly and shook his head.

'Where would he have gone? I looked but there was no where left for him to go.' He drew a cigarette from his coat and lit it. 'Besides, you know Jake. He wouldn't have listened at that moment. I thought he needed time to cool down. He wouldn't have listened, Cat.'

'But, darling, I don't understand how you were tricked by Joseph.' I accepted a cigarette from him and sat on the ledge of the window sill, watching the smoke swirl around the candle flame. 'Wasn't it obvious to you, his little scheme? Why did you go upstairs?'

'I must have loved him once,' Chris said softly, 'in a different incarnation, in another dimension. I pitied him. I understood his loss. It could have been me saying those things.'

'And when he tried to force you – ?'

Chris did not answer immediately. A faint, unnoticed breeze passed through the broken panes. The candle flickered and cast spindly shadows over the walls. Somewhere in the house, in a dark and disused room, the floorboards sighed with the memory of movement. When he did finally speak, he stared at the fireplace as though scrying images in the flames, as though seeing fragments of stories like we used to do.

'I think it's hard to unlearn power,' he said. 'It becomes intrinsic. Joseph once told me a story. He went to a public school, of course. It was on the other side of the Downs; it was the same one my father had been to. It was the type of school you might find in a model village, all the little people standing where they were put in their uniforms, obedient and conformable. In his first year as a junior, he said he was chosen to be the fag of a senior boy, his fag-master. His tasks were menial: warming his master's toilet seat, blacking his shoes, ironing his cricket whites, bringing him tea and lighting his cigars. Whereas the other seniors would beat their fags, often for no reason than a taste their own authority, Joseph's master was mild-tempered. Mostly.

'At the end of his first summer term, Joseph was chosen to be the crucifer in chapel, to carry the processional cross for the end-of-year service. It was a big deal for him, he said. Walking down the aisle, he passed the whole school in rows: the first years at the back, then the second years, the thirds, up to the seniors who sat behind the school masters in the front. Everyone in their place and god in his heaven. When Joseph turned around at the altar, he caught the face of his fag-master beaming with pride. He blushed when his master winked at him.

'After the service, Joseph ran back to the senior dorm. See, it was traditional for fags to receive a tip from their master at the end of term. When he entered the room, his senior was waiting for him. He was holding his cricket whites. There were grass stains on the knees from the match he had played that morning. It should have been clean. He looked up at Joseph and told him to stand at the window. He told him to take his trousers off and wait. It was the only time he beat Joseph, but he did it with such violence that Joseph collapsed. Even when Joseph was on the floor, his master kept going. By the end, they were both crying.

'You could ask why Joseph did as he was told, why he took off his trousers and stood at the window. Why he waited for the inevitable thrashing while the older boy calmly rolled up his sleeves and took off his belt. I asked him why he didn't run away, why he didn't grab something – anything – and throw it at his abuser. He just shrugged. He said he couldn't have done that. It wasn't a consideration. He said the only thing he hoped for was that his senior might be merciful. That's how power works. It programs your options.

'Years later, when he was a senior in his own right, Joseph had his own first-year fag. He said he was patient with his junior, that he never shouted at him, never made him warm his toilet seat or humiliated him in the common room. He said he was lenient towards him too, mostly. Oddly enough, the only time he beat his fag was on the last day of the summer term when his own cricket whites were dirty. He knew that his junior had no time to clean them, as he had had no time to clean his master's all those years before. He said it was a reflex. He said it was instinctive. When it was over, he said he also cried.'

Chris reached down to the hearth and put a book onto the dwindling flames. It was an old book, a battered book with turned down pages that I recognised immediately. The fire leapt at the dry paper and illuminated his tired face from below. He took another book from the pile beside the hearth and then another, and fed them to the fire.

'You remember at primary school, when the teacher would ask us all to line up,' he continued. 'In age order or height order or whatever, you had to jostle about and get into some kind of line. And everybody just did it. The rules were arbitrary, but they were set by the teacher and everyone just accepted that this was the way things were. One way or another, we spend our whole lives being conditioned into accepting some line or order, some position of domination or subjection. It's hard to unlearn such hierarchy, to undo such control. It's implicit.'

Chris ran a finger over his reflection in the mirror, outlining his face. Even in the firelight, I could see the trace he left in the dust.

'I used to think Joseph could channel my father. Towards the end, when we shared nothing but a common dread of being alone, he would use my father's phrases, his ticks, his authority to get his own way, to keep me with him. I used to think he did it deliberately, but perhaps it was just him jostling, unthingingly. Or perhaps I projected those things on him. At the theological college with his other ordinands, sitting around the common room, puffing cigars and sipping gin, sharing power, they all resembled my father. They knew what to say to get their way, how to say it. But perhaps, the whole time, it was in my own eyes.'

'Perhaps,' I said, beginning at last to grasp his meaning. 'Even the Sphinx has eyes.'

'And, consequently, there are many truths,' Chris smiled back and turned to the shadows dancing across the pine floorboards. In the garden, the oak trees whispered a promise of rain. A sleepless blackbird began to whistle. The southern horizon had glowed throughout the night and now the midsummer sun was on the verge of returning.

'Tell me the rest,' I said. 'Tell me what happened after Jake left.'

'The rest. There isn't much that remains. I tried to find him, of course. I left Joseph on the bedroom floor and went to the obvious places: the ruins of Cuthbert's house, the lighthouse, even Diana's Bar. As much as I needed to explain, Jake wouldn't have listened at that time and he was nowhere to be found. I walked back to the cemetery and leaned against a grave stone, trying to sort my thoughts.

'It was while I was there, sheltering from the sun in the shade of an ancient yew, that I looked up and caught someone looking at me. He was only there for an instant, walking along a different path that was parallel to mine but veered to the south. I recognised him immediately, although I hadn't thought about him since our first year. In fact, I only ever thought about him when I was looking at him. And he was there now, looking at me over the tops of the graves. You remember Bisexy Andy from our first year? The timid philosopher? I never knew what had happened to him. I never knew if Paul had ditched him or he had ditched Paul, or whose heart had been broken, if anyone's. I only know that no one spoke about him any more, no one ever mentioned his name. He had disappeared from our lives like he had never existed. I tried to read his expression, but he was too far away. Perhaps he was simply trying to read mine. We held each other's gaze for a moment and then he nodded, embarrassed, and moved on. Perhaps he was looking for his own grave to lean against, I thought. Perhaps I was leaning against his. Either way, it was a strange meeting. Somehow, it settled me.

'When he had gone, I considered what I should do next. Jake would be looking for somewhere to live, I knew. He would return to Joseph's house at some point, if only to collect his belongings, and I would be waiting for him when he did. In the meantime, I had to stop thinking. I had to close my eyes on what happened that afternoon. I had to put everything – Joseph, that look on Jake's face, the oast-house that was waiting for his arrival – all of it into a quiet casket and lock it so delicately that it would not detonate. A single stray thought could have set it off in an instant. I had to survive the next few hours somehow. That's why I went to see Jackie. I had her letter in my pocket. I went to the nearest phone box and arranged to meet her in York.'

Chris rose from his chair and walked towards the fireplace. Leaning against the mantelpiece, he stared closely at his own dark reflection in the mirror.

'Jackie isn't like me.'

'I saw photos of her at your mother's home,' I said, if only to remind him of my presence. 'You both have Calliope's eyes.'

'I don't mean her face. When I think of Jackie, I think of the attic, of my mother's myths in the darkness, the footsteps on the stairs. Jackie reminds me of the iron gates that locked us in the grounds of his castle. She saw herself as a figure from a fairytale, a make-believe heroine trying knitting needles in the lock. The night we ran away, the night

Calliope drove us north, Jackie buried the truth. She put everything that happened down to bedtime tales. Family ghost stories. Childhood fears.

'I arranged to meet her near York Minster. We sat in an expensive teashop sipping coffee and watching the choristers file into the cathedral. I gazed at the clock and counted the passing minutes. I was there in body, Cat, but not in mind. My only thought was for Jake. All I could see was his face in the doorway. No longer flesh and blood for me, his skin had turned to stone, a statue in cold marble. His aortic rhythm had altered, altering his essence. An electric impulse had died in his brain, changing him forever. His name was the only word on my lips. I had to give voice to it and so I began to tell Jackie about him.

'I said that I had been in love with someone for years. Jackie touched my hand and asked for my lover's name. "He's called Jake," I smiled, relieved by the sound. I repeated the name again; it brought me relief. Jackie's eyes flickered uncertainly. She withdrew her hand and lifted the cup to her mouth. She avoided my eyes.

"'I wanted to tell you about him," I said, but hesitated when I saw her reaction. I didn't know what to make of it. "You seem distracted."

"'It's nothing," she replied. "You were saying? What's that name again?"

"'You're crying, Jackie." I reached for her fingers, but she flinched from the contact. She bowed her head and wept silently. "What is it?"

"'I imagine it's just the shock. It's not like I was expecting this turn in the conversation." She wiped her eyes with a napkin and then laughed coldly. "Come on, you're my brother, Chris. It's not like you're effeminate or anything. What did you think I'd say?"

"'I wanted to tell you about Jake. I wanted you to know."

"'Of course you did. How many years has it been since you deigned to speak to me on the phone, let alone meet up? And you saved this up for now? You couldn't just catch up over a coffee, have a chat, could you? You had to have a bombshell. You always have to make an impact. I suppose it's my role to pass this revelation on to Calliope, or will you take pleasure in doing that yourself?"

"'She never told you?" I asked.

"'You can't tell her," Jackie said, suddenly distracted by the thought. "She'll blame herself. No, she'll blame your father. How can you expect a woman of her generation to understand?"

"'She already knows. I told her when I was thirteen."

"'You knew you were a homosexual at thirteen?"

"'Homosexual? Jesus, Jackie, I'm more concerned about which generation you're from.'

"'Calliope knows?" She digested this. "No, she never said."

'"She probably knows that you're an uptight bitch too, but she never told me. I worked that one out for myself."

'I turned to the Minster as the bells chimed nine o'clock. Jackie continued to sob as the congregation spilled onto the streets, shaking hands and saying their peace. I dropped some coins on the table for my coffee and stood up.

'"But how can you be? You're my brother. I know you."

'"You know fuck all about me, Jackie. Don't imagine that you ever will."

'I walked out of the teashop without a backward glance. I wished that it would rain. I wished that the evening sky would well with clouds and wash the heat from the streets. I wanted to feel water on my dry face, cleansing me of the shame and the bitterness. My father used to say that his god scourged the world with drought to punish sinners. I searched the skies for a shadow of a cloud, but the heavens were empty.'

Chris returned to Sunderland station after sunset as the western horizon smouldered. He walked purposefully through the back streets and listened to the rising hum of the night-time city. The evening was cooler now and the slight drop in temperature brought columns of weaving midges into the night air.

He followed the winding path through the cemetery to the northern gate. One by one, the blackbirds in the trees fell silent as he passed. As he approached Joseph's house, the streetlamps were turned on, their orange glow glistened on the holly trees. The lawn crunched beneath his feet, seeming to cry his name to the inhabitants inside. Perhaps because of this signal, perhaps simply by chance, the front door opened and Jake stepped out. He laid a suitcase on the paving slabs and closed the door behind him.

'Thought you'd be back,' he said without surprise when he saw Chris. He glared from beneath his baseball cap. 'Joseph's probably expecting you, isn't he?'

'We need to talk.'

'We've got nothing more to say.' Jake sighed and removed his cap. Running his fingers through his hair, he turned towards the stars and smiled indifferently. 'Doesn't matter anymore. Nothing matters.'

'For us, one last time, please listen.' Chris lowered his face and fingered his hand-fasting ring. 'You need to know what happened. It's such a small thing to ask.'

'I said it doesn't matter.' Jake replaced his cap and nodded towards the cemetery gate. 'Come with me as far as the graveyard. You said we should talk, but it's always you doing the talking, always your words we use. Tonight it's my turn. Come with me to the graveyard.'

Jake led him across the road and through the gates of the burial ground. They walked in silence towards the ruined chapel and listened to the call of the cemetery owl. At a crossroads in the path, Jake leaned his case against a fallen stone and dug his hands into his pockets.

'Is this where you came on New Year's Eve?' he asked casually. Chris nodded. 'Good. I think that's appropriate.'

'What do you want to tell me, Jake?'

'I want to tell you a story in my own words. I want to tell you about Glaucus and Scylla. This past week, while I was waiting for you to come get me, I wanted to know what happened in the story. I wanted to impress you with my knowledge of your stories. Isn't that what you always wanted? To create me in your own image? I borrowed a book from the library, your *Metamorphoses*. I read the rest of that chapter.

'See, you were wrong. Glaucus wasn't just a lonely fisherman. He was also a selfish bastard. I know what the book says. He's made out to be an innocent victim, but there are always two sides to any story, Chris. I'll tell you Scylla's side. She was a nymph who spent her life walking along the cliffs. She was always being bothered by suitors that wanted to own her because she was beautiful. But she knew her own mind and refused to belong to any man. She did her own thing and lived on her own beside the sea, loving her own company.

'One day, or maybe it was early evening when the moon was shining, she swam in the shallow waters of the shore. Because the beach was empty and there was no one to bother her, she closed her eyes and relaxed into the movement of the waves. Just when she thought she'd found peace, this hideous beast rose from the water and clutched her in his arms. His skin was scaled like a fish and he had fins down his spine, but his torso was that of a man. She didn't know if he was a god or a monster, and she didn't really care. She just struggled to be free.

'Eventually, she did fight her way loose and fled to the shoreline. The monster, Glaucus, begged her to return. He told her of his sad past, of his loneliness and longing, and of how much he loved her. He said he would die without her. Sound familiar? When that didn't work, he pretended to drown beneath the waves. Still she didn't come, so he hissed and cursed and went in search of the Old Witch of the Sea to cast a spell on her.

'Your book says that Glaucus only wanted to make Scylla love him. Your book says that the Old Witch of the Sea was cruel and misunderstood his words on purpose. But I say that Glaucus was an evil cunt and wanted to take revenge on the woman who rejected him. I say that the Old Witch listened to Glaucus and followed his wish, word for word. I say that she poured a bowl of his spite into the water and watched the poison spread towards Scylla's feet. As the black liquid touched her skin, the nymph felt a change come over her. Such a horrible transformation is painful, Chris, I can tell you that, but it took a long time in coming. Scylla's body twisted as the spell worked its magic. Her legs were turned into a pack of barking dogs. No man could approach her now, even if she wanted one to, not even Glaucus. Without beauty, without love, she was monstrous. He made her a monster. They say that Glaucus wept for her, but I say he wept for himself.

'So, what do you say, Chris? How monstrous have you made me?'

Chris lifted a cigarette to his lips and flicked the lighter. Jake's white teeth gleamed in the flare, his eyes as cold as moonlight. There was no indifference in his expression now, only hatred. Chris's heart cracked at the sight.

The boughs of the old trees creaked around him, echoing the fracture in his chest. The leaves whispered overhead, seeming to rustle a name in the breeze: Jake-his-name-is-Jake.

'No,' Jake said softly, reaching down for his suitcase. 'I didn't think you'd have anything to say. I'm going away now. Dane said I could stay with him for a while. He's planning a trip to Dublin and wants me to go with him. Said it would cheer me up. Said I could even get me an Irish fling. I doubt it, but who knows what can happen now?'

'Jake,' Chris said, his voice sounding strange in the evening. He did not recognise it as his own. 'Do you remember the cliffs at Whitby? Do you remember the gravestone by the abbey? You carved our names in the rock, you wrote "forever". Do you remember that?'

'No.' He stared into the distance. 'I don't remember that.'

'We first said we loved each other there. Neither of us had said it before. I didn't want to scare you away. And that was ridiculous because we'd already made our vows at the lighthouse months before. Do you remember the hand-fasting? Do you remember the storm?'

'I'm sorry, Chris. It's gone. It's all gone.'

'But the rings, Jake. The moon, the full moon. You drew that picture in charcoal, the one that hung over the piano in the Green Room. You must remember that. You have to remember.'

'That's it now. I said I don't remember any of it.'

'Listen, what happened with Joseph, it isn't what you think.'

'Thing is, nothing is ever because of you, not even Kassi. It's always your ghosts, isn't it? Is that what we call them? Your ghosts?'

'I did what you said.' Chris stared wildly after Jake as he walked away. 'I painted the house for you. There's a Yellow Room and a Green Room and a piano, just like we said. It's all there is left.'

Without turning around, Jake put his suitcase on the ground and adjusted the rim of his cap.

'I don't know if this will help,' said Jake, 'but it might make things easier for you. Dane wasn't lying. I did fuck Gary on the seafront. Four, five times, maybe more. Ten? I can't remember. It doesn't matter. Nothing matters now. Does that help you?'

Jake's footsteps gradually faded as he disappeared into the night. The darkness seemed reluctant to fill the space where he had been. Chris closed his eyes on the lingering shape and held it in his mind. As he traced the smooth line of the jaw in his memory, he heard a familiar cackle in the branches above him.

The gravel crunched as she dropped to the ground. The bones of her fingers pressed deep between his ribs. He pushed her aside and staggered towards the chapel, but her arms were soon wrapped around his neck.

'Open wide,' she said as she pulled him down and pressed her mouth against his breastbone. 'Jake-his-name-is-Jake-his-name-is-Jake.'

He listened to the name thunder in the ground, rising like a wind that left the earth untouched and setting to a deep, convulsing rhythm that counted the stars westward.

* * *

The eastern sky had turned blood red by the time Chris finished speaking. Now, great storm clouds loomed over the rising sun. He stood beside me at the window and gazed across the unearthly coloured Downs. Together, we watched the first drops of rain began to fall.

'Sometimes I can cast her out,' he said as a wave of grey rain swept down from the hills. 'Sometimes, when I close my eyes and see Jake's face, his smile, the blue eyes, I can't stand it and she returns. Sometimes she sits beside me and says his name, and she waits.'

'Is she here now?' I turned uneasily to look around the room.

'No. She comes when I'm alone. She knows that's the best time.' He walked towards the door and beckoned me to follow. 'Come. I want to show you something.'

He led me down the hallway that curved around the Yellow Room towards a low wooden door. Without a word, he turned the handle and opened it. I stepped inside as the first tide of rain hit the windows. Through the dim morning light, I could see that the walls had been freshly painted green. The charred skeleton of the old piano stood against one wall. A vase of dried roses stood on its case. Above it hung a charcoal sketch of the moon, damaged by smoke but still discernable.

'It's a mausoleum,' I said. 'Remnants from a lost civilisation.'

'Relics from before the volcano.'

'Indeed.' I stepped respectfully across the floorboards towards the piano but stopped abruptly when I saw a movement in the corner of the room. As I stared into the shadows, a blanket stirred and sat up.

'Sorry, Chris,' said Day emerging from beneath a pile of bedding. Hugging Richard to his chest, he rose from the floor and rubbed his back. 'We didn't know where else to get some sleep. Hope you don't mind.'

'I mind that you think I'd mind,' Chris said. He looked at me and acknowledged the moment of terror still written on my face. 'This is our castle now, all of ours. I imagine you're hungry. If you find the kitchen, there's milk and coffee. The village shop doesn't seem to stir until nine.'

Day wandered to the kitchen to boil the kettle. Chris led me through the French doors of the Green Room and out into the overgrown garden. The morning rain was warm against my skin, a welcome relief after the drought of the past weeks. The long dry grass seemed to sigh in the deluge. Chris pointed to a cluster of glistening crystals that were hanging from a rose tree.

'Calliope used to call them the tears of Niobe,' he said. 'It was one of the stories she told us in the attic. She said that the power of tears shouldn't be left to sink into the earth; it should be used for wishes. I put these up when I returned, all the wishes of my life. He will come back, Cat. I know I'll see him again one day. And that will be enough.'

Chris walked across the sodden lawn and entered the kitchen door. The sound of Day's voice drifted into the rain. I smelled fresh coffee on the air, drawing me into the house. Before I followed him inside, I took one more look at the rose tree. The crystals chimed quietly against each other, whispering the secret dreams of his life. I watched the streams of rain trickle from the glass and sink into the grateful earth, and then I turned towards the house.

* * *

All that remains to tell you, Jackie, are the stranger things that are unknown. There are places where memory is denied and I stumble among the shadows that giants have cast behind. Sometimes the fabric is threadbare, not through wear and tear but because of poor craftsmanship. Sometimes there are gaps I can never mend, voices I never heard, spaces without numbers and no colours to paint. This is the realm of mythologies. Do not take me at my word, for such things are never literal and truth is no more solid than a meandering daydream. All language is figurative; it is the best we can manage.

Jake found a new religion.

I heard that Diana's Bar closed down. I heard that the builders had blasted through the face of the cliff and fitted uPVC windows where the shields of lost warriors used to hang. As the wrecking ball broke through, the centaurs must have cowered into deeper crevices and the last of the dragons turned to dust, for such creatures cannot survive in daylight. I heard that the limestone walls were smoothed and plastered and painted magnolia. I heard that the marble chessboard was torn up and the floor laminated for the polished brogues of lunchtime diners. I heard that the splintered shards of the mirrored bar glittered for weeks in a moonlit skip, and that Cyane was last seen fleeing north along the midnight shore without her wings.

As Diana's Bar dissolved, I imagine that it reappeared out west on some other misty island, deep within the banks of a river I have never seen. The otherworld does not just disappear like that. It holds one more meeting in my mind before it fades forever.

I imagine the glitterball was spinning slowly above their heads, casting stars over the chequerboard floor. The music was still low because it had only turned six. I imagine Jake sitting at a wooden bench, clinking glasses with Dane and sipping the head of his Guinness.

I imagine Jake glanced towards the bar and saw him at once. The tall man was wearing a charcoal suit. His tie was loosened at the collar and the top of his shirt was unbuttoned. His hair was black, but even from this distance Jake could see the flecks of grey around his temples. The man leant across the bar to order a drink from the flirtatious girl wearing fairy wings. When he looked up, he caught Jake's eyes and held them for an incredible second.

Within that moment, a mere seed containing lifetimes, Jake felt the room sweep close around him. A rush of dark air from the hidden places of the earth drove out the old certainties in his mind and carried a surprising whisper of something different. He waited for Martin Donoghue to pay for his drink and approach his table.

Martin did not smile, he rarely smiled, but he did feel a lightness inside that was unexpected. The problem of his father had finally been resolved: the unstable old man was now safely deposited in a Dublin retirement home. He had watched his father slowly lose his mind in that bedevilled vicarage in Sussex. They had wanted to be close to each other in those last few years, which is why Martin applied to the solicitor's firm in Balwick. Now he was unburdened of that responsibility.

Earlier that day, their goodbyes had not been easy. In his confusion, the old man was convinced that his son was the Devil come to steal him away without a by-your-leave, just like that, in his pyjamas and straw hat. Martin had turned his back on the raving old man and left. He walked along the riverbank all day, sometimes staring into the granite water, sometimes stopping at cafés to watch his coffee grow cold. As the clouds crept inland from the Irish Sea, he decided on a quick drink before heading back to the hotel. He rarely went to gay bars but today was different.

Martin felt uncharacteristically bold as he approached the attractive but sad guy with the white streak in his hair. Politely, in his soft Irish accent, he asked if he might join their table. Jake smiled and reached out to shake Martin's hand. In the shade of the alcove, only the drifting lights from the glitterball passed over their dark faces. For an instant before they sat close beside each other, a moment before their thighs began to touch – a full half hour before Jake's heart quickened when Martin mentioned that he lived in a little Sussex village called Balwick – in that window of time, Jake thought that the man's eyes were like those of an uncomprehending animal; a goat, perhaps, or an ibex.

They say that the Furies rise from the earth to exact revenge whenever a natural law is broken. They say the Furies drive their victims insane by hounding them from one end of the earth to another. They were the most dreaded spirits in ancient times because of their determination to punish. They were so fearsome that you dared not utter their names. To even think of them could be to summon them.

I know of no Furies of vengeance other than the ones we carry inside us. I know of no natural laws, only the unnatural ones we have inherited. It is true there is always cause and effect, the transformation of energy into one form or another, the subtle click of one clog turning another. Jake met Martin Donoghue in Dublin: that much I do know. Some links in the chain are obvious, others we can guess on the balance of probabilities. The rest is pure mythology.

XVI
Of Water

23rd March 2000

I sat at the window in Catriona's bedroom and watched the spring rain drown the wooded plains between the Downs.

My mother used to say that the south wind brings rain from the ocean when the earth cries for the return of her lost daughter. She said that the spring returns because Proserpine has been released from the underworld and the world weeps tears of delight for its resurrected child. The trees will flower and the land shall be green again, at least for a season, until the wheel of time turns and Proserpine descends in the inevitable, unforgiving autumn.

I remember these tales told at bedtime, whispered by my mother in the attic room as the March rain pounded the roof. A daughter's return from the grave, a land released from hibernation for six months of the year. Calliope spoke quietly, careful not to rouse the attention of the priest downstairs.

'But why doesn't Proserpine stay here?' I asked. 'Why not refuse to return to the underworld once she's out?'

My mother smiled and pulled the blanket around my shoulders. She looked to see if Chris was still awake and kissed his brow. In the low candlelight, his eyes gleamed bright and wolf-like.

'You're too young, Jackie,' he said before my mother could answer. 'You don't understand these things. Proserpine has to go back otherwise they'd be no seasons. It has to happen. Isn't that right, Mum?'

'Not always, Chrissy,' she replied, lying down between our bodies. 'Perhaps she could break the cycle, if she really tried. Perhaps she could stay on the earth and refuse to go down to the shades. Or perhaps she simply needs a rest at the end of the summer and wants to go back to the grave.'

'I like graves.' Chris pulled a face at me. 'I'd like to live in a graveyard when I'm older. I'd haunt it like a vampire and have tea with the ghosts in the evening.'

'You're a freak,' I said, turning away.

'No, Jacks. He's occasionally morbid.' Calliope stroked his hair and listened to the rain on the tiles. She paused as a floorboard creaked on the stairs. I watched her jaw set firmly, her chin lift defiantly at the sound of danger.

'Sleep now,' she whispered to her cubs. 'I'll see him off.'

* * *

I sat beside the window in Catriona's bedroom and watched the raindrops trickle down the glass. The daffodils in her garden rocked against the downpour, hanging their faces in the water. Catriona stretched beneath the duvet and muttered my name.

'Are you awake, love?' I asked. 'Did I wake you?'

'Hello, Jacks,' she said without opening her eyes. 'Hello, darling.'

'Day and Lionheart are making breakfast. What would you like?'

'A coffee would do wonders. Is Chris up yet?'

Chris had come back from Greece the previous evening. Now Proserpine had emerged from the underworld and the south wind had carried the breath of Africa to the Downs, all migratory things were returning. Suede had met him at the airport and brought him home in her rusting campervan.

I had waited in the kitchen for him. Lionheart thundered through the cottage, heralding his arrival with the kitten in his arms.

'He's here, Jacks,' he cried. 'Chris is home.'

'I know. I heard the van.'

'Well then, get your arse outside.'

'We say bum, not arse. Remember?' I lit a cigarette and walked to the window. It was barely six o'clock, but the rain clouds loured over the darkening hills. The statues in the garden glowed flesh-like in the light, their faces turned curiously towards the house. I saw a centaur wink in the twilight.

'I hear you say arse all the time. Don't you want to see him?'

'He's my brother. Of course I want to see him. But maybe he won't be over the moon to see me.'

'Why wouldn't I?' said Chris walking into the room. He leaned against the doorframe and smiled. He was always amused when I lost my composure. His skin was dark, really quite sunburnt, and his teeth seemed too white in the dim kitchen light. Catriona followed closely behind and announced a gathering to celebrate his return. She laid an arm around his shoulder and fondly rubbed his stomach.

'We're having a banquet,' she said, brushing the raindrops from his hair. 'A feast for our wandering prince. How was the motherland?'

'It was kind to me this winter, Cat. Who's coming tonight?'

'A handful of witches from the Downs, the usuals. Oh, Conrad and Anna said they'd love to come, but it depends on her workload. She's been promoted again. Director of Directors, Executive of Executives, or something equally memorable.' Catriona turned to me and smiled knowingly. 'I'll leave you two to catch up.'

She disappeared into the hall and called for Lionheart to follow.

'I'm staying put,' the boy replied. He eyed us both expectantly.

'So, what did you get up to in Greece?' I avoided Chris's gaze.

'I fulfilled a promise. I've been looking for Calliope's birthplace in Missolonghi. It wasn't much, when I found it. A ruin in the foothills of a mountain. There are no Mavrocordatos' left, Jackie. We're the last of our line, you and I.'

'I know. She once told me that. Why did you go there?'

Chris took off his damp coat and hung it on the back of a kitchen chair. He sat beside Lionheart and stroked the kitten.

'I talked to Calliope a few years before she died.'

'She never mentioned it to me. She would have told me.'

'I broke all the rules and telephoned her. She didn't want to speak to me, of course. I'd taken the inheritance, I'd bought the oast-house: she couldn't forgive me. Christ, it was hard enough calling her in the first place. I imagine she never even uttered my name, did she?'

'Sometimes, in the first few months after the inheritance she did. Less often after that. After I'd seen you in York, I told her what you said and she became silent. Whenever I said, "I wonder what Chris is doing", she just bit her lip. She worried about you. She wanted to speak to you, but couldn't. How come you broke the rules?'

'It's strange,' Chris said. He walked towards the window and stared at the stone figures on the lawn. 'I knew how she would die, years before it happened. I woke up one morning and had to speak to her. If we didn't at that particular time, I knew we never would again. She was far too stubborn.'

'You both are,' I smiled.

'Thank you,' he said, acknowledging my smile. 'She didn't say anything at first on the phone. I told her about my dream, about the oil slick at Whitby. I said that I'd seen her trying to rescue gulls from the sea, but the rocks were slippery and she fell into the black water. I said I had to speak with her before it happened. She stayed quiet. I was about to put down the phone, but she quietly apologised. I asked her what for.

'"We can't speak, *agapi mou*," she said. If I didn't know how tough she was, I would have said she was crying. "I want to ask you everything. I want so much to see you, but I can't. I can't do that."

'She went silent again and I pressed her to go on. I said, if this was our last conversation, I needed to know why. And so she explained.

'"What that devil did to us, Chrissy, in that house, in those rooms, I can't forgive myself. Every night as I go to sleep, I see his cruelty. I hear his voice when the cottage is silent; the floorboards sing his creaking psalms. Sometimes, when there's no noise but the ticking clock, I think I'm still locked inside those gates. And all the time, every second of every day, I think about what he did to you and I hate myself for not resisting more. All that remains is my resistance. It is all that can ever remain."

"'You did what you could, Calliope. You saved us."

"'You went back to him. And that thought consumes me like a fire. It never goes out. You went back when I could have stopped you. I think of the words I could have used to make you stay and I hate myself for not saying them. I could have taken away your choice."

"'True, you could have locked the gates or chained me in the attic. And I would have despised you, Calliope. I would have tried different keys in the lock each morning until I fled from you."

"'And you would have been right to do so."

"'Then how can you hate yourself?"

"'I failed," she said straightforwardly. "All I can do now is what I should have done then. I fight. I build the walls I should have built earlier. I long for you, Chrissy, I yearn for you with a mother's heart. But you are there in that house. You use his blood money and you live in his house. You took his gifts and, in doing that, you accepted him. You know you didn't have to."

"'I didn't accept him," I said, crying now. "I occupied his land, made it something else. I turned his world upside down. It's over."

"'It will never be over. I live with myself, with the things I've done and the things I've failed to do. I fight."

'Then she said that there was one last thing I could do for her. When she died, she said, when the tide stopped turning and the sea went black, she wanted me not to go the funeral but to visit her in Greece.

"'I won't be here in your father's country," she said. "I want my memory to return to my own land, to the place I was born. Come think of me there, *agapi mou*. Spend a season in our motherland. Return to your father's house if you must, but give me peace in this way. Walk as if you were walking with me along the Ionian shore, let me hold your hand in the olive groves of my childhood home. Listen for me in the song of the honeybees and in the waves against the rocks, but do not speak to me until then. I cannot change until then."

'I tried to persuade her, Jackie. I begged her, but she hung up. I listened to the dead tone for minutes, perhaps hours, who knows. We never spoke again. Sometimes I would pick up the phone and listen to the dialling tone, knowing that she might be doing the same.'

Chris pressed his face against the windowpane. The rain fell relentlessly in the darkness.

* * *

'What is it, sweetheart?' Catriona asked, leaning towards me on her elbows. I pulled the duvet over her shoulder and stroked her cheek.

'Just thinking. Why do you ask?'

'Because you're crying, Jackie. Who is this for?'

I touched my cheeks, felt the tears I did not know were streaming. Nothing, I said. Nothing at all. Just thinking.

I found Day frying bacon in the kitchen. He turned at my approach and came to me, whistling between his teeth.

'Hey,' he sang, swinging his hips. 'Did you happen to see the most beautiful girl in the world?'

I put my arms around his waist and danced slowly around the kitchen to his singing. Through the window, I caught sight of Amber, Suede's daughter, sitting among the branches of an oak tree with Lionheart. They sheltered from the rain beneath the boughs and exchanged cigarettes for dares. Lionheart had obviously lost because Amber was tickling his ear with her tongue. Appalled, he wiped his face and jumped to the lawn. I smiled and closed my eyes.

'Where's Chris?' I stroked Day's golden hair between my fingers.

'Next door, I think. Said he'd come with me later to my house. I've finished a new sculpture for the garden.'

'Why don't you live here all the time, Day? Why bother holding onto that rotten old shack in the Downs? You must get lonely.'

'I'm barely ever there,' he said, pulling away and returning to his frying pan. 'Besides, it's difficult to concentrate here. Impossible to write anything when Lionheart's hovering over each word, contradicting each sub-clause. He wants to be a philosopher now. And I suppose Cat needs some space too, once in a while.'

'Does she?' I looked up the stairs, imagining her lying where I had left her in bed, savouring a moment of solitude. 'From me as well, I imagine?'

He shrugged. 'She'll say, if she needs to.'

Without purpose, I strayed around the garden and sat on the wet stone bench beside the rosemary bushes. Lionheart and Amber conspired from the shelter of oaks. The sound of the downpour was deafening, refreshing. The rain streamed down my hair and cooled my face. All was water, on leaf, on stone, on the pebble path, on the soil.

The return of Chris had brought a change to Catriona's cottage. The world's wheel had turned and my winter sanctuary had been overcome by the arrival of spring. During the darker evenings, Lionheart and I had sat together listening to Catriona's tale beside the fire. He stroked my hair and drifted into dreams on my lap. Catriona's voice had soothed the winter gales to sleep. Sometimes when the wind shook the weathervane, I closed my eyes and imagined that it was Calliope's voice calming the storm, that Chris was resting his head against my shoulder. But with Amber's arrival, Lionheart had become a stranger again. He reverted to that pugnacious imp I had first met in the autumn, guarding his kingdom on the oast-house wall.

Day's hint burrowed into my thoughts. Cat needs some space, he had said, once in a while. Cat will tell you when she needs to. She had said nothing so far, but I could feel the words coming as surely as I could sense the lighter evenings. The love was still there, but her need for solitude was waxing as the days grew warmer and the Downs looked ever more tempting. She loved the hills. She loved her solitude.

And now Chris had returned. He was casually amused by my intimacy with Cat and Day, but ultimately indifferent to my presence in his realm. The previous evening, he had welcomed his guests to the feast dressed as a Romantic poet, wearing a wide collared shirt, loose cravat and a black cape. In another time, at an earlier age, the role of gothic lord would have suited him. Now, he seemed weary of the irony. Catriona, on the other hand, had swept through the house as Catherine the Great, her diamonds gleaming in the candlelight.

'Come on, darling,' she said, bowing graciously before me. 'You know where the costumes are. Even you, Cinderella, shall go to the ball.'

I said I would change into something spectacular and walked listlessly towards the stairs. There is nothing like a house full of people to make you feel alienated. Stepping carefully between a row of cigar-smoking crones on the bottom step, I thought I had left the party behind when I came across four women on the landing. The quartet were indistinguishable. They wore identical red dresses and moved with a collective grace, stroking each other's auburn hair and whispering as I passed. One of the four, one with a serpent brooch on her neckline, looked at me with grey eyes. She did not open her mouth, but I heard, or thought I heard, her voice ring in the air. At her words, all other sounds – the laugher downstairs, the heavy rain – seemed to fade into silence. Come, she said, her eyes holding mine. Come with me into the garden. It's raining now, but the water will wash you whiter than snow. You will shine. I want to see you shine.

'I can't,' I said. 'Catriona's waiting for me.'

The woman smiled and turned to her sisters. They moved towards each other as though drawn by the same impulse. When their lips touched, I looked away and walked into Catriona's bedroom.

The Empress Josephine's white gown lay stretched out upon the bed, waiting for me to wear it. I slipped out of my clothes and into the satin folds of the dress, drawing the fabric around my body like a sheet of elfin chain-mail, steeling myself. I will shine, I thought facetiously. I'll shine like the ghost at the banquet: uninvited, unseen, outstaying my welcome. The sleeves covered the faint red scars on my arms. I lowered the veil over my face and felt invisible behind the mask.

The four women in red had left the landing when I emerged, but I could hear the laughter of young voices from the bathroom. Leaning against the doorframe, I looked inside the candlelit room.

Lionheart and Amber sat fully clothed in the empty bathtub, drinking from a stolen bottle of white wine and enjoying their own party. Amber's blonde dreadlocks flipped from side to side as she shook her head and thumped the enamel rim.

'What's his name then, this *älskling* of yours?' she laughed. Her voice was deep, a contralto like her mother's. Her accent was a curious anthology of inflections, a repository of all the countries she and Suede had passed through on their travels. 'This lion-tamer of yours, who is it?'

'He's no lion-tamer, more like a cat-whisperer,' Lionheart replied, reaching for the wine bottle. He feigned disinterest in the topic of conversation, but his smile could not be suppressed. 'His name is Kevin.'

'Kevin? No, not Kevin. Ah, the shame of it,' she said, refusing to yield the bottle.

'That's not his name, of course. It's what his folks have branded him.' Lionheart grabbed the wine from her hands. 'He's still deciding what his name should be. He's emerging. Besides, you're still Amber.'

'I want to meet him. I have to interrogate my rival.'

'Fuck's sake, Amber, you're so unreconstructed,' he roared.

I backed away from the bathroom as they laughed uncontrollably and fought for the bottle. Turning to the stairs, the fumes from the cigar-smoking crones had settled like a fog on the landing. Feeling my way between the crouching figures, I stepped on bare toes and apologised to each wisely nodding head. The air on the ground floor was clearer, but the rooms were filled with more faces I did not recognise, figures from Chris and Catriona's past. Strangers to me.

In the kitchen, I poured myself a glass of Day's homebrew and picked at the olives that Chris had brought back. Catriona and Suede were leaning against the windowsill, gesturing animatedly as they spoke.

'The last time I saw him was over a year ago,' Catriona said, waving a chicken drumstick in the air. 'In the post office. He looked straight through me as though I didn't exist. It was like he didn't know me, like we didn't have a shared history. Then, he smirks at the clerk.'

'Cock,' said Suede. She stabbed the air with her cigarette.

'And Lionheart was with me, standing behind the postcards. I don't think Jake had clocked him yet. I didn't say anything, but Lionheart had that wicked glint in his eye. You know the one.'

'I know, sugar. Amber has it all the time. Like she's up to something. Like you shouldn't cross her.'

'Exactly. So then Lionheart turns to me, points at Jake and says clearly enough for all the world to hear, "that's him, isn't it? That's the man." I ask him what he means. "That's my father, that man who won't look at us. That's Jake Edlestone."'

'Well, fuck me,' Suede laughed. 'What the hell did you do?'

'What could I do? I admitted that it was. So Lionheart walks over and looks him straight in the eye. He must have stared at him for a full minute before Jake glances down and shrugs. "What do you want, kid?" he says, without any kind of emotion. "Kid," he says.'

'Fucking unbelievable. Intolerable dick.'

'So then Lionheart lifts his fingers, like this.' Catriona raised her hand into the Devil's salute, her first and fourth fingers outstretched. 'And he speaks, but his voice is strange, really quite threatening. You know, it could have been Chris speaking. The post office is silent, except for the newspapers rustling in the breeze. Everyone's looking at Lionheart, even the blue-rinse clerks behind the counter.'

I craned forward to listen to Catriona's words, but a short dark-haired man reached for the olives beside me and blocked my view.

'Witch or atheist?' he asked.

'Both,' I said, avoiding his eyes. I shifted closer to Catriona.

'That's unusual,' he said. 'Anna, my wife, wrote an article about pagan gardeners recently. All the people she spoke to believed in some god or other. Very few atheists among them.'

'Anna?' I looked at him more closely. 'So you would be Conrad?'

We introduced ourselves and shook hands over the table. Conrad chewed a breadstick thoughtfully and studied my face.

'Didn't know Chris had a sister,' he said. 'Then again, there's a lot I don't know about him. Don't see much of him nowadays.'

'I wonder if anyone really knows him, except Catriona, of course.' I listened to Suede's cry of delight as Catriona ended her anecdote. Disappointed, I gave Conrad my attention. 'And so, you're married now?'

'Six years in June,' he nodded and glanced blankly at the window. 'Anna couldn't come tonight. Finishing a last-minute feature for *Allotment Life*. The sex lives of molluscs or something equally riveting. They're hermaphrodites, you know. Sex lasts for days. All very tantric.'

'I see. Hence the article about "pagan gardeners". I thought you were using a euphemism.'

He nodded and stared at the olives. I found I had nothing to say.

'Where's Chris?' we asked simultaneously and laughed at the coincidence. The light rekindled in his eyes. We agreed to go in search of the guest of honour.

Catriona's front garden echoed with the peal of wind-chimes in the rain. Conrad frowned into the darkness.

'Think he's gone for a walk. A fugitive from his own party.'

'Over there.' I pointed at the buddleia. A woman in red gestured beneath the branches, brushing the wooden chimes as she passed. The serpent brooch glittered at her neckline as she turned and moved her lips. Come, she said without words. Come with me into the garden. It's raining now, but the water will make you shine. I want to see you shine.

Leaving Conrad behind, I stepped into the rain and felt the white dress cling instantly to my body. I drew the veil over my head in a futile attempt to keep dry and pursued the woman down the lane.

'Wait up, Jackie,' said Conrad, diving into the downpour after me.

Under the shelter of oaks, we pursued the red dress towards the oast-house gates. Always just a few metres ahead, the figure slipped through the unlocked gates and disappeared into the grounds. We paused at the railings and looked up the deserted driveway. The building towered silently into the rainstorm, lit from below by the dancing glow of Catriona's cottage. The door swung widely in the breeze and tapped against the stone wall.

'Castle Dracula, I presume,' he laughed.

'The keep of the Goblin-King. It used to be my home. I haven't been inside since I was a girl. Chris couldn't keep away tonight, either.'

'Well, he is dressed for the role. You think he's in there?'

'Yes,' I said. As though hearing my voice, the weathervane on the spire turned deliberately to the north, towards where we were standing.

'Are we going in?'

'You can follow, if you want,' I said, pushing the loose gates aside.

I walked over the gravel drive, lifting the hem of my gown above the damp ground. I should be holding a knitting needle, I thought, a long, thin metal needle, cold against the skin, powerful in my hand. But tonight I had no such weapon.

Once upon a time, when the north wind lifted the tiles on the attic roof and made the old weathervane cry a banshee-wail, Chris told me I was the heroine in a fairytale, a make-believe princess in the turret of a wicked count. Once upon a time, in the sepia light of memory, when a younger sun pressed against the windows of this house, I held the iron lock in my hands and turned my back on such childish things. Once upon a time, I would never have imagined myself returning unarmed through the treacherous gates of the house I had buried as a girl.

The guttering creaked in the torrent of spring rain. I listened to the midnight breeze pass through the hall and vacant rooms. Just air, I thought; just wind and water singing through old bones. I looked inside the unlit entrance and stepped over the threshold.

The priest's study was not difficult to find, even in the darkness. The low passages and great halls of this building had recurred in my dreams throughout the years, charting the map of my unconscious. I pressed a palm against the splintered wood of the study door and pushed.

'Wait here,' I said to Conrad, leaving him alone and uncomfortable in the gloom of the dripping hallway.

A low flame burned in the hearth. It threw a vague, grainy glow over the faded yellow walls and dusty mirrors of that great room. The floorboards sighed beneath my feet as I went up to the empty armchair. The warmth of a recent body still lingered in the moth-eaten upholstery.

'Chrissy,' I said, staring into the shadows. 'Chrissy, it's me.'

A movement beside the curtains drew my eyes to the window. His pale face appeared in the shadows as he stood up from the floor. Hesitantly, he stepped across the room, pointing at my veil.

'You,' he said strangely, uncertainly.

'Chrissy.' I retreated to the fireplace and removed the veil. 'It's Jackie. Can't you see me?'

'Jackie?' He paused at the armchair and put his hand down.

'It's me. Who did you think it was?'

'Jackie,' he repeated and came towards me. He pulled me into his arms and pressed his face against my shoulder. We had not touched in years. He felt light, insubstantial. He felt like a stranger.

'I thought it was her. Your dress, it was shining in the rain. In the firelight, I thought – '

We stood in the flickering light of the fire and held each other. He spoke, but his words were drowned by the rain that drummed against the window. I wondered if the storm would ever end.

They say that the Inuit people of the Arctic have fifty words for snow, and the nomadic tribes of the Sahara have countless names for the sandy winds that sweep their continent, yet the English have only one for rain. We should have more, I thought. There should be one for the warm summer rain that falls in vertical lines when no wind breathes, and one for the spiteful icy kind that flies in winter and cuts the skin. And there should be a name for the rain that never ends, the rain that has drowned these islands over centuries of time, as interminable as the tears of an inconsolable goddess.

Chris lifted my arms from his neck and wiped his eyes. He moved towards the window and peered through the broken panes.

'It never gets any easier,' he said without turning. 'Sometimes, when I'm on my own, the house whispers names, phrases, broken sentences that were uttered or should have been uttered or should never have been said at all. Sometimes, there are faces in the darkness, the white teeth of a smile, the blue eyes of a beautiful demon shining in the night. They disappear when I turn on the lights. Sometimes, when I fall asleep in this chair, cold fingers touch my even colder cheek. When I open my eyes, I'm alone and there are tears on my face. I don't know how long I've been asleep, how long I've been crying or if it's the same night at all. But there I am, seeing shadows in the shadows, listening to whispers in the whispers. It never ends.'

I stroked his shoulder, this stranger I had known all my life. He stared outside at a cascade of water from the broken guttering.

'Is it her, the Old Woman? Did she never go away?'

'She's gone, at least for a season. I used to see her all the time when I first moved here. She sat beside me there, next to the armchair, decaying, blind as a broken doll, feeding. I smelt her watching me, waiting for a moment of weakness to climb inside.'

'Ghost stories, Chris. That's all she was. She wasn't real.'

'Real as any emotion.' Chris smiled thinly and strolled around the room. 'Can you keep those emotions out? Can you exorcise them? Guilt, hate, revenge, even love. Can you cast them all out? Sometimes she would creep towards my face and say his name, over and over again. Other times, she rocked quietly on the mantelpiece, clutching the ledge with her fingers and toes, whispering all those things I almost had.'

He untied his cravat and rolled it in his hands.

'There was somebody in my life once,' he said. 'I loved him. He brought a measure of peace. You won't understand, but he made me feel forgiven.'

'It was Jake,' I said. Chris turned and eyed me curiously. 'Catriona told me about him. She said I wouldn't understand you unless I knew about him. Do you mind?'

He shrugged and walked slowly in an anticlockwise arc around the room. He spoke in such hushed tones that I barely caught the words. Conrad emerged from the darkness of the hallway, straining to catch Chris's voice. He stepped quietly across the room and sat on the windowsill beside me. Chris continued his circuit around the empty floor.

* * *

'I remember an autumn here in Balwick,' he said. 'The low, wooded land between the Downs had been flooded by days of rain. The summer had been fierce, but it passed away suddenly that year, the year I returned to this house. I knew it was coming. The end of June saw the arrival of storm clouds. They lined the hills for weeks, a dark army waiting to fall upon the placid plains. I watched their silent presence as the days grew shorter and the sun strayed deeper beneath the midnight horizon. I would lie awake in the darkness, listening to the thunder of distant elements on the Downs, the threat of war-drums echoing between the valleys.

'They say that Vesuvius smoked for weeks before she finally drowned Pompeii in molten rock. They say that she chanted from deep within the burrows of the earth, from the underground halls where dragons slept, long before the age of humans. The people of Pompeii watched the mountain smoulder and yet they stayed in their homes, doing the things they did each day: Pliny writing in his study, a dog barking in the street, a baker and his wife looking through their window. They said the volcano was a goddess who had been angered. They offered her sacrifices in appeasement. But the mountain's appetite was insatiable and she continued to seethe.

'There were no gods in the mountains. No one listens to the prayers of the people. There was nothing but necessity: the everlasting universe of things, a river of molten rock flowing through the streets of the city, taking the faithful and the non-faithful alike, drowning the shoreline with fire. Yet still, I watched the Downs and waited for the clouds to shift, for the drumming in the earth to hush and fall silent.

'When the clouds eventually decamped from the hills, they drove quietly down the slopes. They came in early August and swept the summer away in its prime. The water fell for weeks without end, flooding the fields and towns of the Weald. Autumn was vengeful that year. The harvest was ruined, the seasons were in disarray.

'One evening in September, I was woken by a word against my skin. It was a word of such force, such potency, that I opened my eyes as though I'd been stung. The sound lingered in the air, resounding like the after-ring of a bell. It was simply his name: "Jake". It soon faded, but I sat in that chair and listened to the tap-tap-tap of fingernails against the door. The Old Woman had been gone for days, possibly weeks. She came and went without warning, appearing when I was at my weakest. It was unlike the hag to announce her return, but I recognised the sound of her nails clawing grooves into the door.

'I pressed my ear to the panel. Usually, I could hear her breathing or the slip of her tongue as she tasted the air. This time, there was nothing. I turned the handle and found the hallway empty, but for a trail of woodlice and leaves leading to the front door. I followed her wake down the open drive and into the lane.

'The branches of the oaks bowed beneath the downpour. The bindweed whispered sentences in the evening breeze and spoke with the voice of the old gods, those country spirits that were abandoned long before the mediaeval church was built. Somewhere there, between the hoary oaks, they say a roadside shrine used to mark the crossroads where the cattle path met the highway. Drop a silver coin at midnight for the Old Woman of the night and she will tell you which path to take. Drop a silver coin and listen.

'I had barely pushed a coin into bark of the tree before I heard their voices. Down the lane and over the ancient stone bridge, by my father's old church on the edge of the town, I heard them laughing.

'I followed the sound beneath the dripping canopy of trees. The streetlamps on the high street were beginning to glow dimly as I crossed the bridge over the flooded stream and headed towards the church. Briefly, the bells tolled for Evensong and then fell silent. Within the stone walls and dusty arches, the church organ thundered and the choir began to sing the *Magnificat*.

'I stopped at the wall of the graveyard and waited. The voices that had sounded so close down the lane could no longer be heard. Out in the open, away from the shelter of trees, only the rain spoke. It muted the dirge of the choristers. I turned away from the church and went to look over the edge of the bridge. The river was higher than I can ever remember and roared between the banks of the meadow. Standing there, watching the streetlights dance on the surface of the water, I smiled at the fragmented shadow of my reflection. A phantom from a submerged continent. The memory of a drowned man.

'On a night such as this, I thought, the North Sea would be formidable. The waves would devour the cliffs and the streets would be populated by the ghosts of drowned sailors. Perhaps the cities on the coast had all been washed away by now. Perhaps the tower blocks were pillars of coral in the Sea King's palace. I imagined Penshaw Monument as an island in a wide Arctic ocean, the temple deserted of lovers and besieged by lumbering icebergs. Perhaps the stars would be brighter in a sky forever black.

'The sound of running footsteps brought me back to the bridge. I turned as two figures flashed past me at great speed, holding the collars of their coats against the rain. They sheltered beneath the church porch and pointed at the notice board.

'"It's already started," the tall one said, his Irish accent barely audible above the rushing stream. "Only a couple of minutes late."

'The other one removed his baseball cap and ran his fingers through his fair hair. He glanced uneasily back at the bridge. The light from the church window shone on his damp face, lighting his smile. He shook the rain from his cap and withdrew into the darkness of the porch, but I had seen the white streak.

'"Jake?" I shouted across the bridge. I think I called, although it might have been the river. I know I stepped towards the church.

'In the porch, Jake backed into the shadows and lifted the door handle. Perhaps he had not seen me, I thought. He cannot have seen me.

'I was conscious of the presence of the other man, the tall Irish one. I was vaguely aware that I had seen him some place before. The memory was indistinct, the scene from a half-forgotten dream. I heard him speak but, as in dreams, his words were irrelevant.

'"Jake," I repeated, blinking in the rain. It was the only word.

'The Irish man said something else and this time I understood.

'"Jake, love," he said. "I think this man wants to speak with you."

'Jake emerged from the porch and dug his hands in his pockets. He grinned awkwardly. The Irishman shook my hand and introduced himself. He said his name was Martin. He said he was a solicitor. He said we had met before, on the day I bought the oast-house. He glanced at the sky and said they'd better get into the dry.

'"I'll save you a pew, Jake. Don't be too long now."

'Jake nodded and watched him enter the church. For a moment the graveyard was filled with light and the noise of the choir. Then the door closed and we were alone in the rain. And then, all things became deathly still. Despite the downpour and the screaming stream, the universe went quiet. It is this stillness that I remember most of all, the stillness before the last words are uttered and the world is swept away. It is the calm before the thunder of a parting glance.

'"I thought you were a dream," I said, breaking the silence clumsily. "When I saw you, I didn't think you were real. I still don't."

'Jake nodded and stared distractedly at something down the lane.

'"I dreamed of you coming," I continued. I wanted to touch his clothes, to feel his arms and convince myself that he was real.

'Jake nodded again and turned his face down. His attention was now fixed on a lopsided gravestone that stood beside the path.

'"Do you believe in coincidence?" he asked without looking at me.

'"No, of course not," I replied quickly. I realised that I didn't know what to do with my hands. "How could I after everything that's happened? Especially now?"

'"Maybe you should reconsider." He took a deep breath, preparing himself. "I was on holiday in Dublin. I met Martin there."

'"Of course, you said you'd go away. You needed a break." I took a step closer. "You're looking good. You are looking good."

'"Martin was in Dublin too. He was taking his da to a care home. His da used to be a vicar here in Balwick, you know, at this church. You think that's not a coincidence?"

'"More than that," I laughed, still fathoming the sight of him. "So much more than a coincidence. How could you think it wasn't?"

"'Why do you think I'm here, Chris?" He looked up from the gravestone and peered into my face, scrutinising me dispassionately. "Tell me, what fantasy is going through your head at this very moment?"

"'You're in Balwick, my home town. I knew you'd come."

"'It still hasn't clicked, has it?"

"'What hasn't? You're here, Jake. That's enough for me."

"'Guess your ghosts told you I'd come, didn't they? All those voices in your head, your Old Woman, your old devil. Well, time for that awkward moment of truth. This is what you could have won. I'm here with Martin. He brought me here."

"'I know you're here with Martin." I turned towards the church door. "He was just there."

"'No, Chris." Jake came close until his blue eyes were level with mine. "I'm with Martin. I'm with him."

'I recognised the final words of the *Nunc Dimittis* rising from the choir: the plea for release, the servants departing in peace. The stillness began to dissipate around me. Not yet, I thought. Don't end yet.

"'I painted the Yellow Room," I said as Jake turned to the porch.

"'I know." He removed his cap before entering the church. "You told me already. You've said it all before."

"'You should see it. You should see the Yellow Room."

"'I won't see your Yellow Room. I won't see your house or the people in your life. Or you. This is the last thing I have to say to you. I'm with Martin now. I'm with him." He turned the handle of my father's old church. His face glistened as cold as marble in the rain, silent with the last things that cannot be spoken. And then he was gone and the world was swept away.

* * *

'She came at once,' Chris said, kneeling beside the hearth. The fire was just an ember now. It cast a faint light over his features. 'As soon as Jake closed the church door, she came.'

'The Old Woman?' I asked, although I already knew the answer.

'She brought him here. She wanted to plague me with the one thing I couldn't live with: hope. She knew I couldn't fight that. You can co-exist with despair. That's like sharing a house with a mad dog or a tiger. You get to know the habits of despair, which rooms to avoid, which doors are safe to open, which to close at certain times of the day. It becomes a routine after a while. It's the hope I couldn't resist, not now she had brought him here. Why else would she bring him to this town, if not to give me hope?'

'Chris,' I said, 'there is no Old Woman.' But he did not hear me.

'She revealed him to me again in all his beauty. She brought him here, put him just out of reach on the other side of that church door, so close and so unattainable. Day in and day out, year in and year out. There is no other love, she said – of course there is no other love – and yet there is not love. This is no other hope, she said, and it is no hope at all, though I could feel it and not feel it at the same time, like a ghost that finally understands it no longer has a body but still feels like it does.

'She took my hand, kindly now, and walked me to the edge of the bridge. She wanted to see what I would do. When I went over, she came with me. There is no other hope and there is no hope at all, she said pressing her watery mouth so hard against mine I thought I would never breathe again. There is no other love and there is not love.'

'But you're here,' I said firmly, clenching his hand in mine. 'You're here and you're safe. You survived the worst.'

'Cat and Day found my body on the riverbank the next morning. They brought me home and poured some sickening herbal god-knows-what down my throat. I only got out of bed to escape her medicine. I wouldn't say that I survived.'

'You were strong enough to live through it,' said Conrad, kneeling beside me. He took up Chris's other hand. 'That says something, surely.'

'It says I was too ashamed to die like that, that's all. It was shameful to die while there was hope. Not without his forgiveness.'

Chris rocked gently in the firelight and pressed his fingers to his temples. The cascade from the broken guttering grew calmer as the downpour finally subsided.

'I didn't know,' Conrad said, ruffling Chris's hair. 'You never said any of this to me before. I had no idea.'

Chris flinched from the touch and rose to his feet. The fire gave a final flicker and died, leaving the room in darkness.

'We should return,' said Chris. 'They'll think we've gone to a better party.'

'They'll be stoned,' Conrad replied, hanging on to Chris's hand to delay him. I watched Conrad's fingers stray over Chris's hand-fasting ring in a playful attempt to remove it. 'Stay here, it won't matter. Stay here with me.'

'Why?'

'Because I've missed you,' Conrad shrugged. He tugged at the ring and ran his fingers over Chris's hard knuckles. 'Because we haven't talked in years, not properly. It's difficult to say things when Anna's around. It's hard to talk openly about our past. We did have a past before Jake, don't you remember?'

'You've made your bed and Anna's lying in it.'

'But yours is empty tonight. It needn't be.'

'You haven't been listening. My bed is full of ghosts.'

Chris shook his hand free and walked out of the Yellow Room. His footsteps echoed through the hall and down the solitary lane.

* * *

When the morning shower had passed, I lay my cup of cold coffee on the lawn and shook the rain from my hair. I could hear Catriona talking in the cottage and the sound of the kettle boiling. Smoke from Day's fried breakfast drifted through the window and dispersed in the lightening sky.

I listened to the blackbird's song with relief. Lionheart and Amber dropped to the ground from the branches of the tree and approached me.

'Got any smokes, sister?' asked Amber, glancing coolly at the house. I smiled sadly and shook my head.

'You have, but you're not going to share them.' She sighed and walked back to the tree. 'Wish people would just be honest.'

Lionheart lingered behind and looked at my face.

'You alright, Jacks?' he asked quietly.

'Sure, Man-Cub. Just thinking.'

'Don't mind Amber. She doesn't mean anything.'

'I know. She's a good friend to you, I can see that.'

'She always has been.' Lionheart followed her towards the oaks. He looked back briefly and grinned. 'You're okay, too, you know. I'm glad you're sticking around.'

I watched them climb among the higher branches and conspire behind the green leaves. The spring sunlight glistened on the dewy grass. The statues turned their faces towards the blue sky, surprised by the unexpected sun. The soil crackled as wormholes gasped for air and the floodwaters subsided. Somewhere at the back of my mind, I heard my mother's voice whispering a tale of Proserpine rising from the season of rains, breaking the spell of winter.

XVII
Of Earth

31st March 2000

Chris is still a beautiful man, though his face has begun to show the early signs of ageing. Time and relentless memory have been unkind. From the dark juices of herbs in Catriona's garden, he has tried to infuse sedatives to help the nights pass more benignly, but the dark half-moons grow full beneath his eyes. He sits cross-legged on the edge of the South Downs and gazes at the chalk limbs of the Long Man of Wilmington carved into the hillside. It is here, like this, in this time and in this place, that I like to remember him.

Chris is still handsome, but he rarely smiles now. When he does, it passes as quickly as a shallow break in the otherwise unmoving clouds. He loiters on the ridge between ripe manhood and early middle-age, the crest of the hill where all things that have passed are mapped out in a tapestry of familiar fields and well-trodden paths, and the future is a mist we have not yet mined. Over the heath, follow the spine of the Downs to the edge of the earth where the air is sea-salty and the shoreline ebbs and turns in indecision. There we shall walk along the fluent margins, where the seagulls nest and the frontiers are never the same. Chris smiles briefly, brushing the dark hair away from his blue eyes. And here, like this, he remains forever.

'Is it finished?' I ask, but he does not answer. What with the wind and the gulls and the rolling clouds, I am not even sure he has heard. He is looking the other way at a tiny house in the distance. In its garden, a row of white sheets beckon from a washing line, signalling some frantic message from the floor of the valley.

'Is it done?' I ask, touching his arm so he turns. 'Is it over now?'

I cannot tell if he is frowning or smiling. His face is clenched, his eyes half closed as he accepts the full force of the wind. He sweeps the hair out of his face again.

'I haven't been very kind to you,' he says unexpectedly.

I do not know how to reply or where this thought came from.

'I want you to know,' he looks away, 'I could have been kinder.'

We do not talk for some time. Eventually, I point at the chalk man that was cut into the hillside hundreds of years before.

'What was it for?' I ask. 'Why do you think they made him?'

'Because they could.' His answer is so obvious it barely needs articulating. 'Because they had imaginations big enough for giants.'

'That's not a reason, Chris.'

'What does it matter why they did it?' He pushes himself up from the grass and shields his eyes from the sun to gaze across the rolling green. Conrad and Day are strolling into the distance, casually pointing out landmarks of interest: Cuckmere Valley, Puddingham Wood, the peak of Firle Beacon. Suede, always pursuing her own solitary path wherever she goes, has already disappeared behind the next hill.

'I think it's an epigraph,' Catriona says, linking her arm through Chris's. 'Like words on a tombstone, written in the days before writing made things literal.'

I slide my hand through Chris's other arm and we walk together after the others, like three old friends, although this is new to me. Lionheart and Amber trail behind, their laughter echoing between the slopes. They cheer at the sight of the chalk man on the hillside and then lie down, flat against the edge of the summit.

'If you're going to roll down, love, please don't break anything important,' Catriona shouts. Lionheart grins at us and throws himself over the ridge. My stomach twists as he tumbles down the slope.

'Catriona, why do you let him do that?'

She tries not to smile as she watches the boy's uncontrollable fall.

'Because he can,' she says simply in the same tone that Chris had just used. 'Because it's his body, not mine.' She watches her son rise, bruised but triumphant at the feet of the great chalk figure. He spreads his arms into the air and stands like a victorious 'V' over all my fears. Amber returns the salute and follows his rapid descent. 'Didn't your mother tell you the same thing, Chris?'

'I think you're probably right,' he says, distracted, 'about that epigraph thing. Perhaps they buried the last giants in this place and signed the site with the Long Man. That way, we wouldn't forget that other things have been possible and still are, if we can be bothered to imagine them.'

'Perhaps that's what the Downs really are,' Catriona says. 'The fallen bodies of great monsters, laid to rest and now sleeping under blankets of grass.'

'Perhaps chalk is made from the bones of giants that died when people stopped believing in them.'

'Or the bones of children who rolled to their deaths when they weren't being supervised,' I say, leading them away from the edge.

'Oh, but they were being supervised. We all watched them do it,' says Catriona. She laughs at my caution and then talks of the legendary creatures that were transformed into the landscape around us. Her voice is carried on the wind over the smooth green body of the Downs. It dives sleekly into crevices when the clouds veil the sun.

Chris frowns at the landscape without listening to her words. His thoughts are lost on the horizon, just as they were the morning after he returned from Greece, the morning after the party. At that time, I had come across him unexpectedly in his garden. He had been digging a deep hole beside the dog-rose tree, but stopped to wipe his brow. When I walked around the edge of the house, I found him there, frozen in that position with the back of his hand against his forehead, staring towards the hills that curled southwards to the sea. He did not hear me. The sunlight sparkled on the dewy grass and I thought that I had entered a magic field, that spring had passed this way just seconds before and showered the Selfish Giant's garden with diamonds. As I approached, Chris began whistling a tune between his teeth, a tune with the power of such memories that I too whispered the words involuntarily.

'*Hey dirla, dirladada, hey dirlada,*
Farewell, sir; it's over.
Farewell to the child you're leaving too.
I have only one friend, the river.
She goes dirla dirladada.'

'The ground's waterlogged,' Chris said, scraping the sides of his boot against the tread of the spade. 'Makes it a hell of a lot easier to shift than when it was frozen.'

'What are you hoping to find? Did a rainbow end here?'

'No,' he said, getting back into his task. 'I'm digging a grave.'

'Of course you are. Anyone I know?'

He glanced up for a moment and grinned. That old light danced in his eyes, teasing me to ask more. When I refused, he shrugged and sliced the blade through the moist soil.

'Must be for someone very fat. You could fit a huge arse in there.'

'Uh-huh,' he nodded and picked up the tune where he had left off. '*I have only one friend, the river. She goes dirla dirladada.*'

I dodged the flying clay and followed the path beside the wall until I encountered Lionheart's black kitten stepping gingerly between the tall weeds, her eyes wide, intrigued by the voices in the garden. I stretched my hand in friendly greeting, but she ignored the gesture and peered around me, astonished by the flying clods of earth. I bowed to her, an apology for my impudence, and left the path to walk barefoot on the wet lawn.

The field was smaller than I remembered. In the years of my absence, all things had diminished, the land had shrunk – or else I had grown unnaturally big by eating a mysterious cake that time had marked 'Eat Me'. The great white roof of the oast-house, once the turret of an evil count's castle, now seemed as ridiculous as a child's party hat on senile old man. It was still tall, admittedly, and reached way above me into the clear blue sky – but more like an overgrown toadstool than a menacing tower. And it was in desperate need of redecoration.

'That could do with a coat of paint,' I said, pointing at the paintwork around the windows. 'A different colour this time; perhaps apple-green. It would only take us a couple of days.'

'Us?' Chris asked, frowning as he shielded the sun from his eyes.

'And the garden could do with something to bring it alive. It's a wilderness out here. Perhaps an orchard of fruit trees, plums and pears on either side of the path. Lionheart would love to climb them. Maybe an herbaceous border along this wall.'

'I couldn't help but notice that you said "us", Jackie.'

'So, you were awake. Perhaps lavender and rosemary under the kitchen window. You know, stuff for the kitchen that's easy to reach. And Mediterranean herbs along the southern wall down there; oregano and basil and things like that. It is a suntrap after all. A bay tree even. Chris, did you know that bay is said to protect a house from lightning and plague and every kind of harm? We really should get a bay tree.'

Chris folded his arms and contemplated his hole. A mistle thrush landed beside a clod of upturned earth and pecked for worms. Hidden beneath the rose tree, the kitten eyeballed the bird with delicious outrage, her teeth chattering with the imagined taste of raw fowl.

'Listen, Jacks,' Chris began, carefully emphasising each word. 'I hope you're not asking to move into the oast-house with me.'

I stamped my foot just as the cat pounced for the kill. The mistle thrush escaped, leaving the kitten confused and wondering why she too should not have wings.

'Of course I'm not asking that.' I turned abruptly to the house to hide my face from him.

'Good,' he called out after me. 'Because it's your house as much as mine, always has been. You shouldn't have to ask. I would hate it very much if you thought you needed to ask.'

I felt ashamed again, but this time for a different reason. I went back to him, still blushing. He held out a cigarette and winked as I took it. Sheltering the lighter from the breeze, he nodded toward the porch.

'You could hang wind-chimes from that beam,' he said thoughtfully. 'If you have the front bedroom, they wouldn't keep you awake at night, would they?'

'No,' I replied. 'They wouldn't keep me awake at all.'

'Good. Get me a beer, would you?'

He continued to dig the trench all afternoon, until it was deeper than he was. I strayed through the house, touching the relics of his former empire. In the rooms where I had been too afraid to make a noise as a child, I now clapped my hands and shouted.

'I'm back, *dirlada, hey dirlada,*' I sang. 'I'm back.'

I swept the cobwebs from the high ceilings with a willow broom and listed the repairs that needed to be made. Most of the skirting boards would have to be replaced, and all the windows needed new curtains. The ones that survived were thick with mould. The hallway was especially decrepit where the rain had leaked through the roof. The walls were discoloured and a lung-shaped stain now bruised the pine floorboards. As the setting sun cast a sad lustre over the walls, Chris came to find me. His hands and face were streaked with dirt.

'Are you ready?' he asked tentatively.

'For what?'

'For the burial of the dead. I need your help with the corpse.'

'How many years will I get for being your accomplice?'

'Life.'

He led me through the low door of the Green Room, where the last light lingered on the burnt remains of the piano. He took the vase of long-dead roses from the lid and heaved his shoulder against the frame. Without speaking, we wheeled the instrument through the hallway and onto the lawn, accompanied by the occasional knell of a loose hammer striking untuned strings.

Day's latest stone sculpture had been delivered earlier that afternoon. A crude but recognisable copy of Michelangelo's *David* stood poised beside the graveside, his sling resting harmlessly over his shoulder. The muscular figure gazed over the funeral scene, indifferent to everything except his own languid beauty. How desolate he looks, I thought as we heaved the piano to the edge of the grave.

'Any last words?' I asked.

Chris took a brown cloth bundle from the feet of the statue and carefully unravelled the package. He removed a wooden clothes brush and held it over the grave.

'No, not really.' The brush fell unceremoniously into the hole. 'I don't think there is anything else to say.'

We stood together looking into the earth for some time, until a crow called impatiently from somewhere in the garden, and then Chris moved towards the piano.

'It is strange,' he said. 'I couldn't bear the thought of the piano being destroyed. I salvaged it, you know, from the house fire in Sunderland. I had it brought down here. I knew it couldn't be repaired, but I didn't know I was going to bury it. I suppose it's easier to let go of something when that decision is yours, when you've got the choice.'

He leaned his weight against the side and closed his eyes. The strings growled one last time before it crashed into the hole. For a moment the air was filled with dust, with the cry of splintering wood and roaring chords, and then all was still.

The roosting birds ended their evening songs and settled in their nests. I watched the stars emerge gradually in the sky and noted the appearance of Venus above the Downs. She's with us tonight, Chris, I thought. She's here for this.

Chris lifted the spade from the mound of earth and began to shovel soil over the piano. The thin sliver of a new moon blinked between the branches of Catriona's oaks, granting no light for his task.

'I still love him,' Chris said, turning towards me in the growing darkness.

'But you wouldn't want him back, would you?'

'He wouldn't come back. Sometimes the only desire I have is to see his face again. I never will, of course, though he could be mere metres away from me at this very moment, somewhere in the town. Some nights I think he's standing in the room at the end of my bed, saying things beyond my hearing. When I lean close to catch the words, he tells me I'm forgiven. I know that will never be.'

'Why on earth do you think you need to be forgiven?'

Chris returned to his digging. His silence was unqualified.

There was no evening breeze to turn the weathervane, no movement in the trees. I sat beside the beautiful statue and watched the gravedigger fill the hole. When he had filled about half of the pit, he laid the spade on the trampled grass and turned to the statue.

'I remember all things,' he said. 'Nothing is lost or forgotten, but stays as it always was, unaltered by time, just as it happened.

'I remember the Victorian house. I remember the colours. The hallway was red and purple. There were bronze wall-lamps and cheap Van Gogh and Gauguin prints along the wall. An AGA in the kitchen that heated the water and radiators. First thing in the morning, I'd leave Jake sleeping in bed and creep into the garden to get coke from the shed to fill up the fire. Last thing at night, I did the same. I'd find him curled beneath the duvet, shivering, grinning, waiting for my return. Come to bed, he would say, it's so cold out there. It was freezing, but even the cold contained a promise of his body to come, of skin against skin, bound tightly by warming limbs. Two edges of a wound knitted together.

'Turn off the lamp, Jake, I would say. Look at me and turn off the lamp, so the last thing I see of the day is your face. The light went out, but the darkness felt as thick as his breath against my face, warm and sweet and tasting of toothpaste. I touched my nose to his mouth and inhaled the darkness. In the garden, the crystals chimed against the dream-tree and whispered a song of the Arctic wastes beyond. Out there are dragons, and over there are giants, but here there are lovers under the sea. Deep beneath the ice, I whispered, buried a thousand miles under rock and bones and snow is a palace of hidden treasure. Let me tell you a story of this treasure – '

Chris fell silent and stared at the half-filled pit. I listened to the voices from the cottage drift loosely on the air: Lionheart's laughter, Amber's echo. The sound passed over the stone wall and ruffled the leaves of grass, whispering the secrets of youth to the soil. Chris raised a single rose to his lips and laid it in the grave.

'Are we done here?' I asked.

No, not yet.

* * *

Chris turns to me now and half smiles. He nods towards the roaring sea beyond the edge of the cliffs.

'This is it, for now,' he says.

'Thus far and no further?'

He throws his coat on the grass, a fair distance from the edge, and leisurely sits down beside it. Lionheart playfully grabs his hand and tries to pull him closer, but he resists. There is something wrong in the scene, I think, in Chris's demeanour. Lionheart does not see it or if he does, he wilfully ignores it.

'Come on, darling,' Catriona cajoles. 'It's a stunning view. And we have to go that way to get down the path.'

He turns to me, although I am not sure what for. Does he want me to coax him like the others? He is determined not to move, I can see that much. He has not asked anything of me, but is considering me, weighing up whether I understand. I meet his gaze and know enough not to badger him. Kneeling beside him on the windswept grass, I stretch out my palms on the soil. He closes his eyes and breathes heavily.

'He's not very good with heights,' I say to Catriona. 'He can't bear to be close to the edge. He's all right on the Downs because they're surrounded by earth, but not near the cliffs where there's nothing but a sheer drop and then the water. He never was.'

Catriona does not believe me. I can sense her thoughts probing the surface of my weak explanation. I know that Chris has somehow asked for my help. Is this what he wanted of me?

'But what about Whitby?' she asks.

'That's where we found out, when we first moved there. I think it must have been the day after we arrived, Calliope took us up to the

311

abbey on the cliff-side steps. She said we could reach the sun from the summit, that it was the highest point in the world.'

Most of what I am saying is true, that's what makes it easy to go on. As for the rest, I am not exactly lying. Exaggerating, perhaps, to take the pressure off Chris for whatever reason he needs to be alone here. It is a role I am playing, but I do not know why. I do know that Catriona can see through it.

'Chris ran up the abbey steps without waiting for us,' I continue. 'I held Calliope's hand and walked slowly behind. When we got to the abbey, we couldn't see him at first. Eventually, we found him curled up behind a gravestone, hiding his face in his hands. He wouldn't move from the spot. It took us all evening to persuade him down.'

'But, Whitby?' Catriona says gently. She still does not understand. 'The abbey, Chris, you've been there since. I've seen you there. You used to go up there with Jake. What happened then?'

He shrugs. 'It didn't seem to matter at that time.'

He lowers his face, not embarrassed by this revelation but distracted. His thoughts are elsewhere. This conversation is something he has to endure, an act to sit through before he can be left alone. At last, Catriona seems to understand.

'We'll meet you down there, then,' she says. 'Or back home, if you want to get the train on your own.'

Suede has overheard all. She ambles towards us, smirking.

'Some Prometheus,' she laughs. 'Amber's got to see this.'

'We're going down by the lower path,' Catriona says, glaring at Suede. 'And then the train home from Eastbourne.'

She takes Suede's arm and leads her to the path where Lionheart and Amber have already run ahead, and Day and Conrad before them.

'We'll catch you on the way?' she asks, glancing back at Chris.

'Thank you, Cat.' He holds her gaze for some time and smiles. 'Thank you. You will catch me on the way. Some Prometheus indeed.'

'So much for touching the sun,' she replies, echoing his sad smile.

I stay on the grassy verge above the sea and wait to see if Chris has anything to tell me. A fleet of white-sailed yachts flicker on the sunlit sea, shifting like confetti in the wind. They skim across the surface effortlessly, passing each other by. It is a country-dance of tall white maidens, stripping-the-willow on water.

The seagulls rise on the upsurge, indifferent to my presence. I am no threat to them, they scoff, and slink gracefully to the rocks below. Crawling on my hands and knees, I peer over the edge at their egg-laden nests. Little fuckers, I think, despising them. When I scattered my mother's ashes from the cliffs in Whitby, the gulls had swooped in to catch the remains. I will never forgive them that.

'Just one rock,' I shout down to the nests. 'Just one little stone and then I'll give you something to cry about.'

'I wouldn't do that,' Chris says disapprovingly. He has crawled beside me on his elbows and looks over the edge. 'Remember the Ancient Mariner.'

'That was an albatross.'

He blinks his dark eyelashes, his blue eyes disappearing beneath a frown. 'Calliope never liked them either. You get that from her.'

'I absolutely detest them.' I lie on my back in the grass. 'They invaded her garden in the evenings to pick the seeds she had planted that day. Do you remember, she said they were gargoyles sent by your father to torment her? But they were only seagulls. I watched them doing it. I'd run outside to scare them away, but they worked as a gang, one retreating while another came in. They even nipped me.'

'You hate them more now Calliope's dead.' He says this as a fact. 'Still fighting her battles? You don't need to do that anymore.'

'They came for her when I scattered her ashes. It's my battle now.'

'Then perhaps they are gargoyles of a kind,' he says. He ponders this for a moment and then turns to me. 'I was wrong to leave Whitby. It was a mistake. It's important that you know that. It was wrong of me to go back to the oast-house and leave you both. Things would have been very different if I'd stayed.'

'She let you go. She could have prevented you.'

'She did the right thing. She trusted me to make my own future. It was me that fucked up.' He sighs and stares out at the white sails on the sea. The boats have stopped dancing with each other and are now dispersing, fanning out in uneven flights away from the shore. 'We all do what we think is best at the time, that's the gamble. It's only later we find out whether we were right or wrong. The hardest thing is realising that you don't own anyone. You can't possibly love someone if you think you own them. If she'd locked me up, do you think I wouldn't have tried a knitting needle in the lock every time her back was turned?'

'That's a hard truth.'

'I knew you'd understand.'

* * *

Alone again, I tread carefully down the perilous steps that have been cut into the side of the cliff. I can see why Chris was reluctant to come: the sheer face of crumbling chalk on the left, a single rope guardrail on the right and the churning sea and rocks a hundred metres beneath. I wish he had come nevertheless, or at least let me stay with him. He refused, saying it was time for me join the others.

'What did he say?' Lionheart asks as I pass him. He is hiding behind a sooth slab of fallen chalk, waiting to pounce. I look around but he is on his own. The others have already reached the shore and are wandering in ones and twos, leaving dark footprints in the damp sand.

'He wants to be alone,' I reply, reaching a hand to him. 'As do you, by the looks of things.'

'Did he say anything about earlier?'

'About the train station, you mean? No, not a word.'

Lionheart ignores my hand and gazes at the horizon. His eyes reflect the sea like a mirror, but clearer than the water or the sky. How strange that he should remind me so much of Chris, I think, standing here near the edge. How strange that he should have the same fierce expression, the same defiant lips and proud chin, and yet not be his son – his natural son.

'Did you know I met Jake last year,' he says as though reading my thoughts. He stares without fear at the expanse of air and water around him. 'It was in the post office. I'd never seen him before, but it was like I knew him right away. He looks like me.'

I follow Lionheart as he strolls down the path towards the sandy shoreline. The roar of the sea grows louder as we descend, but I stay close to him and hoard every word. His tale is brief and direct, uttered with the confidence and dignity of someone twice his age.

He says that he was standing behind a rack of postcards when Jake walked into the shop. Although Jake had lived in Balwick for many years by then, they had never actually seen each other. When Lionheart saw Catriona's lips tighten, he knew that this was the man.

'Is that him?' Lionheart asked, glaring at the back of Jake's head.

'We'll come back later, darling,' Catriona said, agitated.

'It is him,' Lionheart said. Catriona nodded and headed towards the door.

Lionheart had never thought about meeting this man. He had heard his mother mention the name to Day and he knew that that one potent syllable was anathema to Chris. For as long as he could remember from overhead conversations late at night, he had absorbed the tones and inflections of those who nurtured him. The memories of the age before his birth lay dormant in his bones. The stories of the past became the stuff of mythology, retold events were coloured with heroic meaning, mortals were transformed into primeval forces of nature.

Chris and Catriona were foremost in his pantheon, of course, casting thunderbolts at those who threatened their realm, defending their castle with garlic and wind-chimes. An army of other gods garrisoned the world of his imagination. Day and Conrad scoured the wilderness beyond his home. Suede, Amber and the Four Mythical Lesbians passed freely between time and space on quests to defeat fire-breathing bulldozers and hydra-headed developers. And yet here, in the wooded levels of the Weald, the man who opened the gates of the underworld smirked and casually bought stamps over a post-office counter.

Lionheart stared at his father. He had heard of the Old Woman of the Downs. He even saw her once, hovering malignantly over Chris's sleeping body. Lionheart knew that she came at the mention of Jake's name, the name Chris uttered in sleep only. He knew that she was summoned by an alchemist's word of ancient power.

Jake opened his wallet and passed coins across the counter to the clerk. He turned suddenly, irritated by the eyes that bore into him, the clear blue eyes that gleamed as a reflection of his own. He shrugged.

'Are you wanting something, kiddo?' he asked.

Lionheart coolly observed the resemblance between this stranger's face and his own features. He could have been looking into a mirror, one that answered the mystery of age and showed his own face in twenty or thirty years' time. I don't want to be like you, he thought.

'They say I was born with a white streak in my hair too,' he said to Jake, 'just like yours.'

'That so?' Jake grinned at the clerk, clearly embarrassed.

'It went away when I was very young, on the night you left Chris.'

Jake collected his stamps from the counter and turned towards the boy. They stood for a moment, facing each other.

'Kid,' he whispered. 'I have no idea what you're prattling on about.'

Lionheart closed his eyes at the sound of Jake's words. They swept across the silence of his mind, echoed down the caverns of half-remembered conversations and touched the crystals that swung between the pillars of his pantheon. Deep within the winding worm-holes of his own underworld, he felt a presence, a distant memory from a Wessex burial chamber, shift and open her black eyes. Lionheart smiled.

Jake straightened his neck and laid a hand on Lionheart's shoulder to move him aside. The boy resisted the pressure and raised his own hand, twisting two fingers and his thumb into a strange gesture. He held it there, his curse, just a few centimetres from Jake's nose.

'They say she comes when you're at your weakest,' said the boy. 'You know what I'm talking about. You've seen her too. Did you think she was just in Chris's head?'

'Sorry, kiddo.' Jake backed away from the youth. He retreated the long way around the counter, glancing apologetically at the post office clerks who watched it all. 'Don't know what you're talking about.'

'She comes at sunset and leaves in the morning,' said Lionheart, following Jake to the door. 'You don't remember her? Of course you do, Jake. Do you think she doesn't know your name?'

Jake grabbed the handle and pulled the door open. The bell rattled loudly against the doorframe. The newspapers rustled in the breeze, seeming to whisper his name. He turned one last time, a shifting glance of awkwardness, apology and agitation at his son – and then he stopped. He focused on something unseen, a figment emerging in the vacant place behind Lionheart's left shoulder.

'She's all yours,' Lionheart grinned. 'I wanted her to come. I willed her. I called her from the Downs, and she came. She's all yours now, father.'

* * *

Lionheart gazes across the flat sands of the shore and grins just like his father used to. The others are seated together in a circle, building sea-gardens with shells and pebbles. Catriona laughs and places a starfish in the centre of her patch. We go to join them.

'Has the Old Woman been back? Has Chris seen her since that day?' I ask quietly as we approach the sea-gardeners. They are concentrating intently on their miniature allotments and fail to notice our arrival. Lionheart shakes his head and speaks in whispers.

'When we got home from the post office, we found that Chris had fixed the weathervane back on the roof. He said he missed its creaking, but wouldn't say any more. He still calls out Jake's name in his sleep, but that's all. Anyway, that was the day I changed my name to Lionheart.'

Catriona waves at our approach and demands that we judge the sea-garden contest. I kneel beside Lionheart and lay an arm casually around his shoulder.

Catriona's garden is by far the most colourful, with seaweed trees marking the boundaries of her territory. She explains that each tree has the name of an ocean nymph and that the starfish is a statue, carved by the wise old man of the sea and offered as a token of his undying love. Suede and Amber's joint creation consists of a pear-shaped path of red pebbles leading to a single white shell.

'What the hell is that?' Conrad asks, laughing at the diagram.

'It's the vulvar garden of our Mother, the Ocean,' Suede says coolly. 'I wouldn't expect you to know your way around it, Conrad. Those red stones are the labia, the shell is the clitoris (I'll tell you what that is later, boys) and this hole is the vaginal orifice through which the world is born. It is the well of the Goddess from which all things issue.'

Kneeling beside her, Lionheart launches into a series of questions about the clitoris. I turn my attention to Day's pile of stones. The abstract construction is chaotic and random, I think. I contemplate the purple mussel that stands upright in the mound of coloured pebbles. I stare at the monument without understanding until Day leans over and whispers a word in my ear.

'The statue,' he says and then I remember.

'Michelangelo's *David* in the garden? Excellent piece of work, by the way, very lifelike. So, this is the oast-house garden? It looks disorderly enough.'

'It's a mussel,' he says, turning the purple shell between his thumb and forefinger. 'A muscle. Get it?'

'I get it, handsome.'

Catriona reaches over to put her starfish in my hand.

'Where's the house then?' she asks and then turns her head to call her son. 'Lionheart? You want to help us make an oast-house sandcastle for Day's garden? I think that apple-green was a good choice, by the way, Jackie. Transforms the atmosphere of the house completely.'

'The outside of it, anyhow. It's going to take a lot more than a lick of paint on the inside.'

'Well, you can always call on your neighbours to help with that. I hear they're a friendly bunch. Not afraid of a little hard graft.'

'You don't mind, do you? That I've moved out of the cottage?'

Catriona shakes her head. 'You're a stone's throw away. I can find you whenever I want. You can't escape from my clutches that easily, Snow White.'

'I mind,' Lionheart says, without looking up from his castle-making at our feet. He uses the empty sandwich tub to mould damp sand into blocks.

'She's only gone next door,' Amber says, kneeling beside him and patting the sides of the sand house into shape. 'You're never that fucking upset when I leave. And we go, like, half-way across the world.'

'Bet you won't even notice when I go tomorrow,' says Conrad. We all turn to him. 'Anna called this morning. She wants me back home in the morning. She says I can't stay any longer. I've got my orders.'

Since Chris's rebuff on the night of the party, Conrad had been increasingly reluctant to leave. He lingered for another week, postponing his inevitable return to London one day at a time. Sometimes, he spoke of how envious he was of our commune in Balwick and then hesitated with a question poised on his lips, but the question never came. He often looked expectantly at Chris, his eyes bright with anticipation, but Chris turned away. Touch me not, his cold silence said. My bed is full of ghosts. That very morning, as we had been setting off to get the train, before Chris and I had even passed through the front gate, Conrad had called him back.

'What is it?' asked Chris.

Standing under the porch, Conrad gestured to Chris with a subtle nod of his head, signalling that he wanted a private word.

'I think your neglected puppy wants some Chris-time,' I said under my breath.

'Go on ahead,' he replied. 'I'll catch you up.'

Walking down that old lane, the sunlight flickering through the trees, it was hard not to imagine my father's black cassock making its purposeful way towards the church, flailing between the dappled shadows of the ancient trunks where only cobwebs and hollow chrysalises remain. A dark memory of the dead, I thought, but we are the living now. We are the meek that inherited your earth, as your church once took it from others before. We are the heirs of this Wealden Eden. Shadows cannot hurt us now.

The church bells chimed nine times as I approached the train station. For the first time this year, I felt the primal presence of spring. The air was teeming with insects and the sun teetered over the red tiles of the station roof. A solitary skylark trembled far above the hills, her distant song echoing on the fields. There was a promise of warmer weather, the hint of a summer sky that stretched as far as the sand dunes of Africa and beyond.

The Downs lay peacefully around the rim of the Weald, cradling the lowlands with rolling muscles of earth. These giants shall not walk again, I thought as I entered the station. These giants shall sleep forever in their chalk halls, dreaming of mortals as we dream of them.

'The others are coming along now,' Chris said, arriving a moment behind me. 'Cat's just seeing to Lionheart. Apparently, Amber trapped his head in the bathroom door or something. It's pandemonium.'

Chris turned to the ticket machine and touched the screen. 'How many of us are there?'

'Six, seven. No, eight. I keep forgetting Conrad. What did he want?'

'To be twenty years old and a student again, I think,' he said without looking up. I noticed a subtle note of sadness in his voice, a whisper of melancholy that seeped through his words.

He pushed his card into the machine and typed his number. The tickets were printed out, but he did not collect them. A half-minute passed and still he did not move.

'What is it?'

318

'She's here,' he said, without looking up from the machine. 'I can smell her.'

'I hope you're not talking about me,' I laughed, but the sound was unconvincing.

I glanced anxiously around the whitewashed walls, half expecting to catch the Old Woman's face leering from the rafters. But the room was quite empty and the walls were painted with the colours of the stained-glass windows. The sudden stench of rotting leaves was merely my imagination, I thought. Perhaps it was the power of Chris's suggestion that made me cover my nose, as I had done in the attic room as a child, listening to the weathervane creak in the wind.

'Can you see her?' I asked.

If Chris had heard me, he did not answer. Instead, he turned to the entrance, his dark eyes staring with some unfathomable emotion. I heard the sound of unsteady footsteps, a suitcase being lowered to the ground. I turned to the doorway, unreasonably afraid of the figure whose arrival now cast a long shadow over the stone floor.

His eyes were the same colour as Lionheart's, as clear and blue as the coloured glass in the station windows. He was shorter than I had imagined, his body much thinner. I had expected him to be more muscled, his shoulders as broad as Michelangelo's *David*, his features as languid and confident as the statue's. I had seen the photographs that were taken years ago, but in the flesh he was slight, stooped and quite like an old man. For a moment, I was unsure if it was actually him at all. But then that distinctive white streak which ran through his thinning, greying hair, confirmed that this was Jake.

Chris mumbled his name so softly that only I, standing close beside him, could have possibly heard it. Coming in behind Jake, I recognised the tall, unshaven Irishman I had almost collided with on the Downs barely five months' earlier. Martin, my erstwhile rescuer, took a momentary look around the waiting room, registered me and Chris without a flicker of acknowledgement and laid his hand on Jake's shoulder.

'I'll wait with you,' Martin said, breaking the silence with his purposefully loud voice. Jake shook his head and turned to kiss his lover.

'You know I hate long, drawn-out goodbyes.'

'It's not even a real goodbye. It's only for a week until I tie up all the loose ends down here.'

'I'll be fine.'

'I'll wait with you.'

'I said I'll be fine.'

'You'll sleep on the train? And you won't do anything before I come up, okay now? I paid the removal company an arm and a leg to

319

unpack everything. It should all be sorted by the time you get to Elliston. Let me know if it's not.'

'I'll be fine.'

'I want you to rest, little man,' Martin said, stroking the dark circles beneath Jake's eyes. 'Rest. And pray for me to get things finished sooner than planned. I'll pray for you too. I'll be with you in no time.'

'I will.'

'God bless.' He kissed Jake's forehead and left the station.

Jake watched his lover disappear down the lane and then he stooped to pick up his suitcase. As he walked past me towards the platform, I knew that the rank smell of decomposing leaves was not in my imagination. It came and went with him.

He kept his eyes fixed firmly ahead on the approaching train as he passed Chris. Between the smooth cleft of the hills, the tracks echoed with the weight of rolling carriages. I watched a golden bead of sweat tremble on Jake's sunlit brow and run tear-like down his cheek. If it were not for the grating rails, I would have heard the droplet shatter on the concrete.

'Jake?' Chris said the ancient name as the train came to a standstill. Jake reached for the push-button of the nearest compartment and the doors slid open. 'Jake.'

Chris emerged from the cool shade of the station shelter and stood in the sunlight. Shielding his eyes, he went up the carriage.

'You knew I always hated goodbyes,' Jake said without stepping aboard. 'You knew I never could.'

'We never needed to say it.' Chris stood beside him now. Without facing each other, they both stared at the carriage window, not at the empty seats inside but at each other's ghostly reflections.

'There's nothing else to say. It's the only thing left to say.'

'So little, it barely seems worth the effort.' Chris smiled at the reflection. 'Yet, to hear anything would be enough.'

'Even when everything's quiet,' said Jake, 'in fact, especially then, the silence is filled with voices. It's funny, but I do sometimes hear you. Sometimes.'

A whistle sounded further down the platform. Jake stepped onto the carriage. He walked heavily, deliberately, as stone might try to move through air.

'And what do I say? When you hear me, what am I saying?'

'What you have always said, of course.' Jake turned to face the man he had known in a different life, the body he had kissed in a thousand places, the lover he had met on a night of snow and full moons. His face looked grey and hard, haunted in the shadows of the compartment.

'And what is that?'

The whistle sounded a second and then a third time.

'You know what it is. You tell me all the time.'

There is an instant between the inevitable closing of the compartment doors and the thunder of the departing train. There is a moment of unforeseen, unexpected time, a crack fractured while the gods are looking away, a rift the size of a rain-stained window between the last glimpse of Jake and the absence thereafter. In that fissure, Jake turned and pressed his palm against the window. His lips twitched faintly into a smile. In that flash of lightning blue, Chris closed his eyes and stole the image – a fleeting face made everlasting before the lamp is switched off.

'It's done,' he said softly, although the northbound train had long-since passed far beyond the Downs and the tracks lay still and empty. The morning sun stood motionless over the hills, drowning the land in golden absolution.

Chris's eyes stayed closed. He did not see the sunlight on the hills, nor hear the distant song of the wavering skylark far above the South Downs. All he could see, all I tell myself he saw, was the image of the face he would take with him to the sea.

'It is done.'

* * *

We are all on the beach now, all except Chris. When I hear the sound, I think of wings and colossal feathers. It is not a cry, nor an exclamation, nor a human voice at all, but the resonance of titanic wings sweeping against the air. It is the sound of the elements splitting, the sound of dragons taking flight.

Day lets the purple mussel fall from his fingers; it lands on the sand and no one reaches for it. He is staring at the sky and the cliffs behind me, a strange, unrecognisable expression on his face. I think that I have never seen him look like this. I did not know he could.

Catriona stands suddenly, bends down, touches her knees, touches her mouth, steps forward, steps back, steps forward again. Strangely, she says the Dharmic 'Om' over and over again, zealously.

'Om. Oh-m. Oh-m. Ohm.'

There is a sound like a seagull, a high cry of nature outraged at some gut-stirring injustice. It is Amber screaming and running to Suede, burying her face inside her mother's arms. Lionheart is on his feet now, his hand shielding his eyes from the blinding glare of the sun. For a moment, I think he is looking at me and I wonder what I have done. I glance down and see that I have stepped through his sandcastle, that I have trodden it into the ground, that I cannot stop myself from walking all over it. My sandals are caked in tenements and turrets, and I cannot stop. There is sand between my toes. Still, I cannot stop.

'I'm sorry,' I say. 'I'm so sorry.' But no one is looking at me. They are staring at the cliffs behind me and I cannot bring myself to turn around. If I do, I know what I will see. Who I will see. And how.

But this is not how it happened, they tell me. They say that I have rewritten events because I wanted a definitive ending. That I needed a final line in the sand rather than the pain of unknowing. They say that I saw these things because dust is all I remember. Perhaps they are right.

Day said that he saw Chris climbing among the cliffs, searching for a way into the dragon nests. That he was last seen scaling a smooth pillar of chalk and he simply disappeared into a secret hollow.

Suede saw nothing, she said. She was seeing to Amber who had cut her foot on a shell. She assumed that Chris had wandered home on his own, as was his way. Conrad did not say what he saw.

Catriona says she saw Chris walking north, back inland over the spine of the winding Downs and towards the Long Man of Wilmington. She said he turned and waved one last time to her, a cigarette hanging from his fingers. She said he had found a way to the underground halls where giants sleep. He would wait there for a season until it was time to return.

But Lionheart tells me something different. He tells me that he saw a golden-winged Icarus leap off the tip of the headland and soar high into the immaculate blue sky. He tells me that Prometheus flew towards the pyre of the gods to bring fire back for the people of the earth. He tells me that Chris runs with the sun and touches the moon. Of bodies changed to other forms, he tells.

* * *

In days when dragons roamed the earth, they burrowed deep into the cliffs to lay their sacred eggs and hoard their stolen treasures. On a night when the moon is full and the snow falls thickly upon the frozen seas, when the dragons have all flown far out to sea, you can stray through underground palaces to see for yourself the sapphire marbles, unicorn horns and vast, unplundered, pearly eggs. And when the ice-age returns and giants walk with gods upon the barren Downs, we ourselves will be the dreams they shall tell each other, sitting around their unimaginable fires in the depths of winter.

I do not know the stories of other people, nor the myths they tell their children. I do not know what reasons they give for the turning of the wheel. I only remember what I think I know: a simple tale told at bedtime, whispered in the candlelight of an attic room. A spell of ice and dragons; a world locked in bitter grief until the sleepers wake and the seasons turn.

Chris speaks quietly now. They did not find his body so why should he not speak? Why should I not hear him? He will talk until I finish writing. And when I have finished, I will go into the garden to bury these words in the earth, in the unfinished pit, in his unfilled grave.

He speaks and I write. I write until the candle fades. I write until the first blackbirds begin to sing. I write until the crystals on the dog-rose tree twinkle in a misty dawn and, at last, the house falls silent.

Lightning Source UK Ltd.
Milton Keynes UK
UKOW04f2335070714

234742UK00001B/241/P